An Introduction to Tonal Theory

PETER WESTERGAARD

An Introduction to Tonal Theory

W · W · Norton & Company · INC
NEW YORK

Copyright © 1975 by W. W. Norton & Company, Inc.

0 393 09342 5

ALL RIGHTS RESERVED
Published simultaneously in Canada
by George J. McLeod Limited, Toronto

This book was designed by Robert Freese
The Typeface used is Times Roman,
set by Communication Crafts, Ltd.

PRINTED IN THE UNITED STATES OF AMERICA

1 2 3 4 5 6 7 8 9 0

Contents

PART I *Problems and Assumptions* — 1

CHAPTER 1. What are we talking about?

1.0 A "theory of tonal music"? What kind of theory? What do you mean, "music"? — 3
1.1 A "scientific" theory? — 4
1.2 "Why don't you just ask him what he hears?" — 7

CHAPTER 2. Notes

2.0 Notes — 11
2.1 Pitch — 11
2.2 Time — 21
2.3 Loudness — 27
2.4 Timbre — 27

CHAPTER 3. Lines

3.0 Lines — 29
3.1 Repetitions, steps, and skips — 29
3.2 Consonance and dissonance — 30
3.3 Linear operations and constructs — 35
3.4 Triads, the tonic, and the diatonic degrees — 41
3.5 Tonal pitch structures — 45

PART II *A First Approximation: Species Counterpoint* — 51

CHAPTER 4. Species counterpoint

4.0 What species counterpoint is and what it's for — 53
4.1 Constructing species lines: some operational rules — 55
4.2 Understanding species lines: structural ambiguity and interest — 63
4.3 Combining species lines: the fundamental voice-leading constraints — 73
4.4 Combining species lines: correspondence between linear structures — 82

CHAPTER 5. Simple species

5.0 Introduction — 99
5.1 Two lines in first species — 99
5.2 Three lines in first species — 105
5.3 Two lines in second species — 111
5.4 Compound lines — 121
5.5 Two lines in third species — 129
5.6 Compound lines, continued — 137
5.7 Three lines in second and third species — 143
5.8 Two lines in fourth species — 147
5.9 Three lines in fourth species — 155

CHAPTER 6. Combined species

6.0 Combining species — 159
6.1 Two lines in second species, one in first
     Two lines in third species, one in first — 160
6.2 Two compound lines moving at the same rate — 165
6.3 Two lines in fourth species, one in first — 177
6.4 One line in first species, one in second, one in third — 181
6.5 Two compound lines moving at different rates — 185

6.6 One line in first species, one in second, one in fourth
One line in first species, one in third, one in fourth — 189
6.7 Dissonant skips and skips to and from dissonant notes: compound lines based on pairs of lines in a higher simple species — 193
6.8 Dissonant skips and skips to and from a dissonant note, continued: compound lines based on pairs of lines in combined species — 205
6.9 Passing tones and dissonant neighbors beginning at the same time as the stable notes against which they are dissonant: combining compound lines with lines in a higher species — 215

PART III *A little closer to the real thing—a theory of tonal rhythm* — 225

CHAPTER 7. Notes, beats, and measures

7.0 Tonal rhythm — 227
7.1 Segmentation, delay, and anticipation — 228
7.2 Thinking of notes in terms of beats — 238
7.3 Secondary segmentations, delays, and anticipations — 245
7.4 Secondary beats — 259
7.5 Establishing beats — 269
7.6 Non-diatonic voice-leading procedures: chromatic neighbors and chromatic step motion — 281
7.7 Some new principles of linear generation: doubling, borrowing and transfer — 289

CHAPTER 8. Phrases, sections, and movements

8.0 Spans longer than a measure: the nature of the problem — 309
8.1 Phrase structure — 313
8.2 The cadence — 325
8.3 Consecutive phrases — 333
8.4 Non-diatonic voice-leading procedures: secondary dominants, diminished sevenths, and augmented sixth chords; mixtures — 345
8.5 Tonicization, structural parallelism, and large-scale span structure — 355
8.6 An overview and some words of warning — 375

CHAPTER 9. Performance

9.0 Some problems we've been avoiding — 379
9.1 Articulation: what the performer does — 379
9.2 Articulation: effect of what the performer does on our understanding of the structure — 384
9.3 Contrasts of loudness and timbre — 391
9.4 Rubato — 401
9.5 Performance strategies and "understanding the structure" — 409

APPENDIX Constructing a pitch system for tonal music — 411

A.0 What the appendix is for — 411
A.1 The physiology of pitch perception — 411
A.2 The primary intervals — 414
A.3 Consonance and dissonance, skip and step — 416
A.4 A preliminary pitch collection — 418
A.5 Diatonic collections and triads — 422
A.6 A final note of caution — 427

ANSWERS TO DRILLS — 429

Preface

This preface is addressed to three different people:
1. the student who wonders whether he ought to take a course that uses this book as a text,
2. the teacher who wonders whether he ought to use this book as a text in his course, and
3. the theorist who wonders whether this book has anything new to offer him.

Obviously, the concerns of these three people need not be mutually exclusive, but to simplify this Preface, let me address them separately.

To the student: This book presupposes no previous training in music theory. However, you will need some acquaintance with the conventions of musical notation. If you are uncertain of your skill, get a copy of John Clough's *Scales, Intervals, Keys, and Triads** and try the problems on page 49. If you can't handle these problems, go back and try some earlier problems, working your way back up to page 49. When you can do that page accurately, you will be able to handle the notation in this book. You will also need some skill at imagining the sounds these conventions stand for. Turn to page 3 of this book. If you can imagine what each note in the example sounds like, in the same way that you can imagine what each syllable of this sentence sounds like, you should have no trouble. If you have to use an instrument, say the piano, to help you know what the passage sounds like, you will probably be able to manage, but you had better make sure you read this book seated at the piano. But if you can only make out the example with some difficulty and need someone to show you "how it goes," you won't be able to use this book unless the course you are taking has an intensive program of practical musicianship built into it.

* New York: W. W. Norton, 1962.

To the teacher: This book was developed for a first-year two-semester college-level course in tonal theory. (I cover either Chapters 1–5 in the first semester and 6–9 in the second, or, if the students are up to it, Chapters 1–6 in the first semester and 7–9 in the second.) You could, however, also use Part II (Chapters 4–6) separately for a one-semester course in tonally oriented species counterpoint for students who have already had at least one year of traditional harmony. You could also use Part III (Chapters 7–9) separately to introduce more advanced students to the problems of tonal rhythm. While the degree of abstraction may seem higher than that of many music theory textbooks, I have not found it too high for college freshmen. On the contrary, college freshmen are conditioned by their other courses to expect this kind of argument. The exceptions are those students who can handle relationships between sounds so well intuitively that they resent the labor of having to think through the implications of those relationships.

To the theorist: This book owes its greatest debts to Schenker, Fux, and Bernhardt. Its central pedagogical means—species counterpoint—is that developed by Fux in the *Gradus ad Parnassum*. But the end to which that means is applied is that developed by Schenker in *Kontrapunkt*. Fux's goal, the Parnassus he wanted to lead the student to, was the ability to write imitation Palestrina. Schenker's goal—and mine—was the ability to understand the complex and varied voice-leading patterns of actual eighteenth- and nineteenth-century music in terms of the simpler patterns available under the artificial constraints of species counterpoint. To that end I have
   a. adapted the linear operations later developed by Schenker in *Der freie Satz* to the rhythmic

limitations of species counterpoint (Sections 4.1, 5.4, 5.6) and

b. tried to show how dissonant skips and skips to and from dissonant notes can arise from species situations in much the same way that Bernhardt shows how such departures in seventeenth-century voice leading had their basis in sixteenth-century practice (Sections 6.7 and 6.8).

Thus, most of the book is at least as old as Schenker, and much is as old as Fux or even Bernhardt. The exceptions are:

a. the modification of traditional species just referred to;
b. an attempt to shift from the acoustic to the physiological domain the assignment of certain interval sizes to certain structural functions (Chapters 1, 2, and the Appendix); and
c. a theory of tonal rhythm (Section 2.2 and Chapters 7–9).

Acknowledgments

Like most textbooks, this one was the outgrowth of a course, or in this case a series of courses. What began as a set of rules in my counterpoint course at Columbia became first the beginnings of a rhythmic theory in my second-year theory course at Amherst and finally the beginnings of a book at Princeton. I have received many helpful criticisms on various preliminary versions of this book both from the students taking the course and from the composers and theorists who have helped me give the course over the past four years—Steven Gerber, Donald Greenfield, Thomas Hall, Jeffrey Kresky, Arthur Margolin, John Melby, Richard Meckstroth, John Rahn, John Rea, Ronald Rouse, David Steinbrook, Gerald Warfield, Daniel Werts, and Mark Zuckerman.

Princeton University
May 1972

PART ONE

Problems and Assumptions

CHAPTER ONE

What Are We Talking About?

1.0 A "Theory of Tonal Music"? What Kind of Theory? What Do You Mean, "Music"?

This book is about the theory of a kind of music—tonal music. What does that mean? What kind of theory is a theory of a kind of music? For that matter, what do we mean by "music"? What kinds of phenomena are we talking about when we talk about music? What can we say about the ways these phenomena are related to one another?*

We use the word "music" to mean a number of different things. We call the black marks on the white page below "music."

(Mozart: *Sonata* K.331, second movement, mm. 1–5.)

But you can also use the word "music" for what you take the marks to signify, or how the air pressure fluctuates when you play what you take the marks to signify, or what you hear when those fluctuations reach your ears.

*I am avoiding for now the question of what we mean by "tonal." That is what all the other chapters in the book are about.

Now, while we can distinguish each of these meanings of the word from the others, we would like to be able to think of them as different stages of a single process. We can think of this process as a form of communication involving three people—a composer, a performer, and a listener—who use two kinds of signals—marks on a page and fluctuations in air pressure—to communicate with one another.

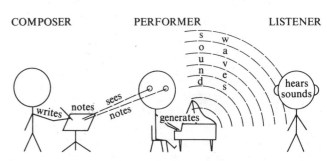

Communication in such a system normally goes in one direction only. Listeners don't usually reply to performers by playing something else that performers can write down and send back to the composer. However, the system is provided with feedback at strategic points. The composer can see what he writes, and the performer can hear the sound waves he generates as sounds. Sometimes the composer is even around to hear them too.

If we think of music as consisting of messages sent through this system, we can distinguish at least eight stages such messages go through:
1. the sounds as the composer conceives of them (that is, as he relates them to one another and to sounds in other messages);
2. the marks as the composer conceives of them (both as he relates them to one another and to marks in other messages, and as he relates them to the sounds as he conceives of them);
3. the marks on the page;
4. what the performer sees when he looks at the page;
5. how the performer conceives of what he sees (how he relates the marks to one another and to marks in other messages, how he relates the marks to what he must do to generate the sound waves, and how he relates the marks to the sounds that will result from them);
6. the sound waves;
7. what the listener hears;
8. how he conceives of what he hears (how he relates the sounds to one another and to the sounds in other messages he has heard).

If we think of music as consisting of such messages, then what is a theory of music? What can we say about the way such messages work? What can we say about the relationship of one stage of such a message to another stage of the same message? How would we go about comparing the same stage of two different messages?

1.1 A "Scientific" Theory?

Suppose you could observe each stage of a message in the same way a physical scientist observes the events he is concerned with. Suppose you could observe each item in each message either as an event or as a systematically related set of events in the physical world. For certain stretches of the system, this is possible. Take what happens when a pianist generates sound waves:
1. his finger presses a key;
2. some levers move;
3. a felt-covered hammer hits a string;
4. the string vibrates;
5. the pressure of the string on the bridge fluctuates rapidly;
6. the bridge vibrates;
7. the pressure of the bridge on the soundboard fluctuates rapidly;

8. the soundboard vibrates;
9. the pressure of the air next to the soundboard fluctuates rapidly;
10. the air pressure at other points in the room fluctuates rapidly;
11. the listener's eardrum vibrates;
12. the listener's ossicles (three tiny bones—the hammer, anvil, and stirrup—in the middle ear) vibrate;
13. the viscous fluid in his cochlea (the snail-shaped tube in the inner ear) sloshes rapidly back and forth;
14. his basilar membrane (the more flexible of the two membranes dividing the cochlea in half) ripples rapidly back and forth.

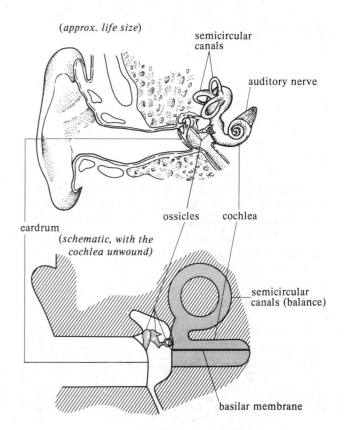

The human ear.

The physicist and the physiologist can measure:
1. the pressure of the fingertips on the piano key;
2. the length, weight, and friction of the levers;
3. the weight of the hammer and its speed at impact;
4. the weight, length, and tension of the string at rest;
5. the motion of the string as it vibrates;
6. the change in the pressure of the bridge against the soundboard;
7. the motion of the soundboard as it vibrates;
8. the change in the air pressure next to the board or anywhere else in the room (including the air next to the listener's eardrum);

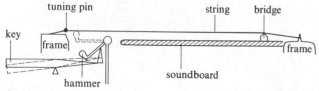

9. the motion of the eardrum and of each of the ossicles;
10. the motion of the cochlear fluid; and
11. the pattern of the basilar membrane's ripples.

They can relate such measurements to one another. For example, the physicist can compare the motions of the string and the soundboard and find that, although the amplitude of the motion (the amount of deviation from the point of rest) is much greater for the string than the board, the motions are similar in many other respects. Both are periodic (that is, after a brief period of irregularity at the beginning, the same pattern is repeated over and over again), and both have the same fundamental frequency (the number of times the pattern is repeated per unit of time). However, he also finds that the response time (the length of time the pattern takes to settle in) is longer for the board, and that the exact pattern being repeated is not identical with that of the string. He can subject both patterns to Fourier analysis and compare them in terms of the relative strength of their partials.* He can apply the same procedures to any of his measurements of vibrations or fluctuations in air pressure. So can the physiologist. He can compare the motions of eardrum and hammer in terms of the same variables: fundamental frequencies and the relative strength of partials.

Further, by comparing a number of cases, the physicist and physiologist can show which relations among variables are independent of one another. For example, suppose the same key were pressed twice, the second time much harder than the first (that is, using greater pressure in the fingertips). They could show that while the amplitudes, response times, and relative strength of partials were markedly different at each point of measurement, the frequencies stayed the same. They could also show that while the height of the highest ripple in the basilar membrane was different at each point of measurement, the point at which the highest ripple occurred remained the same. Or suppose two adjacent keys were pressed in succession, the pressure of the fingertips being equal in both cases. They could show that the amplitudes, response times, and relative strength of the partials were essentially the same at each point of measurement but that the frequencies were different at each point of measurement. They could show that the height of the highest ripple in the basilar membrane was almost identical at each point of measurement, but that the point at which the highest ripple occurred was different.

They can use such information to arrive at a theory of this stretch of the system—from the pressing of the key to the rippling of the basilar membrane. They can explain each adjacent set of events as an independent mechanical system and they can then explain the whole process as a series of connected systems with the output of one system serving as the input of the next.

We can use the same information to arrive at a theory of the kind of *messages* you can send through this stretch of the system. Clearly, since we know that every time a particular key is pressed the ripples in the basilar membrane are at their highest at the same point and that the only key we can press to get the basilar membrane to ripple at that point is that particular key, we can be sure that any message that depends on differentiating between that key and any other will get through this stretch of the system. On the other hand, since we know that a one-pound

---

* The French mathematician Jean Baptiste Fourier showed (1801) that any continuous curve can be understood as the resultant of sine curves. Thus, a complex curve like

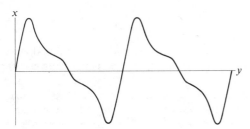

can be analyzed as the sum of three sine curves:

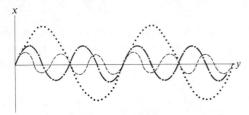

for any value of y the value of x on the complex curve is the sum of the values of x on the three sine curves.

Any sound wave can be plotted as a continuous curve with x representing the displacement of the vibrating medium from position of rest and y representing time. Sound waves that correspond to single notes generally yield curves of the type shown above in that (a) they are periodic and (b) the frequencies of their constituent sine waves (their *partials*) are all integral multiples of the frequency with which the complex pattern is repeated (their *fundamental frequencies*). The relative strength of these partials can be seen by comparing the maximum values of x for their respective sine curves. Thus a sound wave with a curve like the one above would have its energy concentrated at three different frequencies in the following proportions:

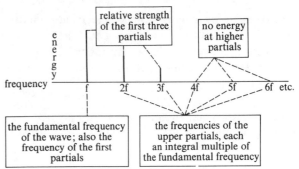

weight dropped on that key from one inch above the keyboard will produce the same pattern in the basilar membrane as a quarter-pound weight dropped from two inches, we can be sure that it is pointless for the pianist to send messages that depend on the difference between pressing the key hard and striking it fast.*

Now, of course, this stretch of the system is not the whole system; it does not even complete one end of the system. The most you can expect of a theory of this stretch of the system is to tell you what kinds of messages won't get through this stretch and hence won't get through to the end. It can't even tell you for sure what will get through to the end, since after all something else may happen to the message in the next stretch. The question is, then, can we extend this kind of inquiry into the final stretches of the system? What can we say about how messages get through to the final stage?

Consider what happens in the next stretch. The hair cells of the organ of Corti are between the basilar membrane and the relatively inflexible tectorial membrane. As the basilar membrane ripples, the hairs are bent and twisted. This makes the cells generate electricity. The neurons of the auditory nerve have their receiving ends anchored among the hair cells.

Section of the cochlea showing Corti's organ.

When the electric charge at one end of these neurons reaches a certain level, the neuron fires, that is, it discharges its own fixed store of electricity, changing the electrochemistry of the other end. The neurons of the auditory nerve are long, thin fibers. They follow the spirals of the cochlea out and lead to the cochlear nucleus where they meet with other neurons to form electrochemical relays called synapses.

When a neuron leading into a synapse fires, it changes the electrochemical state of the tiny space between its end and the ends of the other neurons. If the change is sufficient, a neuron leading out of the synapse fires. In most synapses, however, it takes more than one discharge of an incoming neuron, or the discharges of more than one incoming neuron, to make the outgoing neuron fire. Furthermore, the discharge of some incoming neurons changes the electrochemical state of the space in the opposite direction, inhibiting the discharge of outgoing neurons.

The cochlear nucleus is a maze of thousands of such synapses. It serves as the first switching point for messages on their way from the ear to the brain. Its incoming neurons include those of the auditory nerve as well as others leading from switching points further up the line. Its outgoing neurons lead on to other switching points, each consisting of thousands of synapses. The outgoing neurons from these switching points lead to other switching points, and so on, until the auditory cortex itself is reached. When the neurons of the auditory cortex fire, the listener "hears sounds."

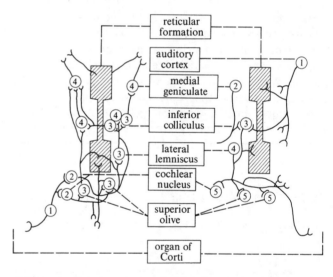

Schematic diagram of the principal neural pathways of the auditory system. For clarity, ascending pathways (neurons taking signals toward the auditory cortex) are shown to the left, descending pathways (neurons taking signals away from the auditory cortex) to the right. A number of by-passes are omitted. (Simplified from Vernon B. Mountcastle, ed., *Medical Physiology*, 12th ed. [St. Louis: C. V. Mosby, 1968], V. II, p. 1508.)

Now, obviously, if you expect to deal with messages going through this stretch of the system with the same degree of certitude that physicists and physiologists can have for the previous stretch, you would have to be able to say

1. which neuron leads into which, and
2. which neuron fires under what stimulus.

---

* In this case the differentiation is lost in the mechanism of the piano, not the mechanism of the ear. No matter how the pianist moves the key, all he can do to vary the shape of the sound wave is to vary the speed with which the hammer is thrown against the string.

That's not easy. In the first place, there are approximately 12,000,000 individual neurons in the human brain and 30,000 neurons in the auditory nerve alone. Furthermore, they all look pretty much alike. You can see the ossicles with your naked eye and guess from their shape and where they are attached what many of their mechanical properties might be. But the brain just looks like an undifferentiated lump of gray putty.

In the second place, if you want to observe how neurons work, you have to observe a live brain. You can remove the middle and inner ear from a recently dead human being and observe its mechanical properties. It will still function because its motive power comes from outside, from the fluctuation in the air pressure against the eardrum. But you can't remove neurons leading in and out of the cochlear nucleus and expect them to function. Their motive power comes from the electrochemical processes of living cells.

These difficulties are not insurmountable. Over the past fifty years, neurophysiologists have developed remarkably complete anatomical maps of the auditory system. During the past twenty years, they have been able to observe the electrical activity of the single neuron by inserting a tiny electrode directly into the living cell. They can show how a particular frequency of the sound wave results in the firing of neurons in a particular area of each switching station and of the auditory cortex itself. They are in the process of developing a consistent picture of the way incoming signals are disregarded or registered, censored or relayed at each station. But they are still far from being able to observe and explain how the brain hears, in the sense that a physicist can observe and explain how a sound wave is propagated. And they are further yet from being able to tell us how the signals to and from the auditory cortex interact with other higher brain centers to produce what we have been calling the way the listener "conceives of what he hears." For our purposes, then, we'll have to find some other way than physical observation of the brain to get at "what the listener hears" and how he conceives of what he hears. But how?

1.2 "Why Don't You Just Ask Him What He Hears?"

Well, why don't we? Suppose we played our listener a recording of these notes

and then asked him: "What did you hear?" He might respond in three different ways:

1. he might play (or sing) what he heard;
2. he might write some marks on music paper that signified to him what he heard;
3. he might try to tell us in words what he heard.

Clearly none of these responses produces the same kind of information as the observations we were talking about in the previous section. It's not that our listener is evasive. He can't say any more than you or I can which neuron fired when, or even which part of his brain was most active. The only way he can get at "what he heard," in order to respond, is by going through "how he conceived of what he heard."

Take his third response, the verbal one, first. Suppose he answers: "Seven notes. The first lower than the second. From the second one on, they make a descending scale." A perfectly good description of "what he heard." Yet note how it reports sounds as related to one another ("lower than") and refers to concepts outside the seven notes ("scale"). And even if our listener was a musical illiterate and could only report that he heard "some notes played on a piano," he has still sorted out the continuous flow of sound into units of sound ("notes") and related these units to others in his auditory memory well enough to identify a common source ("piano"). There really is no way you can *say anything* about what you've heard except in terms of how you conceive of what you've heard.

Or take the second response: notation. Suppose our listener writes

A perfect answer—that is, identical with the symbols the pianist played from—but certainly not just what he heard. Indeed, the degree of conceptualization is far higher than in the verbal response. To get some idea of the number of ways these seven notes are being conceived of in the previous example, just compare it with either of the following possible responses

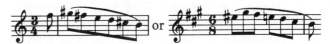

The point is that the notation of this kind of music does not represent sounds but ways of conceiving of sounds in relation to one another. E♯ or F♮ might do equally well to represent the sound you'll hear when you press a particular piano key, but we conceive of the relation of E♯ to G♯ in a very different way from the relation of F♮ to G♯. A note that's on the beat and a note that's off the beat might, taken out of context, sound the same, but in context we conceive of them as very different, and our notation shows it.

Or take, finally, the first response: playing or singing. By making us hear sounds he can hear too, our listener can come much closer to letting us know "what he heard." He can say: "I hear these sounds I'm making and I can remember those sounds you made, and, insofar as I can compare what I hear now with what I remember hearing then, they are the same." But aren't "remembering" and "comparing" part of "conceiving"? That, in any case, was the way we characterized conceiving originally. Maybe our characterization was a poor one. Is it really all that useful to consider "hearing" and "conceiving of what you hear" as separate acts, or "what he hears" and "how he conceives of what he hears" as separate stretches of the message?

The problem is that somehow we have gotten into the habit of thinking of hearing as a passive first step —as though the part of the brain that hears were some kind of electromagnetically sensitized plate that simply receives the imprint of any signals sent to it— and conception as an active second step—as though the part of the brain that conceives of what is heard were some kind of computer that sorts through the signals on the plate, analyzes their relations to one another and to other signals in its storage unit, and catalogs the result. Actually, what neurological evidence we have suggests that hearing is a highly active, not a passive, first step; that the computer operation begins at the first set of synapses; and that the information that reaches the auditory cortex has already been sorted out, analyzed, and catalogued in terms of that brain's experience with previous signals of that sort. While we can't yet explain the exact set of processes by which the brain searches out the information it needs to "hear a sound," these processes appear to be much like those we think it uses to conceive of what it hears. So, for the time being, we might as well scrap the notion of what's heard as an independent preliminary to "how what's heard is conceived of" and concentrate on different ways of conceiving of what's heard. But how do we get at these ways?

Consider again the three different types of response to the question "what do you hear?" First consider the type where the listener actually *plays* or *sings* what he heard. Playing or singing constitutes just as much of a message as the original message, or at least as the last few stages of that message. Consequently, you can observe the same stages of both messages— either by hearing the sounds of each yourself, or, if you want to keep your own conception out of the way, by measuring the sound waves—and compare them.

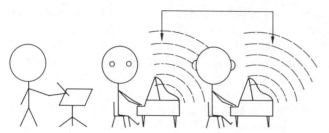

For example, take the case of a listener who, on hearing a recording of a pianist playing

sings "what he heard":

da dee da da da da da

Obviously, neither the sound waves he generates nor the sounds we hear are the same as the original. Yet we can certainly conceive of both as bearing essentially the same message. All seven notes of the original have certain obvious features in common—those features that identify them as notes in the upper-middle range of the piano—that are *not* shared by any of the notes in the response. On the other hand, those features that differ from note to note in the response form patterns that closely resemble patterns in the original.* Presumably when we say that these two versions bear essentially the same message, we are talking about such patterns.

Now consider the second response, where the listener *writes down* what he hears. Here the problems are slightly different. Again the listener has created a stage of another message that can be compared with the same stage of the original message.

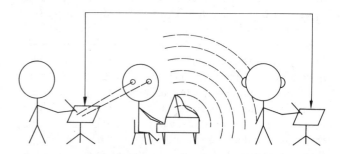

But here the comparable stage occurs much earlier in the system, back where the listener has no way of experiencing it first hand. For example, take the case

---

* The most obvious feature that changes from note to note being, of course, pitch. However, there are others— unfortunately, for our purposes, less explicitly notated—that have a part in bearing the message in question. Here the problem is that to give an example of *sounds* in a book you have to use *written notes*. Our notation of pitch is explicit and precise. Our notation of duration and loudness is explicit only for relatively gross differences. Thus, if you were to measure exactly how long and how loud each note is, you would presumably find that in both versions the G♯ is slightly longer and slightly louder than any of the notes that follow it. For a definition of the critical word "note" and a discussion of the features that differentiate one note from another see Chapter 2. For a discussion of the interrelation of non-pitch factors in projecting pitch patterns see Chapter 9.

of the listener who, on hearing the recorded passage, writes down "what he hears" as:

Presumably this means that he conceives of the same sequence of sounds differently from the composer or performer—he thinks of different notes as falling on the beat. But what do we mean when we say that a note is "on the beat"? And how can we tell from the sounds we hear which notes are on the beat and which are off?

Finally, consider the third response, where the listener tries to *tell* you what he heard. Here the problems are essentially different. Once again another message is involved, but this time it's a message of an entirely different type. None of the stages of this kind of communication can be compared with any stage of the original.

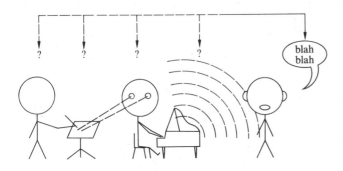

On the other hand, suppose two listeners respond with messages of this type. Or suppose the performer or even the composer were to use messages of this type to talk about the way they conceive of what they imagined, wrote, saw, played, or heard. Obviously such messages can be compared.

When we use one form of communication to refer to another form of communication, we say we apply a *metalanguage* to an *object language*. It might appear that the use of a parallel but essentially different communication system (the verbal metalanguage) gives us a way of getting at just those spots in the original system (the musical object language) that have been eluding us. For example, it might appear that to find out if composer, performer, and listener conceived of a message in the same way, all you would have to do is get them together and ask them. Of course, it's not that easy.

In the first place, to verbalize your conception of a sound, or of the relationship between two sounds, or of the relationship of a sound to some other concept, takes very special skills. There's no reason to suppose that just because a person is good at conceiving of musical messages he's going to be any good at using words to explain his conceptions. (In fact, most people's skill is better characterized by the dialogue illustrated on this page than by the examples on page 7.)

In the second place, even if two people were good at using words to explain their conceptions, how could you be sure the words they used referred to the same conception? How could you be sure they wouldn't use different words for the same conception?

The safest way out of both difficulties would seem to be to develop your own metalanguage and teach it to people by applying it to actual statements in the object language—that is, to passages of music, written or performed. At first you may have to limit your discussion to extremely simple passages—indeed you may have to construct artificially simple passages expressly for the purpose of showing people exactly what you're talking about. But by so doing you should be able to establish a common way of talking about "what you hear" that can then be applied to more and more complex situations.

That is, in fact, just what this book will try to do—develop a metalanguage we can use to talk about tonal music. Fortunately we don't have to invent an entirely new language; ordinary English syntax and, for the most part, ordinary English words will do perfectly well. But we will have to develop a small, closely knit vocabulary of key words—words that pertain directly to the ways in which we think of the music we hear.* In the process of defining and relating these key words we will in effect be exposing the logical framework in terms of which we understand tonal music. That logical framework is what we will mean by the "theory of tonal music."†

---

* Where possible such words will be ones already in use, e.g., "notes," "beats," "line," "step," "consonant," although we may define them somewhat differently.

† As I hope its title makes clear, this book is not intended as a formal presentation of that theory, or even of one such theory, but only as an introduction to the subject. Any theory is useful only insofar as the person applying it can relate its abstractions directly to his own musical experience. Reliability of the metalanguage rather than elegance of theory construction will be our principal concern.

Questions for Discussion

1. How would you expand the communication system described in this chapter to include copying or printing of music or recording of music?
2. The following sentences all refer to the same musical message, but at different stages in its passage through the communication system. Which stage or stages could the speaker mean in each case?
   a. Have you ever seen Bernstein do Beethoven's Fifth?
   b. I bought Beethoven's Fifth today.
   c. Beethoven's Fifth is a hard piece.
   d. It's not easy to record Beethoven's Fifth in Philharmonic Hall.
   e. Why don't conductors take the repeat in the first movement of Beethoven's Fifth?
   f. Beethoven's Fifth is in C minor.
   g. Beethoven took a long time to finish his Fifth Symphony.

CHAPTER TWO

Notes

2.0 Notes

We conceive of music as being made up of units of sound called notes.* To think of a sound as a note we must be able to think of it as
1. having a particular *pitch* and
2. beginning at a particular *point in time* and lasting a particular *length of time.*

We may also think of it as
3. having a particular *loudness* and
4. having a particular tone color or *timbre.*†

(We could, however, also think of the note as having a changing loudness or even as not having any particular loudness at all, and we could think of the note as having a changing timbre or as not having any particular timbre at all.)

---

* This assertion, like many others in Chapters 2 and 3, need not be taken as a statement of fact; rather it is an assumption necessary to a theory of tonal and, indeed, of most Western music. I don't know that everybody thinks of music as being made up of notes, but I do know that you can't get far in thinking about tonal music without making this assumption. In general, assertions of the type "We think of x as y" can be understood either as the axioms of the theory or simply as definitions.

† Each of these attributes of the sound we hear can be correlated with one or more measurable properties of the sound wave that reaches our ears:
1. pitch with the fundamental frequency of the wave;
2. time with time (more properly, subjective time with objective, or chronometric, time);
3. loudness with the amount of energy the wave carries;
4. timbre with (a) the distribution of that energy at various frequencies and
   (b) the rates at which energy is accumulated and dissipated.

What we know about how our ears and brains gauge and encode these properties partially explains how we conceive of the corresponding attributes of sound—but only partially. See the Appendix.

We relate one note to another in terms of these four attributes. We quantify pitch and time relationships with great precision. We can say exactly how much higher one note is than another, or how much later it begins. To do so we refer the notes in question to pre-established *reference systems* of pitch and time. Pitch and time relationships are the primary stuff of the structure of any piece of tonal music.

We do not quantify loudness or timbre with anywhere near the same precision. We say one note is louder than another, but we do not say how much louder. We say two notes have a different timbre, but we are hard put to say what the difference is. Loudness and timbre relationships have a differential role in the structure of tonal music. That is, we use them to help sort out which pitch and time relationships are critical to the structure.

2.1 Pitch

The pitch of a note is how high the note is. If you think of the pitch of any note as a point (P_1) on a vertical axis,

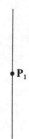

it is obvious that the pitch of any other note would either have to be the same ($P_2 = P_1$) or different

($P_2 \neq P_1$). If it is different, it would have to be either higher ($P_2 > P_1$)

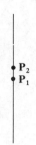

or lower ($P_2 < P_1$).

We think of pitch and pitch relationships in tonal music in terms of certain fixed collections of pitches. We say how high a note is by identifying its pitch with a particular member of a particular collection.* We say how much higher the note is than another by referring both their pitches to the same collection.

The Chromatic Collection: Intervals Measured by Semitones • Think of the pitches available on a piano. Consider how they are related. Press a key. You get a note with a particular pitch. Press the key (black or white) immediately to the right. You get a note a little higher than the first note. Press the key

---

* If a note is too high to be identified with one pitch in the collection and too low to be identified with the next highest note in the collection,

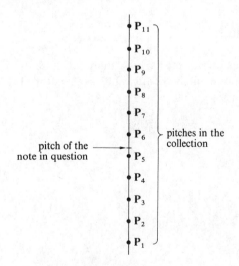

we have no way of thinking of its pitch other than to reject it as "out of tune."

immediately to the right of the second key. You get a note that is exactly as much higher than the second note as the second note is higher than the first. For example:

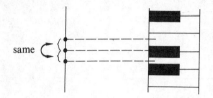

The difference between the pitch of two notes is called an *interval*. The interval formed by the notes you get when you play any two adjacent keys on the piano is always the same size. It is called a *semitone*. A collection of pitches each a semitone from the next highest is called a *chromatic collection*.

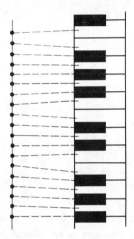

We can use the semitone as a unit interval to measure the size of the interval between any two pitches in the chromatic collection.

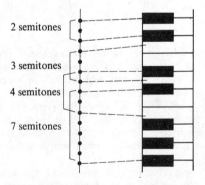

Pitch Class • The interval made up of twelve semitones has a special function in tonal music. Try the following experiment. Press the white key that is eight white keys in from the right end of the keyboard

Then sing a note that seems to you to have the same pitch as the note you just played. Obviously you can't sing a note that really has the same pitch—the piano note is much too high. Try to find a note on the piano that actually has the same pitch. If you're a trained high soprano, you might find it twelve semitones below the one you played. Otherwise you'll find it twenty-four, thirty-six, or forty-eight semitones lower, depending on your age, sex, and vocal prowess. The striking thing is that we accept any and all of these pitches as being *in some sense* the same as the first, even though they are obviously not the same pitch in the simple sense that the two pitches you get by pressing the same key twice are. Nevertheless, we identify these pitches with one another. We call them all "C," or, more properly, "members of the pitch-class C." A *pitch class* is simply the class of all pitches some integral multiple of twelve semitones from a given pitch. If two pitches form an interval of twelve semitones, or twenty-four, or sixty they are members of the same pitch class. If they form an interval of one semitone, or thirty, or seventy-one, they are not.

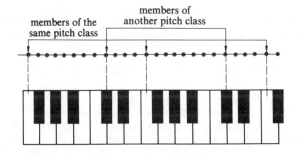

To show pitches as members of pitch classes at a glance, you can curve the straight line we've been using around into a spiral so that every twelfth point is lined up on the same radius.

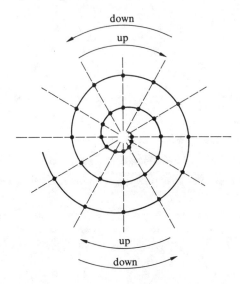

The points still represent pitches a semitone apart; now *up* is represented by clockwise movement and *down* by counterclockwise. Members of the same pitch class are lined up on the same radius of the spiral.

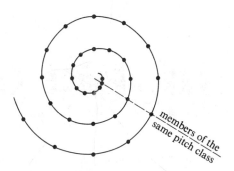

If you're concerned only with pitch class and not with distinguishing between one member of a given pitch class and another, you can tighten the spiral to form a circle so that all the points on a given radius become one point, and each point represents one pitch class.

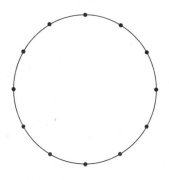

Diatonic Collections • Think of the pitches you can get by using only the white keys of the piano. Consider how they are related. Wherever there is a black key between two adjacent white keys, the interval between the white keys will be two semitones, or a whole tone. Wherever there is no black key between adjacent white keys, the interval will be one semitone. Observe the pattern of intervals between adjacent white-key pitches.

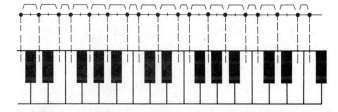

Every seven white keys the same pattern of intervening black keys is repeated: two black keys, no black key, three black keys, no black. Thus, if you start on a white key directly to the left of two black keys, every twelve semitones the same pattern of intervals between adjacent white-key pitches will be repeated: two whole tones, one semitone, three whole tones, one semitone. If you start on some other key, you can get the same pattern of intervals by using black keys as well as white ones. For example:

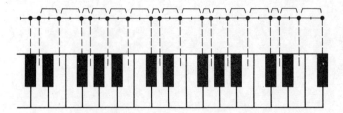

Any collection of seven pitch classes with this particular pattern of intervals between adjacent pitches is called a *diatonic collection*. You can construct a diatonic collection by the following simple method: take a pitch class.

Add another pitch class seven semitones higher (or five lower—it will turn out the same).

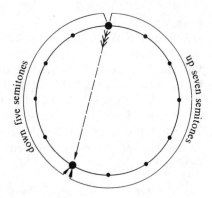

Add another pitch class seven semitones higher (or five lower) than the second.

Repeat the process until you have seven pitch classes.

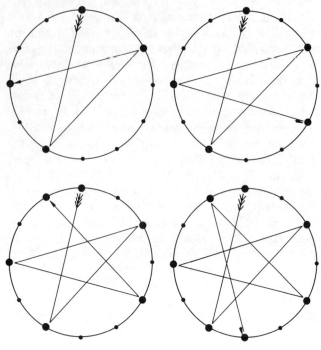

Since there are twelve different pitch classes to start from and since five and seven are mutually prime with twelve, there are twelve different diatonic collections embedded in the chromatic collection.

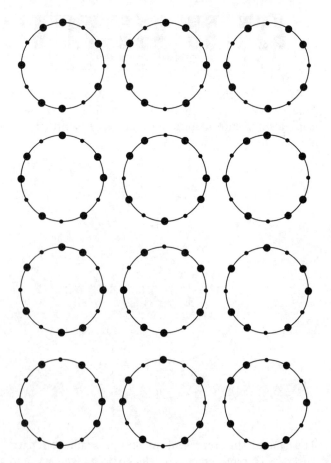

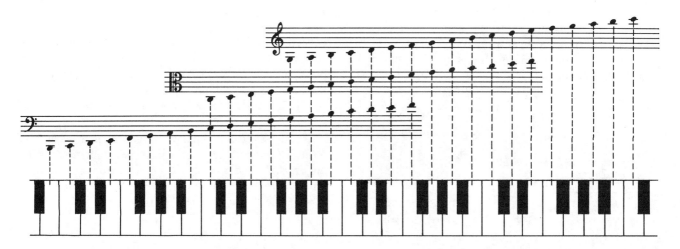

Notating Pitch • We conceive of pitch in tonal music in terms of diatonic collections. Our notation fits this conception. We notate pitch by the position of the note head on a five-line staff: ▤. You can put the note head on a line ▤ or a space between two lines ▤. If you want to show that two notes are to have the same pitch, you put both the note heads in the same position ▤. If you want to show that they are adjacent members of the same diatonic collection you put them in adjacent positions ▤.

To show which pitch in which diatonic collection you mean, you need a clef and a signature. The clef shows which line of the staff would correspond to a given pitch in the white-key diatonic collection.

F clef or bass clef — F below middle C

C clefs: tenor clef, alto clef — middle C

G clef or treble clef — G above middle C

The signature shows which diatonic collection you are using. To get the diatonic collection made up of just white notes you write just the clef (see above). To get the other diatonic collections you must put some sharps or flats right after the clef to form a signature. A sharp (♯) on a line or space just to the right of the clef means that the pitch corresponding to that line or space, and all the other members of that pitch class, are to be read one semitone higher. A flat (♭) in the signature means that the pitch corresponding to that line or space, and all the other members of that pitch class, are to be read one semitone lower. Thus ♯ means that all F's are to be read as F♯'s and ♭ means that all B's are to be read as B♭'s.

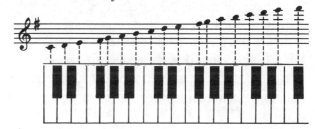

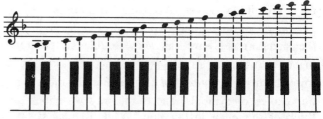

The order of the flats and sharps in a signature shows how that diatonic collection could be generated from a single pitch class by adding other pitch classes seven semitones higher. Flats in a signature show the beginning of the process, although in reverse order. The last flat corresponds to the pitch class from which the diatonic collection could be generated, the next-to-last flat, the first pitch to be added, etc.

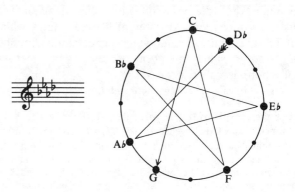

Sharps in a signature show the end of the process. The last sharp in a signature always represents the last pitch class to be added, the next-to-last sharp the next-to-last pitch, etc.

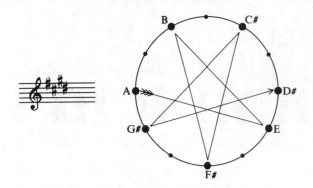

We show pitches that are *not* members of the diatonic collection indicated by the signature by means of *accidentals*. For any pitch that is not affected by a sharp or flat in the signature ⸺ or ⸺ we can show a pitch that is a semitone higher by writing a sharp directly in front of the note ⸺ or ⸺ and a pitch that is a semitone lower by writing a flat directly in front of the note ⸺ or ⸺. For any pitch that is affected by a sharp in the signature ⸺ we can show a pitch a semitone higher by using a *double-sharp* ⸺ and a pitch that is a semitone lower by using a *natural* ⸺. Similarly, for any pitch that is affected by a flat in the signature ⸺ we can show a pitch a semitone higher by using a natural ⸺ and a pitch a semitone lower by using a *double-flat* ⸺. For the most part, our choice of symbols reflects the way we choose to think of the pitch in question.* Thus to play ⸺ on the piano we press the same key we would use to play ⸺, but we think of the first as a *raised* version of an E and the second as a *lowered* version of an F♯.

Naming Intervals • We conceive of intervals in tonal music in terms of the intervals formed by members of a diatonic collection. Our nomenclature fits this conception. An interval between notes whose pitches are identical (and which hence can be thought of as the same member of the same diatonic collection) is called a *unison*.†

An interval between two pitches that could be thought of as adjacent pitches in the same diatonic collection is called a *second*. Because of the intervallic structure of the diatonic collection there are two sizes of second, a larger second of two semitones and a smaller second of only one semitone. We call the larger a *major second* and the smaller *a minor second*.‡

We think of any interval larger than a second in terms of how it can (or can't) be made up of the major and minor seconds of a diatonic collection. Any interval we can think of as being made up of two seconds

[2nd + 2nd = 3rd musical example]

we call a *third*. Obviously, since there are two sizes of second there must be at least two sizes of third: a four-semitone size made up of two major seconds, and a three-semitone size made up of one major and one minor second. We call the larger a *major third* and the smaller a *minor third*.

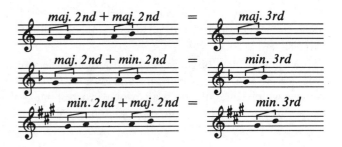

(There is also another, even smaller, two-semitone third that is made up of two minor seconds:

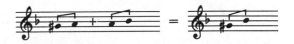

Since the minor seconds in a diatonic collection never come together like this, we think of this third as "too small to be a diatonic third" and call it a *diminished third*.)§

Similarly, any interval that we can think of as being made up of three seconds is called a *fourth*:

[2nd + 2nd + 2nd = 4th musical example]

Again, there are two sizes of fourths available between pitches in a diatonic collection: one of five

---

* For the exceptions see, in particular, Sections 7.6 and 8.4.
† Properly speaking ⸺ and ⸺ are not unisons, but diminished seconds. Our notation shows that although the pitches may be identical, we think of them as belonging to different diatonic collections. Such a relationship is called an *enharmonic equivalence*. We say B♯ is enharmonically equivalent to C.

‡ A second that is too large to occur between two members of any diatonic collection is called an *augmented second* ⸺.
§ The diminished third is also "too small to be a diatonic interval" in that it could be confused with a proper diatonic interval, the major second, since both are the same size, namely two semitones.

16

semitones made up of two major seconds and one minor second

or

and one of six semitones made up of three major seconds

We can think of the five-semitone size as the one basic to the diatonic collection. (It is, after all, the interval you can use to generate the collection.) We call it a *perfect fourth*, or simply a *fourth*. We think of the other size as a special case—the interval between the first and last elements in the generation scheme,

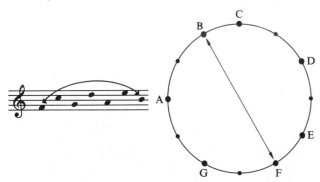

made up of three seconds and therefore a fourth, but too large to be a perfect fourth like the others. We call such a fourth an *augmented fourth*. It is, however, the only augmented interval between members of the same diatonic collection.

Another kind of fourth is made up of two minor seconds and only one major second and hence measures only four semitones:

Since the minor seconds of a diatonic collection are never that close together such a fourth is too small to be a perfect fourth, and we call it a *diminished fourth*.

Similarly, a *fifth* is made up of four seconds. We distinguish between the *perfect fifth* (three major seconds and one minor second and hence seven semitones), the *diminished fifth* (two major seconds and two minor seconds and hence six semitones),* and an *augmented fifth* (four major seconds and hence eight semitones).

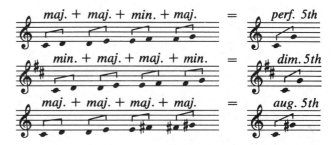

Sixths are made up of five seconds and can be *major* (four major seconds and one minor, hence nine semitones)

or *minor* (three major seconds and two minor, hence eight semitones).

A sixth that is made up of five major seconds (and hence ten semitones) is too large for a diatonic collection and is called an *augmented sixth*:

![maj. + maj. + maj. + maj. + maj. = aug. 6th]

Sevenths are made up of six seconds and can be *major* (five major seconds and one minor second, hence eleven semitones)

![maj. + maj. + min. + maj. + maj. + maj. = maj. 7th]

or *minor* (four major seconds and two minor, hence ten semitones).

![maj. + min. + maj. + maj. + maj. + min. = min. 7th]

A seventh made up of three major seconds and three minor seconds is too small for a diatonic collection and is called a *diminished seventh*:

![min. + maj. + min. + maj. + maj. + min. = dim. 7th]

* The only diminished interval between members of the same diatonic collection.

Finally, an interval made up of seven seconds is called an *octave*.* If the octave is to be between members of the same pitch class it must, of course, be made up of five major seconds and two minor seconds to total twelve semitones. Such an octave is sometimes called a *perfect octave* to distinguish it from an octave made up of six major seconds and only one minor second, which is too large to be a perfect octave

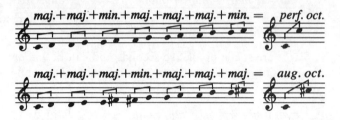

*In English the latinate terms are reserved for the pitch-identity interval (unison, or prime, instead of "first") and the pitch-class membership interval (octave instead of "eighth").

or from an octave made up of four major seconds and three minor seconds and hence too small.

Intervals larger than an octave are called *compound intervals*. We think of such intervals as being made up of some number of octaves plus a smaller interval. We think of a *major ninth* as an octave plus a major second, a *minor tenth* as an octave plus a minor third. Indeed, when the interval is larger than a tenth we usually call it by its compound name—most musicians have to stop and think what an eleventh or a fifteenth is and prefer to say "octave and a fourth" or "double octave." We think of an interval and its compounds as comprising an interval class. Thus, a fourth, an octave and a fourth, two octaves and a fourth, etc., are members of the same interval class, namely that of the fourth.

Exercises

1. Generate a diatonic collection starting from six o'clock.

If you call twelve o'clock C, what would you call the other pitch classes in the collection you have generated?

2. For each of the following give (a) the size of the interval in semitones and (b) the name of the interval in terms of the diatonic collection indicated by the signature.

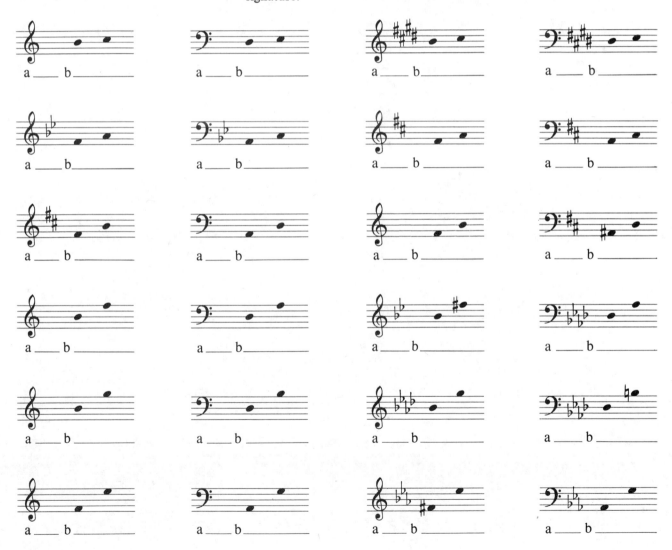

19

2.2 Time

We think of both the point in time that a note begins and the period of time it lasts in terms of a set of reference points in time called *beats*.

Reference Point Systems • Imagine a particular point in time, P_1.

You can use P_1 as a reference point to help you locate the beginnings of notes. Any note, by definition, begins at a particular point in time. That point must either be identical with P_1, or, if it is not, be either before or after P_1. Thus, you can think of any note as beginning before, at, or after P_1.

Now imagine a second point, P_2, some time after P_1.

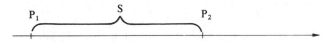

Of course you can use these two points in much the same way you used the single point: to distinguish between notes beginning before P_1, at P_1, between P_1 and P_2, at P_2, or after P_2. But you can do much more now that you have two points. These two points define a period of time, the span, S, from P_1 to P_2.

You can use S to estimate how much before or after either reference point a note begins. For example:

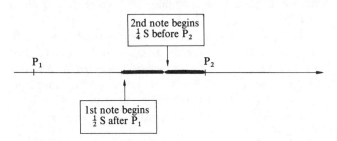

And you can use S to estimate how long a note lasts.

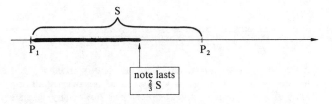

You can make both estimates more accurately and over a longer period of time if you use S to set up a whole system of reference points.

You can use S to extend the pair of reference points P_1, P_2 into a series of equally spaced reference points, P_1, P_2, P_3, P_4, ... Put a point P_3 S after P_2; then put a point P_4 S after P_3. Repeat the procedure as often as you wish.

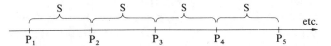

You can also use S to set up secondary reference points. Between each pair of consecutive points, P_1, P_2; P_2, P_3; etc., put one or more points p_1, p_2, p_3 . . . so as to divide S into two or more equal segments, s_1, s_2, s_3, s_4 . . .

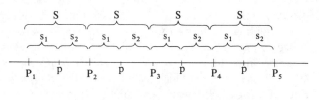

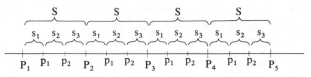

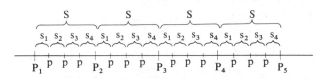

You can then use any of these new points as reference points just as you did P_1 and P_2: any note either begins at one of these points or between two consecutive points. The secondary reference points (the p's) are secondary in the sense that you locate them in terms of the way they divide up the span between two consecutive primary reference points (the P's).

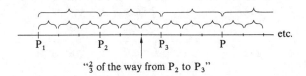

"$\frac{2}{3}$ of the way from P_2 to P_3"

You can also use any of the new spans and segments to estimate how long a note lasts or how much after the most recent reference point it begins.

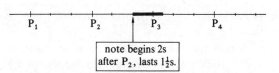

We conceive of time in tonal music in terms of systems of equally spaced reference points like the ones we have just constructed. We call the reference points *beats*. If a note begins at a reference point we say it is "on the beat"; if not, we say it is before or after the beat or simply "off the beat." We call primary reference points *downbeats*. Secondary reference points are sometimes called *upbeats*, but properly speaking upbeat is reserved for that secondary reference point immediately preceding the next downbeat. We call the span between consecutive primary reference points a *measure*. We say that a note that begins on the downbeat and lasts until the next downbeat "lasts a measure." We call the segments formed by the secondary reference points beats.*

If a note begins on one beat and lasts to the next beat we say it "lasts a beat." We call the way the secondary reference points divide the spans between primary reference points the *meter*. One secondary beat dividing each measure into two equal parts is called *duple meter*; two secondary beats dividing each measure into three equal parts is called *triple meter*. We call the rate at which beats occur the *tempo*. A rate of around 85 beats per minute (time from one beat to the next is about $\frac{1}{\sqrt{2}}$ seconds) is usually considered a moderate tempo; most tempos fall between twice and half that rate.

number of beats per minute	time between beats	
30	2^1 sec. (2.0″)	too slow to be useful
42	$2^{\frac{1}{2}}$ sec. (1.414″)	very slow
60	2^0 sec. (1.0″)	moderately slow
84	$2^{-\frac{1}{2}}$ sec. (0.70″)	moderate
120	2^{-1} sec. (0.5″)	moderately fast
168	$2^{-1\frac{1}{2}}$ sec. (0.35″)	very fast
240	2^{-2} sec. (0.25″)	too fast to be useful

Notation • The way we notate time in tonal music fits the conception we have just described. We use a series of *barlines* (vertical lines running through the staff lines) to show the primary reference points. A note symbol written immediately to the right of a barline signifies a note beginning on that downbeat.†

We use the upper number of the *time signature* (two numbers written directly after the clefs and key signatures at the beginning of the piece) to show how many segments the spans are to be divided into.

We use the lower number in the time signature to show which durational symbol will signify a note lasting one such segment. The basic set of durational symbols at our disposal corresponds to a set of durations each of which is half the duration of the next longer duration. They can be distinguished from one another by differences in shape and color of the note head, presence or absence of a stem, and number of flags or beams attached to the stem (see the table on the top of page 23).‡

Another set of symbols—rests—is used to indicate the absence of a note. As with the symbols for notes, different shapes correspond to different durations (see bottom of page 23).

Thus, once you've decided which symbol you will use to represent a note lasting one beat, you also have symbols for notes lasting two beats or four beats, as well as symbols for notes lasting only half a beat, a quarter of a beat, or an eighth of a beat. To represent notes lasting other durations you can use *dots, triplet signs,* and *ties*.

† Except, of course, when the note head is joined by a tie (see page 23) to a note head to the left of that barline.

‡ Note that these durational symbols signify relative, not absolute, periods of time. A quarter note is always half the length of a half note, but that doesn't say how many seconds either lasts. To show how long each segment is we can use a metronome marking which gives the number of such segments per minute. ♩ = MM 84 means that there are 84 quarter notes per minute.

* An unfortunate double use of the same term to mean both a point in time and a period of time between two points.

name of symbol	numerical value, where whole note = 1	symbol	variations in shape and color			
			shape of head	stem	color of head	number of flags
double whole note	2	𝄺	square	no	white	none
whole note	1	o	round	,,	,,	,,
half note	½	♩	,,	yes	,,	,,
quarter note	¼	♩	,,	,,	black	,,
eighth note	⅛	♪	,,	,,	,,	1
sixteenth note	1/16	♬	,,	,,	,,	2
thirty-second note	1/32	♬	,,	,,	,,	3

By putting a dot to the right of the notehead you show that the symbol is to be read at one and a half times its usual value. Thus, if the lower number in the time signature is a 4, ♩. means a note lasting three beats, ♩. means a note lasting a beat and a half, and ♪. means a note lasting three quarters of a beat.

By putting a triplet sign (the number 3, often with a bracket or other sign to show how many symbols it affects) over a series of durational symbols you show that each symbol is to be read at two-thirds of its usual value. Thus, to show three notes each lasting one-third of a beat, you use three of the symbols you would use for half beats and put a triplet sign over them

$\frac{3}{4}$ ♩ ♫ ♩.   or $\frac{2}{2}$ ♩ ♩ ♩

Similarly, to show two notes respectively two-thirds and one-third of the first beat and three notes one half, one sixth, and one third of the second beat you would write $\frac{2}{4}$ ♩♪ ♫ . If such triplet subdivision of the beat is the rule (rather than the exception to the rule), it is much easier to use a dotted symbol to represent notes lasting a beat. In such a case the upper number of the time signature gives the total number of triplet subdivisions per measure (that is, three times the number of beats per measure), while the lower number gives the symbol that will be used for notes lasting one third of a beat. Thus, the preceding example would read $\frac{6}{8}$ ♩ ♪ ♫ .*

By joining two noteheads representing the same pitch with a curved line called a *tie*, you show that

* In other words, $\frac{6}{8}$ does not mean six beats to the measure, the eighth note getting one beat. Similarly for other time signatures where the upper number is a multiple of three:
$\frac{6}{4}$ means two beats to a measure with the ♩. getting one beat;
$\frac{9}{8}$ means three beats to a measure with the ♩. getting one beat;
$\frac{12}{8}$ means four beats to a measure with the ♩. getting one beat.

name of symbol	numerical value, where whole rest = 1	symbol	variations in shape and position on staff
double whole rest	2	𝄺	square, between third and fourth lines
whole rest	1	𝄻	rectangular, just below fourth line
half rest	½	𝄼	rectangular, just above third line
quarter rest	¼	𝄽	
eighth rest	⅛	𝄾	one flag
sixteenth rest	1/16	𝄿	two flags
thirty-second rest	1/32	𝅀	three flags

both durational symbols are to be read as one note with a total duration equal to the sum of the two. Thus, when the lower number in the time signature is a 4, 𝅘𝅥𝅮𝅮 means one note lasting two and a half beats.

By using these symbols to represent consecutive notes we show not only how long each note is to last, but when the next note is to begin.* This way the point in time at which any note is to begin can be measured from the frames provided by the barlines. A symbol directly to the right of a barline means a note on the downbeat; if that symbol corresponds to a note lasting a beat, the next symbol means a note beginning on the second beat; if the first symbol corresponds to a note lasting a beat and a half, the next symbol means a note beginning halfway between the second beat and the next beat.

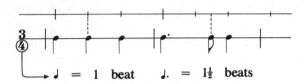

Similarly, if a symbol corresponding to a note lasting a beat is placed immediately to the left of a barline, it means a note beginning on the upbeat. If two symbols corresponding to durations adding up to a beat are placed to the left of a barline, the first of the two means a note beginning on the upbeat.

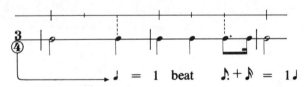

* This leaves us free to alter the duration of a note by articulation marks without affecting the period of time between beginnings of notes. Thus a staccato dot over the notehead indicates that the note stops well before the beginning of the next note and a legato curve connecting two noteheads indicates that the first note lasts until the very instant the next note begins, but the time elapsed between the beginnings of the notes is still that indicated by the durational symbols.

We will deal with these problems in Chapter 9.

Two further notational conventions help make our conception of notes in terms of beats clear:

1. Beams
   Eighth-, sixteenth-, and thirty-second notes that are subdivisions of a single beat are written with common beams rather than separate flags.†

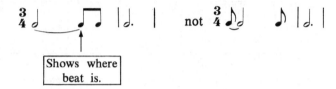

2. Ties and dots
   Tied symbols are written so that the second symbol would correspond to a note falling on the beat.

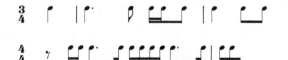

We reserve dotted symbols for on-the-beat notes

and for those off-the-beat notes that do not last beyond the next beat.

† In vocal music flags and beams were formerly used to show where syllables begin and end. This can be confusing.

Die See-len — empfinden die kräf - - - tig - sten Trie-be—

(old notation: beams show extent of syllable)

Die See-len — empfin-den die kräf - - - tig - sten Trie-be—

(new notation: legato marks show extent of syllable)

(J. S. Bach: *Cantata* No. 1, *Wie schön leuchtet der Morgenstern*, BWV 1, Aria 1, mm. 36–37.)

Exercises

1. In the following a dot (•) represents a point at which a note begins while a wedge (⋎) represents a beat. Transcribe this information into musical notation, letting a quarter note equal one beat.

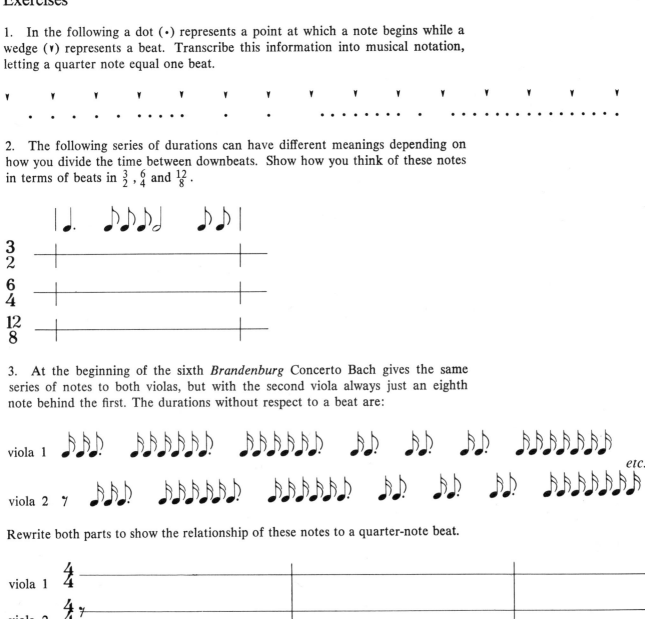

2. The following series of durations can have different meanings depending on how you divide the time between downbeats. Show how you think of these notes in terms of beats in $\frac{3}{2}$, $\frac{6}{4}$ and $\frac{12}{8}$.

3. At the beginning of the sixth *Brandenburg* Concerto Bach gives the same series of notes to both violas, but with the second viola always just an eighth note behind the first. The durations without respect to a beat are:

Rewrite both parts to show the relationship of these notes to a quarter-note beat.

2.3 Loudness

Imagine a note. Now imagine a second note exactly as loud as the first. Next, imagine a note that's louder than the first note. Can you imagine a fourth note that is as much louder than the third note as the third note was louder than the first?

It's not that the idea of the relationship is so hard to grasp, it's just that that kind of relationship is not characteristic of the way we think of loudness in tonal music, and consequently it is not part of what most musicians are trained to do. It would be difficult to get a musician to play three notes that two or more people will agree fulfill these relationships.

Now, of course, if you ask a musician to play a note exactly as loud as a note you played (or louder, or softer), he can, and he can play it so that other people will agree that his note was as loud as (or louder, or softer than) your note. Such relationships are part of the way we think of the loudness of a note in tonal music on those occasions when we are specifically aware of loudness as an independent characteristic. The striking thing is how rare those occasions are.

Why should this be? It's not that the energy level of the sound waves performers generate doesn't vary from note to note—it usually does. Nor is it that the variations in the energy level of the sound waves are too small to be perceived as variations in loudness. In fact, if we hear the sounds out of context, we have no difficulty discriminating among them. Rather, it's because most of the time we use these variations in amplitude to communicate something other than the idea of loudness *per se*.

Suppose you had a way of generating a series of clicks, one every second. They are to be identical in all respects save one: the clicks on odd seconds have a slightly greater energy level than the ones on even seconds. Most people will find it easier to think of those clicks as all being equally loud but coming alternately on downbeat and upbeat. Of course, there's a good deal more going on in real music than just clicks. There are many other signals that tell the listener where the downbeat is. Most of the time there's no need for the performer to step up the energy level of the sound waves that become notes on the downbeat. (Indeed, when he does, the effect is usually crude, and we accuse him of "coming down heavy on the downbeat.") Occasionally, however, there is. Occasionally, for example, the pitches you would expect to find on the downbeat are on the next beat, and the pitches you might expect to find on the upbeat are on the downbeat. In such a case the performer automatically "leans on the downbeat" a little and lets up on the next beat.

The exact variation in amplitude depends on many factors: the length of the notes, their particular pitch relationships, the physical capabilities of the instrument, and so on. The performer senses how much is needed to make the location of the downbeat clear without creating the impression that the notes on the downbeat are louder than the others. None of this need be notated by the composer. He assumes that the performer understands the note-to-note context from the pitch durations, barlines, and beams on the page and will know what to do to communicate that context. Neither he, nor the performer, nor the listener normally thinks of such note-to-note variations as changes in loudness. The variations they do understand as changes in loudness are the ones that affect a wider context. They are also the ones the composer is more apt to notate as such. For example, suppose the composer wants the performer to think of two passages as being at different levels: one moderately loud and one soft. He marks the first passage *mf* and the second *p*.* If you were to measure the energy level of the sound waves the performer generates in playing each of these passages, you would find that they were far from equal, that is, there would be a considerable range in any one passage. While the average level of the *p* passage might be distinctly lower than that of the *mf* passage, the highest level of the *p* passage might be above the lowest level of the *mf* passage. Nevertheless, performer and listener would agree that two distinct levels had been maintained. Similarly, if the composer wants a given note to stick out of the note-to-note context of a passage so that its influence will be understood to go beyond that context, he may mark it with a >, a *sfz*, or, if the marking for the passage is *p*, an *f*. The performer then understands that such a note is supposed to stick out, supposed to be heard as louder than you might expect it to be. How much louder will have to depend on the performer's understanding, not just of the symbol, but of the larger context, that is, what that note sticking out has to do with the way all the notes in that part of the piece are related.

2.4 Timbre

Play middle C on the piano. Now sing the same note. How do you conceive of the difference between these two notes? Can you compare them at all beyond saying they had the same pitch, the same length, the same loudness, but different timbres? Different in what sense? When two notes have different pitches,

---

* The letters used to mark contrasting levels of loudness are abbreviations of Italian words.
   f=forte, "strong" and hence loud.
   p=piano, "level, not raised" and hence soft.
Intermediate gradations are made possible by
   m=mezzo, "medium"; thus *mf* means medium loud, that is loud, but not as loud as *f*, while *mp* means medium soft, not as soft as *p* but softer than *mf*.
Repeating the *f* or the *p* increases the degree of loudness or softness implied. Thus *ff* stand for *fortissimo*, very loud, while *pp* stands for *pianissimo*, very soft.

or different lengths, or different loudnesses we can say that one is higher, or longer, or louder than the other. Can you say that the piano note is more—well, more what?—than the voice note? Certainly more piano-like if you want, but that doesn't tell you any more than you knew when you called one note a piano note and the other note a voice note. Now this may seem at first like a linguistic problem rather than a musical one. Perhaps we just don't have a word for the quality by means of which we distinguish piano notes from voice notes. On the other hand, if there is such a quality, you ought to be able to imagine another note that has less of that quality than a piano note and more of it than a voice note. But you can't, or at least I can't. Why should this be?

The trouble is that the variables by which we distinguish piano notes from voice notes are many rather than one. When we use the word timbre, we are simply including all these variables in one grab-bag term.

Try the following experiment. Lift up the lid of the piano, put your foot on the pedal, and pluck the middle of one of the shorter strings with your fingernail. Then pluck it again, this time a little closer to the bridge. And again, and again until you reach the bridge. The timbre of the notes will change gradually. What happens is that as you change the position of initial maximum displacement of the string, you also change the pattern of motion the string makes when it gets going and therefore the distribution of energy among the various frequencies at which the string is vibrating. The closer toward the end of the string you pluck, the weaker the lower partials (including the fundamental) get and the "twangier" and "more metallic" the timbre becomes.

Now you also generate different-shaped sound waves when you play the piano the ordinary way, although we don't think of the change as a change in timbre. Try striking a key on the piano. Hit it again a little harder. Again, even harder. And again, harder than that. Keep on until you think the next one will break the piano and then stop. The harder you hit the key, the faster the hammer hits the string and the greater the energy of the string's vibrations. The greater the energy of the string's vibrations, the greater the distortion of their pattern by the time the pattern is radiated by the soundboard. The relative strength of the partials becomes more and more markedly altered as you hit the key harder and harder, but you probably didn't think of the change as a change in timbre, until the last few tries when the notes began to get jangly.

Actually such changes prove very useful in getting some sense of how loud a pianist is playing. When he's 200 feet away from you on the stage of a concert hall, the amplitude of the sound waves that reach your ears may be less than when he's 10 feet away in your living room, but the pattern of distortion is the same.

Or try playing each note on the piano, one after another, rather softly, from the lowest A to the highest C. Listen to the timbre of each note and see if you can detect any change. Next look inside the piano and note the dividing line between the hammers that strike two wound strings and the hammers that strike three unwound strings. Play a series of notes that crosses the dividing line. Did you hear a difference in timbre? Presumably the difference in the pattern of motion of the heavy, wound strings and the light, unwound strings should produce different-shaped wave forms and hence different timbres, but on most pianos the difference is barely, if at all, detectable, and then usually only after you know where the dividing line is. The piano manufacturer has, of course, done his utmost to minimize the difference—or rather to distribute it along the whole range of the instrument—by adjusting other variables such as the shape of the hammers, the tension and length of the strings, and so on.

What is done for the pianist by the manufacturer, the performer must learn to do for himself on most other instruments. When a beginner first blows a clarinet, for example, there is a marked difference in the timbre of the highest note he can play by opening up all the holes, a note with the pitch 𝄞 and the note a semitone higher 𝄞 . What the clarinetist learns is to minimize the difference. He learns to alter the air pressure and the position of his mouth so that the difference in timbre between 𝄞 and 𝄞 is no more noticeable than the difference in timbre between 𝄞 and 𝄞 or between 𝄞 and 𝄞 . In other words, by making changes in timbre as much as possible one-to-one with changes in pitch, he tries to create a sense of timbral identity—his "sound" as he puts it—throughout his entire range. His attitude is highly indicative of how we think of timbre in tonal music. Even though the timbre of high notes on the clarinet is markedly different from the timbre of low notes on the clarinet, we still think of the timbre of both primarily as clarinet timbre—that is as a basically different quality from flute timbre, or violin timbre, or voice timbre, in short, a quality identifiable only with itself.

CHAPTER THREE

Lines

3.0 Lines

We think of the notes in a tonal piece as being connected into chains of consecutive notes called *lines*. In order for two notes to be consecutive:
1. the two notes must begin at two different points in time,
2. no other note in the line can begin at a point between those two points, and
3. the first note must not last beyond the beginning of the second note.

By saying that the notes must be connected, we can distinguish those pairs of consecutive notes we choose to consider as being in the same line from those we don't. Take the notes

If we consider the lines to be

we are in effect saying that there is a special sense in which the first E and F are connected, or the C and the D, that is not true of the first E and the D, nor of the C and the F.

If, on the other hand, we consider the lines to be

we are saying that the E and the D or the C and the F are connected in this special way and that the C and the D or the E and the F are not.

Thus, only one note is present in a given line at a given time. This means that we can conceive of the notes as appearing one by one in a succession, each note replacing the one before it and each note in its turn being replaced by the next note until the last note occurs. Or, to put it another way, we can think of the line itself as progressing from one note to the next. Thus, we can think of the line as an entity with its own structure, unfolding in time.

This in turn means that we can conceive of a piece of music as being made up of two or more such lines unfolding simultaneously. We can relate these lines to one another, both in terms of their respective structures taken as wholes,

and in terms of the ways their individual notes may come into contact with one another.

3.1 Repetitions, Skips, and Steps

Thinking of notes as being connected in separate lines affects the way we think of the intervals between notes. The same interval may serve an entirely different function, depending on whether it is formed by consecutive notes in the same line or by simultaneously sounding notes in two different lines.

The intervals between consecutive notes in the same line can be divided into three distinct functional categories:

a. repetitions
b. steps
c. skips.

In a *repetition*, the interval between the two notes is a unison.*

We think of both notes as maintaining the same pitch. When the second note occurs, there is no doubt about the conceptual status of the pitch of the first note; it is explicitly confirmed.

In a *step*, the interval between the two notes is a major or minor second.†

We think of the pitch of the second note as *displacing* the pitch of the first. When the second note occurs, there is no doubt about the conceptual status of the pitch of the first note; it is explicitly denied.

In a *skip*, the interval between the two pitches is larger than a major second.

We think of the pitch of the first note as being *left hanging*. The conceptual status of the pitch of the first note is left in doubt during the second note: although the first pitch is not actually present, it has not been displaced. We retain a sense of it until it is subsequently either explicitly reconfirmed

---

* Normally, of course, a perfect unison. In the special case of an augmented unison, we think of the note that is not in the diatonic collection as inflecting the other pitch. We call this special case an *inflected repetition*.

† Note that neither diminished seconds nor augmented seconds are considered as steps. In the first case the two pitches are not so much different pitches as different ways of conceiving of the same pitch. We say the two pitches are *enharmonically equivalent* and call the linear relationship an *enharmonic repetition*. In the second case, we think of the pitch of the first note as being left hanging, rather than as being displaced by the second pitch.

or displaced

3.2 Consonance and Dissonance

We think of the intervals between simultaneously sounding notes in two lines in terms of two distinct functional categories:

a. consonance
b. dissonance.‡

The classes of intervals we think of as *consonant* are §

1. perfect unisons;
2. perfect octaves;
3. perfect fifths;
4. perfect fourths, where the lower of the two notes is not the lowest note sounding;#
5. major and minor thirds; and
6. major and minor sixths.

When the pitches of two notes form a consonant interval, we can think of the two notes as stable with respect to one another. Such a stable relationship is reciprocal and conceptually self-sufficient: we require no further information to grasp the relationship between the two notes.

The classes of intervals we think of as *dissonant* are:

1. perfect fourths, where the lower of the two notes is the lowest note sounding;
2. major and minor seconds;
3. major and minor sevenths; and
4. all augmented and diminished intervals.

When the pitches of two notes form a dissonant

---

‡ As we'll see in Section 3.3 we also use these categories for certain skips.

§ For a discussion of the complicated question of why we should choose to regard some intervals as consonant and others as dissonant see the Appendix, particularly Sections A.3 and A.5.

\# Consonant fourths:

Dissonant fourths:

interval, we cannot think of the pitches of the notes as stable with respect to one another. Furthermore, we think of *one* of the notes as unstable with respect to the other. Such a relationship is one-sided and conceptually incomplete. We need to know

a. which note is the unstable one and
b. how we can understand it in terms of some other note (or notes) in its line that *are* stable.

For example:

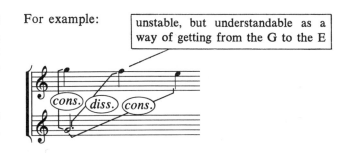

Exercises

1. Mark the steps.

(Mozart: *Symphony* No. 40, first movement, mm. 1–8.)

2. Mark the dissonant intervals between simultaneously sounding notes.

(Corelli: *Sonata* Op. 3, No. 11, first movement, mm. 1–4.)

3. Mark the dissonant skips.

(J. S. Bach: *Mass in B Minor*, Kyrie, mm. 5–7.)

(Mozart: *Die Entführung aus dem Serail*, Act II, "Traurigkeit," mm. 22–27.)

(Verdi: *Aida*, Act IV, finale, mm. 92–94.)

3.3 Linear Operations and Constructs

Rearticulations • Take a note in a line: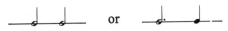
By definition we think of it as
1. beginning at a particular moment in time,
2. lasting a particular length of time, and
3. having a particular pitch.

Now suppose we were to divide the duration of this note into two parts so that we would have two notes such that
1. their durations together equal that of the original note

2. they both have the same pitch as the original note

3. the first note begins at the same moment in time the original note began.

We will call both the linear structure that results and the operation that produces it *rearticulation*.

In a rearticulation we think of the pitch of the second note in terms of the pitch of the first: the second note prolongs the first. We think of the moment in time the second note begins as an interior dividing point of the total duration of both notes. In short, we think of the second note in terms of the first note. We say the first note has conceptual priority over the second note.

Note that while repetition is a necessary condition for a rearticulation it is not a sufficient one. Imagine a line with two consecutive notes with different pitches:

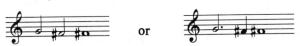

Suppose you were to borrow some later part of the duration of the first note for a new note with the same pitch as the second note:

Suppose that the new note were to begin at a moment in time that we would want to think of in terms of the moment in time that the second note in the original line began:

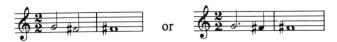

In such a case, we would think of the first of the two notes forming the repetition in terms of the second. We would think of the added note as *anticipating* the pitch of the second. The second note has conceptual priority over the first. As we shall see later, anticipations have a much more limited role in the structure of tonal music than do rearticulations.

Neighbors • Take two notes of a rearticulation:

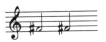

Consider their common pitch as a member of a particular diatonic collection:

Now suppose you were to borrow some later part of the duration of the first note for a second note that would have a pitch that is an adjacent member of that particular diatonic collection:

We will call the added note a *neighbor*, and the linear structure that results a *neighbor embellishment* or a *neighbor structure*.*

In a neighbor embellishment we think of the neighbor temporarily displacing the pitch of the first note, only to be displaced in turn by a note with the same pitch as the first note. This means we can still think of the third note as prolonging the pitch of the first. Thus, we think of the neighbor in terms of the notes forming the original rearticulation. We think of the notes with the same pitch as having conceptual priority over the neighbor. Note that while the relationship between two notes forming a rearticulation depends on our sense of pitch identity, and hence can be independent of the notion of a particular diatonic

---

* When we use the word neighbor to talk about a relationship between people, we are talking about a reciprocal relationship: if Smith is Jones' neighbor, Jones must necessarily be Smith's neighbor too. But when we use the word to talk about a relationship between notes, we are talking about a one-way relationship. In our example the G is the neighbor of the F#'s; neither of the F#'s is a neighbor to the G.

collection, the relationship between neighbor and rearticulated notes depends on our sense of pitch adjacency and hence on which diatonic collection we have in mind. Sometimes a neighbor has a pitch that is not a member of the diatonic collection under consideration:

Where the neighbor is a *minor* second away we can think of the pitch of the neighbor as having been raised or lowered to intensify the sense of its adjacency to the pitch of the rearticulated notes. But when the neighbor is a *major* second from the rearticulated notes, we must consider the neighbor embellishment in terms of a different diatonic collection.

Arpeggiation • Take two notes beginning at the same time and having the same duration but with different pitches that form a consonant interval. Since they sound simultaneously they must, by our definition of line, belong to two different lines. But suppose we want to use their pitch relationship in a single line. Then obviously we have to state their pitches in two consecutive notes such that the first note begins at the moment that both notes in the original began and the durations of both notes together equal the common duration of the original notes.

We will call both the linear structures that result and the operation that produces them *arpeggiations*.*

In an arpeggiation we do not think of the first pitch in terms of the second pitch or the second in terms of the first. Neither has conceptual priority over the other. We think of both in terms of a simpler temporal situation in which their relationship is reciprocal

---

* In common usage "arpeggiation" means the practice of attacking the notes of a chord in rapid succession, usually from the bottom up. Thus, what is written [notation] is played [notation]. In this book the word is used to mean the consecutive statement of notes that could have been simultaneously stated. Thus, we will consider [notation] an arpeggiation of [notation]. More important, we can consider [notation] as an arpeggiation of [notation].

and self-sufficient. Thus

has conceptual priority over

However, since the moment the first note in the arpeggiation begins marks the moment that both notes begin in the conceptually prior situation, we do think of the moment the second note begins in terms of the moment the first begins.†

Step Motion • Take two notes forming an arpeggiation:

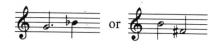

Consider their pitches as belonging to the same diatonic collection:

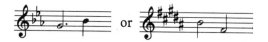

Now suppose you were to borrow some later part of the duration of the first note for some new notes that would have all the intervening pitches of that collection:

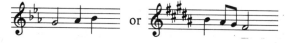

We will call the linear structure that results a *step motion* and the operation that produces it *connection by step motion*.

In a step motion we think of the intervening pitches as ways of getting from one pitch in the arpeggiation to the other. As the pitch of each note displaces the one before it, each new note carries the line farther away from the point of departure—that is, the first note of the arpeggiation—until finally, with the last

---

† By analogy to the principle of anticipation it is also possible to construct what we will call *anticipatory arpeggiations*. In an anticipatory arpeggiation, the second note of the arpeggiation marks the original beginning of the two simultaneously sounding notes, so the duration of the first note of the arpeggiation is taken from the duration of the preceding note.

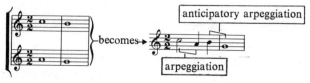

displacement, the goal is reached. Thus, we think of the notes with the intervening pitches in terms of the notes from the original arpeggiation. The notes from the original arpeggiation have conceptual priority over the other notes and thus retain their original sense. No one of the intervening pitches has conceptual priority over any of the others, since no one of them by itself can function as a way of getting from one arpeggiated pitch to the other. Sometimes a step motion uses pitches that do not belong to the diatonic collection under consideration. Where the minor second comes at the end, that is, as the final step,

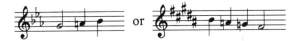

we usually think of these pitches as substitutes for members of the original diatonic collection, altered so as to intensify the sense of getting there, rather than as members of a different diatonic collection. Where the minor second comes somewhere else:

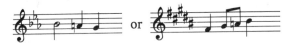

we have no alternative but to think of it in terms of a different diatonic collection.

Delay • Take a note in a line: . Suppose you were to *substitute for it* a different note—a note with the same pitch as the original and occurring during the time occupied by the original but beginning at a later point than the original note: . We will call both the rhythmic situation that results and the operation that produces it a *delay*. In a simple delay, the part of the time occupied by the original note that is not used by the new note (the delay period) is added to the duration of the preceding note or rest.*

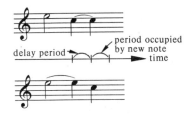

Often, however, the point at which the original note

* Obviously, if the original note is the first note in a line, delaying it would result in a rest.

would have begun is marked by another note arrived at by some other operation.

Operations and Constructs • We shall use these four structures—rearticulation, neighbor embellishment, arpeggiation, and step motion—together with anticipation and delay both to compose and to understand tonal lines. Taken as compositional operations we can use them to construct a tonal line. For example:

But we can also use them as conceptual constructs to understand the tonal lines we know. We can use them to think of all the notes in a line in terms of an even smaller set of conceptually prior notes. For example, in the passage

we can understand the C♯ in as a neighbor to the two B's in and both B's and both D's as rearticulations of . We can in turn think of those two notes as an arpeggiation of the middle notes in and of those middle notes as the interior elements in a step motion from C♯ to A and from E to C♯

Exercises

Write two versions of each of the following (use a different rhythm for each version, but make the total time span of both versions the same as the given original):

1. Rearticulate

2. Embellish by neighbor

3. Rearticulate  and then embellish the result by neighbor.

4. Arpeggiate

5. Connect these notes by step motion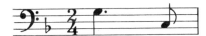

6. Arpeggiate  and connect the two notes of the arpeggiation by step motion.

7. Arpeggiate  and connect the two notes of the arpeggiation by step motion, embellishing the second with a neighbor.

8. Arpeggiate  embellish the first note of the arpeggiation with a neighbor and connect it to the other by a step motion.

3.4 Triads, the Tonic, and the Diatonic Degrees

Triads • Choose a pitch class. Now choose another pitch class whose pitches can form consonant intervals with those of the first. Now choose a third pitch class whose pitches can be consonant with the pitches of both the other pitch classes. What you have is a *triad*.

Whatever pitch class you started with, there were six different triads you could have ended up with. Say you started with C. There are six different pitch classes whose pitches can be consonant with the pitch class C, namely: E♭, E, F, G, A♭, and A. Any one will do. However, having chosen one of them, you have further limited your choice of the third. Say you chose E♭. Then the only pitch classes whose pitches can be consonant with both E♭ and C will be G and A♭. If you chose E as the second pitch class, then only G and A will do. And so it goes. The only collections of three pitch classes available are: C+E♭+G, C+E♭+A♭, C+E+G, C+E+A, C+F+A♭, and C+F+A. All six possible collections have two pitch classes forming a fifth.

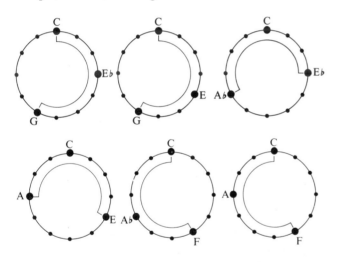

And in all six collections the other pitch class breaks up the fifth into a major third and a minor third. In three of them the major third is on the bottom.*

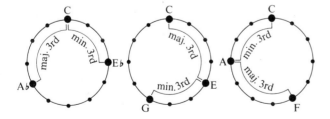

In the other three the minor third is on the bottom.

---

* Remember that **clockwise** is up, **counterclockwise** down on the pitch-class diagrams.

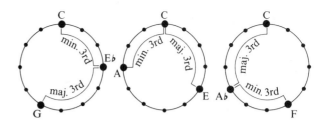

We think of the triad as defined by its fifth. We think of the upper of the two pitches forming the fifth in terms of the lower of the two pitches, and the other pitch in terms of its relation to both. Consequently, we think of the class of the lower of the two pitches forming the fifth as the *fundamental pitch class* of the triad, and we name the triad accordingly. Thus our example has two C triads (C+E+G and C+E♭+G), two F triads (F+A+C and F+A♭+C), an A♭ triad (A♭+C+E♭), and an A triad (A+C+E). In each of the six triads shown, the only intervals other than the fifth are thirds, one major and one minor. We think of the interval type between the fundamental pitch class of the triad and the one a third above as giving the triad its "color". When the third is a major third, we call the triad a *major triad*. When it's a minor third, we call the triad a *minor triad*. These two types of triads—major and minor—are the only two intervallic structures that fit our definition of a triad, that is, a collection of three pitch classes such that the pitches of each are consonant with the pitches of the other two.†

We can think of all the pitch classes represented in any tonal piece in terms of their relationship to a single pitch class. That pitch class is called the *tonic*.

When we say a piece is in C or in the key of C we mean that the pitch class C functions as the tonic of that piece. Other pitch classes serve other functions, but all these functions are defined in terms of the tonic. The tonic, the pitch class called the *dominant*, whose pitches lie a fifth above the tonic, and the pitch class called the *mediant*, whose pitches form thirds with the pitches of the tonic and the dominant together comprise the tonic triad. If the tonic triad is a major one, we say that the piece is in the *major mode*, or in a *major key*; when the tonic triad is minor, we say the piece is in the *minor mode*, or in a *minor key*. Each tonic triad, major or minor, is associated with a particular diatonic collection. The pitch classes of that collection form the seven *diatonic degrees* of that key. To find the diatonic degrees add to the three pitch classes of the tonic triad four more

---

† Note that two collections of pitch classes that are commonly called triads are **not** triads by this definition.

"augmented triad"   "diminished triad"

pitch classes, such that each is a fifth above or below some triad member.*

Major:

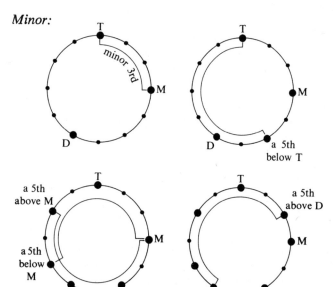

Minor:

* Thus maximizing the number of consonant intervals available between tonic triad members and other members of the associated diatonic collection. For the advantages of this property see Section A.5 in the Appendix.

Calling the tonic I and stretching out the circle we get

Major mode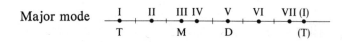

Minor mode †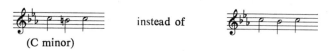

† In fact, as we shall see in Section 5.1, the sixth and seventh degrees in minor are normally altered according to the principle explained in Section 3.3. Thus, where the seventh degree functions primarily as a neighbor to the tonic it is normally raised a semitone so as to be a minor second from the tonic:

(C minor)

When the sixth and seventh degrees are used in ascending step motions

they are normally raised. However, when the seventh degree is used as a neighbor to the tonic and forms a downward arpeggiation with the dominant the only step motion possible is through the raised sixth degree:

And when the sixth degree is used as neighbor to the dominant and forms an upward arpeggiation with the tonic only the unaltered seventh degree will make step motion possible:

Exercises

1. Indicate the six different triads that include the pitch class at eight o'clock.

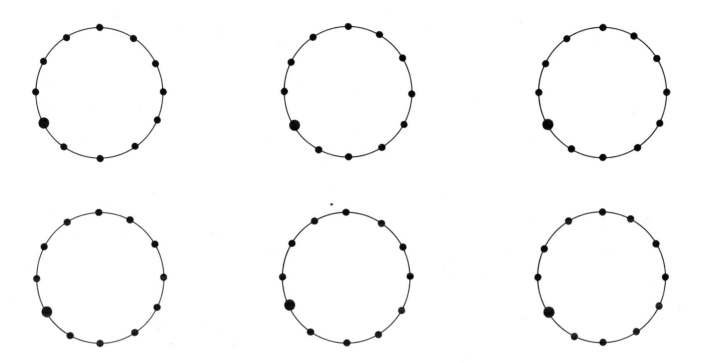

2. On the diagrams above write the names of the other pitch classes in each triad if the pitch class at eight o'clock is called A♭.
3. On the diagrams below write the names of the other pitch classes in each triad if the pitch class at eight o'clock is called G♯.

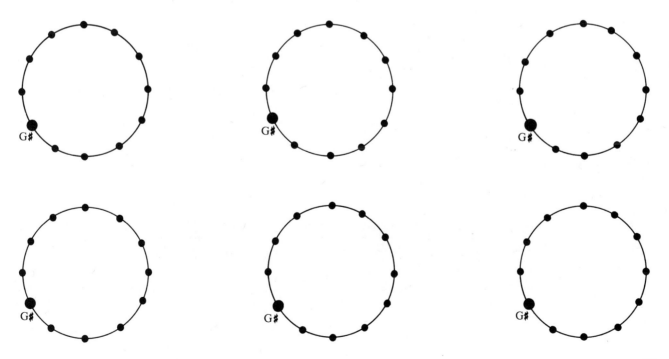

4. Copy the six triads you get in No. 1 without the pitch class names you get in No. 2. Then label the fundamental pitch class of each triad as I, the pitch class a fifth above as V, and the pitch class a third above as III. Now taking each triad as the tonic triad, add the intervening diatonic degrees.

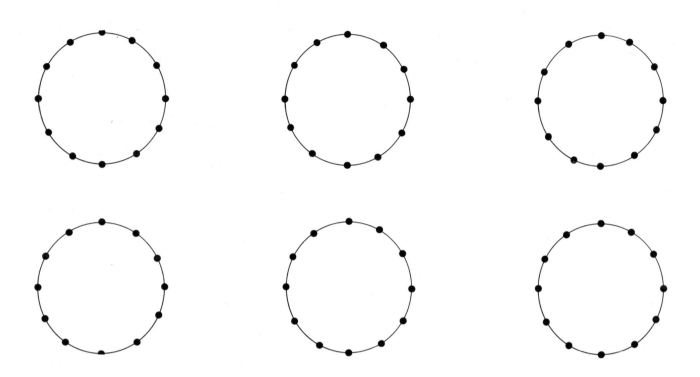

5. For each of the keys indicated in the circle diagrams above write out the degrees of the diatonic collection in whatever notational form involves the least sharps or flats.

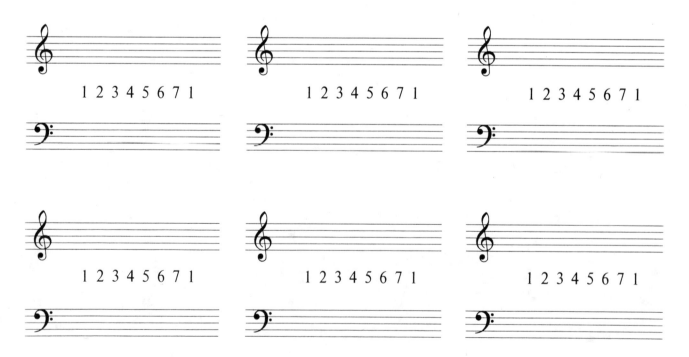

3.5 Tonal Pitch Structures

The pitch structure of any tonal piece can be thought of as being based on an underlying, or basic, structure. The lines of this structure consist of arpeggiations, rearticulations, and neighbor embellishments of triad pitches (members of the pitch class of the tonic triad) and step motions from one triad pitch to another. Characteristically, the lowest line, the bass, consists of a simple arpeggiation of triad pitches beginning and ending on the tonic, with the dominant next to last, either tonic-dominant-tonic or tonic-mediant-dominant-tonic. At least one of the upper lines consists of a descending step motion from a triad pitch down through the pitches of the intervening diatonic degrees to a tonic pitch. Thus, the simplest form these two lines can take is

The other lines of a basic structure consist of neighbor embellishments, arpeggiations, or rearticulations of triad pitches. For example:

Note that intervals between simultaneously sounding notes are all consonant. This means that we can use them for further arpeggiations and step motions, not to mention repetitions and neighbors. If we arrange the new notes in such a secondary structure so that they too form consonant intervals, the new notes may also become the basis for yet another set of structures. In this way a whole phrase, a whole section, a whole movement, or even a whole piece can be built up. The following diagram shows the essential steps in building up a short, simple tonal piece* from a basic structure.

* Purcell: "A Trumpet Tune" from *A Choice Collection of Lessons for the Harpsichord or Spinnet,* originally a piece for trumpet and strings from *The Indian Queen.* While this diagram is largely self-explanatory, there are still a number of notes you will have no way of understanding until you have read Chapter 7. Thus, for example, the F in the bass in the next to last measure is an *incomplete neighbor* of the type explained on page 235. The notes in parentheses can be generated with the *doubling* and *borrowing* operations explained in Section 7.7.

47

Exercises

For each of the following, show how the line on the fifth staff can be derived from the simple structures on the first staff by labelling each new configuration.

PART TWO

A First Approximation: Species Counterpoint

CHAPTER FOUR

Species Counterpoint

4.0 What Species Counterpoint Is and What It's For

From the description at the end of Chapter 3 you might suppose that all you have to do is plug the principles of linear structure discussed on page 37 into a triad-oriented diatonic collection and out will come tonal music.

Of course, it isn't that easy. Chapter 3 tells you very little about the way these linear structures are to be combined: What happens when two or more lines are stated simultaneously? What kinds of intervals can occur between a note in one linear structure and a simultaneously sounding note in another? How do we understand two or more different linear structures at the same time? What effect does a note's duration or its relationship to the beat have on its structural role?

Working out answers to these questions is a complicated business. To simplify the job we will make use of a special kind of tonal music—a highly simplified first approximation to the real thing—called *species counterpoint*.

This kind of music uses many of the same pitch structures that tonal music uses, but the way these structures happen in time—their rhythm—is much simpler. In a species composition each line sticks to a single rate of flow: the time between the beginning of one note and the beginning of the next note in that line is always the same. Each species is simply a different format for combining such lines and relating their notes to a regular beat.

In the simplest species—first species—all the notes in all the lines occur on the beat. Thus, each note begins at the same time that a note in the other line does and lasts the same amount of time.

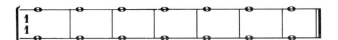

The time signature $\frac{1}{1}$ means that there is one beat per measure and a whole-note span between beats. Thus, there is no differentiation between downbeats and other beats, since all beats are downbeats. In the higher species (second, third, and fourth), one or more lines have all their notes on the beat, just as in first species, but one line (the *species line*) does not. In second species, all the notes in the species line but the last are half notes, and every other note is on the beat.*

species line

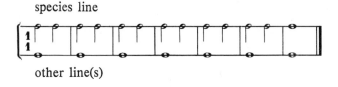

other line(s)

In third species, either every third note in the species line is on the beat,

species line

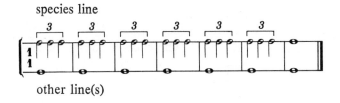

other line(s)

or every fourth note in the species line is on the beat.

---

* The following diagrams show the higher-species line as the top line, but it may equally well be the bass or middle line.

species line

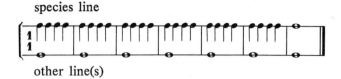

other line(s)

In fourth species, only the last note in the species line is on the beat; all the rest are off the beat.

species line

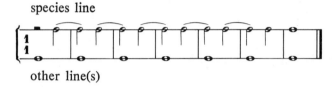

other line(s)

Note that in each species the last note in the species line is a whole note just like the other lines; in fourth species this means that the next-to-last note must be a half note.

In mixed, or combined, species, two higher species lines are used at once. They can be either from the same higher species,

second species line

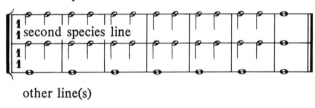

other line(s)

or from two different higher species.

fourth species line

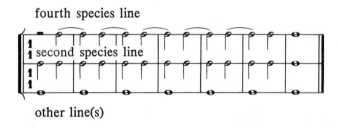

other line(s)

Taken as a kind of music in its own right, species counterpoint seems remarkably limited. Why should we bother to consider pieces that use the same few ways of relating notes to one another and to the beat over and over again, measure after measure, when any piece of tonal music uses a rich variety of such relationships? But taken as a means for studying just such relationships, species counterpoint is remarkably efficient. Consider the different orders the beginnings and ends of two simultaneously sounding notes might have:

(a) both notes begin at the same time; both notes end at the same time

(b) both notes begin at the same time but one lasts longer than the other

(c) one note begins before the other but they both end at the same time

(d) one note begins before and ends after the other note

(e) one note begins before the other note begins and ends before it ends

Then consider the different relationships the beginning or end of either note might have with a beat:

1. both notes begin on the beat;

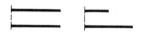

2. one note begins on the beat, the other note begins after the beat;

3. the beat occurs just as both notes end;

4. the beat occurs just as one of the notes ends and after the other has already ended;

5. the beat occurs during the course of both notes;

6. the beat occurs during the course of one note and after, at the end of, before, or at the beginning of the other note.

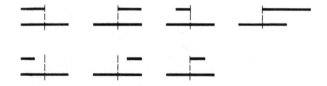

You will see that there is a species or combination of species that covers each possible situation. For example:

occurs in the combination of second and third species:

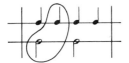

So does

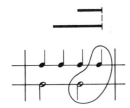

If the beat falls both at the beginning and the end of the longer note

you have a situation that occurs in second species:

But

occurs in the combination of second and fourth species:

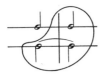

To put it another way, each species or combination of species consists of a limited set of such situations:

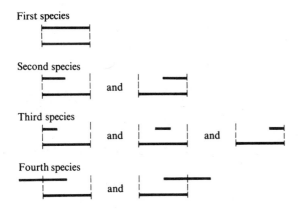

Combinations of higher species consist of the remaining situations plus, in some cases, several other situations in which the beat does not coincide with the beginning or end of either note:

Second and second

⊢═ and ═⊣

Third and third

⊢═ and ¦═¦ and ═⊣

Fourth and fourth

═
═

Second and third

⊢═ and ─── and ─── and ───

Second and fourth

═⊣ and ⊢═

Third and fourth

═ and ═ and ⊢═ and ═⊣

Thus, not only do the collected formats of species counterpoint cover all the ways the beginnings and ends of two simultaneously sounding notes might be ordered in time and related to a beat, but each separate format allows us to concentrate on the problems posed by a limited number of such situations.

4.1 Constructing Species Lines: Some Operational Rules

As we saw in the preceding section, any species composition consists of the simultaneous statement of two or more lines. These lines may or may not be differentiated according to species, but they are always differentiated according to range and underlying structure.

The lowest line is called the bass line or, simply, the bass. No bass note is ever higher than any simultaneously sounding note in one of the other lines. The structure of the bass line is always based on the arpeggiation of the tonic and dominant degrees. This arpeggiation is called the *basic arpeggiation*.

The structure of one of the other lines is always based on a descending step motion from the mediant, dominant, or tonic down to a tonic. Such a step motion is called the *basic step motion*. The structure of any other line may be based on the repetition of, neighbor embellishment of, arpeggiation of, or step motion between, tonic triad pitches.

We can construct simple species lines of each type by using one of the following three sets of operational rules.

I. *Operational rules for constructing an upper line with a basic step motion*
   A. *The basic step motion*
      1. The final pitch in the basic step motion must be a tonic. Thus, for example, a basic step motion in C major must end with a C.

      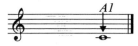

      2. The first pitch in the basic step motion must be a tonic triad member a third, a fifth, or an octave above the final pitch. That is, if—as in the above example—a basic step motion in C major ends on middle C, it must begin on the E, the G, or the C above middle C.

      either

      or

      or

      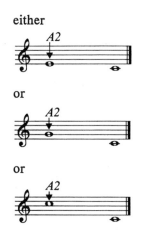

      3. These two pitches must be joined by inserting the pitches of intervening diatonic degrees to form a descending step motion.

   Thus, given ... the basic step motion will be

   given ... the basic step motion will be

   given ... the basic step motion will be

   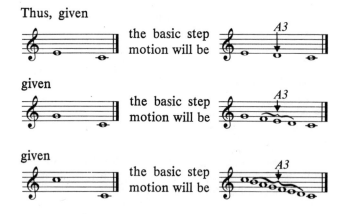

   B. *Secondary structures*
      1. Any triad pitch may be repeated.

   Thus,

   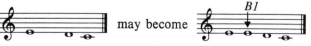

   may become

      2. A neighbor may be inserted between consecutive notes with the same pitch.

   Thus,

   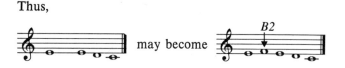

   may become

   (The pitch of the neighbor is always a member of the diatonic collection, except where it is the lower neighbor to the tonic in a minor key, in which case it is altered so as to be a minor second from the tonic it embellishes.) For example, if you want to put a lower neighbor between the two C's in

   you must use a B♮

   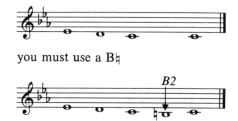

      3. Any triad pitch may precede the first pitch or may be inserted between any two consecutive pitches as long as no dissonant skip and no skip larger than an octave is created.

   Thus,

   may become either

   or

   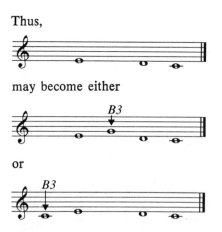

   (We will consider a skip of a perfect fourth in an upper line to be consonant.)

      4. Any two consecutive notes forming a skip may be joined by a step motion.

Thus,

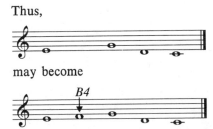

may become

The pitches of the inserted notes are those of the intervening diatonic degrees, except for the following mandatory use of the raised sixth and seventh degrees in a minor key:

a. a rising step motion from the fifth degree to the tonic

(If you want to join the G and the C in

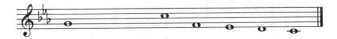

by a step motion, you must use A♮ and B♮).

b. a rising step motion from the fifth degree to the seventh degree

(If you want to join the G and the B♭ in

by a step motion, you must use an A♮)

c. a falling step motion from the raised seventh degree to the fifth degree

(If you want to join the B♮ and the G

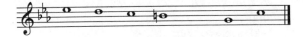

by a step motion, you must use an A♮).

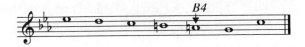

Note that rules *A1*, *A2*, and *A3* use the word "must"; they are to be applied once and in the order they appear above to generate the underlying basis for the structure of the whole line. Such an underlying structure must always be present. Rules *B1* through *B4* use the word "may"; once the basic step motion is established, any of these rules may be applied any number of times and in any meaningful order. Obviously, you must have already applied rule *B1* before you can apply rule *B2* or you won't have any repeated pitches to put a neighbor in between. Similarly, you must have already applied rule *B3* before you can apply rule *B4* or your won't have a skip to fill in with step motion. However, you don't need to have already applied rule *B1* or rule *B2* in order to apply rule *B3* or rule *B4*. Furthermore, once having applied rules *B1* and *B2*, you can always apply rule *B1* again, and once having applied rules *B3* and *B4*, you can always apply rule *B3* again.

The operational rules for a bass line are similar, except that the basic structure of a bass line is an arpeggiation rather than a step motion, and the *A* rules are therefore different.

II. *Operational rules for constructing a bass line*

   A. *Basic arpeggiation*

   1. The final pitch of the basic arpeggiation must be a tonic. For example, in C major

   2. The first pitch of the basic arpeggiation must be a tonic. For example,

   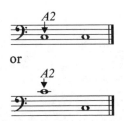

   or

   3. The middle pitch of the basic arpeggiation must be a dominant either a fifth above or a fourth below the final tonic. For example,

   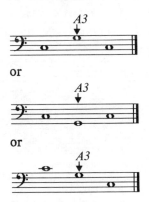

   or

   or

   (If the middle pitch is more than a fifth from the first pitch, other pitches will have to be added under the *B* rules, so that no skip greater than an octave remains. Thus, given a basic arpeggiation like

some subsequent operation like

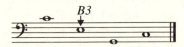

would be necessary.)

B. *Secondary structures*
1. Any triad pitch may be repeated.

For example,

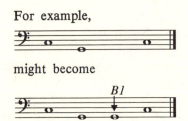

might become

2. A neighbor may be inserted between consecutive notes with the same pitch.

Thus,

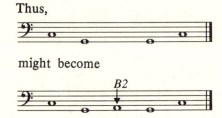

might become

3. Any triad pitch may be inserted between any two consecutive pitches as long as no dissonant skip and no skip larger than an octave is created.

Thus,

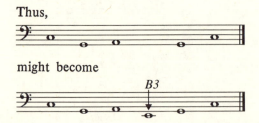

might become

(Warning: inserting the mediant between the final statement of the dominant and the final tonic of the basic arpeggiation may obscure the fundamental relationship of dominant to tonic—if in doubt, don't do it.)

(We will consider a skip of a fourth in the bass to be consonant unless the other notes present allow the interpretation that the lower of the two pitches forming the fourth represents the lowest pitch of a single triad with its fifth in the bass.

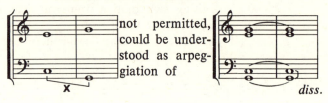

not permitted, could be understood as arpeggiation of

diss.

permitted, D is stable with respect to G, but not a member of the C triad.

Methods of preventing this interpretation vary with the rhythmic situation and will be treated separately for each species.)

4. Any two consecutive notes forming a skip may be joined by step motion. (The added pitches are subject to the same limitations as those in rule *B4* for upper lines.)

Finally, the operational rules for any other line are simply a weaker version of the rules for an upper line with a basic step motion.

III. *Operational rules for constructing another upper line*
A. *Basic structure*
1. The final pitch in the basic structure must be a tonic triad member. In C major, for example, the basic structure may end with a C, an E, or a G.

2. The first pitch must be a tonic triad member no more than an octave from

the final pitch. In C major, therefore, any of the following are possible:

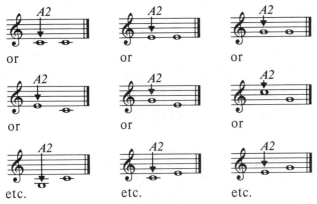

3. If identical, these pitches may be embellished by neighbor, as in rule *B2* in I and II above. If different, these pitches may be connected by step motion as in rule *B4* in I and II above. For example,

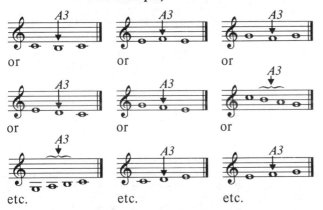

B. *Secondary structures*

As in rules *B1*, *B2*, *B3*, and *B4* for an upper line with a basic step motion (I).

These operational rules are for the most part just a working version of the principles of linear structure introduced in Chapter 3, tailored to fit the limitations of species rhythm. In both this chapter and Chapter 3 we used successive operations to produce more notes. But in Chapter 3 we kept the total time taken by all of the notes at any state of construction the same, so that each successive operation divided the total time into smaller units.

In any given species we keep the durations of all the notes in a line the same, so that each successive operation adds more and more to the total time.

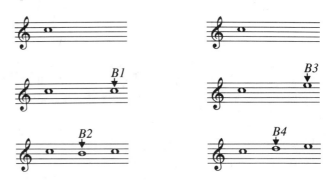

This means that if you want to think of a repetition created by operation *B1* as the re-articulation of a note, you will have to think of that note as being twice as long as the other notes in the line: And if you want to think of the results of rules *B1* and *B2* as a neighbor embellishment of a note, you will have to think of that note as three times as long as the other notes in the line: However, rule *B1* guarantees that the long note will be a tonic triad pitch. Thus, the only pitches that are prolonged in the course of a species line are just those we want to think of as the reference points for the other pitches.

Similarly, if you want to think of the skip created by operation *B3* as an arpeggiation of two simultaneously sounding notes, you will have to introduce the idea of another line:

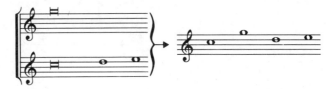

However, rule *B3* guarantees that such a line will consist solely of tonic triad pitches. Thus, those pitches that are left hanging at the end of a species line are just those we want to think of as the reference points for the other pitches. (The other pitches that are skipped from are subsequently displaced.)

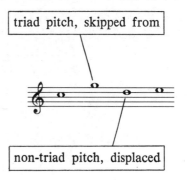

59

Drills

Find the error in each of the following schemes for generating an upper line with a basic step motion.

60

Exercises

Generate a line with a basic step motion according to the following scheme.

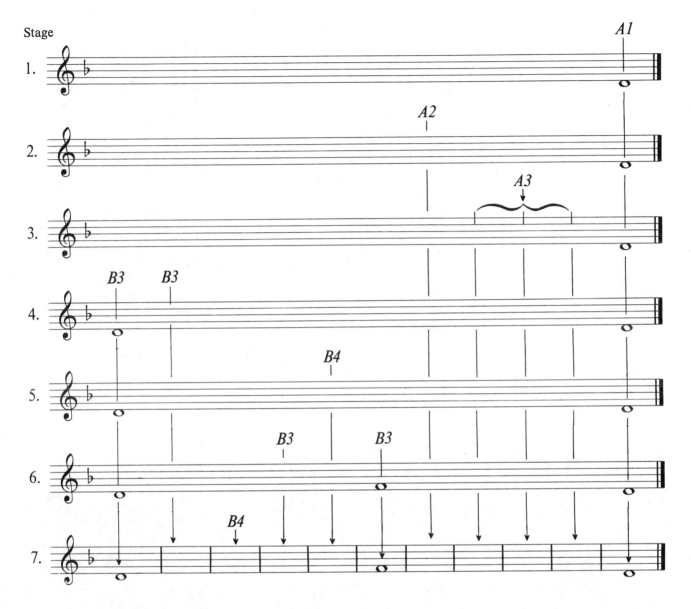

Stage 2: What pitch could you generate under rule *A2* that will allow you to generate three pitches under rule *A3* at stage 3?

Stage 4: What pitch could you generate with the second application of rule *B3* that would allow you one pitch under rule *B4* at stage 5?

Stage 6: What pitch can you generate with the first application of rule *B3* that will allow you to generate one pitch under rule *B4* at stage 7 but will not allow anyone to construe the pitch you generated at stage 5 as making a step motion from the fourth to the sixth measure?

4.2 Understanding Species Lines: Structural Ambiguity and Interest

In the last section we used the operational rules to construct species lines. In this section we will use the same set of rules as a method of understanding the structure of a species line someone else has constructed.

Now, obviously, constructing and understanding are two very different processes. But our rules are so formulated that showing how a given line might have been constructed is in fact simply an efficient way of describing how you conceive of its structure. By stating the particular rule by which you add a note to the line, you are defining the function of that note with respect to the key and to other notes already present in the line. By stating the order in which you apply the rules, you are showing the conceptual priority you use to conceive of the notes and structures of the complete line. Thus, to say that you think of the line

as being constructed

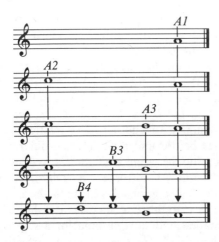

is a kind of shorthand notation for saying that you think of:

- the D as a way of getting from the C to the E, to form a secondary step motion;
- the E as a tonic triad pitch inserted between the C and the B, to provide a goal for the secondary step motion;
- the B as a way of getting from the C to the A, to form a basic step motion;
- the C as a tonic triad pitch, to provide a point of departure for the basic step motion; and
- the A as the final tonic, the goal of the basic step motion.

Of course, saying that you conceive of a line in a certain way says nothing about how you arrived at that conception. After all, you hear the notes of a line in the order in which they occur, not in the order of their conceptual priority. And the notes you hear don't have any rule *A1* or rule *B4* attached to them. Nor do you hear the key signature at the beginning. Then how do you come to understand a particular pitch class as the tonic, how do you come to assign particular functions to each note, and how do you arrive at an order of conceptual priority for the notes?

Different people approach these problems in different ways. Imagine, for the sake of the argument, two extreme types of listeners. Both know our rules, and that is all they know about music. Neither has ever heard the line on this page before. The first listener perceives all five notes in one gulp. He then tries to see how what he has perceived fits with what he knows the rules will produce. He knows that no rule will generate a non-triad pitch at the beginning or end of a line and that no combination of rules will leave a non-triad note hanging at the end of a line. So he figures that the tonic triad must consist of the pitch classes A, C, and E. He knows that the only way to generate a non-triad pitch is as a neighbor to a triad pitch or as part of a step motion to or from a triad pitch. In either case, there must be a note a step away both before and after the non-triad note. Since the only two notes that form steps with the D are the C and the E, and since the D comes after the C and before the E, he has to take the D to be part of the step motion C-D-E. Likewise, since the only two notes that form steps with the B are the C and the A, he has to take the B to be part of the step motion C-B-A. Finally, he knows that the only way to generate two step motions that share the same first note is to generate the one that's going to end last before generating the other. Since the A comes after the E, he takes C-B-A to be the basic structure.

The second imaginary listener is a completely different sort of person. He considers each note as he perceives it and tries to assign it some possible function or functions in terms of the notes he has already heard and the notes he might hear next. He knows that the initial C must be a tonic triad pitch, but he has no way of knowing whether it is a tonic in C major or C minor, a mediant in A♭ major or A minor, or a dominant in F major or F minor. On hearing the D he can eliminate A♭ major, but he cannot be sure whether the D is an upper neighbor in C major, C minor, A minor, or F major, or the second note in a step motion in C major, C minor, A minor, F major, or F minor. On hearing the E he can eliminate C minor, and he has every reason to believe that the D was indeed part of a step motion, but he still does not know whether the E is the goal of the step motion or just another interior element. On hearing the B he can eliminate F major and F minor. He can also be sure that the E was indeed the goal of the initial step motion, since such a structure would have to have been completed before the line could move on to a non-triad note. He still has no way of knowing whether the B is a neighbor to the C in C major or A minor, or part of a descending step motion from the C in C major or A minor. On hearing the A he knows that the B must have been part of a descending step motion, but he still does not know whether or not the A is the goal, and he still does not know whether the line is in C major or A minor. It is only when he hears the silence after the A that he can be sure.*

Despite their different approaches, both listeners arrived at a conception of the structure of this line that can be identified with the construction on page 63. In fact, they were bound to, for given our rules, there is no other way this line could have been constructed. We can therefore consider such a line as *structurally unambiguous.*

On the other hand, suppose there were more than one way to construct the line in question. Take the line

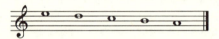

You can generate these notes by using the same set of rules we used for the example on page 63, just reversing the direction of the secondary step motion between E and C.

But you can get the same notes in less moves by using a five-note basic step motion.

---

* Of course, there's no point in pretending that any real listener ever listens to actual tonal music in either of these ways. Actual tonal compositions have far too many notes in them for anybody to perceive them all in one gulp, that is, without subjecting them to some form of structuring along the way. On the other hand, the notes come and go far too quickly for anybody to weigh the possible alternative functions of each note as he hears it. What real listeners confronted by actual tonal music do is mix the two approaches, applying intuitively a much more complicated set of constraints, of which our rules are just a highly simplified first approximation.

These two ways of constructing the line correspond to two possible ways of conceiving of the structure of the line, but chances are the first way would never even occur to either of our imaginary listeners. The first listener simply hears that the last note is a fifth below the first and that the intervening notes form a series of steps in the same direction. Consequently, the last note is the tonic and the first is the dominant, and the whole line can be understood as a single step motion. Why should he bother to go through the extra conceptual steps needed to think of two step motions, one basic and the other secondary? The second listener registers the E as a tonic triad pitch. He can't tell whether the D is a neighbor to the E or a part of a step motion from the E to some lower pitch until he hears the C, at which point he assumes the latter. When he hears the B he can't tell whether it's a neighbor to the C, the goal of the step motion, or just one more pitch on the way down to a lower pitch. When he hears the A, he assumes it's one of the latter two and when he hears the silence he knows it's the last—the A must be the lower pitch in question. At no point would he have any reason to consider the possibility that the C was the end of one step motion and the beginning of another. The relationship of C to the notes before and after it is no different from the relationship between any other two consecutive notes in the line. In retrospect he might, of course, think of the C as consonant with both the E and the A and hence a tonic triad member capable of being both destination and starting point of a step motion; but why should he? He already has a perfectly satisfactory way of understanding the line.

Thus, although the example on this page could be constructed in more than one way, both our imaginary listeners would find one particular way the most efficient way of understanding the structure of the line. In general, where a line can be constructed in more than one way, we will consider the way that uses the least number of constructive stages to be the most efficient way of understanding the line.

But suppose there is more than one way of constructing the line, and the different ways are equally efficient. Take the line

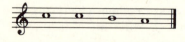

You can generate these notes with our rules in any of three ways:

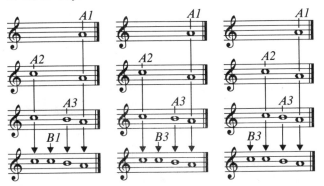

But the first is certainly preferable as a way of understanding the line in that it offers a more complete explanation of each note in terms of the others. Why be content with thinking of a pitch as being simply a triad pitch, when you can specify that it is the same triad pitch as the preceding pitch? The latter two constructions are best reserved for the lines that they alone explain, for example:

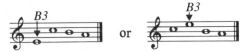

The principle of preferring the more complete explanation has important implications for how we group notes into structures. Take the line segment*

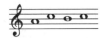

Starting with an A and a C we could generate the other two notes in two different ways:

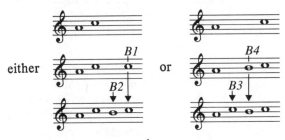

Or take the segment 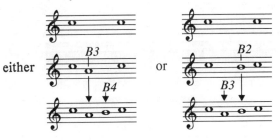. Starting with the two C's we could get the other two notes in two different ways:

In both cases the first way gives a tighter explanation. In the first case the only note rule $B1$ will explain is C, and the only notes rule $B2$ would explain are B and D, so the only successions of four notes these rules will account for are:

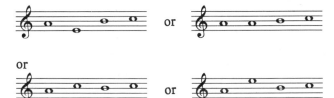

The second way will account for four different segments:

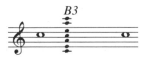

In the second case, applying rule $B3$ first would account for no less than seven possible pitches,

but of these, only two would allow a single note under rule $B4$.

Applying rule $B2$ first would account for two possible pitches

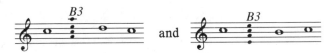

and for each of these, applying rule $B3$ would account for four different pitches:

Note also that in both cases the preferred explanation completes a neighbor structure or step motion in a shorter period of time.

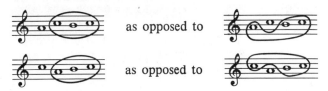

---

* By line segment we mean any succession of notes for which we can assume that structures generated by the B rules are complete but structures generated by the A rules are not. Thus, for the segments that follow, we have no way of knowing what functions the C's or the A's might have in the basic structure.

In general, we will find that when a note forms seconds with two other notes either before it

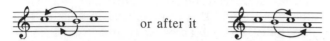 or after it

in such a way that either but not both the seconds can be construed as a step in a step motion or neighbor structure,

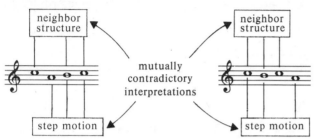

we will choose as forming a step whichever pair of notes is closer in time. Or take the line

The two most efficient ways to generate these notes are:

The second explanation is preferable as a way of understanding the line in that it shows more consistently the regularity of the intervallic succession—skip up, three steps down, skip down, three steps up. It allows us to understand the first five notes as having the same structure

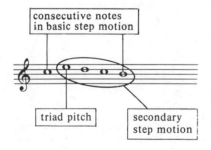

as the last five:

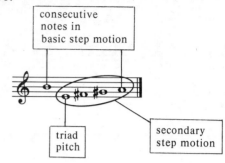

Finally, take the bass line

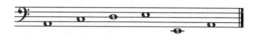

You can generate these notes with our rules in two equally efficient ways:

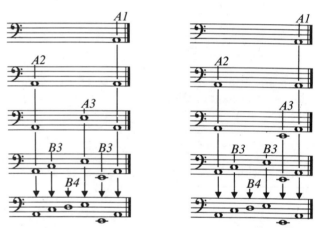

The first is preferable as a way of understanding the line in that it offers a more connected or unified way of thinking of the whole structure. We have to think of the C-D-E as a secondary step motion. By thinking of the goal of the secondary structure as an element in the basic structure, we give the secondary structure a *raison d'être*. Instead of the secondary structure simply filling up the time between two elements of the basic structure

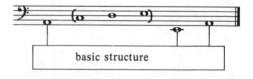

it leads us toward and thus draws our attention to an element in the basic structure

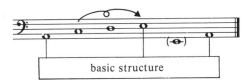

We can consider the structure of each of the four lines discussed on pages 64, 65, and 66 as essentially unambiguous. Although each line could be constructed in more than one way, for each of the lines there is always one way that has at least one advantage over the others. Either (1) it uses fewer stages to construct the line and therefore provides a more efficient explanation, or (2) it determines the pitches of the line more closely and therefore provides a tighter explanation, or (3) it corresponds more closely to any regularities in the pattern of the line and therefore provides a more consistent explanation, or (4) it attaches secondary structures to more basic pitches and therefore provides a more connected, unified explanation. As long as such advantages do not conflict with one another, there is no problem. But suppose they do. Take the line

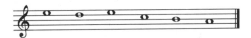

There are at least two ways of generating these notes with our rules:

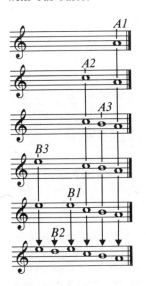
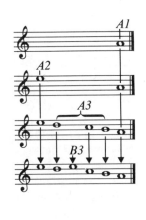

The advantage of the first is that it shows the D as forming a step with the note immediately following it. The advantage of the second is that it is more efficient. There is no way of constructing this line that would have both these advantages. Hence there is no way of resolving the conflict.

Or take the line

We could generate these notes with our rules in two ways:

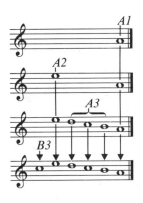
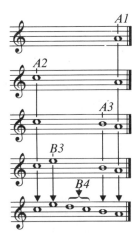

The advantage of the first way is that it is more efficient. The advantage of the second is that it provides a more unified structure. Here again, there is no way of resolving the conflict. In both these cases we have to consider the line as structurally ambiguous.

Now, of course, when we say that a line is structurally ambiguous or unambiguous, we are only talking about the line as we conceive it. We are not talking about how the line was composed. We are saying that there are advantages to conceiving of the line in terms of a certain method of construction. We are not saying that the composer must have constructed it that way. In fact, there is no way we can tell by looking at the notes of a line how the composer arrived at that line. The way we have chosen to understand the line may be the most efficient way of constructing the line according to our rules, but how do we know the composer necessarily used the most efficient way? For that matter, how do we know he used our rules?*

On the other hand, suppose you were the composer and wanted to construct lines for people who are like our two imaginary listeners. They know our rules and that is all they know about music. You want to communicate to your listeners not only which note follows which but how you conceive of the notes in your lines in terms of one another. To do that you must stick to unambiguous structures.

If you want to write a line that will be understood as a three-note secondary step motion leading into a three-note basic step motion with the last note of the secondary structure also acting as the first note of the basic structure, you will have to write

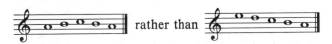

---

* The line you constructed by our rules as an exercise on page 61 was first written more than 200 years before our rules were formulated.

If you want your listeners to understand the second note of a four-note line as the first note of the basic motion, you can't give the first two notes the same pitch. You will have to write

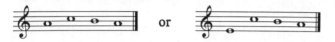 or

instead of

If you want your listeners to understand a particular structural grouping, you can't use patterns that make another grouping easier to grasp. If you want them to understand a five-note basic step motion, you will have to write

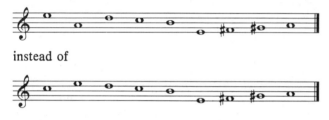

instead of

And if you want your listeners to understand the the second of two dominants as the dominant of a basic arpeggiation, then you will have to construct a secondary step motion that leads to or from it

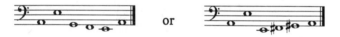 or

rather than

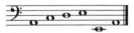

Of course if you are composing lines for somebody else to listen to, you are presumably concerned that he find them not just structurally unambiguous but interesting as well. Unfortunately, it is more difficult to state what makes a line interesting than it is to state what makes it clear. The problem is not that we can't agree that some lines are interesting and others are dull. Rather the problem is that it's difficult to specify which structural procedures will always produce interesting lines and which dull. Like the other operational rules in this chapter, the following set of principles should be understood as a first approximation: Given two lines that are the same in other respects, we will find more interesting the line that:

1. makes us understand its structure in terms of a greater number of stages;
2. makes us understand its step motions and neighbors as occupying longer time spans;

3. makes us understand the same pitch or the same interval in different ways on successive occasions.

For example, compare the lines

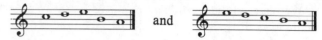 and

Both have the same number of notes and use the same pitches. But it takes five stages to construct the first and only three to construct the second. Therefore, we think of the first line as having a deeper structure, that is, one which requires more conceptual steps.

Compare the lines

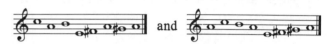 and

Both have the same number of notes, use the same pitches, and take the same number of stages to construct.

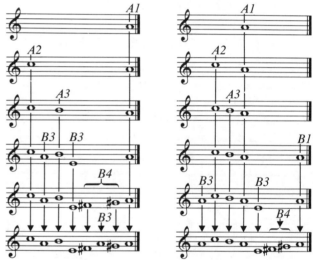

But in the first the secondary step motion from E to A is inserted between two elements of the basic step motion, thereby stretching out the time span of the basic step motion. Similarly, the first two notes of the basic step motion are kept apart by the insertion of the first A and even the F♯ and G♯ of the secondary step motion are kept apart by the insertion of the second A. In the second line the basic step motion is finished by the fourth note, and the secondary step motion is just tacked on to the end.

Compare the lines

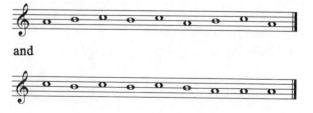

and

Both have the same number of notes, use the same

pitches, require the same number of stages to construct, and have the same time spans for their basic and secondary structures.

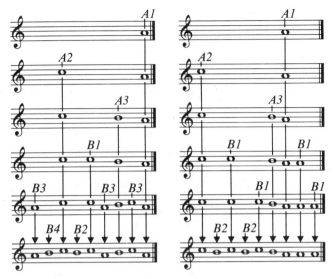

time spans

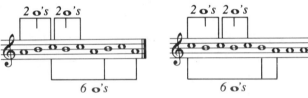

In both lines one C, one B, and one A belong to the basic step motion. In the first line the two other C's have different functions as do the other B's and the other A's. But in the second line both of the other C's have the same function, as do both the other B's and both the other A's.

Or compare the lines

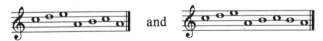

Both repeat an intervallic pattern (two upward steps) at different pitch levels (C-D-E followed by A-B-C). However, in the second line we can understand both patterns as having the same structural sense. We can construct the line

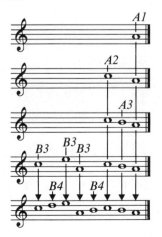

That is, we can understand the first three notes as forming the same kind of structure the second three do. In the first line we cannot. There is no B after the final C. Therefore the B that precedes the final C is a part of the basic step motion and is not available for a secondary step motion regardless of the regularity of pattern between the first three notes and the second three notes. The only way to construct this line with a basic step motion is

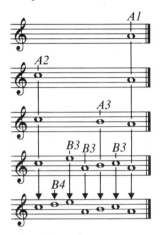

To sum up, note that each of the foregoing three principles is in direct conflict with one of the principles we used to decide between possible ways of understanding a line.

> Given two ways of understanding the same line, we choose the one that lets us use fewer steps. But given two lines, we find more interesting the line that makes us use more steps.

> Given two ways of understanding the same line, we choose the one that lets us determine the pitches more closely and consequently the one that lets us understand its secondary step motions and neighbor structures as taking less time. But given two lines, we find more interesting the line that makes us understand its secondary step motions and neighbors as taking more time.

> Given two ways of understanding the same line, we choose the one that explains any regular patterns in a consistent way. But given two lines with regular patterns, we find more interesting the one that makes us understand a structure that seems to contradict the regularity.

Such conflicts seem to me to be intrinsic to the concept of interest.*

---

* Note that the fourth principle used for resolving ambiguities of structure is not included in this set of conflicts. It stands, so to speak, above the battle. Indeed, we could even include it among the principles for determining the relative interest of two lines, thus:
> Given two lines that are alike in other respects, we will find more interesting the one that presents a more unified structure.

Drill

Which of the following lines
   a. cannot be constructed from a basic step motion using our rules?
   b. can be constructed from a basic step motion in only one way?
   c. can be constructed from a basic step motion in two or more ways, only one of which has conceptual advantages over the others?

1.

2.

3.

4.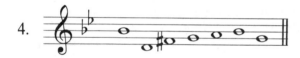

5.

6.

7.

Exercises

1. The line you generated as an answer to the assignment on page 61

is the first *cantus firmus* (a given line, to which other lines are to be added) used by Fux in his *Gradus ad Parnassum*. Show two other ways it could have been generated using our rules and compare the conceptual advantages of all three ways.

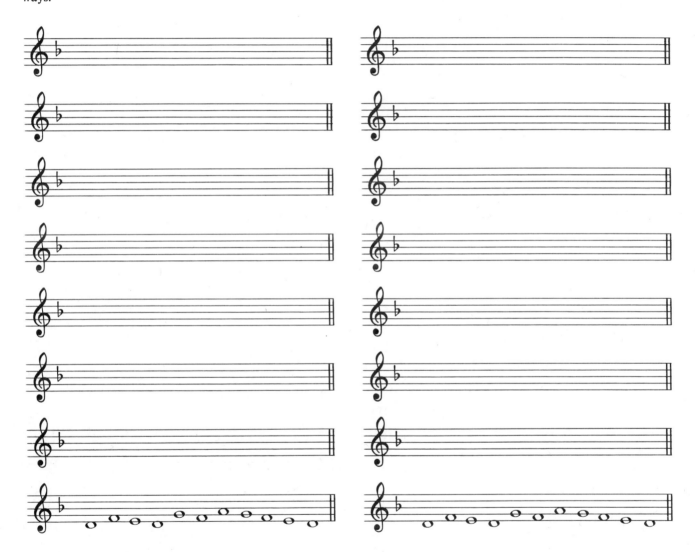

2. Here are four other Fuxian *cantus firmi*.

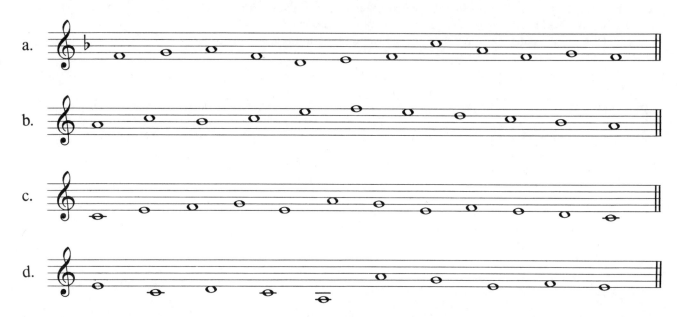

Not all of them can be generated by our rules. (Indeed, not all of them are strictly speaking tonal.) Which can be generated by our rules and how?

3. Using a three-note basic step motion in G major, write lines of 7, 8, 9, and 10 notes each. Make each line as interesting as you can.

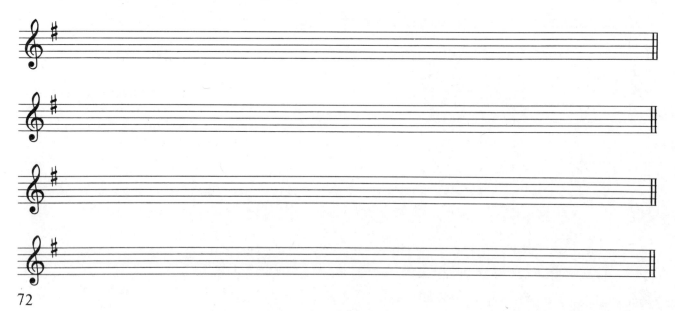

4.3 Combining Species Lines: The Fundamental Voice-Leading Constraints

Now we must consider what happens when we combine, that is, state simultaneously, two or more lines. We will approach this problem from two points of view. The first, dealt with in this section, is essentially local. It is concerned solely with the way the notes that actually come into contact with one another are related to one another. The second point of view is longer range and will be dealt with in the next section. It is concerned with the relationship between the structure of one line taken as a whole and the structure of another line, and with how this relationship affects our understanding of the structure of each individual line.

Local Relationships • Consider the kinds of local relationships that can exist between the notes in each of the four species. There are relationships between consecutive notes in the same line:

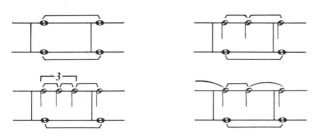

There are relationships between simultaneously sounding notes in different lines:

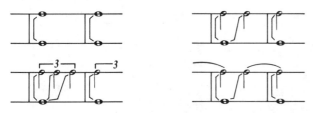

These are of two types: a stronger type in which the two notes actually begin together, and a weaker type in which they don't. First species consists entirely of the stronger type, fourth species of the weaker type, while second and third species use both. Finally, there are the relationships between contiguous notes* in different lines:

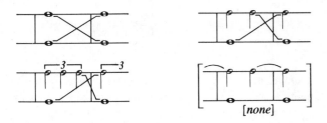

* By contiguous I mean that one note ends just as the other begins.

Intervals Between Consecutive Notes • The intervals used for consecutive relationships are controlled by the operational rules of Section 4.1. These rules limit the intervals between two consecutive notes in a line to perfect unisons, fourths, fifths, octaves, and major or minor seconds, thirds, and sixths. No augmented or diminished intervals, no dissonant skips, and no skips larger than an octave are permitted.

Intervals Between Simultaneously Sounding Notes: Control of Dissonance • The intervals used between simultaneously sounding notes are subject to a number of constraints. Chief among them are those that limit dissonant intervals to particular rhythmic and intervallic situations. Since each species or combination of species consists in effect of a different set of rhythmic situations, we will state these constraints in detail later, separately for each species. These constraints are designed to make it possible

1. to tell which of the two notes forming the dissonant interval is the unstable one, and
2. to have some way of understanding the unstable note either as
    a. subordinate in pitch and rhythmic function to other notes in its line (that is, as a neighbor or interior element in a step motion falling off the beat)

or b. left over from a previous period of time during which it was stable.

Intervals Between Simultaneously Sounding Notes: Sonority Controls • Of secondary concern are those constraints that help control the level of sonority.† It is easier to define the factors that influence our sense of the collective sonority of two or more simultaneously sounding notes than it is to define what we mean by sonority itself. There are three factors involved:

† These sonority constraints are intended only as rules of thumb for avoiding difficulties. Unlike the constraints pertaining to generation of lines (pages 55–59), control of dissonance (this page), and forbidden forms of motion (pages 76–79), they are not absolute. See in particular page 100.

1. *interval class:* we think of perfect intervals (unisons, octaves, fifths, fourths) as creating the thinnest sonority, imperfect consonances as creating a fuller sonority, and dissonant intervals—particularly seconds and sevenths but excluding perfect fourths—as creating a dense sonority;
2. *interval sizes:* the smaller the interval, the fuller the sonority. We think of thirds as fuller than tenths, twelfths as thinner than fifths;
3. *register:* the lower the range, the fuller the sonority. We think of a twelfth between two lines, the lower of which is in the middle register, as thin, but the same interval between two lines, the lower of which is in a low register, as not so thin. We think of a third in the middle range as producing a nice fat sonority, but we think of a third between two lines in a low range as dense, even difficult to grasp.

If we were to vary each of these factors one at a time, we could arrive at all sorts of fine gradations of sonority.

But in fact we usually vary more than one factor at a time.

The idea of sonority is not well enough defined to answer these questions. In other words, sonority is simply too rough an idea for us to make use of it as a compositional resource at this stage. We can, however, formulate a few rules of thumb to prevent any gross discrepancies of sonority from getting in the way of the tonal structure proper.

1. Spacing
    a. If you can make your intervals smaller by shifting one or more lines up or down an octave without violating any voice-leading constraints, then do so.

is preferable to

b. With three lines, if the interval between the bass note and the middle note is less than an octave, and the interval between the middle note and the top note is more than an octave, watch out—this spacing can have the effect of dissociating the bottom two notes from the top, particularly when these notes are in a relatively low register. Thus,

2. Interval control

Once you've reached the sonority level you are going to use for most of the piece, maintain it, at least on downbeats. A perfect consonance in the midst of imperfect consonances will draw attention to the pitches forming the perfect consonance. Unless these pitches have a particularly critical role in the structures of their individual lines, you may find the sense of flow is broken.

Compare

with

The pitches forming the octave and the fifth in the third and fifth measures in the first version are interior elements in secondary structures. The pitches forming the octave in the seventh measure of the second version are both elements in the basic structures of their respective lines and can both be understood as goals of secondary step motions.

Intervals Between Contiguous Notes: Cross Relations • The idea of line rests on a fundamental distinction between two ways of understanding the phenomenon of one note following another. Suppose, just as one note ends a second note begins; nothing comes between them. If we consider the two notes as members of the same line, we call them consecutive and make much of their connection. But if we do not consider them members of the same line we call them contiguous and don't bother with their relationship. Or, rather, we only bother with their relationship when it bothers us.

One such relationship is the so-called *cross-relation*, in which a diatonic-degree pitch and a chromatic alteration of that pitch appear contiguously. With our rules this can happen in minor where the sixth degree is used in an ascending step motion in one line and in a descending step motion or as an upper neighbor in the other,

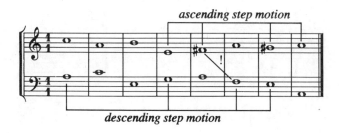

or where the seventh degree is used in a descending step motion in one line and in an ascending step motion or as a lower neighbor in the other.

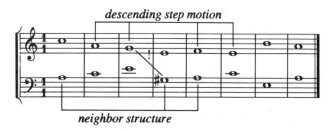

Within the circumscribed world of species, a cross-relation is bound to come as something of a shock. The shock is somewhat less when the second of the cross-related pitches is approached by step, thereby creating a dissonance with the first of the cross-related pitches;

when a simultaneously sounding note in another line forms a dissonance with one of the cross-related pitches;

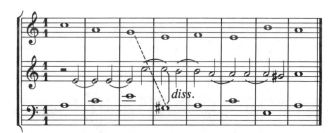

or even when another line moves by step at the moment the second of the cross-related pitches occurs.

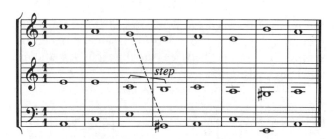

Types of Motion: Nomenclature • We think of the intervals between consecutive, contiguous, and simultaneously sounding notes as defining the motion of the lines at any one point. When two consecutive notes in a line have different pitches, we think of the line as *moving* to the second pitch. When two lines move at the same time* and by the same interval in

---

* Note that "two lines move at the same time" means that the second note under consideration in one line begins at the same time that the second note under consideration in the other line begins. Where the other notes begin or end is immaterial.

the same direction, we say the two lines move *in parallel* or are in *parallel motion*.

 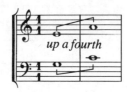

Indeed, even if the intervals are not exactly the same size (are not made up of the same number of semitones) but we can think of them as being made up of the *same number of seconds* (as, for example, a third is made up of two seconds whether it is a major, minor, or even diminished third) we think of them as diatonically equivalent and consider the motion parallel.

Obviously, if the interval between consecutive notes in one line is made up of the same number of seconds as the interval in the other line,

the interval between the two notes at the moment of motion must be made up of the same number of seconds as the one between simultaneously sounding notes just before it.

We often name parallel motions by this interval.

"parallel thirds"   "parallel sixths"   "parallel fifths"

When two lines move at the same time and in the same direction but by an interval made up of a different number of seconds, we say their motion is *similar,* or that they are in *similar motion* at that point.

When as a result of parallel or similar motion the second note of the lower of the two lines is higher than the first note of the upper (or the second note of the upper is lower than the first note of the lower), we say the motion is *overlapping*.

When the two lines move at the same time but in opposite directions,

we call the motion *contrary.* When one line moves and the other doesn't,

we call the motion *oblique.*

Types of Motion: Constraints • Parallel and similar motion are subject to the following constraints:
  A. Forbidden parallel motion

No parallel unisons, octaves, or fifths.*

It might seem that parallel unisons and octaves occur all the time in actual tonal music.

(Beethoven: *Quartet* Op. 18, No. 1, first movement, mm. 1–2.)

But we don't think of such parallels as occurring between lines with separate identities; we think instead of the lines in question as *doubling* one another—that is stating the same line in another octave or another timbre. In species counterpoint, we are trying to study lines as independent structural entities, each with its own identity. That identity would be destroyed if we allowed parallel octaves.

Parallel fifths, on the other hand, do not occur often in actual tonal music. When they do, we usually think

* Note that octaves and fifths include any interval of their interval classes. Thus

constitutes parallel fifths. However

does not, since the motion is contrary rather than parallel. Similarly

cannot be considered parallel fifths since there is *no motion*—that is, neither line moves.

of them as crude, unfinished, or perhaps deliberately archaic.†

Parallel motion is so basic to the structure of tonal music that we stretch the concept to include what we will call *non-consecutive parallels*.

We defined motion in terms of the way a line goes from one note to the next. But, of course, we think of the notes of a line as going not just from one note

† Fifths as well as octaves were used as a basis for doubling in the ninth and tenth centuries.

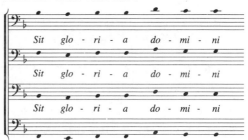

In the twelfth to the fourteenth centuries composers seem to have had no qualms about parallel fifths in otherwise independent lines.

(Machaut: *S'il estoit nulz*, mm. 5–7.)

From as early as 1450 on—that is a good 150 years before the kind of tonal structure we are talking about became commonplace—the most influential composers considered the avoidance of parallel fifths an elementary part of their craft. In the late nineteenth and early twentieth centuries, mimicking the early doubling practice for programmatic effect became popular among some composers.

(Debussy: *Préludes*, Book I, "La Cathédrale engloutie," mm. 28–30.)

to the next but from one note in a linear structure to the next note in the same linear structure. And where notes occur both on and off the beat, we will find we think of the notes of a line as going from one beat to the next. So you can see how if two lines were based on the same structure and were combined so that members of the same pitch classes were serving the same functions at the same times,

the sense of separate identity of the two lines might suffer. And you can see how if the same perfect intervals were to fall on consecutive beats, their weak sonority in a strong rhythmic position might make them seem awkward, even if they were not the result of the same linear structure in both lines.

The weaker the sonority of an interval, the stronger the structural bond between the notes forming it: the dangers of parallelism are most acute for unisons, a little less so for octaves, and considerably less so for fifths. Furthermore, the smaller the interval between two non-consecutive notes, the greater the potential for structural connection they will have: repetitions cannot create parallel motions, but steps are distinctly more dangerous than skips.

Specific methods for handling these dangers—for *breaking* non-consecutive parallels—vary with the rhythmic situation and hence will be dealt with separately for each species. All these methods, however, are based on two simple strategies:

1. denying the prolonged sense of the first pitch before the second is arrived at

2. weakening the arrival of the second pitch by having a member of the same pitch class occur between the parallels

B. Restrictions on similar motion

When the notes in two lines begin at the same time, the relationship between the two pitches is emphasized. When the two notes are approached by similar motion, the emphasis is increased, particularly when the two notes fall on a downbeat or when the upper note is approached by a skip.* If the interval formed by the two notes is a unison, octave, or fifth, a problem arises in that these intervals create a strong sense of structural bond but a weak sense of sonority. As we pointed out above, the stronger the structural bond, the weaker the sonority, and hence the more sensitive the interval. The acuteness of the problem varies with the sensitivity of the interval, how it is approached in both lines, what the other lines—if any—are contributing to the sonority, and whether or not the motion occurs on the beat. Methods for handling the problem will be given separately for each species, but in general note that:

The *unison*—the most sensitive interval—is never approached by similar motion. (In actual tonal music

---

* We are used to smaller intervals being toward the top. Having the smallest interval between simultaneously sounding notes in the lowest two lines sounds abnormal and unbalanced and thus draws our attention to the relationship involved.

In the same way, having the larger interval between consecutive notes of the upper of two lines in similar motion sounds unusual and draws our attention to the motion.

it sometimes is, but usually the effect is buried in the midst of more notes than we'll be using in species.)

The *octave*—a somewhat less sensitive interval—can be approached by similar motion, but only if the upper note is approached by step,

and either both notes forming the octave have critical roles in the structure of the respective lines

Both C's are final elements in their lines' basic structures

or the effect is compensated for by other factors.

The *fifth*—the least sensitive of the three problematic intervals—has the widest latitude. It can be approached by similar motion with a step in the upper line when both notes forming it have critical roles in the underlying structures of their respective lines

Both notes are elements in their lines' basic structures

or simply when another line contributes enough sonority.

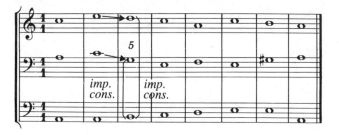

It can even be approached by similar motion with a skip in the upper line if the effect is compensated for by other factors.

C. Restrictions on crossing and overlapping motion

When two lines cross or overlap there is always a danger that the listener will lose the sense of the functional identity of the individual line. In the case of the bass, whose function is, after all, by definition to be the lowest sounding line at any moment, crossing is out of the question,

while overlapping creates an awkward situation which is best avoided entirely.

In the case of the upper lines, the problem is not so acute, since neither line need be the higher or the lower of the two in order to carry out its function. Nevertheless, crossing and overlapping may sound awkward or confusing unless care is taken to make the total situation as easy to grasp as possible. For crossing, the simplest way to make sure the lines are easy to follow is to use oblique motion:

If the motion is contrary or similar, it is safest to

79

have one of the lines move by step. It also helps to have the other line skip an octave or continue in a step motion or neighbor structure from some previous note.

The easiest kind of overlap to grasp is where the lines move in parallel thirds or sixths or where one line skips an octave,

but under no condition should a unison be left by similar motion.

Drill

Mark the errors in the following using the symbols indicated below.

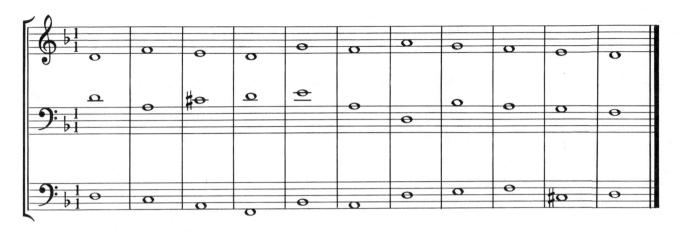

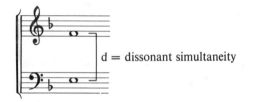 = dissonant skip   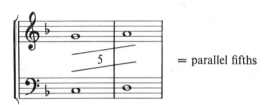 = non-generable note

 d = dissonant simultaneity   = parallel fifths

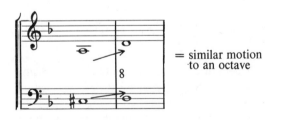 = similar motion to an octave   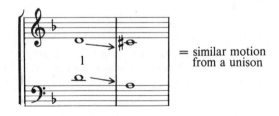 = similar motion from a unison

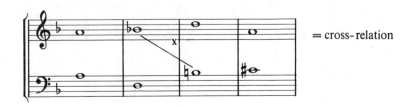 = cross-relation

81

4.4 Combining Species Lines: Correspondence Between Linear Structures

In this section we will be concerned with the way we understand the structure of one line in terms of its relationship to the structure of another, simultaneously stated line.

Types of Correspondence • Consider the different ways that two simultaneously unfolding structures can be related to one another. Take two lines that begin

Here the two structures correspond as closely as is possible without producing parallel octaves or unisons. We would generate the notes of each segment in the same order, using the same rule for both lines at each point.

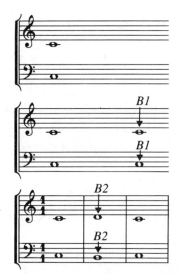

We will call such a correspondence between structures *aligned*. When structures are aligned, simultaneously sounding notes have the same order of conceptual priority in their respective lines. We will also call such a correspondence *functionally parallel*, in that simultaneously sounding notes serve the same function in their respective lines.* Now, take two lines

---

* Note the distinction between parallel motion and parallel structures:
In

the motion is contrary but the structures are parallel. From the second to the third measure of

beginning

Here the structures correspond less closely. We can generate the notes of each line in the same order, but different rules are used for the last notes to be generated in each line.

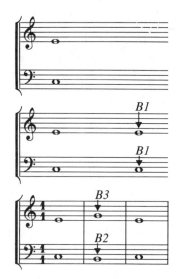

We can say that the structures are *aligned* but *not parallel*. Finally, take two lines that begin

In order to generate both segments in the same number of stages using the same rules, we would have to generate the third note before the second note in the top line and the second note before the third note in the bottom line.

the motion is parallel but the structures are not. In

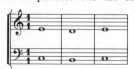

both motion and structure are parallel.

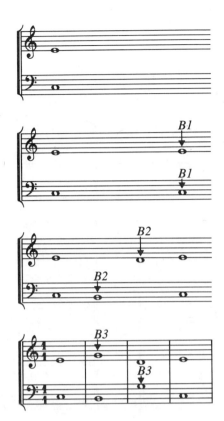

This means that the second and third notes of the top segment are in a different order of conceptual priority from the simultaneously sounding notes in the bottom segment. We say that the structures are *unaligned*.

We can use the same set of distinctions to deal with structural relationships between complete lines as well. Since there is no way a basic step motion can be functionally parallel to a basic arpeggiation, the closest correspondence possible would be alignment.

Secondary structures might then be parallel,

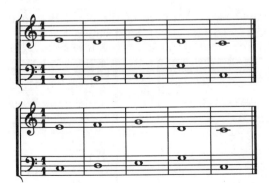

aligned but not parallel,

or unaligned.

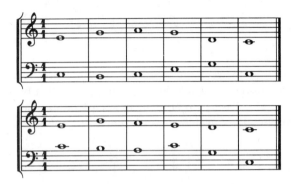

On the other hand, any of the three notes of the basic step motion might be unaligned with the corresponding note in the basic arpeggiation.

Indeed, all three might be.

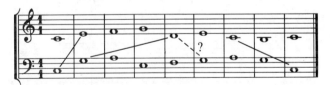

Correspondence and Ambiguity • All the lines in the above examples are structurally unambiguous. But take the line

If we did not have to interpret this line in terms of a basic step motion, we might understand it in terms of two neighbor embellishments, constructing it thus:

83

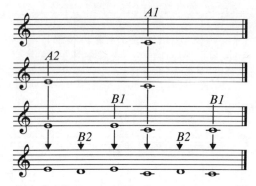

But if there were no other line present with a basic step motion, we would have to understand this line in terms of a basic step motion. In such a case, there are two equally plausible ways of generating the line

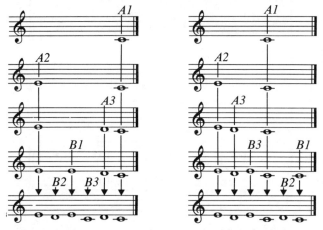

Taken by itself, therefore, the line is structurally ambiguous. Suppose, however, it were combined with such a bass:

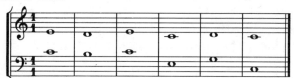

The structure of this bass is unambiguous; the only way you can construct it is

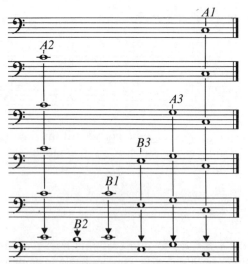

This structure corresponds closely with one of the ways of understanding the structure of the upper line but not with the other.

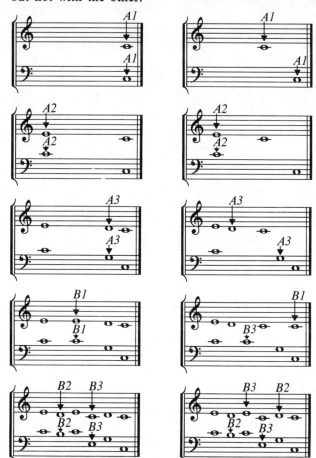

Consequently, since we must conceive of the structure of both lines *at the same time,* it is much easier to understand the upper line in terms of the first method of construction.

If this same upper line were combined with a bass line whose structure unambiguously corresponded to the second way of understanding the structure of the upper line, namely,

we would have conceived of the upper line in terms of the second method of construction.

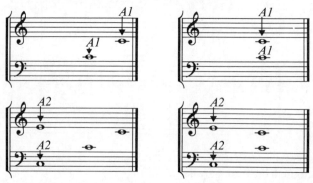

84

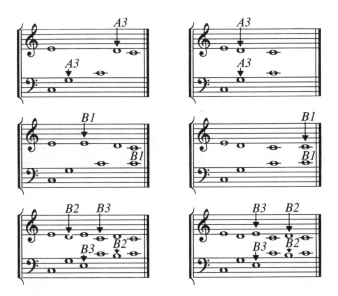

Now, take the combination of lines

Taken separately, each line is structurally ambiguous, that is, each line can be constructed in at least two distinct ways. Starting from a three-note basic step motion

we can construct the top line in three more stages:

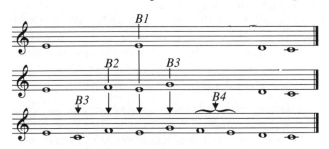

But starting with a five-note basic step motion

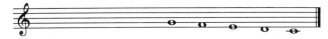

we can generate the same notes in an equal number of stages

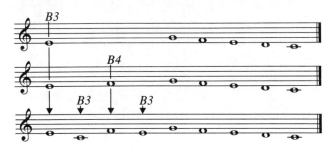

and arrive at an essentially different way of understanding the line. The advantage of the first way is that it allows us to understand the first F-E as part of a structure that requires a step. The advantage of the second way is that it allows us to understand the E-F-G as a regularly spaced motion directed toward the first note of the basic step motion. As for the bass, if we want to understand the step E-D as the beginning of a neighbor structure, it takes seven stages to construct the line.

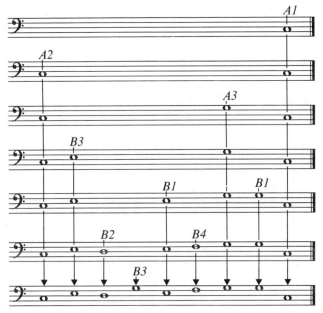

If we are willing to accept the less immediate C-D as forming the beginning of a step motion, we can construct the line in five stages.

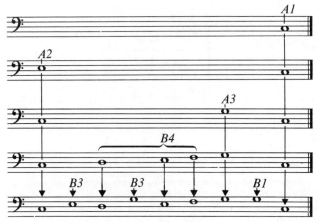

Taken in combination, however, the ambiguity of the individual lines disappears. Consider the four available combinations of the above structural interpretations, shown on the next page. In none of these combinations

85

are the basic structures aligned, but at least in the third combination the opening secondary structures are.*

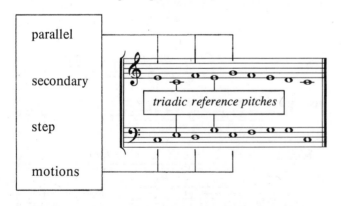

In general then, we may say:

> Given the combination of an ambiguous line with an unambiguous one, we will prefer to understand the ambiguous line in terms of whatever structure corresponds most closely to that of the unambiguous line.

> Given the combination of two ambiguous lines, we will prefer to understand them as having whatever available structures correspond most closely to one another.

---

* Note the shift in the rate of flow from every other note, in the C–D–E part of the secondary motion in the bass, to every note, in the E–F–G part; and note the possible structural parallelism with the upper line. The fit is even tighter if we construct the lines

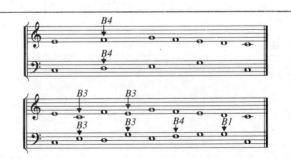

Correspondence and Interest • Compare the following two combinations of lines:

and

While the spacing-out of the opening step motion in the upper line of the second example, and the even more extensive spacing-out of the neighbor structure in the bass in the first example, might make us prefer these as individual lines, the real difference between the interest of the two combinations comes from the way the linear structures are related. The relationship between the linear structures of the first example is itself of interest precisely because these structures are unaligned. Compare the relationship between the neighbor structures at the ends of the two examples.

There is nothing so interesting about a neighbor structure per se. Nor are two simultaneously sounding neighbor structures any more interesting. But when they are staggered so that the neighbor note of one comes at the same time as the embellished note of the other (as in the first example), we have at least a minimal basis for interest. To sum up, other things being equal:

> Given two ways of understanding a combination of lines, we will choose whichever way gives the closer correspondence between linear structures. But given two combinations of lines, we will find that combination more interesting that maintains a less close correspondence between linear structures.

Thus, just as with the principles discussed in Section 4.2, there is a direct conflict between the way we use the principle of correspondence to avoid ambiguity and the way we use it to create interest.

Exercises

For each of the following, (a) show how you would understand the structure of the bass line by generating it. Then (b) show which of the available ways of understanding the upper line corresponds most closely to that structure. Finally, (c) answer the following questions: Which bass makes you understand the upper line in the most interesting way? Which combination do you find the most interesting and why?

1.
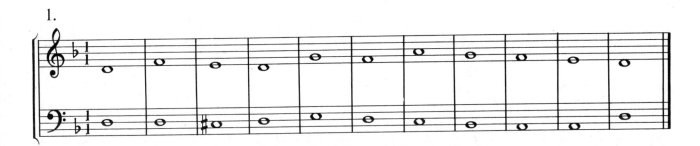

2.
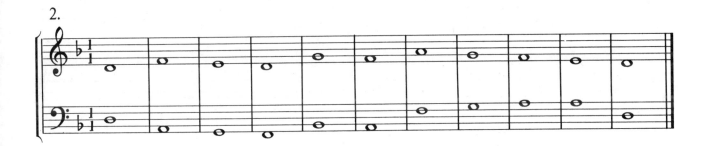

3.
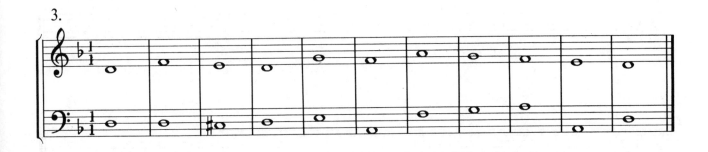

4.
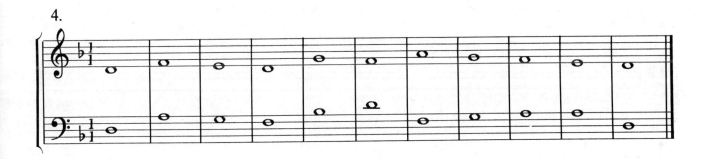

89

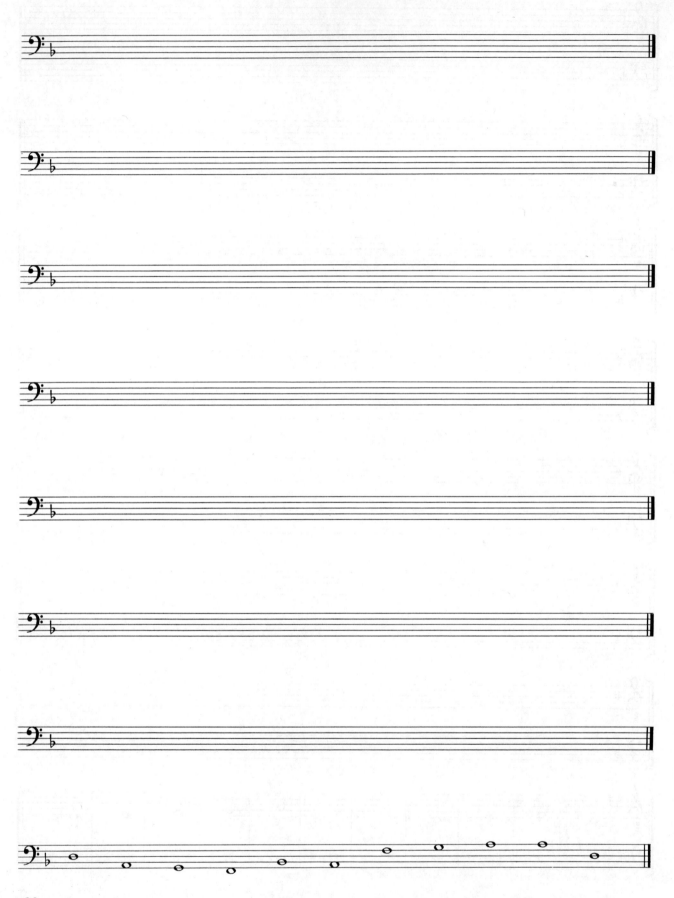

2b.

3a.

3b.

4a.

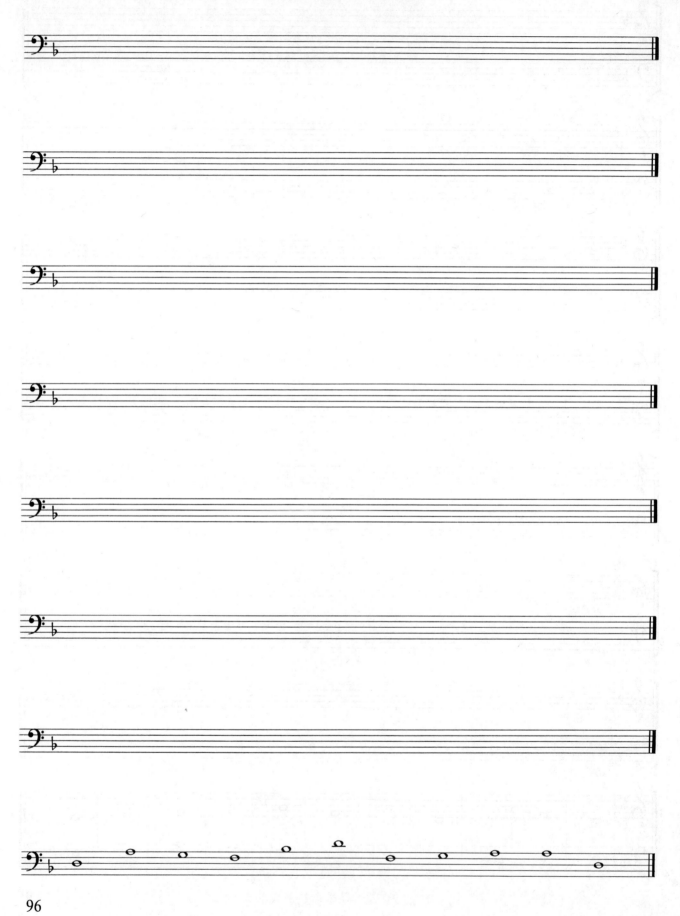

96

4b.

CHAPTER FIVE

Simple Species

5.0 Introduction

In the first four chapters of this book I used a lot of words to try to show you where I think certain critical problems of musical structure lie and how I think solutions to these problems might be formulated. In the next two chapters I will no longer rely so much on words but on musical problems, which are intended for you to solve, not with words, but with notes.

For each species or combination of species I will discuss briefly the different kinds of rhythmic relationships that can obtain between notes in the given format and then give a set of rules governing the kinds of intervals proper to each kind of rhythmic relationship. You will then work out a series of exercises in the given format following the given rules. What I hope you will learn from these sections is not so much the rules themselves as a sense of how the rules affect the way the notes of one line interact with the notes of another.

5.1 Two Lines in First Species

Rhythmic Format • Both lines use only whole notes. Both lines begin and end together, and all notes are on the beat.

These lines must be generated by the operational rules stated in Section 4.1. They are to be combined according to the voice-leading constraints of Section 4.3. Since many of the considerations presented there do not apply to the limited circumstances of first species, a resume of the relevant constraints follows.

Rules for Two Lines in First Species

Intervals between consecutive notes in a line:
  In general, as covered by the operational rules of Section 4.1.
  Skips of a fourth in the bass
    No skip of a fourth in the bass unless there is a note in an upper line that sounds simultaneously with one of the notes forming the fourth and forms a second or seventh with the other.

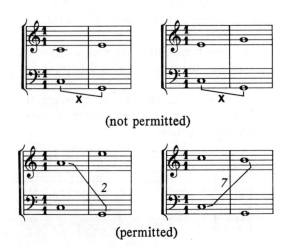

Intervals between simultaneously sounding notes:
  Dissonance
    Two simultaneously sounding notes may not form a dissonant interval. (Remember that since there are only two lines, one of the notes must always be the lowest sounding

note; consequently, fourths and, of course, elevenths, or any other interval of the fourth class, are considered dissonant.)

Sonority

Once the fullest available sonority (imperfect consonances) is reached, maintain it except where octaves or fifths would clarify the structure. Avoid unisons except in the first and last measures. If intervals larger than a tenth occur, check to see if it would be possible to shift the bass up an octave or the upper line down an octave.

Forbidden forms of motion:

No parallel unisons, octaves, or fifths between consecutive pairs of simultaneously sounding notes.

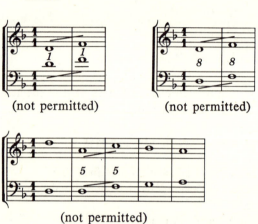

No non-consecutive parallel unisons or octaves that are the result of parallel structures in their respective lines, unless between the unisons or octaves one of the lines has a pitch that is dissonant with one of the pitches forming the first unison or octave.

(permitted)

(not permitted)

(structures not parallel, hence permitted)

No similar motion to or from a unison.

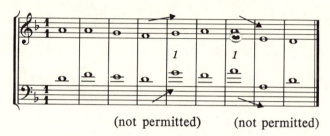
(not permitted)   (not permitted)

No similar motion to an octave except where the upper note of the octave is approached by step and both notes forming the octave are final tonics in their respective basic structures.

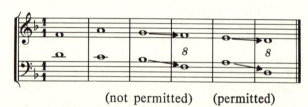
(not permitted)   (permitted)

No similar motion to a fifth except where the upper note of the fifth is approached by step and is either the dominant or the second degree.

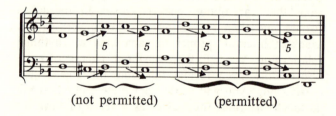
(not permitted)   (permitted)

No voice crossing, overlapping motion, or cross-relations.

It is essential to realize that constraints in species counterpoint carry slightly different weights from one another. Voice-leading constraints (forbidden forms of motion, conditions under which a dissonance may occur) are taken as absolute—no parallel fifths means that *no* circumstances will mitigate parallel fifths. The methods of linear construction are equally absolute—you must be able to generate each line by the *A* and *B* rules of Section 4.1. The sonority constraints, however, are much weaker—your basic task is to write the most interesting lines you can, combined in the most interesting ways available under the voice-leading constraints. The purpose of the sonority constraints is to avoid unintended emphases on intervals between lines caused by sudden shifts to weaker sonorities. They are to be considered as convenient rules of thumb rather than as absolute laws.

Drills

1. Show why there is no way that either of the following could be completed.

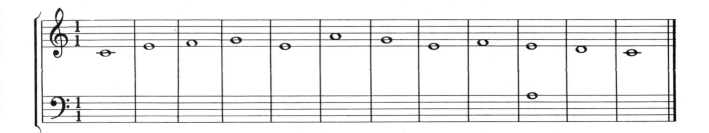

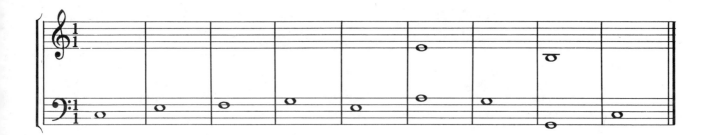

2. Complete each of the following.

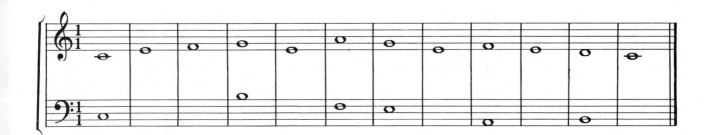

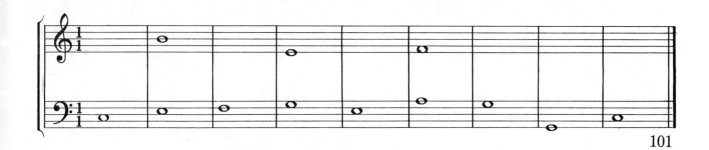

Exercises

1. For each place the given line has a skip, show all the steps available for the other line.

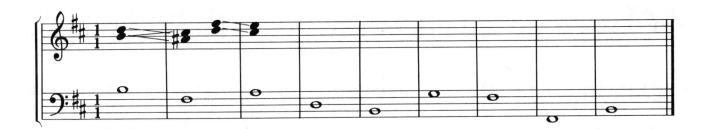

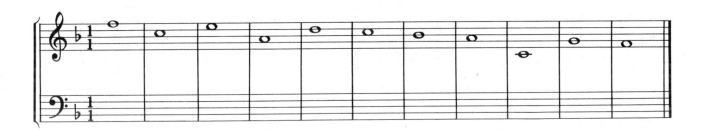

How many of these steps can you use in a line constructed according to our rules?

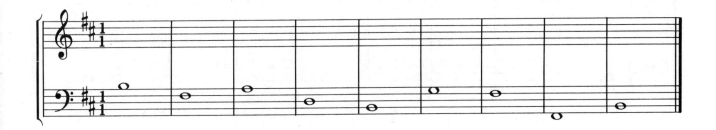

2. Write two basses for the following upper line: one that makes the listener hear the upper line in terms of a three-note basic step motion, and another that makes him think of it in terms of a five-note basic step motion.

3. Write two different upper lines for the following bass: one that would be understood in terms of a three-note basic step motion, and another that would be understood in terms of a five- or eight-note basic step motion.

5.2 Three Lines in First Species

Rhythmic Format • All three lines can use only whole notes, which fall on the beat, and all three lines begin and end together.

The relationship of any two of the three lines to one another is subject to essentially the same set of constraints as those for two lines in first species.

Rules for Three Lines in First Species

Intervals between consecutive notes in a line:
   Already covered by the operational rules of Section 4.1.
Intervals between simultaneously sounding notes:
   Dissonance
      Two simultaneously sounding notes must not form a dissonant interval. (Remember that fourths—and other intervals of that class—between the bass note and any simultaneously sounding note in an upper line are considered dissonant, but that fourths between simultaneously sounding notes in the upper lines are considered consonant.)

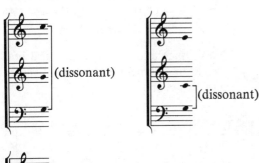

Exception to the rule against dissonant intervals:
   An augmented fourth or diminished fifth between simultaneously sounding notes in the upper two lines is permitted if the bass note forms a sixth with one note and a third with the other.

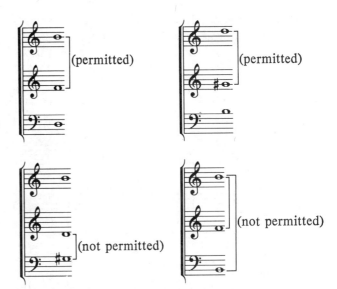

(The practice of allowing "diminished triads" to function locally as consonant combinations corresponds to that of actual tonal music. As long as the third is in the bass, the diminished fifth or augmented fourth is treated as though it were consonant. Note, however, that this practice is not extended to augmented triads.)

Sonority
   Maintain the fullest available sonority (three different pitch classes) where possible, except where linear interest or coherence would suffer. Where the structures of the individual lines make it impossible or undesirable to do this, use the next fullest sonority (two pitches that are members of the same class, the third pitch forming an imperfect consonance with them). Avoid collections that form only perfect intervals except at the beginning and the end. Keep the upper two lines close together (usually no more than an octave apart, under exceptional circumstances a tenth). (See below.)

(the tenth emphasizes the principal interior destination points of the two upper lines)

Forbidden forms of motion:

The bass may not cross or overlap with either of the upper lines. The upper lines may cross or overlap as long as the structure of each remains clear. (See Chapter 4, pages 79–80.)

No parallel unisons, octaves, or fifths between consecutive notes in any pair of lines.

No non-consecutive parallel unisons or octaves that result from parallel structures in their respective lines unless between the octaves or unisons a pitch occurs in any of the three lines that is either

    a. dissonant with the pitches of the first octave or unison

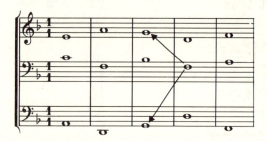

or b. a member of the same pitch class as the pitches of the second octave or unison.

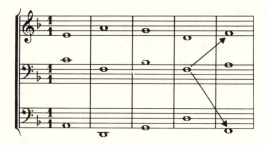

No similar motion to or from a unison.

No similar motion to an octave except where the upper note is approached by step and both notes are the final notes in their respective basic structures.

No similar motion to a fifth except where the upper note is approached by step and either

    a. the upper note is the dominant or the second degree

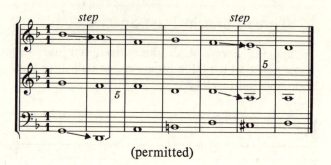

(permitted)

or b. the fifth is in the upper two lines and the bass note is a member of a different pitch class.

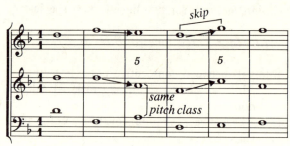

(not permitted)

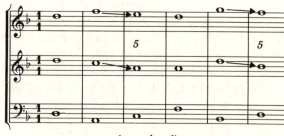

(permitted)

No cross-relations unless the third line moves by step at the moment the second of the cross-related pitches occurs.

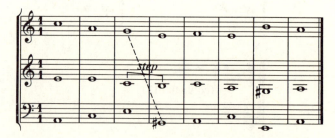

Drills

1. Find the errors in the following.

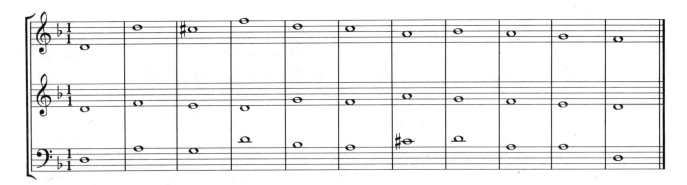

2. Complete the following.*

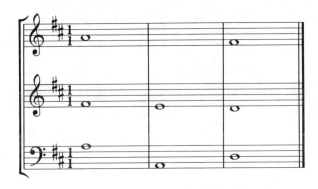

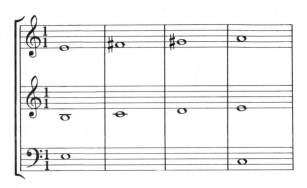

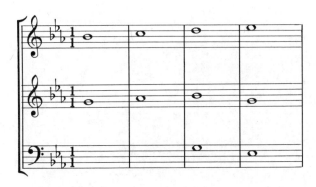

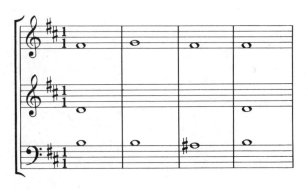

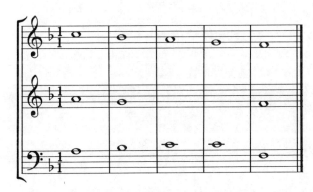

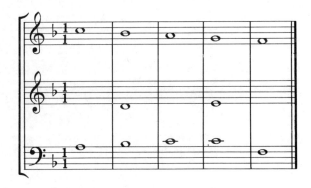

* All linear structures must be complete. If the segment ends with a double bar you must have a completed basic arpeggiation in the bass and a basic step motion in one of the upper lines.

Exercises

1. Add a bass line.

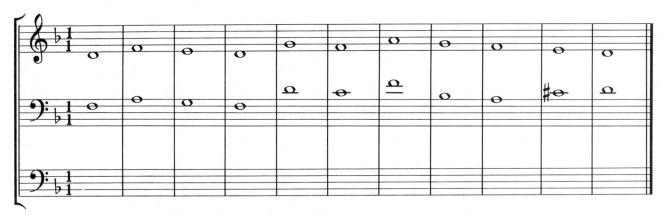

2. Add an inner line.

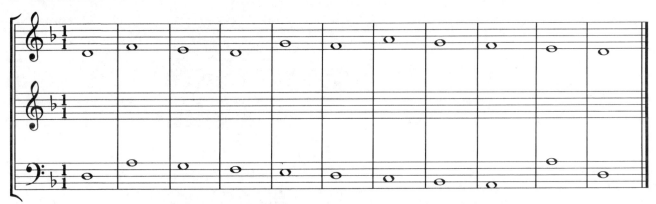

3. Add a bass line and a top line.

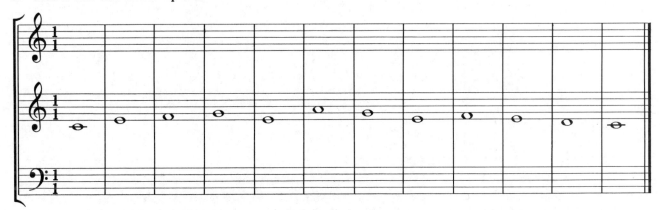

5.3 Two Lines in Second Species

Rhythmic Format • The species line is made up of half notes, the other line of whole notes. The meter is $\frac{1}{1}$ so that all the whole notes are on the beat, but only every other half note is on the beat. The species line may begin on or off the beat.

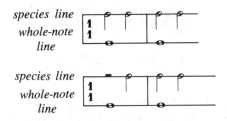

The last note in the species line is a whole note on the beat.

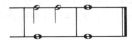

The species line may serve as bass or upper line.

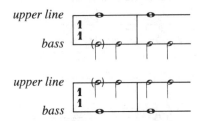

This rhythmic format has important implications both for the way we understand the structure of the species line and for the local intervallic relationships between the species line and the other line.

On the Beat and Off the Beat: Ambiguity and Interest • Consider the following line:

If all these notes have the same relationship to the beat, say they are all on the beat,

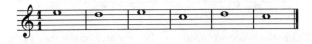

the structure of the line is ambiguous. (Which D is a neighbor and which the middle element of the basic step motion? See Section 4.4) But suppose only every other note is on the beat:

The ambiguity disappears. It is much easier to think of the second D as a neighbor because it is off the beat and the first D as an element in the underlying structure of the line because it is on the beat. To see the strength of these factors consider the line

Now it is much easier to hear the first D as a neighbor and the second D as an element in the basic structure. Why should this be so? Consider our definition of a beat: A beat is simply a moment in time in terms of which you think of other nearby moments in time. You think of the moments you describe as off the beat in terms of those moments before and after it that you describe as on the beat. Similarly you think of the pitch of a neighbor in terms of the pitches before and after it. Given a choice, it is easier to associate conceptually prior pitches with conceptually prior points in time and conceptually dependent pitches with conceptually dependent points in time. Of course, you are not always given the choice. Compare the lines

and

The structure of these two lines is almost identical. Yet the first line is clearly more interesting. In the second line, for every pair of consecutive notes but one, the note with the conceptually prior pitch is on the beat and the note with the conceptually dependent pitch is off the beat.

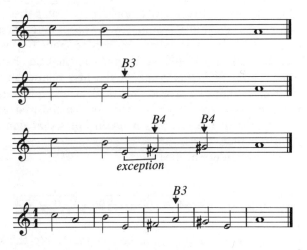

In the first line, virtually the opposite is true:

The conflict between how we conceive of a note's place in time and how we conceive of its place in a pitch structure is itself a source of interest. The absence of such conflict is almost guaranteed to produce a dull line.

We can then add one more pair of general principles to those stated in Sections 4.2 and 4.4:

> Given two possible ways of understanding the pitch structure of a line, we will choose whichever way assigns conceptually prior pitches to conceptually prior moments in time and conceptually subsequent pitches to conceptually subsequent moments in time. But, given two lines alike in other respects, we will find more interesting whichever assigns conceptually prior pitches to conceptually subsequent moments in time and conceptually subsequent pitches to conceptually prior moments in time.

On the Beat and Off the Beat: Passing Tones and Dissonant Neighbors • Consider the two kinds of relationships that can occur between simultaneously sounding notes in second species. One occurs between two notes that begin together, that is, between whole notes and on-the-beat half notes: . The other occurs between two notes that don't begin together but do sound simultaneously because the first note is still sounding when the second note begins, that is, between whole notes and off-the-beat half notes: . We think of the first relationship as stronger than the second. We think of the intervals between notes that begin together as emphasized at the expense of the intervals between notes that don't begin together.

Now, consider the line:

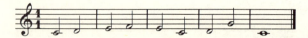

Take the second note in the first measure. We think of its pitch entirely in terms of its relationship to the pitches of the notes immediately before and after it.

Similarly, we think of the moment it begins in terms of the moments that the notes before and after it begin. Since the C and the E are on-the-beat half notes, they are the ones that will form the strong relationships with the whole notes. Thus, as long as the C and the E are stable with respect to the whole notes, there is no need for the D to be.

When such an interior element in a step motion is dissonant with a previously established note in another line, we call it a *passing tone*. Note that a passing tone is immediately preceded and succeeded by the other elements in its structure. In generating lines we might subsequently add a note between elements of a step motion.

But in such a case the D cannot be a passing tone

(not permitted)

because although we think of its moment in time in terms of the beats before and after it, we can't think of its pitch in terms of the pitches before and after it. We must think of the D in terms of the C and the E, not in terms of the C and the G.

Now let's go back to the original form of the line.

Take the second note in the second measure. Here again we think of both its pitch and the moment in time that it occurs in terms of the notes immediately before and after it. For the same reasons adduced before, there is no reason why such a note has to be stable with respect to a simultaneously sounding whole note. Therefore, the interval can be either consonant or dissonant. If dissonant, we would call it a *dissonant neighbor* to distinguish its linear function from that of the passing tone.

Now take the second note in the third measure. Like all the other off-the-beat notes, its moment in time is conceptually dependent on the beats before and after it. But although its pitch is conceptually subsequent to the E before it and the D after it, it is not dependent on the E and the D. Any other triad pitch would have worked as well.

Consequently, unlike the D and the F, it cannot be dissonant with a whole note in another voice,

but must be consonant.

Thus, under no condition may a dissonant half note be approached or left by skip.

On the Beat and Off the Beat: Non-Consecutive Parallels • In first species, there is only one kind of moment where motion can occur: on the beat, when all the lines start new notes. In second species there are two kinds of moments: on the beat—when all lines move and any kind of motion can occur—and off the beat—when only one line moves and therefore only oblique motion can occur. Motion at the second moment offers no problems—all motion is oblique. Motion at the first moment offers no new problems—we can use the same restrictions we used in first species. What is new is the problem of motion from one moment to the next like moment, particularly from one strong relationship to the next strong relationship

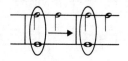

and to a lesser extent from one weak relationship to the next weak relationship.

Given this rhythmic format, there is really no way to hide parallel unisons and octaves on consecutive downbeats. When the parallels are the result of parallel structures in their respective lines, there is simply no way that either of the methods for breaking the sense of parallelism (see page 78) can be used.

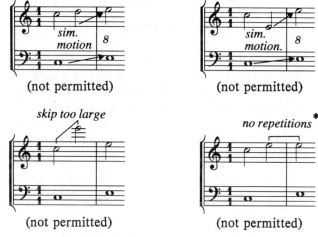

But even if they are not, the combination of weak sonority and strong metric position brings out the octaves or unisons at the expense of the real structure

(Later, when we have a third line to add sonority, such a passage will be possible.)

* See page 114.

Parallel fifths on consecutive downbeats present no problem as long as the species line makes it clear that the fifths are not the result of parallel linear structures.

(permitted)

(not permitted)

Parallel octaves off consecutive beats may stick out despite the fact that one of the pitches forming the second octave occurs before the octave itself. Where the pitches forming the octaves are a second apart, the danger is particularly strong. It can usually be averted by approaching the two off-the-beat half notes from opposite directions.

(not permitted)

(permitted)

Where the octaves are related by some interval other than a second, it is sufficient to leave the first off-the-beat half note by step.

(not permitted)   (permitted)

It is virtually impossible to use parallel unisons on or off consecutive beats without their sticking out.

Rules for Two Lines in Second Species

Intervals between consecutive notes in a line:

As in first species, these intervals are controlled by the operational rules of Section 4.1. There is one exception for the half-note line.

No direct repetitions. Rule *B1* may be used to generate a pitch, but another rule must be subsequently applied so that no direct repetitions of a pitch occur in the final line.

The prohibition against skips of a fourth in the bass varies with the rhythmic situation:

a. half notes in the bass, skip of a fourth within a measure.
   Not permitted under any circumstances.

b. half notes in the bass, skip of a fourth over the barline (from the last note in one measure to the first note in the next).
   As in first species.

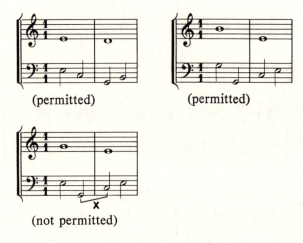

(permitted)   (permitted)

(not permitted)

c. whole notes in the bass
   Permitted where there is a half-note in the upper line that forms a second or seventh with one of the notes forming the fourth, sounds simultaneously with and is consonant with the other, and fulfills at least one of the following conditions:
   i. falls on the beat
   ii. is approached by skip
   iii. is contiguous with the note it forms a seventh or second with.

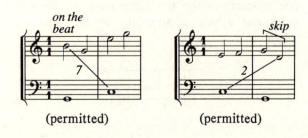

(permitted)   (permitted)

contiguous
(permitted)   (not permitted)

Intervals between simultaneously sounding notes:
  On the beat:
    Must be consonant.
  Off the beat:
    May be dissonant where the half note is a passing tone or neighbor

(permitted)

(permitted)

(permitted)   (permitted)

but *not* where the half note is approached or left by skip.

Forbidden forms of motion:
  On the beat to off the beat:
    All motion is oblique; consequently the only restriction is against the bass crossing.

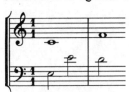
(not permitted)

  Off the beat to on the beat:
    As in first species (see page 100) except that cross-relations are permitted if the half notes form steps.

(permitted)

(not permitted)

On the beat to on the beat:
No parallel unisons.

(not permitted)

No parallel octaves.

(not permitted)

No parallel fifths except where the second note is an interior element of a step motion moving in the opposite direction.

(permitted)

(not permitted)

No cross-relations between an on-the-beat half note and the whole note in the next measure unless the half note is first displaced by step.

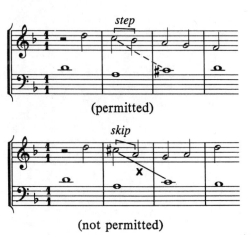
(permitted)

(not permitted)

Off the beat to off the beat:
No parallel unisons.
Parallel octaves related by seconds are permitted only if the two off-the-beat half notes are approached from different directions.

(permitted)

(not permitted)

(permitted) (permitted)

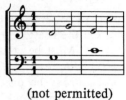
(permitted) (not permitted)

Parallel octaves related by any other interval are permitted if either
    a. the two off-the-beat half notes are approached from opposite directions
or b. the first off-the-beat half note is left by step.

Sonority
  On the beat:
    As in first species.
  Off the beat:
    Any interval, dissonant ones preferred.

Drill

Complete each example as follows:
Add a half note wherever you see an asterisk. If a dissonant half note is possible, write it. If a dissonant half note is not possible write a consonant one. Assume the key is C minor. Try to complete any structures generated by the *B* rules within the given measures. Where this is not possible you may use extra measures before and after the given measures.

Exercises

1. Here are two second-species versions of Fux's D-minor cantus:

For one of them, there is no way to generate a bass in whole notes that doesn't break some rule of second species. Show which version this is true of and why. For the other, there is only one whole-note bass available. Write it.

2. Add a top line in second species to the following bass:

3. Complete the bass line in the following:

Can you connect the D and the A by step motion? (If you wish, you may shift the D off the beat and begin with a rest.)

Supplementary Exercises

1. Write an upper line in second species to go with the following bass:

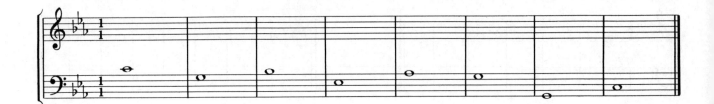

2. Write a bass line in second species to go with the following upper line:

5.4 Compound Lines

The rhythmic format of second species affords a convenient way of attacking the problem of compound species lines. Take the combination of three lines above. Each line has been generated according to one of our three sets of operational rules, and the three lines have been combined according to the constraints of first species. This means that in any one measure the pitches of the upper two lines are consonant with one another and with the bass. Consequently, as long as these two pitches form neither a unison nor an interval greater than an octave, they can also be used as two consecutive half notes in a single second-species line.

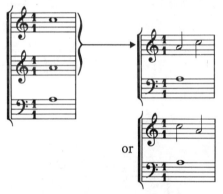

No matter which order we put the two half notes in, the skip they form is bound to be consonant, and both the note skipped to and the note skipped from are bound to be consonant with the bass.

We can apply the same procedure to the next measure.

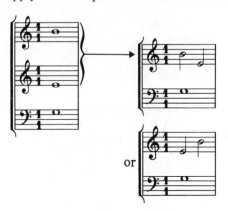

Furthermore, for these two measures we can state either second-species version of the first measure with either second-species version of the second measure without violating any of the constraints of second species.

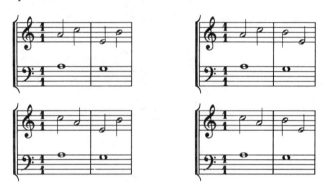

This is not always possible. For example, the fourth measure of our original first-species example yields two possible second-species measures.

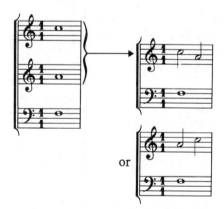

So does the fifth measure.

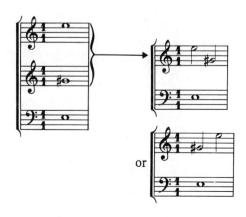

But here only three of the four combinations of available second-species measures will work.

The other has a dissonant skip between the last note of one measure and the first note of the next.

Similarly, of the four possible combinations of the available second-species versions of mm. 5 and 6,

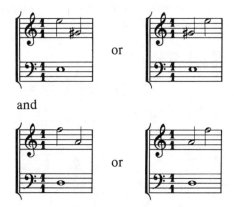

only two will work:

Of the other two, one has a dissonant skip

and the other has similar motion to a fifth.

And of the four possible combinations of the available second-species versions of mm. 7 and 8,

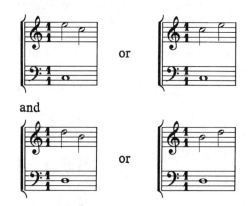

two work

and the other two don't.

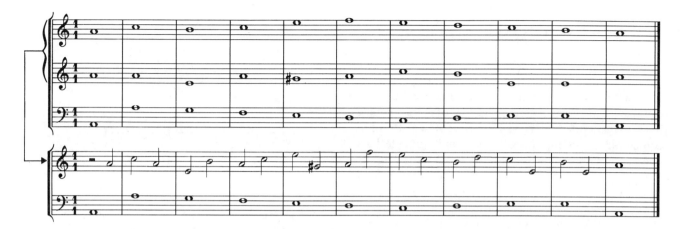

But as long as there is even one combination of second-species versions that will work for each pair of consecutive measures in the original, we can apply the same process to the entire original example, converting three lines in first species into two lines in second species (see above). The half-note line that results is called a *compound line,* as opposed to lines generated by the rules of Section 4.1 alone, which will be called *simple lines.*

Generating a single second-species compound line from two first-species simple lines is simply a more inclusive application of the concept of arpeggiation, as defined in Chapter 3. Up to now, we have always used at least one triad pitch in any arpeggiation. What is new here is that any pair of pitches that could be stated simultaneously in first species can also be stated consecutively in a single second-species line. Thus, as long as both the original lines stick to triad pitches,

there will be nothing in the resultant compound line that we could not have generated in a simple line.

Indeed, as long as *one* of the original lines sticks to triad pitches,

there will be nothing in the resultant compound line

that we couldn't have generated in a simple line.

However, whenever both original lines use non-triad pitches at the same time,

the resultant line is bound to include successions of pitches that could not have been generated in a simple line.

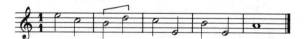

Indeed, whenever one of the original lines begins a structure involving non-triad pitches before the other line has finished a previously initiated structure involving non-triad pitches,

the resultant line will include pitch successions that could not have been generated in a simple line.

To sum up, the preceding example shows how you can use a first-species combination of three simple lines to generate a second-species combination of a compound upper line in half notes and a simple bass line in whole notes. It works because all three original lines are subject to the constraints of first species *and* because the two upper lines of the original are subject to the following additional constraints:

1. simultaneously sounding notes of the upper two lines of the original may form no augmented fourths or diminished fifths and no interval greater than an octave;

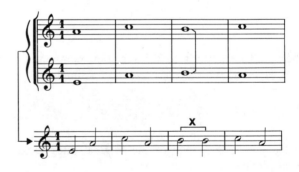

2. the final notes of the upper two lines of the original must form a unison. The only other permissible unison formed by simultaneously sounding notes in the upper two lines of the original is that formed by the notes in the first measure.

You can also use a first-species combination of three simple lines to generate a second-species combination of a compound bass line in half notes and a simple upper line in whole notes. Here the additional constraints are somewhat more limiting:

1. simultaneously sounding notes of the bottom two lines of the original must form no interval greater than an octave;

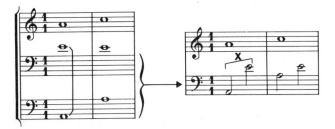

2. the final two notes of the two bottom lines of the original must form a unison. The only other unison permitted between simultaneously sounding notes of the original is in the first measure;

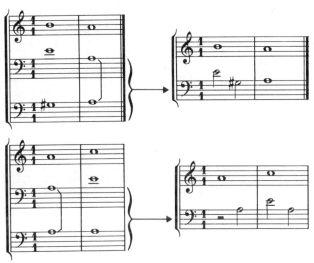

3. the upper two lines of the original must not cross;

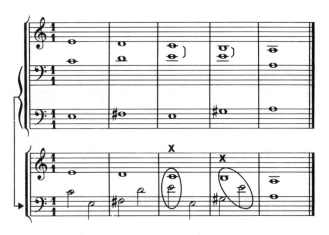

4. simultaneously sounding notes of the upper two lines in the original must form no fourths.

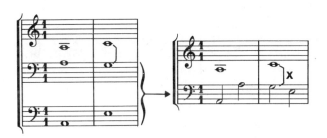

Drill

The half-note line has been generated from the upper two lines in the three-line example. Find the errors in the half-note line and in its relationship to the bass.

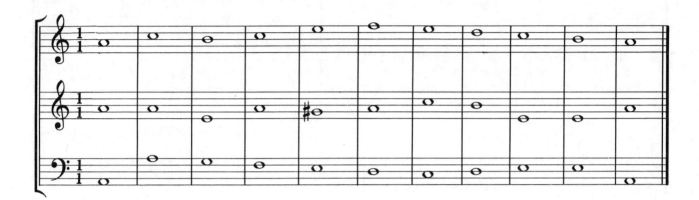

Exercises

1. Generate a compound line in half notes from the upper two whole-note lines.

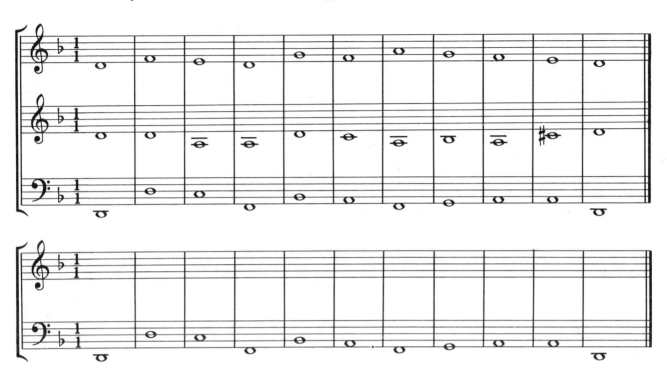

2. Write an upper line in whole notes. Then use your two upper lines to generate a single upper line in half notes.

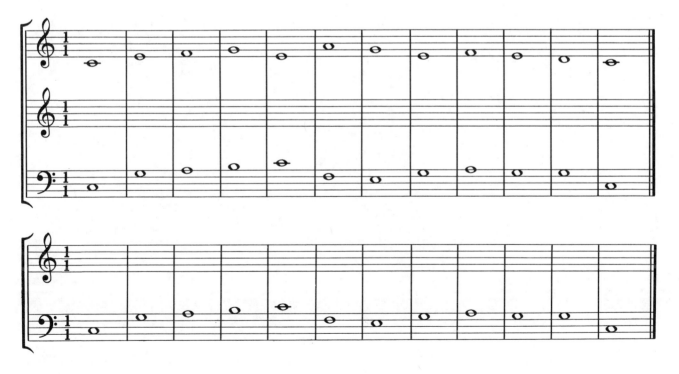

5.5 Two Lines in Third Species

Rhythmic Format • The chief difference between third species and second is simply that in third species there are more notes in the species line: either three to the whole-note beat

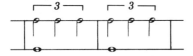

or four.

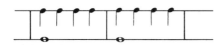

As in second species, the species line may appear either as the bass

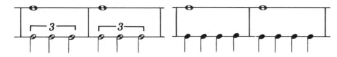

or as the upper line.

As in second species, the species line may begin on any part of the first measure:

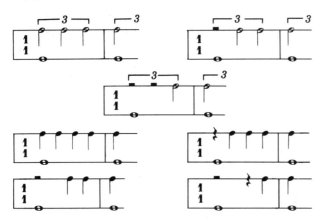

The fact that there are more notes per beat affects the way we understand both the species line and its relationship to the other line.

1. Having fewer notes on the beat than off increases the tendency to understand pitches that fall on the beat as prior elements in the structure.

2. Having three or more notes per measure makes it possible to complete a neighbor structure within a measure. This means that it is now possible to understand a non-triad pitch as being embellished by a neighbor. Take the succession of pitches

In first species they would be understood as

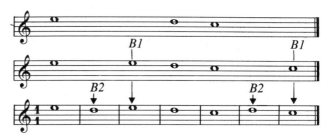

In third species, with three notes to the measure, the second group of three notes would be understood as forming the same kind of neighbor structure as the first group of three notes,

but there is no way we can generate such a structure with the rules of Section 4.1. We will, therefore, have to amend rule *B1* to read: "Any triad pitch may be repeated and any non-triad pitch may be repeated within a measure." Now we can generate the line to conform with our understanding of it.

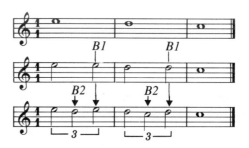

3. Having three or more notes per measure makes it possible to generate a complete step motion within a single measure. Of course, where possible we will still prefer to understand step motion as moving from beat to beat,

but where there is no choice we can certainly understand step motions as moving from off the beat to on the beat,

from on the beat to off the beat within the same measure,

or even from off the beat to off the beat in the same measure.

Note that in each case the interior element in the step motion may be dissonant.

Rules for Two Lines in Third Species

Relationships between consecutive notes in a line:
As in first species, these relationships are controlled by the operational rules of Section 4.1. There are a few exceptions and addenda for the species line.

No direct repetitions. Rule *B1* may be applied only if some other rule is subsequently applied to insert a note between a pitch and its repetition.

Rule *B1* may also be applied to non-triad pitches where both notes are in the same measure.

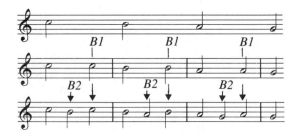

When rule *B2* is used to create a lower neighbor to the seventh degree in minor, the raised form of the sixth degree must be used.

As in second species, the prohibition against skips of a fourth in the bass varies with the rhythmic situation:

a. triplet half notes or quarter notes in the bass, skip of a fourth within a measure
No skips of a fourth within a measure unless the same measure also includes a lower pitch that is consonant with both pitches forming the fourth.

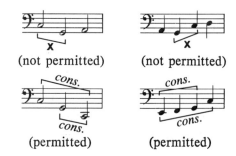

b. triplet halves or quarters in the bass, skip of a fourth over the barline
As in first and second species.

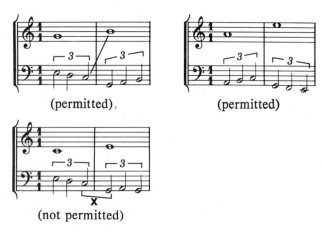

c. whole notes in the bass
A skip of a fourth in the bass is permitted only where there is a note in an upper line that either
i. sounds simultaneously with and is consonant with the first of the two notes forming the fourth, forms a seventh or a second with the

second of the two notes forming the fourth, and either comes at the beginning of the measure, at the end of the measure, or—if it comes in the middle of the measure—is not subsequently displaced by a step-related, consonant note within that measure

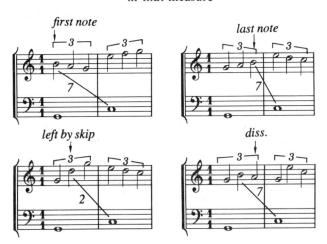

or ii. sounds simultaneously with and is consonant with the second of the two notes forming the fourth, forms a seventh or second with the first of the two notes forming the fourth, and either comes at the beginning of the measure, or is not preceded in that measure by any consonant, step-related note.

Intervals between simultaneously sounding notes:
As in second species.

Restrictions on motion:
On the beat to the following off the beat, or off the beat to the following off the beat:

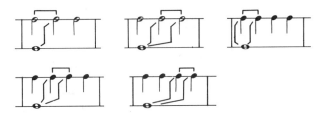

As in second species, on the beat to off the beat, all motion is oblique; consequently the only restriction is against crossing.

Off the beat to immediately following on the beat:

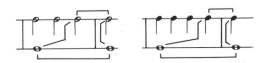

As in second species.

On the beat to on the beat:

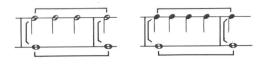

No parallel unisons.
Parallel octaves and fifths are permissible only where the half note or quarter note forming the second octave or fifth is an interior element in a step motion moving in the opposite direction to that of the parallel motion,

or where the pitch of the half note or quarter note forming the second octave or fifth appears in the preceding measure and is consonant with the whole note.

(permitted)

(permitted)

Off the beat to next (but not immediately following) on the beat:

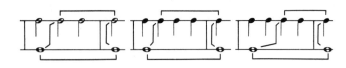

No parallel unisons.
Parallel octaves are permitted only where the half note or quarter note forming the second octave is an interior element in a step motion in the opposite direction to that of the parallel motion,

or where the pitch of the half note or quarter note forming the second octave appears as a consonant note in the preceding measure.

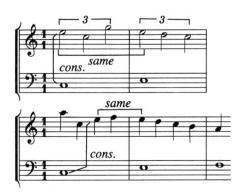

Drill

What pitches, if any, are available for the whole-note line in the first measure of each of the following? (Assume the key is A minor and that the two measures are somewhere in the middle of the composition.)

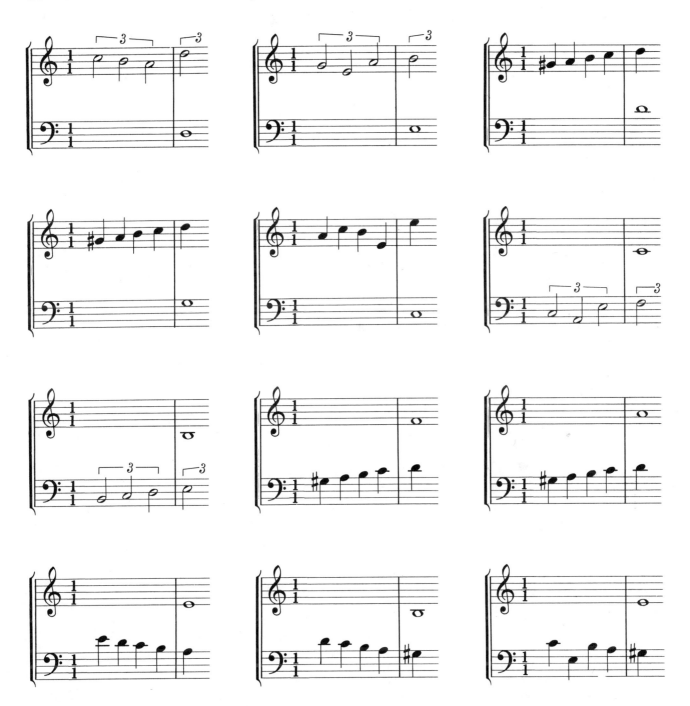

Exercises

1. For some of the following, a bass in whole notes is not possible. Which, and why?

2. Of the possible bass lines for the upper lines in 1. which is the most interesting?

3. Complete the bass.

4. Complete the upper line.

5.6 Compound Lines, Continued

In Section 5.4 we used the two-notes-against-one rhythmic format of second species to generate a single compound second-species line from two first-species lines.

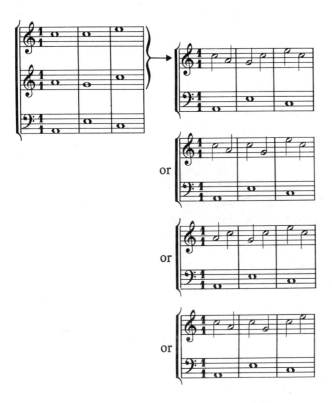

We can use the three-notes-against-one and four-notes-against-one formats of third species in the same way.

It is, however, much more interesting if we use the added notes to create secondary step motions between the skips. Take the two notes of the initial third in our example:

If we have three notes to a measure instead of two, we can connect the two notes in the arpeggiated third with a secondary step motion.

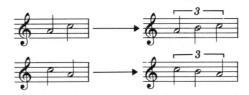

The fact that the B is dissonant with the bass

helps clarify its subordinate role.

Similarly, if we have four notes to a measure instead of two, we can connect two notes of an arpeggiated fourth by a secondary step motion.

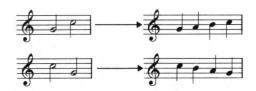

This third and this fourth were both between simultaneously sounding pitches in the original:

137

But the other thirds and fourths are also available for this kind of treatment: There are those that were originally intervals between consecutive whole notes in the same line.

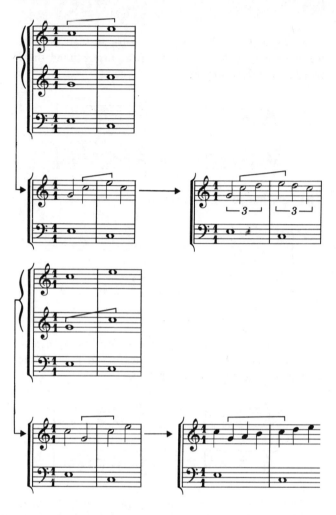

There are also those that were originally intervals between contiguous whole notes in the two generating lines.

Where the interval that would result in the right number of notes for the given rhythmic format is not available, embellishment by neighbor can be applied. In a four-notes-against-one format, neighbor embellishment is always possible and is certainly more interesting than repeating the arpeggiation would be.

In a three-notes-against-one format, however, embellishment by neighbor is available only where there is a unison in the generating combination, between simultaneously sounding notes,

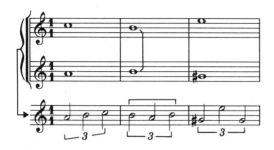

or between consecutive notes,

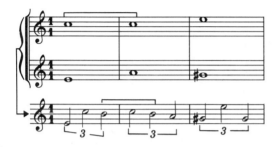

or between contiguous notes.

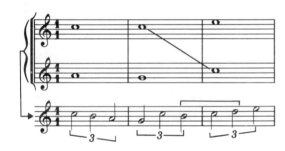

Furthermore, where a note in a simple line does not contribute anything to the structure of the line—that is, when no other note depends on a note generated by rule *B1* or rule *B3*—that note may be omitted in the compound line and its place in time taken by a neighbor.

Applying these principles, we can further transform the compound second-species line arrived at in Section 5.4 as shown below.

Exercises

1. a. Write a middle line in whole notes to go with the given outer lines.
   b. Mark all the *thirds* between consecutive, simultaneously sounding, or contiguous notes in the upper two lines.

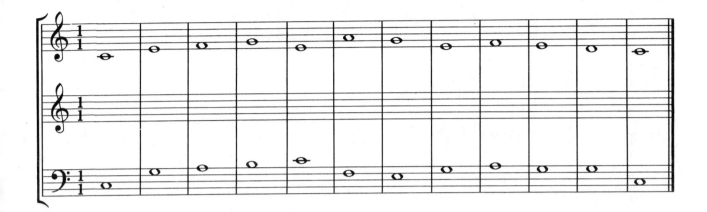

   c. Use the upper two lines to generate a single compound line in triplet half notes. Fill in as many of the thirds with step motion as you can.

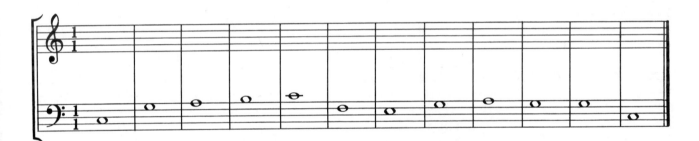

2. a. Make a new copy of 1a.
   b. Mark all the *fourths* between consecutive, simultaneously sounding, or contiguous notes in the upper two lines.

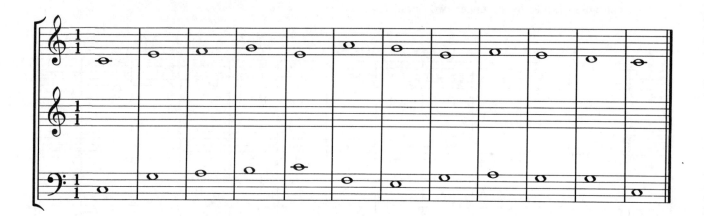

   c. Use the upper two lines to generate a single compound line in quarter notes. Fill in as many of the fourths with step motion as you can.

5.7 Three Lines in Second and Third Species

Rhythmic Format • Any line may be the species line.

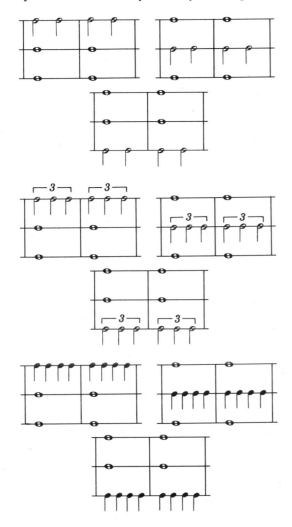

Combining one line in shorter durations with two lines in longer durations poses no essentially new problems. Each line and each pair of lines simply behave according to the rules of the relevant species.

Rules for Three Lines in Second and Third Species

Relationships between consecutive notes in a line:
    Whole-note lines: as in first species.
    Species line: as in that species.
Intervals between simultaneously sounding notes:
    Species line and either whole-note line:
        On the beat: as in first species, three lines.
        Off the beat: consonant or dissonant, but if dissonant, the note in the species line must be a passing tone or a neighbor. Under no condition may the dissonant note be approached or left by skip.

Restrictions on motion:
    Between the two whole-note lines: as in first species, three lines (Section 5.2).
    Between the species line and either of the whole-note lines: as in the relevant species (Sections 5.3, 5.5), with the following emendations:
    1. Parallel octaves on consecutive downbeats are permitted where the second on-the-beat half note is an interior element in a step motion in the opposite direction from the parallel motion and forms an imperfect consonance with the third line.

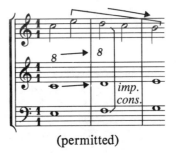

(permitted)

    2. The upper two lines are free to cross and overlap as in first species, three lines (Section 5.2).

Sonority
    On the beat: as in first species, three lines.
    Off the beat: no restrictions.

Exercises

Given

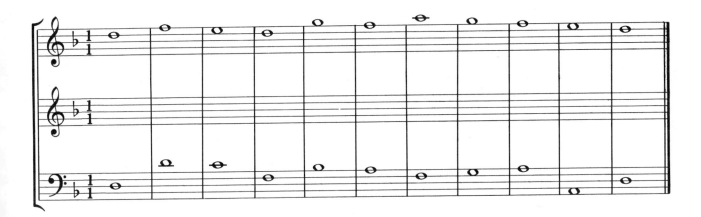

1. Write an inner line in second species.
2. Write an inner line in third species, triplet half notes.

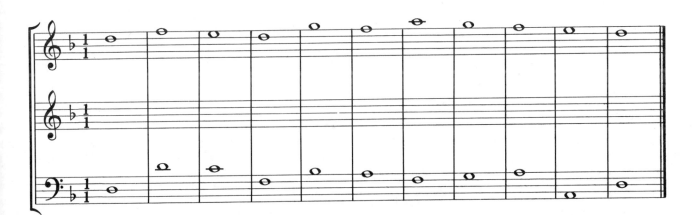

5.8 Two Lines in Fourth Species

Rhythmic Format: Suspensions • In first species the notes in both lines had the same duration. We lined up these notes so that there was only one possible relationship between simultaneously sounding notes. This relationship is the strongest kind possible: both notes begin and end at the same time.

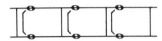

In second and third species we used shorter durations in one of the lines. The notes were lined up so that there were two possible relationships between simultaneously sounding notes, a stronger one between the notes that began at the same time,

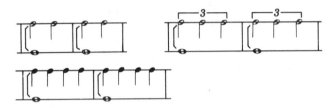

and a weaker one between notes that sounded simultaneously but did not begin together.

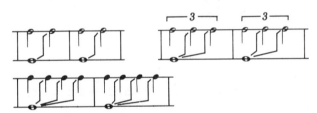

In fourth species we will again use notes of the same length in both lines. But instead of lining up the notes so that each note in one line begins at the same time as a note in the other,

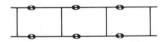

we will delay, or *suspend*, each whole note in one line so that it begins (and ends) a half note later.

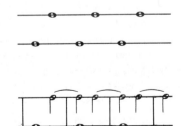

This means that we think of the intervals between simultaneously sounding notes falling off the beat as presenting the basic relationship of the two lines,

while the intervals falling on the beat are simply a by-product of the delay.

Thus, while second and third species place conceptually prior pitch relationships at conceptually prior points in time, fourth species does the opposite: it places conceptually prior pitch relationships at conceptually secondary points in time. In fourth species the intervals between simultaneously sounding notes that fall off the beat have conceptual priority over the others and therefore must be consonant. The other intervals, however, may be either consonant or dissonant. If the interval is consonant, it causes no further problem, but if it is dissonant, it is the leftover part of the tied note that is thought of as unstable

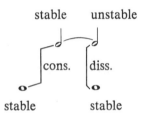

and it is the suspended line that is subject to further constraint. We think of the motion of the whole-note line to a note that is dissonant with the tied-over note as creating a state of tension. This tension can only be resolved when the suspended line moves down by step to a consonant pitch.

We think of the downward motion as helping to relax the state of tension. The motion must be by step in order to displace the unstable pitch. (If it were by skip, the unstable pitch would be left hanging.)

Thus, the whole process consists of three successive stages: a *preparation*, in which the suspended note is presented as a stable element; the *suspension* itself, in which the suspended note is made unstable by the action of the other line; and the *resolution*, in which the tension created by putting an unstable pitch relationship at a stable point in time is resolved by downward step motion to a note that is consonant with the other line or lines.

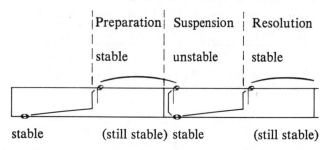

Each note in the suspended line is first stable with respect to the other line, and then, if dissonant, unstable with respect to the other line. Each resolution is a potential preparation for the next suspension.

(The only exception is, of course, the next to last note, for the last note is, as in second and third species, a whole note on the beat.)

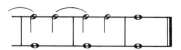

We refer to suspensions by pairs of consecutive numbers. We speak of a 7–6 suspension or a 2–3 suspension. The numbers refer to the classes of intervals formed by simultaneously sounding notes at the suspension proper and at the resolution. Since the suspended line always moves down by step, if the second number is smaller than the first, the suspended line is the upper line,

but if the second number is larger than the first, the suspended line is the lower of the two lines.

We distinguish among different suspension patterns in terms of their clarity and self-sufficiency. 7–6's and 2–3's are easy to grasp:

There is a clear contrast in the level of sonority and the resolution pitch is not doubled with a pitch of the same class. 2–1's and 4–5's, however, are hard to grasp: the 2–1 because of the way the two lines seem to collide at the unison; the 4–5 because the level of sonority of the two intervals is so nearly the same.

This lack of clarity is dispelled where there is room to keep the lines clear of one another, as in a 9–8,*

where the dissonant interval is an augmented interval, as in an augmented 4–5,

or where either suspension is coupled with a 2–3 or a 7–6.

We distinguish, then, between three classes of suspensions: *strong suspensions*, which can stand by themselves and indeed can even clarify a confusing situation caused by a weak suspension; *intermediate suspensions*, which can stand by themselves but are not strong enough to clarify a weak suspension; and *weak suspensions*, which cannot stand by themselves and need further clarification in the form of a strong suspension. The strong suspensions are 7–6's (including

---

* Note that we distinguish between the unison class consisting of unisons only and the octave class consisting of any number of octaves. We call the first interval class of a 9–8 a 9 instead of a 2 to make it easier to grasp that the suspended line moves down by step. (2–8 would be confusing.)

diminished 7–6's) and 2–3's (including augmented 2–3's).

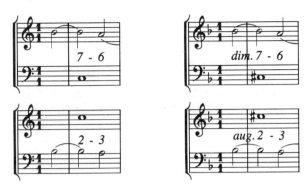

The intermediate suspensions are 9–8's, 4–3's (including both augmented 4–3's and diminished 4–3's), augmented 4–5's, and augmented or diminished 5–6's.

The weak suspensions are 2–1's, 7–8's, and 4–5's.

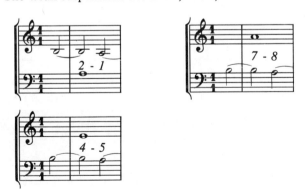

Rules for Two Lines in Fourth Species

Intervals between consecutive notes in a line:
   Whole-note line: as in first species, but with the exception that a skip of a fourth in a whole-note bass line is possible only if either
   a. the first of the two notes forming the fourth is dissonant with the second note in the next measure

or b. the second of the two notes forming the fourth is dissonant with the suspended note.

   Species line: as in first species, but with the exception that skips of a fourth in a fourth-species bass line are not permitted except at the end.
Intervals between simultaneously sounding notes:
   Off the beat: must be consonant
   On the beat: may be consonant or dissonant, but if dissonant, the suspended line must move down by step to form one of the strong or intermediate suspensions. 2–1's, 7–8's, and 4–5's are not permitted.

Restrictions on forms of motion:
   Last two measures:

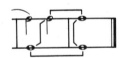 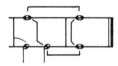

   No parallel unisons, octaves, or fifths.*
   No similar motion to a unison. Similar motion to an octave is permitted only if the upper line moves by step.
   Elsewhere, the lines are always in oblique motion.

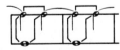 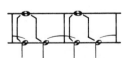

   Off the beat to next off the beat:

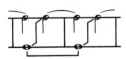

---

* Actually, since both a bass line and an upper line with a basic step motion *must* end on the tonic, fifths cannot occur with only two lines.

No parallel unisons.
Parallel octaves are permitted only if the intervening interval is consonant.

(not permitted)

(permitted)

On the beat to next on the beat:

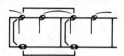

No parallel unisons.

Sonority

On the beat: other things being equal, the fullest level of sonority (seconds and sevenths) is preferable.

Drills

1. Locate the errors.

2. Complete the following.

Exercises

1. For one of the following cantus firmi there is no fourth-species bass that will fit our rules. Which cantus is it? And why is there no bass available?

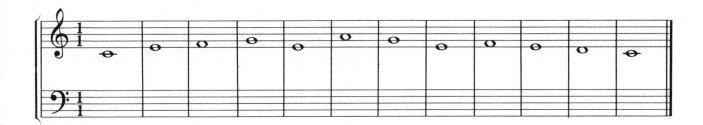

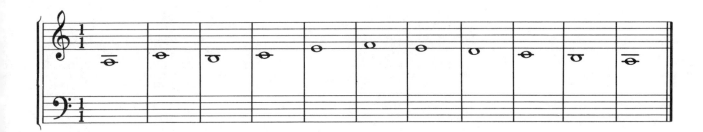

2. Add an upper line in fourth species with an eight-note basic step motion.

3. Add a bass line with a step motion that connects two dominants an octave apart.

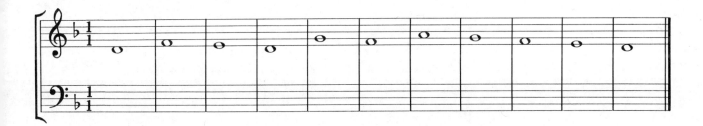

5.9 Three Lines in Fourth Species

Rhythmic Format • Any line may be the species line.

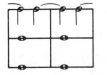

Each line and each pair of lines behave essentially according to the rules of the relevant species.

Rules for Three Lines in Fourth Species

Intervals between consecutive notes in a line:
    As in fourth species, two lines.
Intervals between simultaneously sounding notes:
    Between two whole notes:

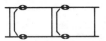

    As in first species, three lines.
Between a tied note and a whole note:
    Off the beat:

    As in fourth species, two lines.
    On the beat:

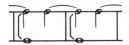

They may be consonant or dissonant, but if dissonant, the suspended line must move down by step. If the suspension formed is either strong or intermediate, there are no further restrictions. But if it is a weak suspension, the suspended line must form a strong suspension with the other whole-note line.

  (permitted)   (permitted)

(permitted)

(not permitted)   (not permitted)

Restrictions on forms of motion:
  Whole-note lines: as in first species, three lines, with two exceptions.
    1. Similar motion to a fifth is possible even when the upper note is approached by skip, if that note forms a dissonance with the note in the species line.

    2. Cross-relations are permitted when the second of the cross-related pitches makes the suspended note dissonant.

  Species line and either of the whole-note lines:
    As in fourth species, two lines.
Sonority
  On the beat: maintain the fullest sonority wherever possible.
    Avoid collections of all perfect intervals except at the beginning and end.

Drills

1. Fill in the missing notes.

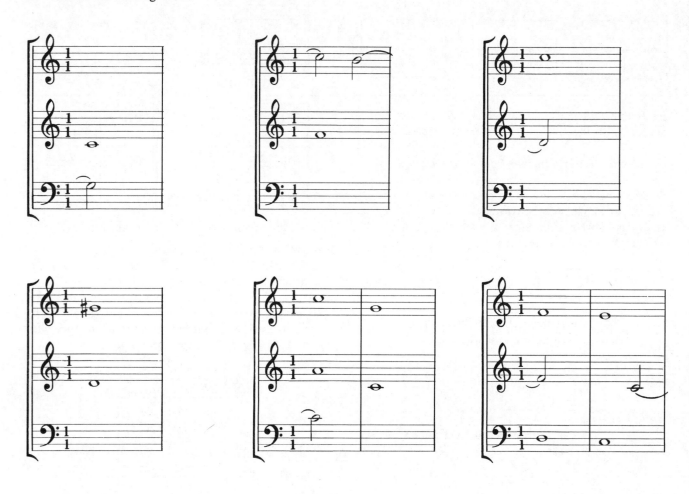

2. Complete the middle line.

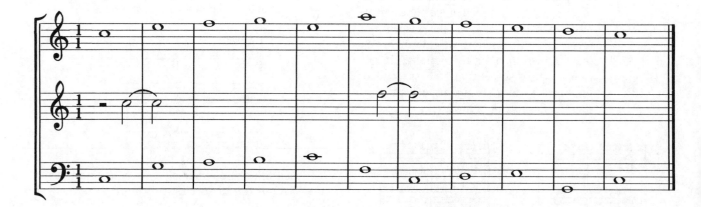

Exercises

1. Write a middle line in whole notes.

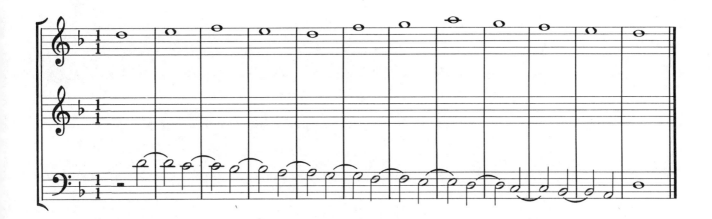

2. Add a bass in fourth species and a middle line in whole notes.

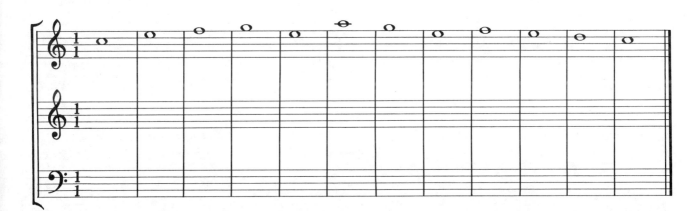

CHAPTER SIX

Combined Species

6.0 Combining Species

In the last chapter we dealt with simple species. In simple species one line at most is in a higher species; all the others are in whole notes. Thus, if there are three lines, the rhythmic relationship of the higher-species line to each of the other two lines will be exactly the same, and the intervallic constraints governing the combination of the higher-species line with either of the other lines will be the same.

We are now ready for the next stage: combined species. In combined species we combine two lines in higher species with one line in first species. Thus each higher-species line will have a different rhythmic relationship to each of the other two lines, and the intervallic constraints will be different in the two cases.

The rhythmic relationship of each higher-species line to the first-species line, however, will still be the same, no matter what species the other line is in. The notes of a second-species line, for example, will still fall alternately on and off the beat and hence begin alternately at the same time as and after the whole notes no matter what the notes in the other line do.

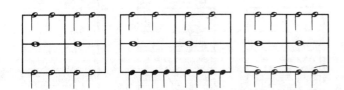

Consequently, the constraints governing the intervals between the notes of each species line and those of the whole-note line will be essentially the same as in simple species. What is new is the rhythmic relationship of the two species lines to one another.

The simplest kind of relationship between two species lines occurs when the two species are the same.

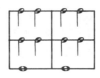 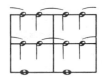

In such a case the rhythmic relationship between the two species lines is essentially the same as that between two lines in first species. That is, for any pair of simultaneously sounding notes, both notes begin and end at the same time. Consequently, the constraints governing the intervals formed by these lines will be essentially the same as those of first species. (The only exceptions are due to the fact that some pairs of simultaneously sounding notes fall off the beat: for example, restrictions on similar motion to a fifth falling off the beat are considerably relaxed.)

More complicated are the relationships between two species lines where the species are not the same.*

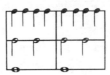 

The rhythmic relationship between a line in second

---

* Note that we avoid combining second or fourth species with third species in triplets:

species and one in third is essentially the same as that between the half-note line and the whole-note line in simple second species: every other note in the faster-moving line begins at the same time as a note in the slower-moving line.

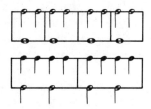

Consequently, those quarter notes that begin at the same time as half notes must be consonant with those half notes, but the others may be dissonant with the simultaneously sounding half note, as long as they form passing tones or neighbors. The rhythmic relationship of a line in second or third species to one in fourth shares attributes of the species involved. Where simultaneously sounding notes begin together, they must be consonant with one another and must not create forbidden forms of motion.

But the first half note or first quarter note in a measure may make the suspended note dissonant to form a suspension,

and the second or fourth quarter note may form a dissonant passing tone or neighbor.

6.1 Two Lines in Second Species, One in First. Two Lines in Third Species, One in First

Rhythmic Format • The first-species line may serve as top, middle, or bass line. The other lines may begin at any point in the first measure. For example:

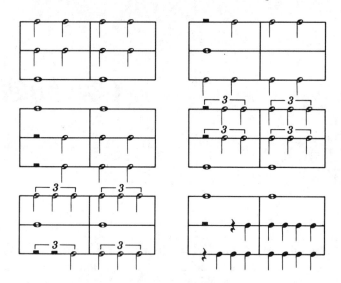

All three lines end with a whole note.

Rules for Two Lines in Second Species, One in First; Two Lines in Third Species, One in First

Intervals between consecutive notes in a line:
As in the relevant species. Exception: A second- or third-species bass line may skip a fourth within a measure

if the other species line has a note that is simultaneous with one of the notes forming the fourth and is a second or seventh away from the other note forming the fourth.

Intervals between simultaneously sounding notes:
Between notes in either higher-species line and the first-species line:
As in the relevant species.

Between notes in the two higher-species lines:
  As in first species.

Restrictions on forms of motion:
  Between the higher-species line and the first-species line:
    As in the simple higher species.
  Between the two higher-species lines:
    As in first species, with two emendations:
      1. Similar motion to a fifth falling off the beat is permitted even when the upper note of the fifth is approached by skip.

      2. Parallel unisons on consecutive beats are not permitted.

  Parallel octaves on consecutive beats are permitted only if
    a. one of the notes forming the first octave is left by step in the opposite direction from the parallel motion

  or b. one of the notes forming the second octave is an interior element in a step motion moving in the opposite direction from the parallel motion

  or c. one of the notes that comes between the parallel octaves has the same pitch as one of the notes forming the second of the octaves.

Sonority
  As in simple second and third species, three lines.

Drill

Fill in the missing whole notes.

(Hint: work on mm. 3 and 5 first.)

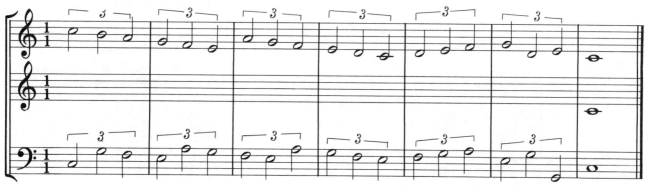

(Hint: work from the last measure back.)

Exercise

Write bass and middle lines in half notes. Use as many steps as you can: use as much parallel motion as you can. Mm. 9 and, particularly, 3 will give you trouble if you don't figure out what you're going to do there *before* you write the rest of your lines.

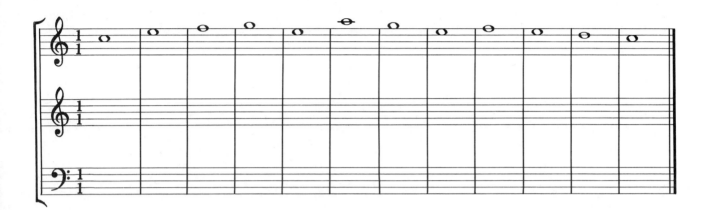

6.2 Two Compound Lines Moving at the Same Rate

In Sections 5.4 and 5.6 we developed the idea of a compound line and showed how it could be used in second or third species. Now that you know how to combine two second-species lines with a first-species line or two third-species lines with a first-species line, the next step is to combine two compound lines at once.

Two Compound Lines in Second Species • It might seem that in order to have two compound lines in second species and one simple line in first species, you would need five independent lines in first species—two for each compound line and one for the simple line.

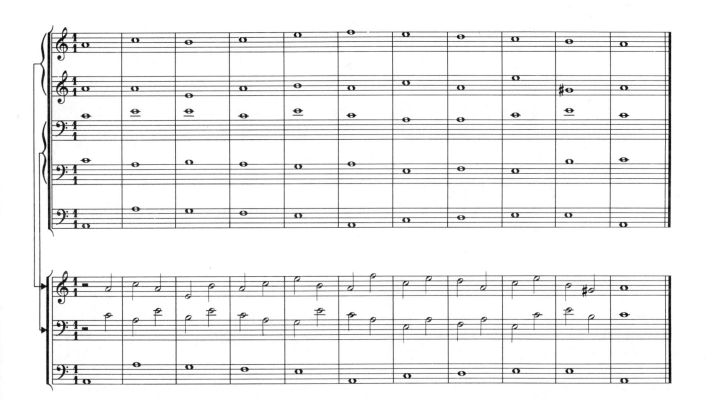

While this is one way to arrive at such a combination, it is neither the easiest nor the most satisfactory.

In the first place, it is by no means easy to produce five independent first-species lines. Since each of the five notes sounding at any given moment must be consonant with each of the other four, and since the maximum number of pitch classes that can be consonant with one another is three, in any measure at least two of the five notes will have to be members of the same pitch class as one or two of the other three. While parallel octaves and unisons *can* be avoided under such circumstances, in order to avoid them you usually have to settle for at least one fairly dull first-species line. (Consider the middle line in our example. A line like that contributes little interest to a compound line based on it.)

In the second place, even if you manage to produce five clean, even moderately interesting first-species lines, it is extremely difficult to follow their underlying structures in a compound line. There is simply too much going on.

For these reasons, in this section we will concentrate on generating two compound second-species lines and one first-species line from only three independent first-species lines. To see how this works take the same combination of three lines we used to generate one compound upper line with a simple bass.

This time we want to use the two upper simple lines to generate two compound lines by arpeggiating pairs of simultaneously sounding notes. Clearly, if the direction of the arpeggiation is the same in any measure of both compound lines, we will end up with parallel unisons.

Indeed, if it is the same in all measures, we simply get identical lines.

 etc.

On the other hand, if in each measure we arpeggiate in opposite directions for the two lines, the result is two independent lines, each of which is based on the same pair of simple lines.

Admittedly, the way the lines cross in every measure and move by identical intervals in every measure gets a bit tedious. However, the progress of the underlying simple lines is clear, and despite the fact that both compound lines are based on the same structure, there are no problems of parallel unisons or

* Note that a minor repair is needed in mm. 1 and 2 because of the repetitions. One way out would be to use an E in the middle line and put both A's in the bass in the same register.

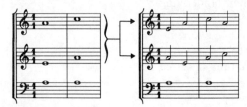

octaves.* We can avoid the constant crossing by transposing the top compound line up an octave.

This means that the simple lines on which the compound lines are based are both doubled at the octave.

But obviously there are no parallel octaves between compound lines any more than there were parallel unisons in the earlier versions, since all octaves are between contiguous rather than simultaneously sounding notes.

Finally, we can avoid the constant contrary motion by like intervals and substitute the smoother effect of similar motion by intervals that are octave complements of one another by doubling one of the simple lines at the octave and keeping the other at the unison.

---

* Played on the piano, the combination makes no sense at all. There is almost no way a pianist can differentiate the version with compound lines crossing from one with simple lines in repeated notes.

sounds like

To get a better sense of how the compound lines work *as lines,* try singing one and playing the other.

This procedure, however, creates a problem in that what is a final unison between the pair of simple lines will have become an octave between the other pair, and while a unison can be used to generate a single whole note, two whole notes forming an octave cannot.

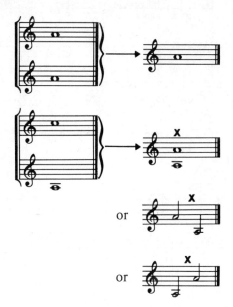

Neither of the octave-related A's can be omitted in the middle line. If the line ends on the upper A, a dissonant skip will be created, and the B in the next to last measure will be left hanging.

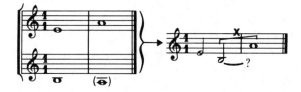

If the line ends on the lower A, the B in m. 8 will be left hanging.

Therefore, one or more of the simple lines must be altered so that both pairs arrive at a unison in the last measure without leaving any structures incomplete. Suppose, for example, the upper of the two simple lines that underlie the middle compound line read

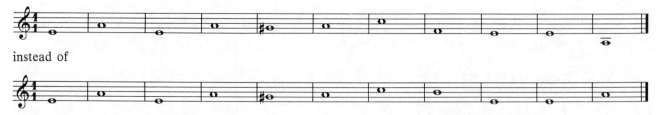

instead of

Then the two simple lines end on a unison and the compound line can be complete, ending with a whole note.

Two Compound Lines in Third Species, Three Notes to a Beat • If both pairs of simple lines are moving in parallel thirds,

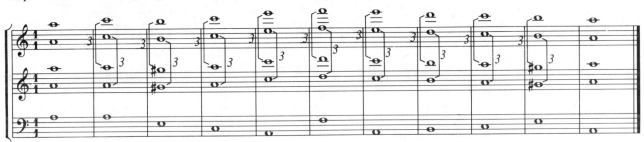

it is easy to derive two compound lines with secondary step motions: just arpeggiate the thirds in opposite directions and insert the intervening diatonic degrees to form a step motion. The two interior elements in the step motion will be consonant, since they will be either unisons or octaves, and, being interior elements in their respective step motions, cannot cause any awkward parallelisms.

Other step motions are available wherever both simple lines move up or down a third.

If the pairs of simple lines do not form thirds, three other techniques are available:
1. an arpeggiation in which the third note returns to the pitch of the first;

2. neighbor embellishment of one of the notes in the simple lines and omission of the other. This is only possible when no other notes in the simple line depend on the omitted note; it cannot be used in both lines in two consecutive measures without creating parallel octaves or unisons;

3. further application of rule *B3*.

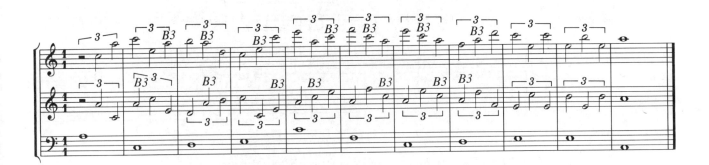

Where the registers of the simple lines are switched so that the pairs of lines
form complementary intervals,

arpeggiations with a return to the first pitch are almost always possible.

* See page 168.

Combinations of neighbor embellishment or step motion from one measure to the next with further application of rule *B3* may be used to vary the relationship of the two lines.

Two Compound Lines in Third Species, Four Notes to a Beat • When the compound lines have four notes to the beat, the most generally useful pattern is formed by embellishing one of the arpeggiated notes by neighbor.

You can use this pattern for any consonant interval except, of course, the unison. Furthermore, such patterns are easy to combine. If both compound lines use the same pair of pitch classes, arpeggiate these pitches at the same time either in contrary motion if the intervals are equal, or, if the intervals add up to an octave, in similar motion. If the interval of arpeggiation is a perfect consonance, make the neighbor embellishments move by contrary motion. If the interval of arpeggiation is an imperfect consonance, make the neighbor embellishment move in parallels.

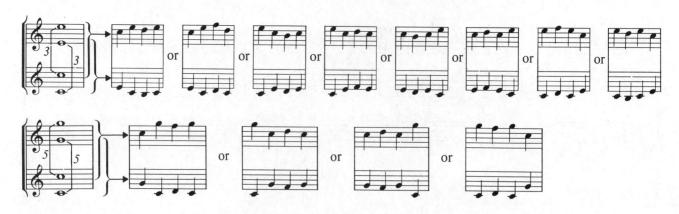

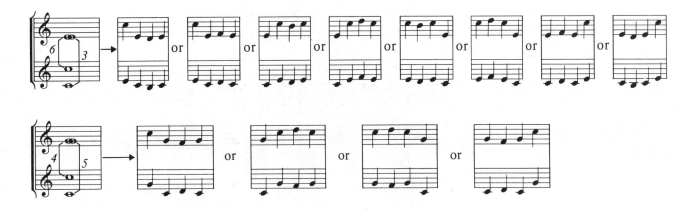

This technique is particularly useful for pairs of simple lines forming complementary intervals.

Step motions between arpeggiated pitches are limited to places where the two simple lines form thirds. In such cases, the first pitch in a measure is repeated at the end of the measure.

Patterns in contrary motion may be combined.

If both pairs of simple lines move in parallel thirds, contrary motion of this type can be used exclusively.

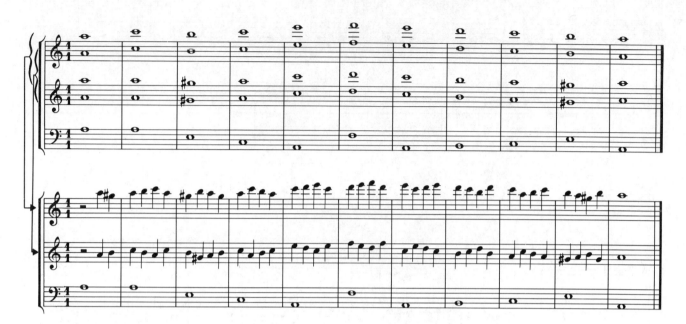

Where both pairs of simple lines are in parallel motion, secondary motion over a third or a fourth may be possible from one measure to the next.

Exercises

1. Given:

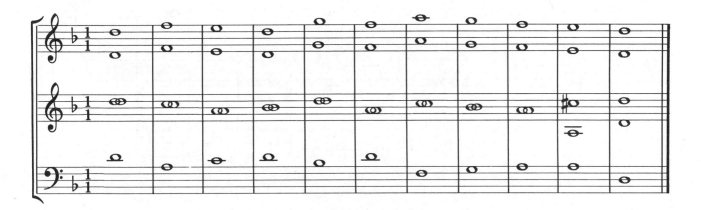

use the simple lines to generate two compound lines in half notes.

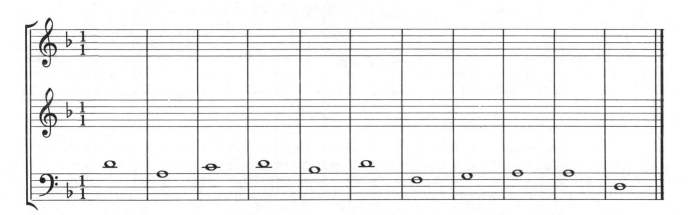

2. Complete the simple lines in whole notes.

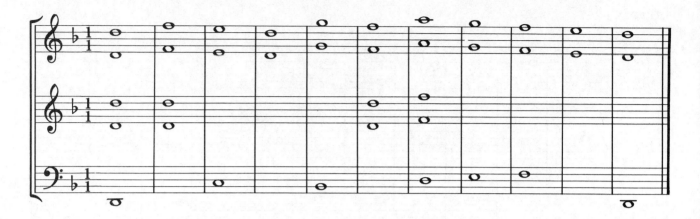

3. Use the whole-note lines of 2. to generate two compound lines in triplet half notes.

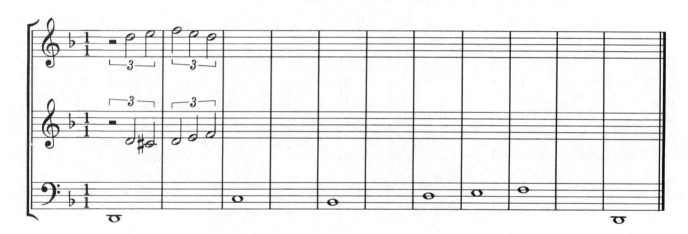

6.3 Two Lines in Fourth Species, One in First

Rhythmic Format • The first-species line may be the top, middle, or bass line.

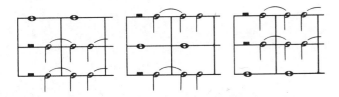

All three lines end with a whole note.

Rules for Combining Two Lines in Fourth Species with One in First

Relationship of the fourth-species lines to one another: As in first-species. Exception: a resolution must not be doubled. That is, if a note in one of the two fourth-species lines is dissonant with the first-species line

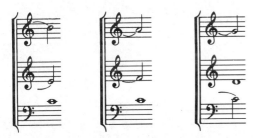

the next note in that fourth-species line must not form an octave or a unison with the note in the other fourth-species line.

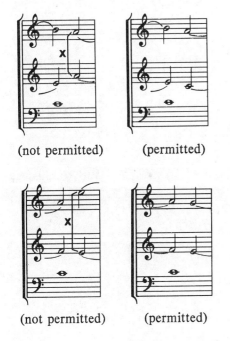

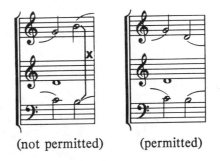

(not permitted)   (permitted)

Relationship of either fourth-species line to the first-species line:

Essentially as in fourth species, three lines.

The first part (the off-the-beat part) of the tied note is always consonant with the simultaneously sounding whole note. The on-the-beat part of the tied note may be consonant or dissonant with the whole note, but if dissonant the line must move down by step to the next note. If one fourth-species line forms a weak suspension, the other must form a strong suspension.

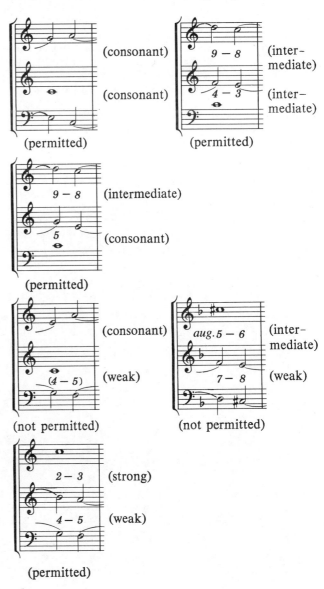

177

Exercises

1. Add a bass in whole notes.

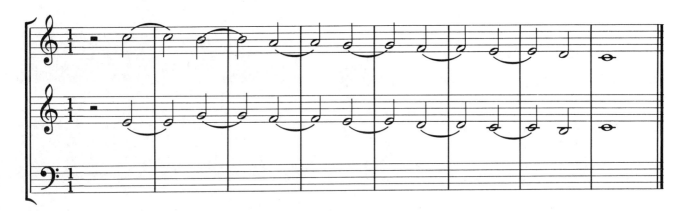

2. There is no middle line in fourth species that will fit the following. Why not?

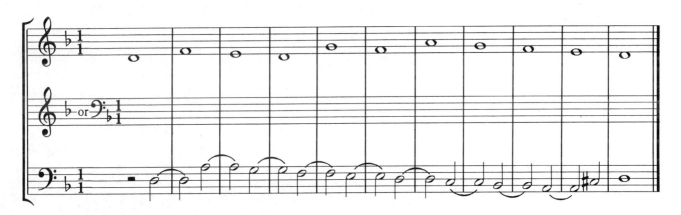

3. Add a bass and a top line in fourth species.

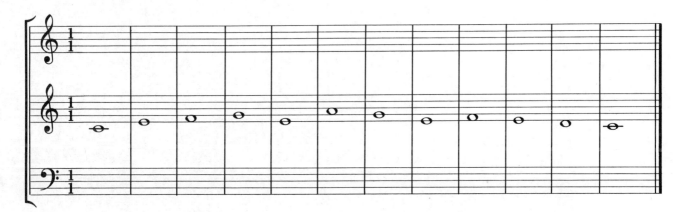

6.4 One Line in First Species, One in Second, One in Third

Rhythmic Format • Any species may appear as top, middle, or bass line. The third-species line is in quarter notes.

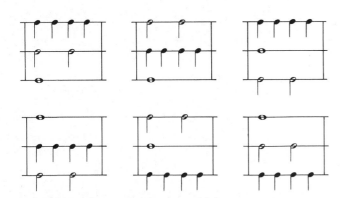

The higher-species lines may begin on any beat in the first measure. All lines end with a whole note.

Rules for Combining One Line in First Species, One in Second, and One in Third

Intervals between consecutive notes in a line:
  As in two lines in second species, one in first or two lines in third species, one in first. (Section 6.1)

Intervals between simultaneously sounding notes:
  a. Half notes and whole notes: as in second species.
  b. Quarter notes and whole notes: as in third species.
  c. Quarter notes and half notes: as in second species; that is, the first and third quarters must be consonant with the simultaneously sounding half note.

The second and fourth quarters may be consonant or dissonant with the simultaneously sounding half note, but if dissonant, they must be either passing tones or neighbors.

Restrictions on forms of motion:
  First- and second-species lines: as in second species.
  First- and third-species lines: as in third species.
  Second- and third-species lines: as in second species.
  Exception: similar motion to a fifth on the third quarter is permitted.

Exercises

1. Add a bass in whole notes and a top line in half notes.

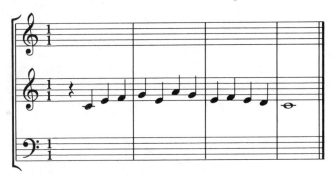

2. Add a top line in whole notes and a bass in half notes.

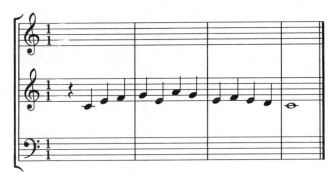

3. Add a top line in whole notes.

4. Add a bass in whole notes and a top line in quarter notes.

6.5 Two Compound Lines Moving at Different Rates

Combining two compound lines, one in second species and one in third, takes a little extra care. When both compound lines are moving at the same rate, it is relatively simple to arrange that one line have the pitch of one of the simple lines while the other two have the other, necessarily consonant, pitch.

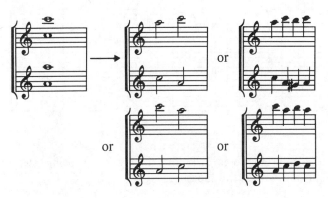

But when one compound line is moving twice as fast as the other, collisions at dissonant intervals

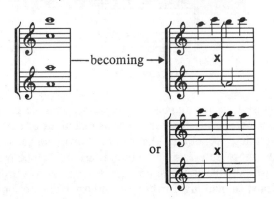

and inadvertent parallelisms

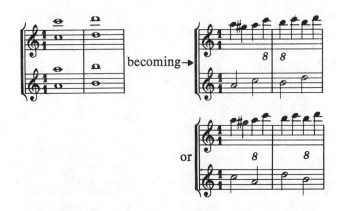

are more likely to arise, and care must be taken to avoid them. Octaves can be avoided by embellishing the second note of the arpeggiation in the quarter-note line rather than the first.

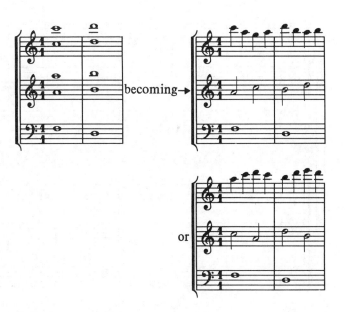

Dissonances between the second half note and a neighbor on the third quarter can be avoided as long as the intervals formed by the pairs of simple lines are not all octaves and unisons.

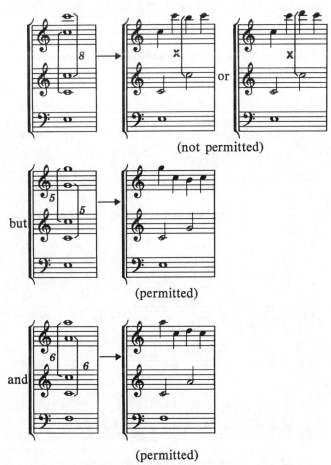

Note, however, that where the bottom simple line of one pair is at the unison with the top simple line of the other, similar motion from a unison may occur.

185

(not permitted)

This may be avoided by substituting a neighbor in a different direction

(permitted)

or, if the interval between the pair of lines creating the quarter notes is a fourth, by substituting step motion within the measure.

(permitted)

Applying these techniques to the pairs of simple lines we have been using for our previous examples of compound lines, we obtain the result shown above. Of course, more interesting combinations of compound lines are possible if the simple lines form more thirds and fourths, making further secondary step motions possible (see below).

186

Exercise

Use the given simple lines in whole notes

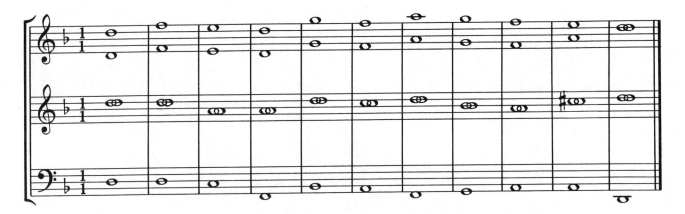

to create two compound lines—a top line in half notes and a middle line in quarter notes.

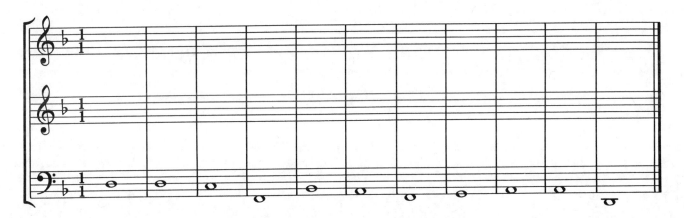

6.6 One Line in First Species, One in Second, One in Fourth. One Line in First Species, One in Third, One in Fourth

Rhythmic Format • The third-species line is in quarter notes. Any species may be the top, middle, or bass line. The second- or third-species line may begin at any point in the first measure. For example:

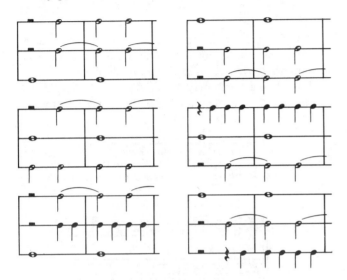

All three lines end with a whole note.

Rules for Combining One Line in First Species, One in Second, and One in Fourth; or One in First, One in Third, and One in Fourth

Intervals between consecutive notes in a line:
  As in the relevant species.
Intervals between simultaneously sounding notes:
  a. Each higher-species line to the first-species line: as in that higher species.
  b. Second-species line and fourth-species line: Off the beat: intervals must be consonant. The resolution of a dissonant suspension must not be doubled. That is, if a note in the fourth-species line is dissonant with either the first- or the second-species line on the beat, the next note in the fourth-species line must not have a pitch that is a member of the same pitch class as that of the other half note that begins at the same time.

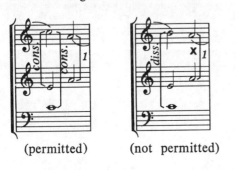

(permitted)   (not permitted)

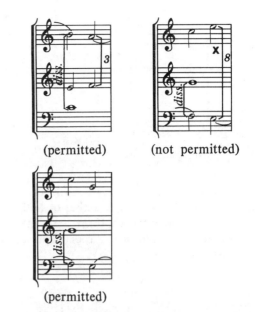

(permitted)   (not permitted)

(permitted)

On the beat: essentially as in fourth species, three lines. That is, the interval may be consonant or dissonant, but if dissonant, the fourth-species line must move down by step. If the fourth species line forms a weak suspension with one line, it must form a strong suspension with the other.

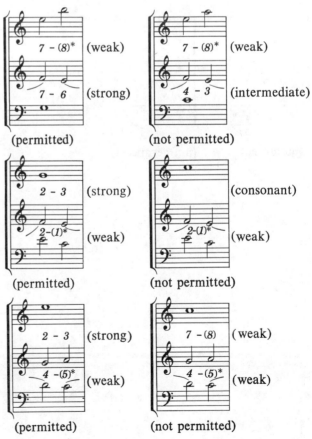

* Parentheses around the second interval in a suspension pattern indicates that by the time the suspended line moves, the other line has also moved. The number inside the parentheses indicates what the interval would have been, had the other line not moved.

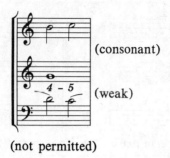

(consonant)

(weak)

(not permitted)

A second-species bass line may skip a fourth from on the beat to off the beat as long as either or both of the half notes forming the fourth form a seventh or a second with either or both of the fourth-species notes in that measure.

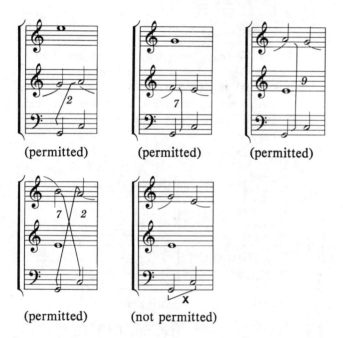

Relationship of the third-species line to the fourth-species line:

First quarter: as in second and fourth species, on the beat.

Second quarter: may be any interval, but if dissonant, the quarter note must be either a passing tone or a neighbor. Exception: if the quarter note is dissonant with the half note, and the quarter note forms a unison or an octave with the whole note, the quarter note is considered the consonant note and hence may be approached or left by skip or step.

Third quarter: as in second and fourth species, notes beginning at the same time must be consonant. A resolution must not be doubled.

Fourth quarter: may be any interval, but if dissonant, the quarter note must be a passing tone or neighbor.

Exercises

1. Add a top line in whole notes.

2. Add a middle line in whole notes.

3. Add a middle line in fourth species and a bass in first.

4. Add a middle line in fourth species and a bass in first.

6.7 Dissonant Skips and Skips to and from Dissonant Notes: Compound Lines Based on Pairs of Lines in a Higher Simple Species

In Section 5.4 we learned how to generate a single compound line from a pair of simple lines in first species by arpeggiating the simultaneously sounding pitches.

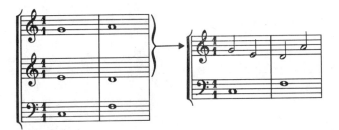

Since simultaneously sounding notes are consonant in first species, we avoided for the time being the problems posed by dissonant skips and skips to or from a dissonant pitch. Such problems are the subject of this section.

Consider the dissonance between the upper two lines in each of the following:

Each dissonance is controlled according to the voice-leading constraints of the relevant species. In each case it is clear which pitch is the stable one and which the unstable one. In each case the structural sense of the unstable pitch is clear either as a passing tone or neighbor *conceptually dependent* on the pitches directly before and after it, or as a suspension resulting from the *delay* of one of the lines.

Now, suppose we were to arpeggiate the simultaneously sounding notes in the upper two lines to form a single, compound line:

In each case, although the dissonance becomes more noticeable by being a *skip* in a single line, instead of a de-emphasized interval between two lines in oblique motion, *the structural role of the unstable pitch is preserved.*

Similarly, consider the dissonance between the outer lines in the following:

When we arpeggiate simultaneously sounding notes in the upper two lines to form a single line

the dissonances become more noticeable because the unstable pitches are approached or left by skip, but the unstable structural role of the unstable pitches is preserved. Note that the only dissonant skips included in the preceding examples are those resulting from the arpeggiation of simultaneously sounding notes in the original. In no case is a dissonant skip generated from intervals between contiguous notes. (Compare the following:

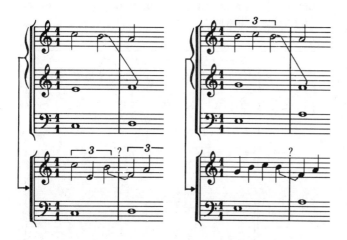

Here we have no way of understanding the dissonant skip as an arpeggiation of two simultaneously sounding notes, one of which is a dissonant neighbor or passing tone.) Note also how those properties of order that are essential to our understanding of the function of the dissonant pitch are preserved:

1. The order of notes in the higher-species simple line is preserved in the compound line. Although some consecutive notes in the simple line may cease to be consecutive when notes from the other simple line are inserted between them to form the compound line,

in no case does the second of two consecutive notes in a simple line appear before the first in the compound line. (Compare the following:

How are we to understand the dissonant skip? For B to be a passing tone from C to A it must occur *after* the upper C.)

2. The order in which pitches forming a dissonance first appear is preserved. (Compare the following:

One of the reasons we understand the B in the original as the unstable note is that the C in the middle line is established as a stable pitch *before* the B appears. If this order is reversed in the compound line, we have no way of telling which of the two pitches forming the dissonance is the unstable one. Note, however, that once the stable pitch is introduced before the unstable pitch, it may occur again after the unstable pitch.)

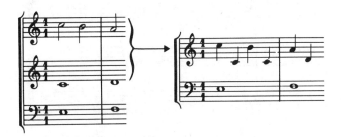

3. Where, in the original, a passing tone or dissonant neighbor immediately precedes an on-the-beat note, the on-the-beat note must fall on the beat in the compound line as well.

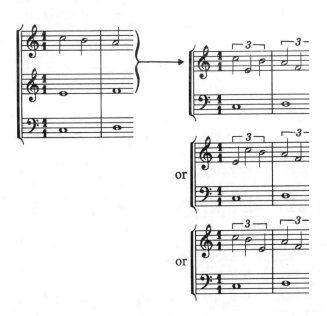

Thus, no unstable pitch is left hanging beyond the measure in which it first occurs.

If you keep these principles in mind, it is relatively easy to generate compound lines with dissonant skips and skips to and from dissonant notes from simple species combinations.

Simple Lines in Second Species • Take the combination

To transform the top two lines into a single compound line in triplet half notes, just represent the on-the-beat half notes by the first note in each measure,

the whole notes by the second note in each measure,

and the off-the-beat half notes by the third note in each measure.

Then, should the off-the-beat half note in the original be dissonant,

the next on-the-beat half note will be represented by an on-the-beat triplet half note

and the stable note against which the triplet half note is dissonant will have already appeared.

195

Of course, where the off-the-beat half note is consonant, the order may be varied

as long as

1. repetitions in the whole-note line do not appear as consecutive notes in the compound line,
2. repetitions or dissonant skips do not result from using contiguous notes in the original as consecutive notes in the compound line, and
3. forbidden parallels or similar motions do not result from using contiguous notes in the compound line.

It is just as easy to transform the same second-species combination into a compound line in quarter notes. In this case the three notes of each measure of the original combination of lines (two half notes in one line and one whole note in the other) must become four notes in each measure of the compound line. Thus, one pitch must always be stated twice. One scheme that always works is to represent the on-the-beat half note by both the first and third quarter notes, the off-the-beat half note by the fourth quarter note, and the whole note by the second quarter note.

Such a pattern avoids all problems, but it also sacrifices the interest inherent in dissonant skips and skips to and from a dissonant note. A pattern that works most of the time represents the on-the-beat half note by the first quarter note, the off-the-beat half note by the third quarter note, and the whole note by both the second and fourth quarter notes.

Where the off-the-beat half note in the preceding measure is consonant, the whole note may be represented by the first quarter note,

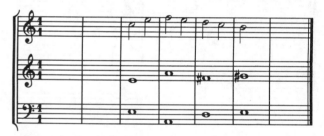

but care must be taken to avoid voice-leading errors created by converting contiguous notes into consecutive ones.

Thus a considerable variety of patterns may be used in the compound line without losing the sense of motion of the simple lines from which it was generated.

196

Simple Lines in Third Species • In much the same way, you can transform a third-species combination of simple lines—one in triplet half notes and one in whole notes—into a single compound line in quarter notes. The safest procedure is to represent the whole notes by the second quarter notes of each measure.

Where the third triplet half note of the preceding measure is consonant, the whole note may be represented by the first quarter note.

Where unwanted dissonant skips or forbidden forms of motion occur, the whole note in the preceding measure may be represented by the last quarter note of that measure.

Simple Lines in Fourth Species • The problems involved in transforming a pair of simple lines in fourth species into a compound line are slightly different. The procedure varies with the number of notes per measure in the compound line. When there are only two notes per measure, obviously each note in the original can be represented only once and the order must be the same as in the original (see below). In such a case the intervals from on-the-beat to off-the-beat notes in the compound line represent the intervals between simultaneously sounding notes off the beat in the original, and the intervals between off-the-beat notes to the following on-the-beat notes represent the intervals between simultaneously sounding notes on the beat in the original. Thus, the suspensions themselves are represented by dissonant skips from off-the-beat notes to the following on-the-beat notes. The first note is thought of as left hanging during the second note, only to be displaced by the next note.

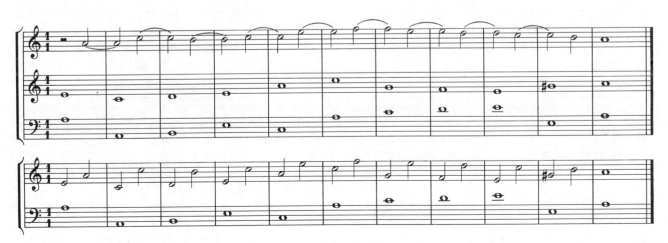

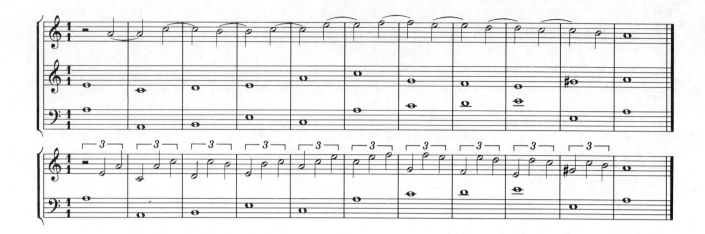

Note, however, that a 2–3 dissonance is apt to be misunderstood, since the second becomes a step rather than a dissonant skip.

Furthermore, the interval formed by an off-the-beat note to the next on-the-beat note may create a forbidden form of motion with the other line.

In such a case the only alternative is to alter one or more of the original lines.

If, on the other hand, there are more notes per measure in the compound line, there is more freedom. Where the compound line has three notes to a measure, the safest procedure is to represent the whole notes in the original by the first note in each measure of the compound line and the two halves of the tied note by the notes before and after it (see above). As long as there are no dissonances, this order may be varied, but as soon as the first dissonance occurs, it becomes the only possible order for the rest of the line.*

When the compound line has four notes to the

---

* Thus

is the only solution for m. 3, because of the dissonance. Consequently

is the only solution for m. 4, since the other solution would create a repetition.

measure, the simplest procedure is to represent each whole note by the first and fourth quarter notes and the suspended line by the other two quarter notes (see above). Then each pair of consecutive notes in the compound line will represent either a pair of simultaneously sounding notes or a pair of consecutive notes in the original.*

* Therefore the change in the bass. Had we used the same bass as the two previous examples, the similar motion to an octave at m. 4 would have been obvious.

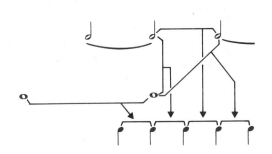

Exercises

1. Use the upper two simple lines to generate a single compound line

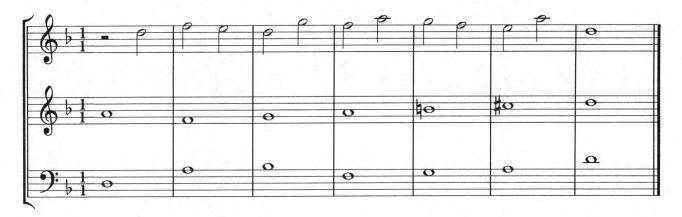

   a. in triplet half notes

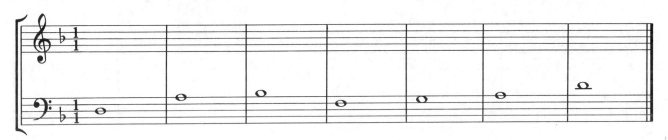

   b. in quarter notes.

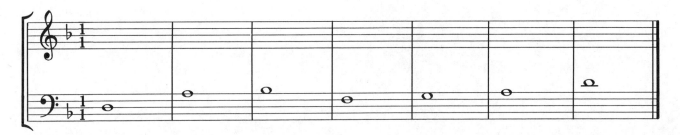

(In both cases, get all the dissonant skips and skips to a dissonance you can, but make sure you de-emphasize the octaves in mm. 4 and 5.)

2. Add middle and bass lines in whole notes

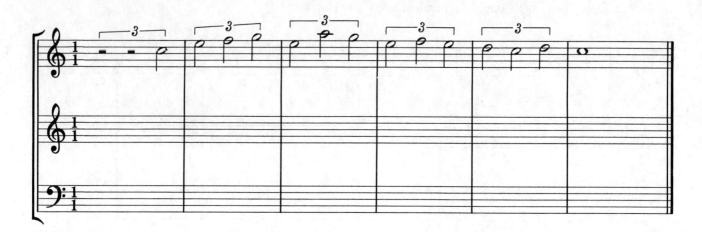

and then convert the top two lines into a single line in quarter notes, preserving where possible the sense of any dissonances in the original.

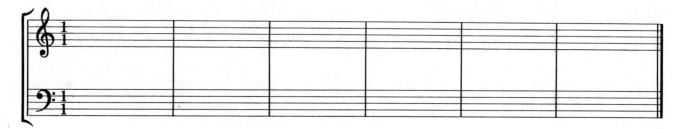

3. Try using the upper two lines of the following to generate a simple line

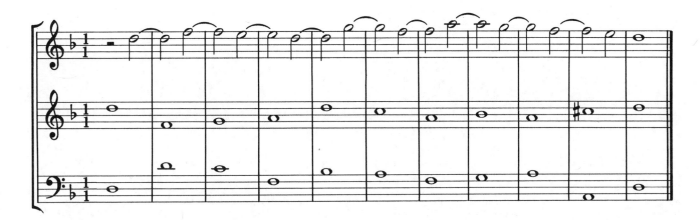

   a. in half notes

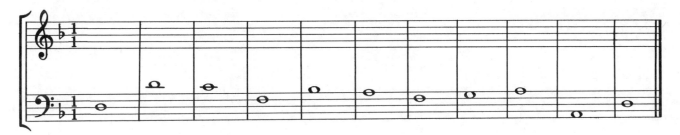

   b. in triplet half notes

   c. in quarter notes

(They won't work for at least one of these at at least one point. Which, where, and why not?)

6.8 Dissonant Skips and Skips to and from a Dissonant Note, Continued: Compound Lines Based on Pairs of Lines in Combined Species

Generating a single compound line from two simple lines, both of which are in a higher species, creates relatively few new problems.

Simple Lines Both in Second Species or Both in Third Species • Consider what happens when both simple lines have an unstable note at the end of a measure.

The third principle established in the previous section states that where a passing tone or dissonant neighbor immediately precedes an on-the-beat note in the original, the on-the-beat note must fall on the beat in the compound line as well (see page 195). But obviously there is no way that *both* on-the-beat notes can fall on the beat in the compound line, since there is no way that two notes can occur at the same time in a single line.

This is less of a problem than it might at first seem. Because both simple lines were in the same species, the underlying rates of flow of the two constituent threads of the compound line are the same. Consequently, there is no particular difficulty in grasping which notes are unstable or which notes they are connected to.

The problems you will have to worry about are principally the old ones of proper voice leading. Note, however, that most voice-leading errors are due simply to representing contiguous notes consecutively.

They can be avoided by alternating the source of your notes in the following pattern: top line, middle line, middle line, top line, etc.,

or the reverse.

In this way, only intervals between consecutive or simultaneously sounding notes find their way into the compound line.

Note that since there can be no dissonant intervals between simultaneously sounding notes of two second-species lines, there are no dissonant skips in the resultant compound line. The same is true when both the original lines are in third species.

Both Simple Lines in Fourth Species • The chief problems in generating a compound line from two simple lines both of which are in fourth species arise from the fact that both simple lines consist of notes that change their structural sense with the arrival of the on-the-beat note in the third line. The safest way to make sure that both senses of the tied notes in both simple lines are preserved in the compound line is to use quarter notes, arpeggiating each pair of simultaneously sounding notes twice—both before and after the barline.

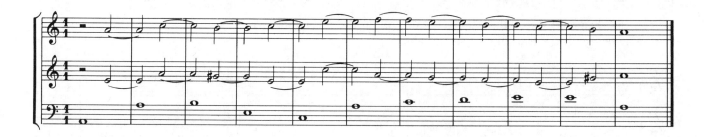

This way each dissonant suspension is properly treated: preparation, suspension, and resolution are explicitly stated and in the correct order.

Unfortunately, the resulting line, while perfectly coherent, is apt to be tedious. To make the compound line more interesting, locate those consecutive or contiguous tied half notes that form unisons or thirds.

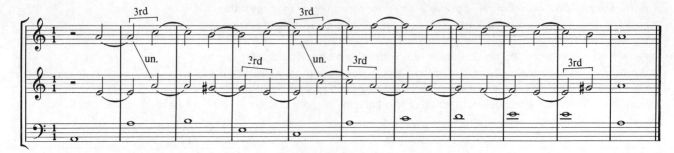

You can then omit the on-the-beat tied half note in the other line to leave a quarter note free for a neighbor or step motion.

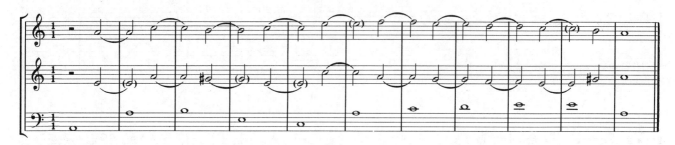

Generating a single compound line in triplet half notes from two suspended lines is a little trickier. With only three notes to a measure, there is no way you can represent both suspended notes in both measures. However, if the last triplet half note in a measure is left by skip, it can be considered as left hanging in the next measure and so need not be explicitly represented.

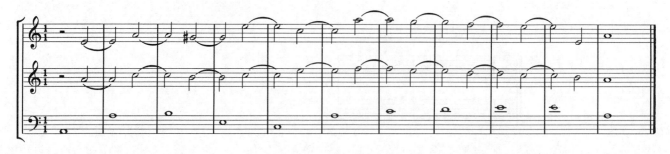

Simple Lines in Different Higher Species • The basic problem in generating a compound line from two simple lines each in a different higher species is to maintain the sense of two underlying rates of flow in a single line. The easiest way to do this is to keep the same correspondence between parts of each measure in the original and each measure in the compound line. Thus, to generate a compound line in triplet quarter notes from a pair of lines, one in half notes and one in quarter notes, you can always represent the first quarter by the first triplet quarter, the first half by the second triplet quarter, the second quarter by the third triplet quarter, repeating the same correspondence for the second half of the measure.

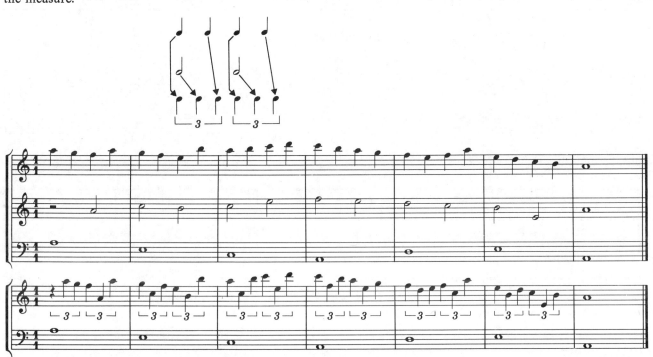

Where notes in both simple lines form dissonant intervals with the third line, or where they are dissonant with one another, this correspondence guarantees both coherence and the interest provided by dissonant skips and skips to and from dissonant notes. Where one or more off-the-beat notes are not dissonant, other patterns can, of course, be used.

To generate a compound line in quarter notes from a pair of simple lines, one in second species and the other in fourth, the safest pattern of correspondence is usually

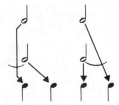

The principal exception is where the two simple lines form a 2–(3) or 2–(1) suspension. For the suspensions to be understood as such, the suspended note

must be represented on the beat. Thus the 2–(3) between the top two lines in m. 8 of the following

disappears when we use the same correspondence throughout,

but if we put the E on the beat,

there is no other way to understand the dissonance.

To generate a compound line in triplet quarters from simple lines in third and fourth species the safest pattern is

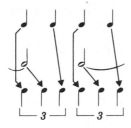

Thus, a combination like

becomes

Where no dissonance is involved, other patterns are possible, but there is little need for variety of pattern where the *underlying* rhythm is itself so complex.

Exercises

1. Use the two upper lines in half notes to generate a single compound line in quarters.

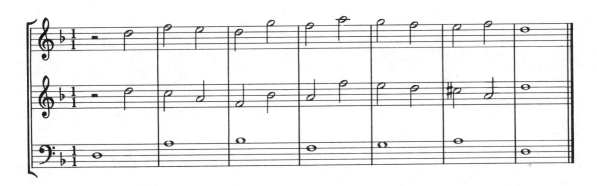

2. Use the two upper lines in triplet half notes to generate a single compound line with six quarter notes to the measure.

3. Use the two upper lines to generate a single compound line

   a. in triplet half notes

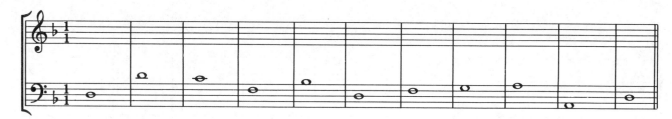

   b. in quarter notes

4. Use the top two lines to generate a compound line in triplet quarter notes.

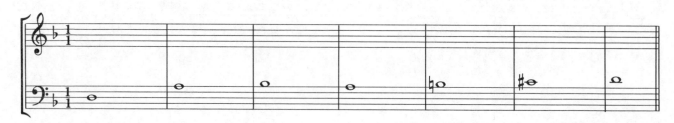

5. Use the top two lines to generate a compound line in quarter notes.

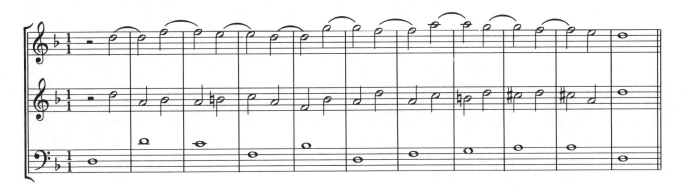

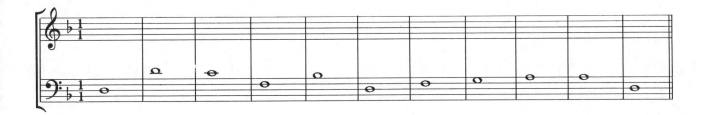

6. Use the top two lines to generate a compound line in triplet quarter notes.

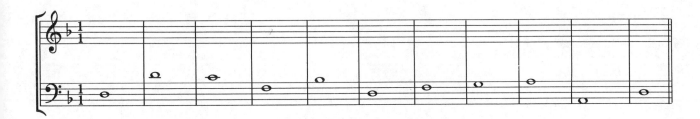

6.9 Passing Tones and Dissonant Neighbors Beginning at the Same Time as the Stable Notes Against Which They Are Dissonant: Combining Compound Lines with Lines in a Higher Species

Take the following combination of three simple lines in simple second species.

Now suppose you were to try to transform the top two lines into a single compound line in half notes.

Clearly, the result does not fit our rules for combining two lines in second species. Nor is there any way it could. Obviously, any time the second bass note in a measure is dissonant with both the whole notes above it, it won't make any difference which order you arpeggiate the whole notes in—that bass note will be dissonant with the half note that begins with it.

On the other hand, there is no doubt as to which note is the unstable one, even though they both begin at the same time. Despite the fact that both lines appear to be moving at the same rate, the underlying rate of flow of the compound line is clearly in whole notes. Consequently, even though the second half note in each measure of the compound line may begin simultaneously with a dissonant passing tone or neighbor in the bass, we understand it as belonging with the first half note in the measure and thus have no difficulty in understanding it as the stable note and the bass note as the unstable one.

Now consider what happens when we transform the same pair of upper lines into a compound line in quarter notes complete with its own passing tones and dissonant neighbors.

* The similar motion to a fifth can be avoided when the top two lines become one compound line.

Again the result does not fit our rules for combining lines in second and third species. Yet each time two notes forming a dissonance begin together it is clear which of the two is the unstable one and how it is to be understood as a passing tone or dissonant neighbor in terms of its own line. Here we have three rates of flow: the underlying rate of flow of the compound line is at the whole note, the bass moves at the half note, and the note-to-note motion of the compound line is at the quarter note. Thus, we can understand off-the-beat half notes as being dissonant against the underlying whole notes (which may or may not be stated simultaneously with them) and off-the-beat quarter notes being dissonant against either half note. In determining which note is the stable one we must take account of many factors: Is the note on the beat? Is it consonant with notes on the beat? Is it approached or left by skip? Can it be construed as a neighbor or an interior element in a step motion?

Thus, in the first measure of the top line the A and the E are the stable pitches, the A because it is on the beat and the E because it is skipped from. The G and the F are passing tones, unstable with respect to the bass notes they sound simultaneously with. The G in the bass, however, is dissonant with respect to the A in the top line. In the second measure the A's and the C in the top line and the F and the A in the bottom line are stable pitches. The B is, of course, unstable with respect to the F; it is a passing tone. In the third measure the B and the D's in the top line are stable pitches. The E is unstable with respect to the F in the bass; it is a dissonant neighbor. The F in the bass is itself unstable with respect to the B at the beginning of the measure; it is a passing note, but this relation is not made explicit since the two notes never sound simultaneously. If, instead, we embellish the B with a neighbor the relationship becomes explicit.

In the fourth measure the C's are the stable notes in the top line and the D in the bass is unstable with respect to them. The B in the top line is simply a neighbor; in this case it happens to be consonant with the simultaneously sounding note in the bass. But note how the fact that the last C is left by skip leaves no doubt that it, and not the B, is the stable pitch.

Now consider the following combination of three lines in simple fourth species:

When we transform the two whole-note lines into a single compound line in half notes,

we get a pair of lines that fit our rules for combining lines in second and fourth species in at least two respects—all notes off the beat are consonant with one

216

another, and any time the notes on the beat form a dissonant interval, the suspended line moves down by step. However, note how the suspensions formed by the on-the-beat half note are not always strong or intermediate ones.

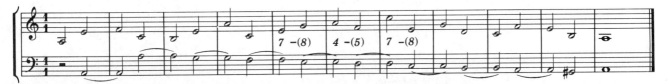

On the other hand, consider what would happen if we reversed the order of arpeggiation in these measures to make sure that the pitch that creates the strong arpeggiation is the one that falls on the beat:

Clearly, it is more important to avoid doubling the resolution than it is to make the strong suspension the explicit one.

Finally, consider what happens when we use the two whole-note lines as the basis for a compound line in quarter notes:

Again, such a pair of lines does not fit the rules for the combination of fourth and third species. Yet if you bear in mind the same set of considerations we used for the previous example with quarter-note motion, you will see that each time two simultaneously sounding notes form a dissonant interval, it is always clear which note is the unstable one.

Thus, in the first measure the A in the bass and the B in the upper line form a dissonance. As in the combination of lines in third and fourth species, the B is the unstable pitch functioning as a dissonant neighbor to the C's before and after it. In the second measure, however, the D in the top line forms a dissonant interval with the upper A in the bass. Both notes begin simultaneously but because the C and the E have been established as stable in the beginning of the measure, it is easy to understand the D as a passing tone between the E and the second C.

Exercises

1. a. Write a middle line in whole notes.

b. Use the top two lines to generate a single compound line in half notes. Write two versions: in the first, wherever possible avoid dissonance between notes that begin at the same time; in the second, try to get as many dissonances as possible between notes that begin at the same time.

c. Use the top two lines to generate a single compound line in quarter notes. Write two versions as in 1b.

2. a. Write a middle line in whole notes.

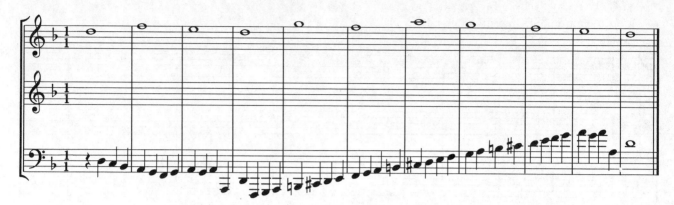

b. Use the top two lines to generate a single compound line in half notes. Write two versions as in 1b.

3. a. Write a middle line in whole notes.

b. Use the top two lines to generate a single line in half notes. Write two versions as in 1b.

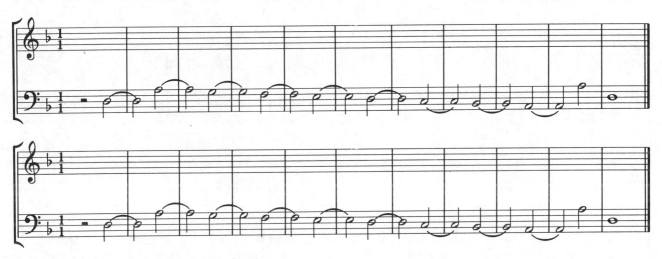

c. Use the top two lines to generate a single line in quarter notes. Write two versions as in 1b.

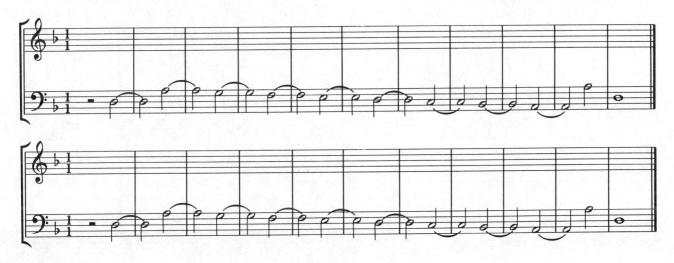

4. a. Write a middle line in whole notes.

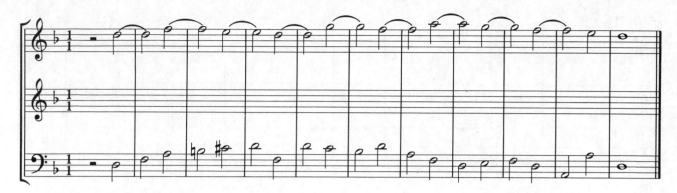

b. Use the top two lines of 4a. to generate a compound line in half notes. Write two versions as in 1b.

c. Use the top two lines of 4a. to generate a single compound line in quarter notes. Write two versions as in 1b.

5. a. Write a middle line in whole notes.

b. Use the top two lines of 5a. to generate a single compound line in half notes. Write two versions as in 1b.

PART THREE

A Little Closer to the Real Thing— A Theory of Tonal Rhythm

CHAPTER SEVEN

Notes, Beats, and Measures

7.0 Tonal Rhythm

In Part II we used a highly oversimplified version of the rhythmic structure of tonal music in order to concentrate on two aspects of its pitch structure—how lines can be built up and how they can be combined. Now we must deal with the actual rhythmic structure of tonal music.

In doing so, we will not neglect pitch structure. Indeed, there is no way we could, for rhythmic structure and pitch are so dependent on one another in tonal music that to consider one without the other would be meaningless. Rather, we will use our study of rhythmic structure to open up new possibilities of pitch structure, possibilities unthinkable in the narrow confines of species counterpoint.

In general, the course of our discussion will lead from details—what happens from note to note and beat to beat (Chapter 7) to the large—what happens in a whole phrase, section, or movement (Chapter 8), reserving the special problems of the role of performance in making it happen for the end (Chapter 9).

We will begin by picking up a few loose ends from Part I. In Section 3.3 we showed how a given set of notes could be rearticulated, embellished by neighbor, arpeggiated, or connected by step motion to get more notes.

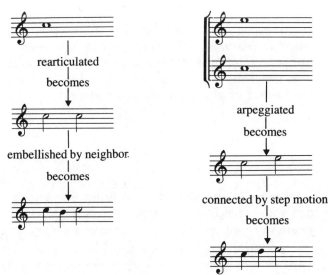

In our examples the new set of notes always divided the duration of one of the given notes into equal segments. That is one possibility in tonal music, but it is only one of several alternative possibilities. In Section 7.1 we will show that the length of the segments normally follows the constraint that $s_1 \geq s_2 = s_3 \ldots = s_n$; that is, the first segment is no shorter than any subsequent segment and all subsequent segments are equal to one another. In this section we will also show that the minimum period that the beginning of a note can be delayed is normally half the duration of the original note (or $d \geq \frac{1}{2} S$, where d is the delay period and S the span defined by the original note) and the maximum duration of an anticipation is half the span defined by the note it anticipates ($a \leq \frac{1}{2} S$).

In Section 2.2 we showed how we think of the point in time at which a note begins and the period of time it lasts in terms of a set of reference points called beats. In Section 7.2 we will use the relationships discussed in Section 7.1 to show what the pitch of the note has to do with how we think of a note in terms of a beat. Sections 7.3 and 7.4 deal with the complications and ambiguities introduced by secondary pitch structures and secondary beats. In Section 7.5 we will try to show how a composer uses pitches and durations to establish a particular set of reference points. The last two sections of this chapter will deal with extensions of the line-building principles introduced so far —Section 7.6 with the introduction of pitches outside the diatonic collection, and Section 7.7 with the use in one line of a pitch that originated in another line.

7.1 Segmentation, Delay, and Anticipation

We think of a note as beginning at a particular point in time and lasting a certain period of time. We think of the beginnings of notes as articulating points in time. We can think of the beginnings of two consecutive notes in a line as defining a span, S, that stretches from the point, P, at which the first note begins, to P′, the point at which the second note begins.*

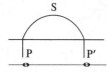

When we rearticulate a note, embellish a rearticulation with a neighbor, arpeggiate a pair of notes, or connect two arpeggiated notes with a step motion, we

---

* In the following examples, the second of the two notes defining a span is often omitted. This is possible because, in our notational system, each durational symbol (half note, whole note) shows the period of time between the beginning of that note and the beginning of the next, rather than the period of time the first note lasts. The two periods may, of course, be equal, but they need not be. We can show roughly how much of the span a note occupies by using articulation marks.

first note lasts entire span

first note lasts substantially less than entire span

See Sections 9.1 and 9.2.

---

increase the number of articulation points, thereby cutting up the original span into two or more segments.

And when we understand notes in a line as forming one of the four fundamental structures, we are in effect thinking of the durations of these notes as segments of a longer span of time and thus thinking of the points in time that cut the span into segments in terms of their relationship to the points in time that articulated the original span. That is, we think of

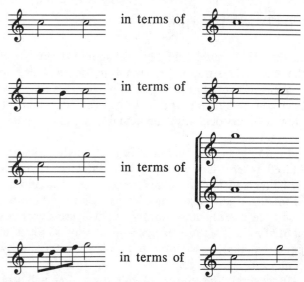

Now the question is: What durations can the composer give his notes and still be reasonably sure that his listener will in fact understand them as segments of a longer span? † The answer, of course, depends on what kind of understanding the composer can expect of "his listener." For now, let us assume that the listener we're talking about is a rather simple-minded person who understands notes in time according to two principles: an order principle and a size principle:

1. Given two different points in time, it is easier

---

† In species we avoided this problem by making all notes in a line of equal duration.

to think of the second point in terms of the first,* and

2. Given two unequal periods of time, it is easier to think of the shorter in terms of the longer.

Consider the simplest possible case. You want to write two consecutive notes with the same pitch beginning at points p_1 and p_2

such that our imaginary listener will understand the spans defined by these notes as two segments, s_1 and s_2, of a single large span, S†, beginning at P

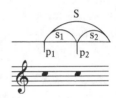

Clearly, the extent of S will simply be the sum of s_1 and s_2, and P will have to be located at p_1. In other words, we are in effect asking our listener to understand the point at which the second note begins *in terms of* the point at which the first note begins. We are asking him to think of p_2 as an interior point of articulation within the span of time that begins at p_1. Now the question is: How will the relative length of these two notes affect the way he thinks about them?

Obviously, if we may make s_1 longer than s_2, our listener can use both the principles we have ascribed to him.

For example, where S is a whole note

If we make s_1 and s_2 the same length, he can use only the first.

---

* Presumably, because the listener can refer back to his memory of the first while experiencing the second. Of course, if we give him some reason to expect the second point—that is, to know when it's coming before it arrives—the situation changes.

† Here, as elsewhere in this book I am using upper case letters to denote conceptual priority. Thus, the symbols s_1 and s_2 denote two shorter periods of time, which we can think of *in terms of* (in this case, as segments of) the longer period of time denoted by S. Similarly, p_1 and p_2 denote points in time that we can think of in terms of P. (That is, we identify p_1 with P, and we understand p_2 as an interior point of articulation within the span initiated at P.)

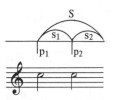

However, if we make s_1 shorter than s_2, the two principles are in direct conflict.

The listener has no way of telling whether he is expected to think of the first note in terms of the second because the second is longer, or the second in terms of the first because the first is first. In general, then, the safest procedure for two notes is to follow the rule that

$$s_1 \geq s_2$$

The same rule applies to any operation that cuts an existing span into two segments, that is, when you add a neighbor,

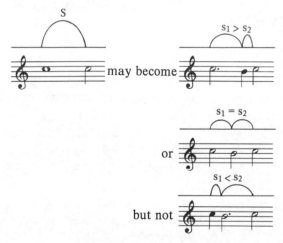

arpeggiate two simultaneously sounding notes,

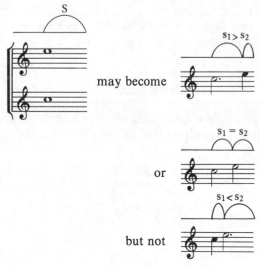

or create a step motion between two notes a third apart.

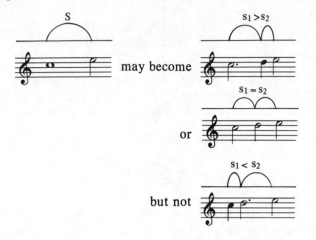

It also applies to successive applications of any operation: what is considered a segment at one stage is considered a span at the next.

Now suppose you wanted to cut the span into more than two segments by a single operation. Say you wanted to connect two notes a fourth apart

by step motion. By adding two notes you articulate the span originally defined by the first of the two notes a fourth apart

into three segments.

You want your listener to understand the first three notes as segments of a single span. He will have to understand both p_2 and p_3 directly in terms of p_1 and the whole structure as the result of a single operation.

Clearly, from the argument presented for spans with two segments, you can't make s_1 less than s_2 or s_1 less than s_3 if you want him to understand both p_2 and p_3 in terms of p_1.* But what about the relationship of s_2 and s_3? The problem is that you must prevent the listener from thinking of p_2 in terms of p_3, or p_3 in terms of p_2. You want him to relate both p_2 and p_3 directly back to p_1. If you make s_2 greater than s_3

he has every reason to think of p_3 in terms of p_2

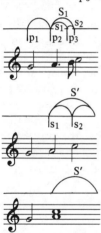

since both his principles support that approach.

On the other hand, if you make s_2 less than s_3

* Actually he can understand p_3 in terms of p_1 even though s_1 is less than s_3, but only by understanding the whole structure in terms of more than one operation. Say that $s_1 = s_2$ and $s_1 + s_2 = s_3$, for example:

He can then understand s_1 and s_2 as forming a span, which in turn forms the first segment of a span together with s_3:

However, in such a case he is not understanding the whole structure in terms of a single operation.

you might suppose that by putting the two principles into conflict you could force him not to think of p_2 in terms of p_3 or vice versa. But he has another way of resolving the conflict. He can think of s_1 and s_2 as forming a span and can then use the first principle to think of p_2 in terms of p_1 (which defines the beginning of the span segmented by p_2) and the second principle to think of p_2 in terms of p_3 (which defines the end of the span segmented by p_2). That, of course, means he thinks of the total span as being segmented at p_3 into two segments, $s_1 + s_2$ and s_3.

The safest course is to make $s_2 = s_3$. Then he has no reason for thinking of p_2 in terms of p_3, and his only reason for thinking of p_3 in terms of p_2 (that p_2 comes first) is just as true of the relationship of p_3 to p_1.

Where three segments are involved, then, the rule reads

$$s_1 \geq s_2 = s_3$$

For more than three segments, the same considerations would affect all the segments from the second one to the last one, so we can state the general form for n segments as

$$s_1 \geq s_2 = s_3 \ldots = s_n$$

This *law of segmentation* applies equally to all four operations—rearticulation, embellishment by neighbor, arpeggiation, and connection by step motion.* In each case the segments are the duration of the new, shorter notes that divide up the time originally occupied by a longer note: in the case of a rearticulation, the note being rearticulated

---

* Later it will prove useful to include, as a special case of rearticulation, the *shortening* of the duration of a note by dividing its span into two segments; s_1, the duration of the new note and s_2, a period of silence.

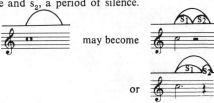

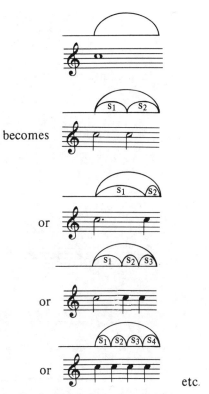

in the case of a neighbor embellishment, the first of two notes with the same pitch

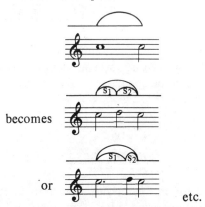

in the case of an arpeggiation, both the notes being arpeggiated

and in the case of a step motion, the first of the two notes being connected.

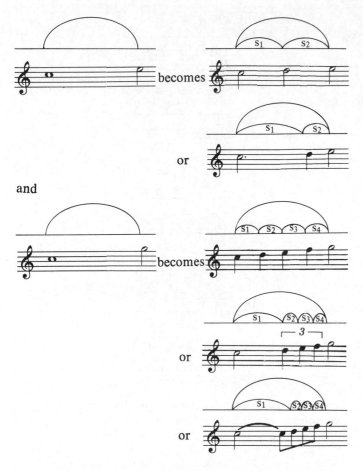

Delay • Take a note beginning at a particular point in time, P, and lasting for a particular period of time so as to define the span, S.

You want to transform this note into another note that your listener can think of as a *delayed representative* of the original note.
The new note will

1. begin at some later point, p, a given period, d, later than P,

and

2. last a particular period of time, s.

Now consider what you are asking your listener to do. To understand the new note in terms of the original note he has to be able to think of p in terms of P and s in terms of S. But how is he going to know where P is or how long S lasts, once the original note isn't sounding anymore? Suppose, however, he had a way of knowing where P was and had reason to expect a note at that point, but no new note began there and the next note began at p. Then if d is shorter than S and s ends where S would have ended,

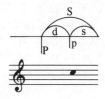

he can relate s to S by thinking of s as the second of two segments of S and the one which is articulated by the note expected at P. Furthermore, if the two segments of S follow the rule of segmentation, that is, if $d \geq s$, then he should be able to think of p in terms of P, and hence understand the new note as the delayed representative of the missing original. For example:

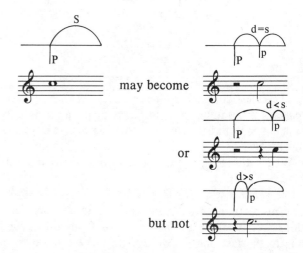

Thus, the law of relative durations for delays is no more than a special case of that for segmentation. Since there are never more than the two segments, d and s, involved, we can express the relationship between the delay, d, and the span, S, directly:

$$d \geq \tfrac{1}{2}S.$$

Note, however, that while segmentation affects only notes within the span segments

delaying a note affects the note before as well.

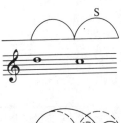

Delaying the point in time at which the second note begins increases the length of time the first note lasts by the period of delay.

Anticipation • Take a note beginning at a particular point, P, and lasting a particular period of time so as to define a span, S.

Suppose you want to anticipate that note—that is, you want to add another note with the same pitch beginning at some point, p, a particular period of time, a, before P, such that your listener thinks of p in terms of P and a in terms of S.

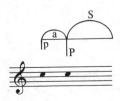

Now consider what you are asking your listener to do when you expect him to understand these two notes the way you intended them. You are asking him to think of a point, p, in terms of another point, P, that hasn't even occurred yet. (In a segmentation or a delay, the conceptually prior point always occurs first.) Furthermore, you are asking him to think of a period of time, a, in terms of another period of time, S, of which it is not even a part. (The s's and d's in segmentation and delays are always parts of the span, S.)

But suppose he has some way of knowing when P is coming—and some way of knowing how long S will last. He could then imagine a span, S′, equal in length to S but beginning at point P′, ending at P, divided by p into two segments, s′ and a.

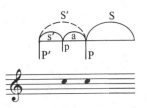

In that case he could think of p when it happens in terms of the expected P and, if $a \leq \frac{1}{2}S'$, think of a as a segment of S′, which he in turn thinks of as being equal to the span in question, namely, S.

Or, suppose that although he had no way of knowing when P was coming, he knows how long S will last. He could then imagine a point, P′, marking the end of the S and another point, p′, bearing the same relationship to P′ that p bears to P and defining two segments of S, s′, and a′, equal to a.

Then if $s' \geq a'$, he could think of a′ as a segment of S and hence think of a in terms of S by thinking of it as equal to a′. While he would have no way of thinking of p in terms of P at the moment p occurs, he could in retrospect understand it as being related to P in the same way that p′ is related to P′. In either case, then, to have a way of thinking of the anticipation in terms of the anticipated note, $a \leq \frac{1}{2}S$. This rule of anticipation is, in effect, another special case of the rule of segmentation. However, two important differences must be noted.

1. In an anticipation the new note is added outside the original span. Consequently, other notes may be affected and other spans involved. Suppose that preceding the note defining span S there is a note defining span S′.

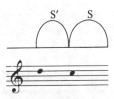

Then a note anticipating S would segment S′ into two segments, s and a.

233

Thus, not only must $a \leq \frac{1}{2}S$, but $a \leq \frac{1}{2}S'$ as well. If $S' < S$, it means the length of a is limited by the length of S'.

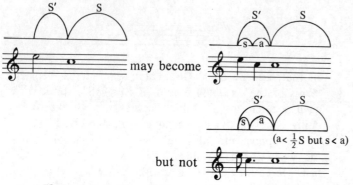

If, however, $S' = S$

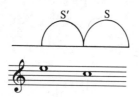

or $S' > S$,

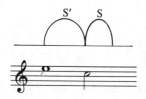

then no further constraint is imposed.

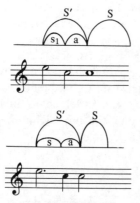

2. Expecting a listener to grasp the relationship of anticipatory note to anticipated note by the procedure outlined above is expecting a great deal. We can make it much easier for him by supplying actual notes to articulate those heretofore imaginary points P' and p',

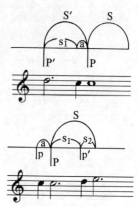

but unless he has some way of sensing the location of P or the length of S ahead of time, he will not be able to understand the note at p as an anticipation. The same set of requirements holds for an *anticipatory arpeggiation* and for an *incomplete neighbor*. In an anticipatory arpeggiation both the pitches are thought of as originally associated with the span S beginning at point P.

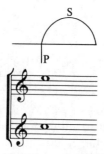

Instead of one of them beginning at P and one at some later point, p, thereby segmenting S as in an ordinary arpeggiation,

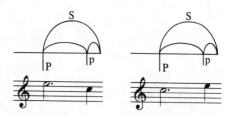

one of them begins at an earlier point, p, and the other at P, as in an anticipation.

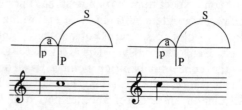

In an incomplete neighbor, the note being embellished begins at P

234

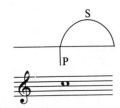

and the neighbor begins at p.

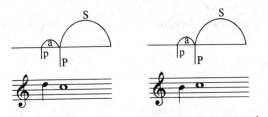

The neighbor is incomplete in that there is no prior statement of the pitch being embellished.*

("complete" neighbor)

In both cases the listener needs some way of predicting the location of P and the duration of S, and in both cases the anticipatory segment, a, must be no longer than half of S.

* Note that the term "incomplete neighbor" as used in this book always means that the notes appear in the order: neighbor followed by note being embellished.

Drills

1. Which of the following are *not* subject to the constraints presented in this section?

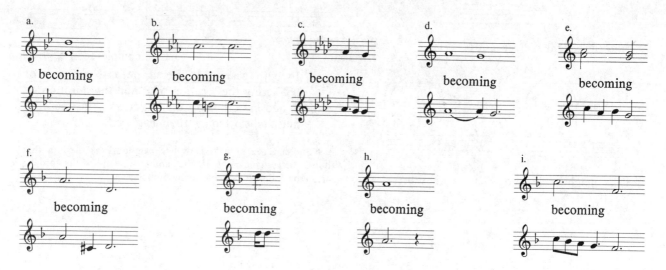

2. Connect the pitches of the two given notes, segmenting the span defined by the first given note and giving the maximum duration possible to each interior element in the step motion.

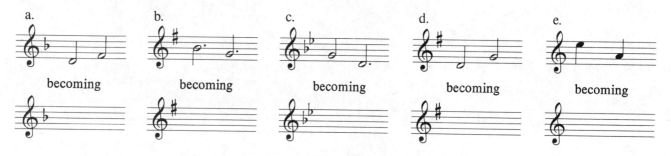

3. Delay the second note by the minimum possible delay period.

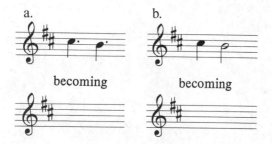

4. Anticipate the second given note, giving the maximum duration possible to the anticipation.

5. Approach the second given note by an incomplete neighbor, giving the maximum duration possible to the neighbor.

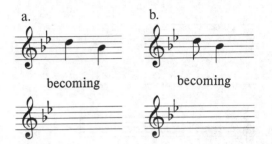

6. Arpeggiate the two given notes in two different ways: in a. so that the lower of the two pitches is stated first and the upper receives the maximum duration possible under the law of segmentation, and in b. so as to form an anticipatory arpeggiation in which the upper pitch is stated first and the anticipatory segment is as long as possible.

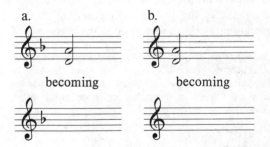

7.2 Thinking of Notes in Terms of Beats

In the last section we talked about notes as though they were floating about in a kind of limbo—in a time without beats. In tonal music, however, we think of notes in terms of their relationship to beats. We defined beats in Section 2.2 as "reference points in time" and showed how we can think of both the point in time at which a note begins and the period of time it lasts in terms of such reference points.

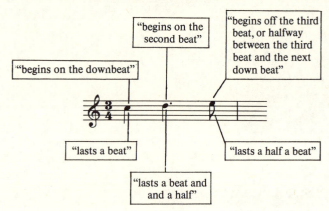

But such a way of thinking of notes in time is incomplete, for it takes no account of pitches.* The advantage of using the approach introduced in Section 7.1 to think about notes in time (that is, thinking of them as segments, delays, or anticipations of longer notes) is that this approach takes account of the pitches of the notes right from the beginning. Our next job is to fit these two ways of thinking of notes in time into a single, unified conception.

Suppose your listener conceives of a period of time in terms of two reference points, the beats B_1 and B_2.† They define a span, Z_1, stretching from B_1 to B_2 and, by extension, a second span, Z_2, starting at B_2 and lasting as long as Z_1. Suppose also that you were to give him two consecutive notes, pitches a third apart, beginning at points, P_1 and P_2, and defining spans, S_1 and S_2, such that P_1 and B_1, P_2 and B_2, S_1 and Z_1, and S_2 and Z_2 are identical with one another. For example:

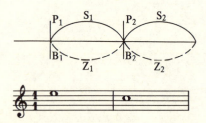

Obviously he would have no difficulty thinking of your notes in terms of his beats. Not only are the notes on the beats but their spans are the same as the spans defined by the beats.

Now suppose you were to segment either or both of the spans defined by your notes by a step motion and a rearticulation.‡‡ For example:

Obviously the fact that your listener thinks of the points, P_1 and P_2, at which your notes begin as his reference points, B_1 and B_2, is not going to get in the way of understanding p_1 in terms of P_1 and p_2 in terms of P_2. On the contrary, by definition he must think of the off-the-beat notes in terms of the beat. The fact that he already identifies P_1 and P_2 as the beats, B_1 and B_2, only makes the job of understanding s_1^1 and s_2^1 as segments of S_1 and s_1^2 and s_2^2 as segments of

‡‡ Given these pitches, step motion and rearticulation are the only pitch structures possible for the first span. Lacking a third note, rearticulation is the only pitch structure possible for the second span. Given other pitches or more notes, other structures would be possible,

but the argument would be the same in any case.

---

* It is, of course, advantageous in a notation system to keep these two attributes of notes separate.

† Getting him to use the particular set of points you want him to is another problem. See Section 7.5.

S_2 all the easier.* Thus, in each case he can think of your notes in terms of his beats by thinking of them as segmenting the spans that would have been created by the notes on the beat.

Or suppose you were to delay either or both your original notes. For example:

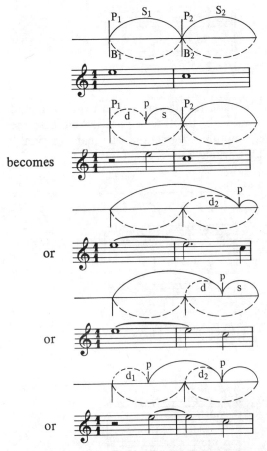

As we pointed out in Section 7.1, to think of a note beginning at a point, p, as a delayed representative of a note that would have begun at an earlier point, P, your listener needs (1) some way of knowing where P is once the original note is no longer there to articulate it and (2) some reason for thinking of p in terms of P. Obviously, if he is already thinking of each P as a beat, B, both conditions are satisfied. In each case he can think of your notes in terms of his beats by think-

---

* In fact, so much easier that we even find cases where the first segment is shorter than the second, thereby breaking the law of segmentation.

(Purcell: *The Fairy Queen*, Act II, "Secrecy's Song", mm. 12–15.)

Because such "unstable segmentations" require special attention on the part of the performer, we will deal with them in Chapter 9.

---

ing of either or both notes as delayed representatives of notes that would have been on the beat. Notice, however, that when you delay the second note, its delay period is of course added to the first note, making it last beyond the second beat. Your listener will understand the span, S_1', defined by this new note as being made up of two segments, the part before the second beat (the old $S_1 = Z_1$, or, if the first note is also delayed, the segment, s_1) and the part after (the delay period of the second note, d_2). If only the second note is delayed, no new problems are created: the first segment is bound to be longer than the second since $S_1 = S_2$ and d_2 is part of S_2. But if both notes are delayed, you could create a situation in which the first segment (s_1) is shorter than the second (d_2).

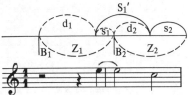

Such situations are hard for your listener to grasp. To avoid them make both delay periods equal half the span period.

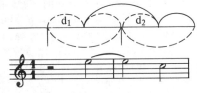

Or, finally, suppose you were to anticipate either or both your original notes.†

---

† You could, of course, also supply them with incomplete neighbors.

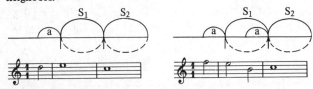

Or, had your original notes included a pair of simultaneously sounding notes,

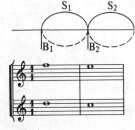

you could have used them to create an anticipatory arpeggiation.

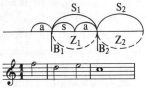

In either case the same argument would follow.

239

For example:

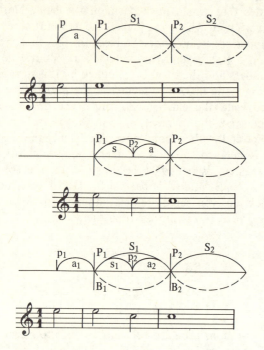

As we pointed out in Section 7.1, to think of a note as anticipating another note, your listener has to think of a point, p, in terms of another point, P, that hasn't even happened yet, and a period of time, a, in terms of another period, S, of which it is not even a part. Now, obviously, if your listener is already thinking of each P as a beat, B, the first condition is already met; if he's made up his mind when B is going to happen, it won't matter that it hasn't happened yet when p occurs. Furthermore, if he has already made up his mind when two such beats are going to happen, then he already has set in his mind a span between them, Z_1, as well as a span of equal length, Z_2, following B_2. He can easily imagine an earlier span of the same length, Z_0, ending at B_1.

Thus, a_1 and a_2 are automatically segments of spans equal in length to the spans they anticipate, and the inherent difficulties in thinking of one note as anticipating another are considerably diminished. Thus, in each of the above cases your listener can think of your notes in terms of his beats by thinking of each off-the-beat note as anticipating the span defined by a note that is on the beat and lasts a beat.

Just as you can use the ideas of segmentation, delay, and anticipation to understand the relationship of consecutive notes in a line to one another in terms of a simpler set of notes beginning on the beat, so too you can use these ideas to understand the relationship of simultaneously sounding notes to one another. We have already dealt with many such relationships in our study of species counterpoint; the range of possibilities in actual tonal music is simply greater.

Suppose you gave your listener a combination of lines like

He can understand the dissonance between the D and the C by thinking of the D as connecting the E to the C by step motion, segmenting a span originally occupied by a whole-note E.

becomes

The passing tone as we know it from species is simply a special case of the off-the-beat passing tone found in real music: in real music the segment occupied by the passing tone itself is either the same length as the on-the-beat segment or shorter; in species it is always the same length.*

---

* The same is of course true for dissonant neighbors.

either

or

may be thought of in terms of

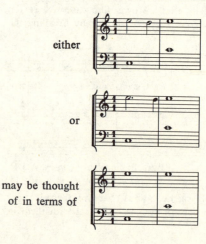

Similarly, suppose you gave your listener a combination of lines like

He can understand the dissonance as the result of the delay of the second note in the top line from the simpler

becomes

The suspension as we know it from species is simply a special case of suspensions found in real music: in real music the delay is either half the length of the span or longer: in species it is always half the length.*

Finally, suppose you were to give your listener a combination of lines like

He can understand the dissonance of the quarter-note C against the whole-note B by thinking of the C as anticipating the whole-note span of the second measure and using a part of the span originally defined by a whole-note D in the first measure.

---

* Occasionally you find suspensions resolving up by step in real music, particularly where the step is a minor second.

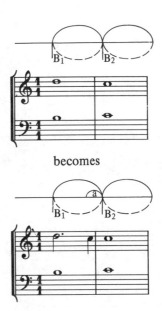

becomes

There were no dissonant anticipations in species, since there were no anticipations, but they abound in tonal music.†

To sum up: we can use the ideas of segmentation, delay, and anticipation to understand situations involving off-the-beat notes and notes lasting less than a beat in terms of simpler note-per-beat situations. However, it does not follow that any off-the-beat note can be understood in terms of an on-the-beat note in this way. For example, suppose you had given your listener off-the-beat notes like these:

He would have no way of understanding these notes as segments, delayed representatives, or anticipations of notes with the same spans as his beats. Beyond saying that they were simply off the beat or at such and such a point between two beats, he would have no way at all of thinking of these notes in terms of his beats.

†As do dissonant anticipatory arpeggiations

and dissonant incomplete neighbors.

Exercises

1. Segment the span defined by the first note by connecting the two pitches to form a step motion (a) such that $s_1 = s_2$ and (b) such that $s_1 > s_2$.

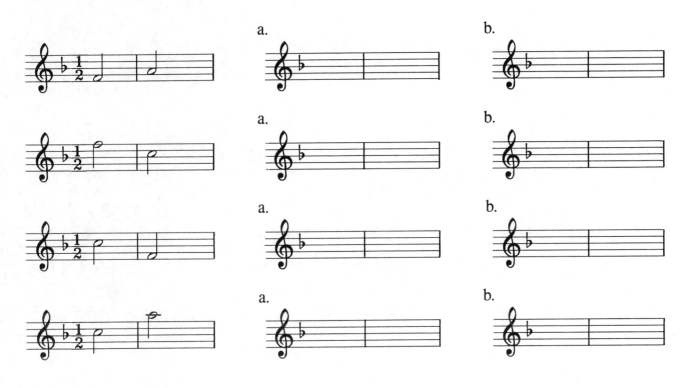

2. Delay the B♮ in the bass (a) such that $d = \tfrac{1}{2}S$ and (b) such that $d > \tfrac{1}{2}S$.

3. Anticipate the E in the top line.

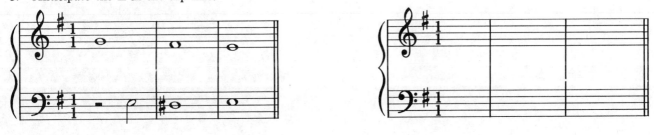

4. Generate the following line from a set of on-the-beat notes.

7.3 Secondary Segmentations, Delays, and Anticipations

In the preceding two sections we took units that we thought of as defining spans and subjected them to segmentation, delay, or anticipation to produce new notes.

Now any of these new notes could, of course, also be considered as defining a span and subjected to further segmentation, delay, or anticipation. However, such procedures do bring up a few new problems.

Alternative Ways of Understanding the Same Notes: Ambiguities and Resolutions of Ambiguities • As we saw when we first constructed species lines (Section 4.2, Ambiguity and Interest), just because you arrived at a series of notes in a particular way does not necessarily mean that your listener will understand them that way. If there is another way of constructing the same series of notes, he may well prefer the other way.

Take the notes

You (and your listener), by using the idea of delay, can conceive of these notes as a simple note-per-beat situation.

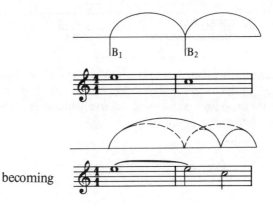

245

becoming

You could, of course, arrive at these notes in this way, but would your listener understand them in this way? Why should he go to the trouble of using two conceptual stages to understand your notes in terms of his beats,

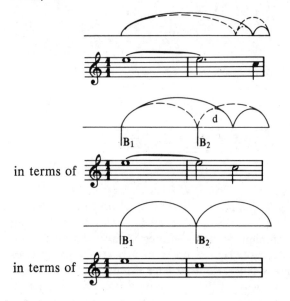

in terms of

in terms of

when he can understand the same notes in one step?

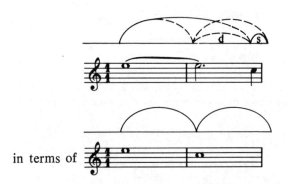

in terms of

In general, we can say that given the choice of two ways of understanding the same notes, the listener (other things being equal) will choose whichever way requires fewer conceptual steps.

Take the notes

You (and your listener), by using the idea of segmentation, can conceive of these notes in terms of a simple note-per-beat situation.

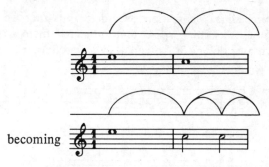

becoming

Now suppose you wanted to anticipate the second C.

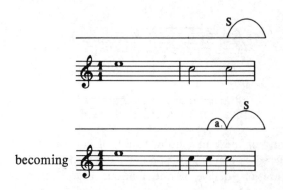

becoming

Again, it is possible to arrive at these notes in this way, but why should your listener understand them this way? Why should he go to the trouble of using a conceptually problematic construct like the anticipation, when he can understand the same notes in terms of the conceptually much less problematic segmentation?

in terms of

In general, we can say that given the choice of two ways of understanding a given passage, the listener (other things being equal) will choose whichever one depends on the conceptually less problematic constructs.

Take the notes

You (and your listener) can conceive of them in terms of a simple note-per-beat structure as

becoming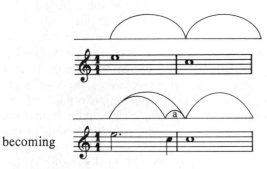

Suppose you wanted to connect the E to the C by step motion, segmenting the span defined by the dotted-half E.

becoming

Again, you could arrive at these notes in this way, but would your listener understand them in this way? Wouldn't it be easier for him to think of these notes in terms of the simple note-per-beat situation as

in terms of

in terms of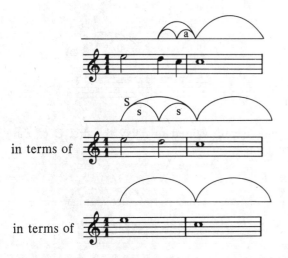

This way, instead of having to base something that is easy to grasp (a segmentation) on something that is difficult to grasp (an anticipation), he can use the easy one as the basis for the hard one.

In general, we can say that given the choice of two ways of understanding the same note, the listener (other things being equal) will choose the way that makes the unproblematic concept prior to the problematic, rather than vice versa. The effect of this principle is particularly evident in the case of a dissonance between two simultaneously sounding notes. A dissonance is by its very nature problematic. It can never be self-contained the way a consonance can be; it always demands an explanation. Thus, if you were to add a lower line to the previous example, making the D consonant but the quarter-note C dissonant,

the dissonance would make it even more obvious to your listener that the D is conceptually prior to the quarter-note C. It is much easier to understand the passage as

than as

On the other hand, if you add a lower line that makes the D dissonant and the quarter-note C consonant,

the dissonance has the opposite effect. It makes it harder for your listener to arrive at a single best way of understanding your notes. Both the dissonant D and the anticipatory C are conceptually problematic, but he must use one of them as the basis for the other.

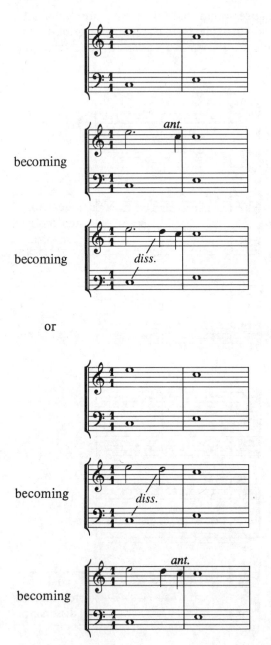

In this particular case he would still probably prefer the second way, but for different reasons. Note that in the second way each successive operation divides a span into equal segments and each successive stage creates shorter segments than the one before. It is easier to think of the quarter-note C as beginning halfway between the D and the whole-note C and the D as beginning halfway between the two beats than to think of the D as beginning two-thirds of the way from the E to the quarter-note C and the quarter-note C as three-fourths of the way from the E to the whole-note C.

In general, we can say that given the choice of two ways of understanding the same notes, the listener (other things being equal) will choose whichever way generates equal segments at any one stage but smaller and smaller segments with each successive stage.

Finally, take the notes

You (and your listener), by using the idea of delay and segmentation, can conceive of these notes in terms of a simple note-per-beat situation.

Now suppose you wanted to delay the first C of the segmentation

You can arrive at these notes in this way, but would

your listener understand them this way? He could, after all, also understand them this way:

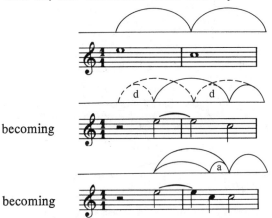

becoming

becoming

Both ways use the same number of steps; both ways segment whole notes into half notes and half notes into quarters. The advantage of the second way is that where two spans are involved at the same stage, the same operation is used on both.*

In general, we can say that given a choice of two ways of understanding the same notes, the listener (other things being equal) will choose whichever way allows him to use the same operation at the same stage. This principle applies not only to consecutive spans in the same line (as in the previous example) but also to simultaneous spans in two different lines.

To sum up: whenever there is more than one way of arriving at the same notes, the possibility always exists that your listener may understand your notes in a way different from the way you intend. However, we can assume that given the choice of two ways of understanding the same notes, he will choose the easier way. Specifically this means that he will choose the way that

1. requires fewer stages;
2. avoids problematic constructs (or, if they are unavoidable, postpones them to as late a stage as possible); and

---

* If he shifts the delay of the E down a stage to put it at the same stage as the delayed C shown in the first interpretation

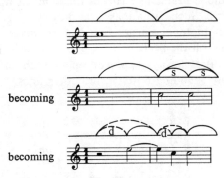

becoming

becoming

he then creates unequal segments.

3. generates segments of the same size at the same stage or uses the same operation at the same stage.

When none of these distinctions leads the listener to favor one interpretation over the other, or when two or more lead him to favor opposing interpretations, which thus cancel each other out, the structure of the passage is ambiguous.

Segmentation of a Note by a Beat • Take the notes

You (and your listener), by using the idea of delay, can understand them in terms of a note-per-beat situation.

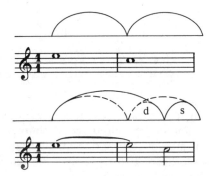

becoming

Now suppose you wanted to connect the E to the C by step motion. The question is when to begin the D. You want your listener to be able to understand the D in terms of the E and the C. To do this he has to be able to understand the point, p', at which the D begins in terms of the points, P_1 and P_2, at which the E and the C begin, and the periods of time the E and the D last as segments, s_1' and s_2', of S'. Obviously s_1' cannot be shorter than s_2'. But notice what happens when you make s_1' equal to s_2'.

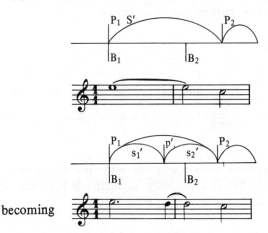

becoming

How can your listener be expected to understand p' in terms of P_2 when one of his own reference points, B_2, comes first? It's much easier for him to understand the D as going to a C on that beat, which is subsequently delayed.*

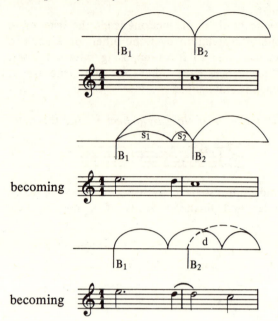

becoming

becoming

The problem is that the span, S', defined by the tied-over E, cannot be considered a simple span. Your listener thinks of it in terms of his beats, that is, as being made up of two segments: the part before the second beat and the part after.

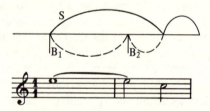

You must therefore either use these segments for your notes, putting the D on the beat,

or divide the second segment into two subsegments, beginning the D at or after the midpoint between the beat and the C.

* Even this way of thinking of the D is far from satisfactory, since it forces him to think of the span defined by the D as divided into two segments (the part before the beat and the part after), the second of which is longer than the first.

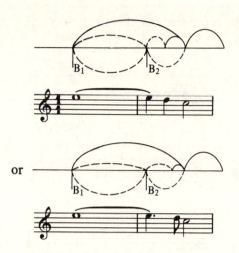

or

In the first case your listener can think of the D as marking the place where the C would have been if it hadn't been delayed.

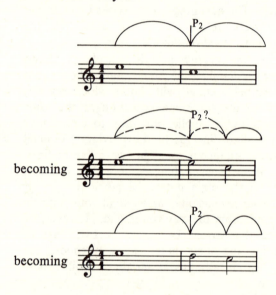

becoming

becoming

In the second case he can think of the D as creating a step motion from the second part of the E to the delayed C.

The first case is, of course, harder for him to grasp in that it involves thinking of the pitch of the D in terms of that of the C, but thinking of the point at which the C begins in terms of the point at which the D begins. Such situations are, however, extremely common in tonal music. In order to make it clear that the off-the-beat note is the *goal* of the step motion, it is always kept consonant with the simultaneously sounding notes in the other lines.

The on-the-beat note, however, is only an interior element in a step motion and thus may be dissonant.*

Whenever the second of two notes in a note-per-beat situation is delayed, the duration of the first note is extended beyond the second beat, so the span defined by the new first note is always segmented by the second beat. Any secondary operations must take account of that fact. Thus other operations that create segmentations are subject to the same constraints as the step motion. The second note of a rearticulation can occur on the beat†

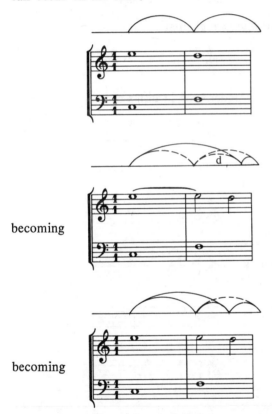

or off the beat (at any time from halfway between the beat and the delayed note to just before the delayed note).

---

* In order to make it clear that the point at which the on-the-beat pitch begins is indeed the beat and not (as it might appear because of the pitches associated with it) off the beat, the on-the-beat note is frequently played a shade louder and the off-the-beat notes a shade shorter. See Chapter 9.
† And can, if the delay produces a dissonant suspension, as in our example, create a dissonance between two on-the-beat notes.

may become

or

etc.

The same is true of a neighbor.

may become

or

etc.

Indeed, the same is even true of an incomplete neighbor.

may become

or

etc.

Arpeggiations and anticipatory arpeggiations, on the other hand, are limited by the length of the delayed note.

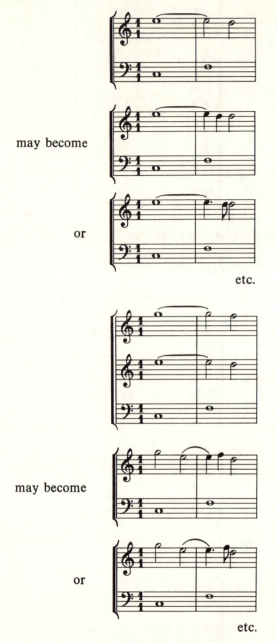

may become

or

etc.

may become

or

etc.

For note-per-beat situations with two primary beats and no secondary beats, the problem of segmentation of a note by a beat can only arise as the result of a delay, since only a delay will leave a beat unarticulated. However, as we shall see in Section 7.4, once we add secondary beats, this problem arises all the time.

Interest • Again, as we saw when we first constructed species lines, being able to predict how your listener will understand a series of notes says nothing about whether he will find your notes of any interest. As we saw in species, the problem of interest is much more elusive than that of ambiguity. However, we can at least state some rough guidelines that may prove useful later.

In the first part of this section we stated a general principle for resolving ambiguity: given two ways of understanding the same set of notes, your listener will choose the easier way. By turning this principle around we can come up with a general principle for creating interest that seems to work pretty well: given two comparable sets of notes (the same number of notes referred to the same number of beats), your listener's interest will be more engaged by the set of notes he has to work harder to understand. Specifically, this means the set of notes that makes him use

1. more stages to understand,
2. more problematic constructs,
3. unequal segments at the same stage or equal segments at different stages.

Thus, for example,

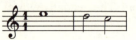

is "more interesting" than

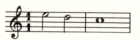

Both can be understood in terms of

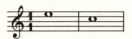

but the first passage makes your listener use two stages instead of one.

becoming

becoming

and

becoming

Similarly,

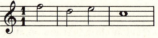

is "more interesting" than

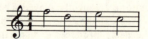

Both can be understood in terms of

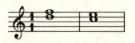

but the first passage makes your listener use anticipatory arpeggiations. And finally,

is "more interesting" than

Both can be understood in terms of

but the first passage makes your listener use unequal segments at the same stage and equal segments at different stages.

Drills

For each of the following operations, use the maximum duration available for any note or rest that begins at some new point in time. If you apply each operation to the notes that you got by the previous operation, you should end up with the first two measures of a line by Mozart.

1.

Delay the second C.

Embellish the two C's with a lower neighbor.

Arpeggiate the first pair of simultaneously sounding notes, stating the lower note first.

Subject the second pair of simultaneously sounding notes to an anticipatory arpeggiation, stating the upper note first.

Segment the final C into a note plus a rest (see the footnote on page 231).

Anticipate the last C.

Add an upper neighbor to the last two C's.

2.

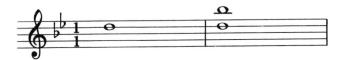

Rearticulate the first D and segment the notes in the second measure into half notes followed by a half rest.

Approach all three D's by incomplete upper neighbors and arpeggiate the simultaneously sounding notes stating the lower pitch first.

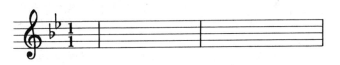

Anticipate all the D's.

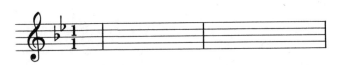

Exercises

1. In each of the following cases show how the passage on the bottom staff could be generated from the on-the-beat notes on the top staff:

2. Here are two ways of generating the same passage from a set of on-the-beat notes. Write a bass line to fit each way of understanding the passage. Limit both bass lines to the pitch succession G – F♯ – G.

7.4 Secondary Beats

So far, the only beats we have been concerned with have been a pair of independent reference points, B_1 and B_2. We have represented them as downbeats in a meter ($\frac{1}{1}$ or $\frac{1}{2}$) in which there are no other beats, our purpose being to avoid for the time being the problem of secondary beats—of thinking of one beat in terms of another. Of course, in actual music we do think of one beat in terms of another. Not only do we think of non-downbeats in terms of the downbeats before and after them, but, as we shall see in Chapter 8, we think of some downbeats in terms of other, conceptually prior, downbeats.

Suppose your listener conceives of the time between B_1 and B_2 as measured off by $n-1$ points, $b_1, b_2 \ldots b_{n-1}$ into n equal segments, $z_1, z_2, z_3, \ldots z_n$.* For example:

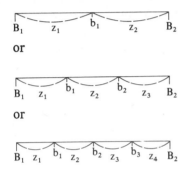

He could extend the series of equidistant points beyond B_2 or, if necessary, start them before B_1.

He can then use these points as secondary beats. That is, he can think of notes not on B_1 or B_2 in terms of their relationship to one or more b's, and then, in turn, think of the relationship of those b's to the primary beats, B_1 and B_2. These secondary beats are beats in that he can use them as reference points for conceiving of the points at which notes begin and the period of time they last. They are secondary in that he thinks of them in terms of other points of reference, the primary beats, B_1 and B_2.

When notes fall only on the primary beats, he uses the secondary beats as a way of measuring the spans defined by the notes.

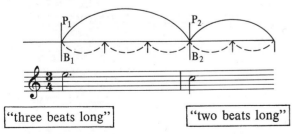

* Giving him reason to do so is another problem. See Section 7.5.

When a note falls on one of the secondary beats, he uses the secondary beats both to measure the period of time the note lasts and to locate the point at which the note begins with reference to the primary beats.

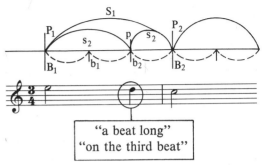

"a beat long"
"on the third beat"

(Thinking of p as being at b_2 gives him an immediate grasp of the comparative sizes of S_1, s_1, and s_2. He understands the segmentation of the span by the note at p in terms of the segments made by the points b_1 and b_2.) Now suppose your listener has divided the period between the two primary beats into four equal segments by creating three secondary beats. Suppose there are notes on both primary beats.

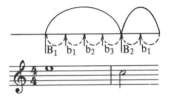

Suppose you want to segment the span defined by the first note by a step motion. If you put the D on the beat, you make it easy for your listener to grasp the situation.†

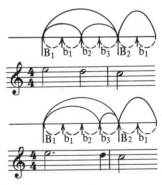

He can relate the D to the E and C and the primary beats on which they fall by means of the secondary beats between them. He can think of the E as lasting two (or three) beats and the D as lasting two (or one) beats. He can think of the D as beginning on the

† Putting the D on b_1 would create an unstable segmentation.

third* (or fourth) beat and know by this exactly how the point at which it begins is related to the two primary beats.

But if you put the D off the beat, you make it harder for him—indeed, in some cases impossible. Consider

In either case he can think of the E as consisting of two parts: the part before the fourth beat and the part after. Because the D lasts no longer than the part of the E after the fourth beat, he can think of the D either

1. as segmenting a span

which he in turn thinks of as a segment of a larger span

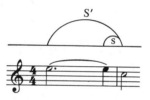

or 2. as a delayed version

of a note that would have begun on the previous beat.

On the other hand, consider

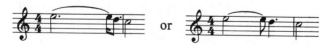

In neither case has your listener any way of thinking of the D in terms of b_3. In the first case he cannot consider the D as segmenting the span between b_3 and B_2, nor can he think of it as a delayed version of a D beginning at b_3 because the part of the E after b_3 is shorter than the D. In the second case he cannot think of the D as segmenting the span between b_2 and b_3, since no note begins at b_3,

(cf. )

nor can he think of it as a delayed version of a D that would have begun on b_2, since no note begins at b_3 nor could one have been delayed from b_3.

(cf. )

The same considerations apply when there are more than two segments to a span. Take

Suppose you want to connect the G to the C by step motion. If you put all the notes on the beat

your listener can use the secondary beats to understand the temporal relationship of the interior elements in the step motion to the goal and to the point of departure. If you put some—or even all—of the notes off the beat, he can still use the secondary beats to relate the interior elements to the **exterior** elements, as long as he can think of the segments you have created with your notes as segments of the spans he has defined with his secondary beats.

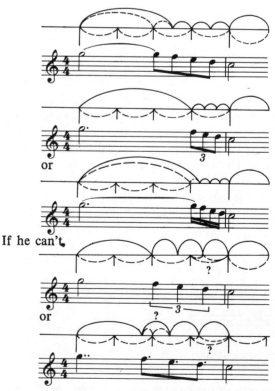

If he can't,

he can't use his secondary beat to relate your notes

---

* Counting the primary beat itself as the first beat.

to one another because he can't relate some of your notes to his beats.

You can avoid such difficulties by following these rules:

When one or more notes falls between two consecutive beats

1. there should be a note on the second of the two beats (or a note after the second beat that could be understood as a delayed version of a note that would have fallen on the second beat);
2. the note or notes falling between the two beats should segment the span defined by the two beats so that $s_1 \geq s_2 = s_3 \ldots = s_n$.

The same considerations apply to delays and anticipations. Suppose you want to delay the second note of

Your listener can extend his series of regularly spaced beats beyond the second primary beat.

Then if you put the delayed note on the first secondary beat after the second primary beat,

he has no trouble using the relationship of the secondary beat to the primary beat to understand the delay. If you begin the delayed note at a point halfway between that secondary beat and the next secondary beat

or at any point between that point and the next beat

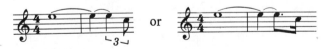

he can still use the first secondary beat as a way of relating the point at which the note actually begins to the point at which it would have begun.

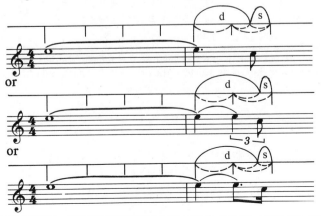

But if you begin it at some other point

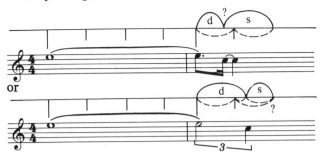

he can't.

Suppose you wanted to delay both notes in

If the secondary beats divide the spans between primary beats into two or four equal segments, there is no problem, since you can simply make each delay half of its respective span.

But if the secondary beats divide the spans into three equal segments, you can't.

The best you can do is either delay both notes by one beat, in which case the relationship of the delay to the original span is wrong,

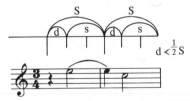

or delay both notes two beats, in which case the relationship of the part of the note that falls before the primary beat to the part of the note that falls after the primary beat is wrong.

Both are hard for your listener to grasp, but the latter is the easier of the two since segmentation is less problematic than delay, and the span defined by the primary beats is conceptually prior to the span defined by the new note.

Or suppose you want to anticipate the first note of

If your listener can extend the series of regular beats before the first primary beat,

then if you put the anticipation on the last or next to last secondary beat,

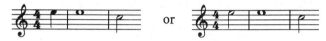

he can use the relationship of the secondary beat to the coming primary beat and to the span defined by both primary beats to help him understand the relationship of the anticipation to the anticipated note.

Or if you begin the anticipation halfway between the last secondary beat and the primary beat,

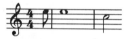

or at any point between that point and the primary beat, he can use the relationship between the secondary beat and the coming primary beat to relate the anticipation to the note being anticipated. Indeed, in all these cases, the secondary beats give him exactly what he needs to make the hard job of thinking of a note in terms of another note that hasn't happened yet relatively easy.

On the other hand, if you begin the anticipatory note somewhere else,

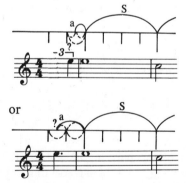

he has no way of using his secondary beats to understand your added note. They contradict each other.

Finally, the same considerations also apply to secondary segmentations, delays, and arpeggiations.

In applying secondary operations, make sure that the new notes either fall on secondary beats,

may become

or, if not, that there is either a note on the next beat

or at least a note after the next beat that can be construed as having been subsequently delayed from the next beat.

And make sure that any off-the-beat notes segment the spans defined by any two consecutive beats, secondary or primary, according to the rule $s_1 \geq s_2 = s_3 \ldots = s_n$

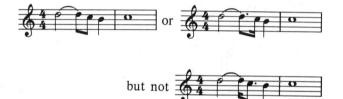

but not

If you do, your listener can use his beats to understand your notes. If you don't, he can't.*

---

* I am ignoring here rhythms like

(Beethoven, *Sonata* Op. 31, No.1, first movement, mm. 1–5.)

The tied notes can be understood as on-the-beat notes with anticipations

in which the attacks of the on-the-beat notes have been suppressed. This is possible because the notes in the left hand articulate the points at which the on-the-beat notes would have occurred.

Drills

1. Which of the following are *not* subject to the constraints presented in this section?

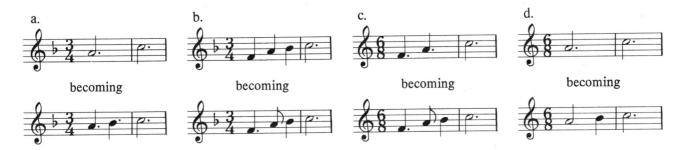

2. Connect the pitches of the given notes by step motion, segmenting the span defined by the duration of the first given note and giving the maximum duration possible to each interior element in the step motion.

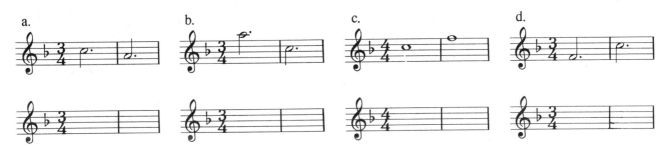

3. Delay the second note by the minimum possible delay period.

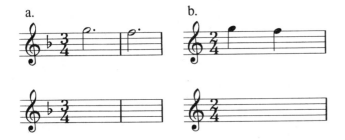

4. Add an incomplete neighbor to the second note so as to create an anticipatory segment of maximum duration.

Exercises

Show how each of the following passages from *The Marriage of Figaro* could be generated from the given note-per-measure models.

(Mozart: *The Marriage of Figaro*, Act I, "Non più andrai," mm. 1–5.)

(*Ibid.*, Act II, "Voi che sapete," mm. 9–12.)

3.

(*Ibid.*, Act II, "Porgi amor," mm. 18–21.)

Supplementary Exercises

Here are the opening two measures of Haydn's Quartet, Op. 64, No. 3.

1. Show how the violin and cello lines can be understood as generated from the following measure-long span pitches:

2. Suppose that these two measures had been in $\frac{6}{8}$ instead of $\frac{3}{4}$. How could they be understood as generated from the same set of span pitches?

267

7.5 Establishing Beats

In the last two sections we dealt with beats as though the listener's choice of which points in time to use as references were an arbitrary decision over which the composer had no control. Now it is true that each listener creates his own set of reference points in his own mind and understands your notes in terms of them. Just because you think of your notes in terms of a particular set of reference points needn't mean that your listener will use the same set. Nor do you have any way of telling him directly, "Use this point as a point of reference," or "Don't use this point."*

On the other hand, his only reason for creating a set of reference points is to understand the notes you've chosen. Unlike the listener in Sections 7.3 and 7.4, he is hardly likely to establish his reference points before he has heard a note of music. Presumably he will wait until he's heard a few of your notes and then choose those points that will give him the simplest, most complete way of understanding your notes.

Establishing an Initial Beat • The first question is then: how do you get your listener to think of a particular point in time (P) as his first reference point or beat (B_1)? You could, of course, just give him a note that begins at P.

But that is not really enough. The beginning of a note may articulate for him the point in time you have in mind, but it gives him no reason to think of that point as a reference point. What you need is another note that begins at another point, p, that he must think of in terms of P. For example:†

---

* Actually, this is exactly what the "rhythm section" does to establish "the beat" in traditional jazz. The fact that the beat is explicitly presented by the instruments with the most clearly defined attacks (percussion, bass, guitar, and piano) means that the other instruments are free to project rhythmic structures that make the Beethoven example on page 262 seem like child's play.

† Note the absence of the delay operation here. You might be thinking of the note at p in terms of the point P, but how would he know where P was?

Given these pitches and these durations, he has no other way of understanding these notes except in terms of a span beginning at P.†† He has to understand p in terms of P. This being the case, he might as well locate B at P, since he is already using P that way anyway.

Indeed, putting B anywhere else would leave him with either

a. no satisfactory way of understanding your notes in terms of his beat,

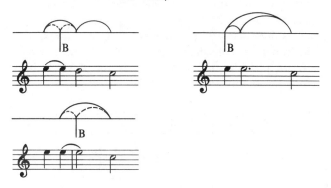

or b. a much more complicated way of understanding your notes in terms of his beat,

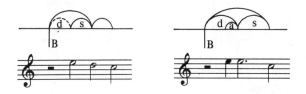

or c. a way of understanding your first three notes that will only work if the third note turns out

---

†† Compare what happens when you give him a succession of notes like

that he can understand in two different ways.

In such cases he'll put his beat wherever he chooses to think the span begins.

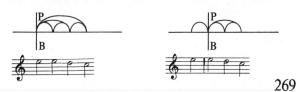

to begin a second span at least twice the length of the first.*

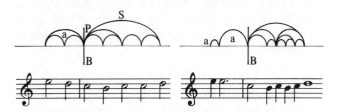

Establishing Subsequent Beats • Having established the first reference point, the next problem is to get your listener to think of specific subsequent points in time as subsequent points of reference. Essentially, the methods at your disposal are not that different from those you used to establish the initial beat. There is, however, one important further consideration: your listener will want to make his reference points equally spaced so that he can use some of them as secondary beats measuring off the time between the others, which he can then consider primary beats. Now, obviously, if you provide him with a succession of spans beginning at equally spaced points, P_1, P_2, P_3 . . .

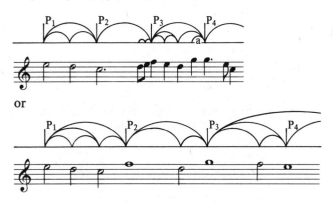

there is no problem. He can simply put his beats at these points.

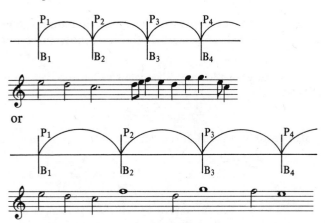

* Note that in both the examples the secondary beat at P is implied anyway.

On the other hand, if you give him a series of spans beginning at unequally spaced points,

he will resist putting his beats at those points.

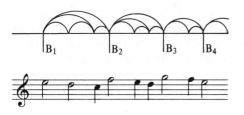

Instead, he will do everything he can to think of your notes in terms of an equally spaced set of beats—even though this may entail understanding your notes in a much more complicated way. For example:

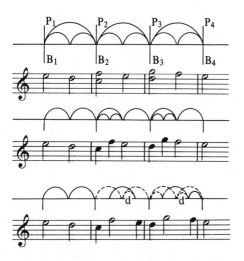

In effect, then, all you have to do to establish a particular set of equally spaced beats is to give your listener a series of notes that can most efficiently be understood in terms of those beats, and only those beats.

More Than One Line at a Time • So far, all our examples have been single lines. However, the same principles that hold for one line hold for more than one line as well. Obviously, if you give both your lines the same span structure,

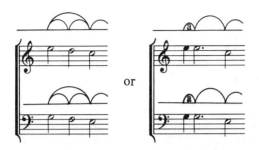

your listener will use as beats the same points he would use if he heard either line separately.

Indeed, if you just make the principal spans of both lines start at the same points,

he will use those points as beats even though the details of structure are different.

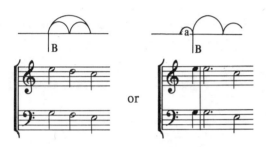

If anything, such differences make it easier for him to arrive at the one choice of reference points that will work for both lines. For example, if one of the lines could be understood in two ways,

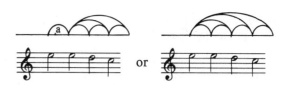

but the spans in one of the ways start at the same points as the spans in the other line,

and

the ambiguity is resolved.

If you give your lines principal spans beginning at different points in time,

and

your listener will have to work a little harder. He will have to find some way of understanding these different points in terms of a single set of reference points, either by considering the earlier of the two points as the reference point and the second as the result of a delay,

or by reinterpreting the earlier of the two spans as the result of anticipation or anticipatory arpeggiation.

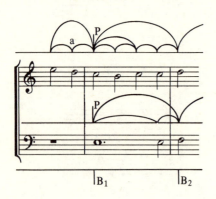

Secondary Beats and the Problem of Tempo • So far, we have been ignoring secondary beats. Suppose you gave your listener a line that he could understand in terms of a series of equally spaced beats. For example:

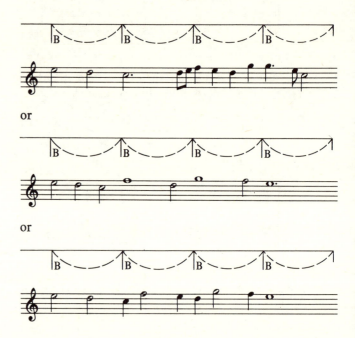

And suppose that between these beats there were other points that divided the time between beats into equal segments;

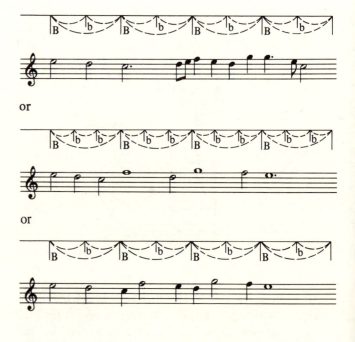

such that no other notes divided a segment improperly

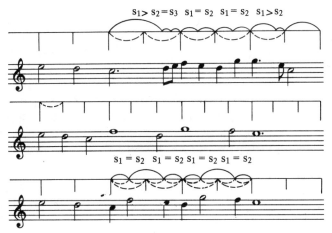

and no other point divided a note improperly.

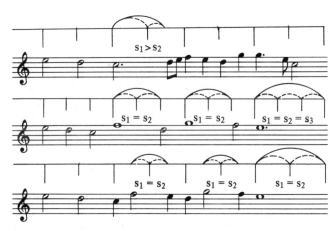

Now the question is: under what conditions will your listener want to use these other points as secondary beats? This question is not easy to answer. The answer depends largely on how useful such points are to your listener in understanding these notes. That, in turn, will depend on two factors: structural considerations and tempo. As for structural considerations, take the first example:

Obviously, he doesn't really need b_1 to think of the D in terms of B_1 and B_2. But b_1's presence doesn't make the conceptual process any more difficult. On the other hand, b_2, if anything, makes the process of relating the second D and E to B_2 more complicated. The first of the b's to prove distinctly useful to him is b_3. He has to think of the E just before it in terms of the F and the D, and he has to have some means of measuring the time taken by the G just after it to make sure it is no longer than half the coming span. Although not absolutely necessary, b_3 is helpful to him in both cases. On the other hand, take the second example:

Here the b's are of no particular help in understanding the structure, beyond giving your listener a convenient unit for measuring how long each note is.

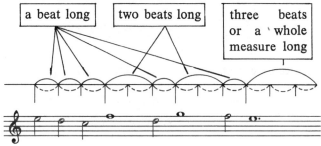

Finally, take the third example:

The first b is not particularly useful, but the next two are because they mark the points at which the delayed E and F would have begun.

The tempo brings in a number of factors we have been ignoring since Part I. Suppose the half notes in the first example lasted one second each.

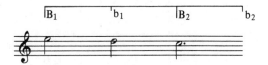

That would mean that the time elapsed between B's would be two seconds. Most listeners find this a very long time to keep track of without some interior sub-

Prestissimo*

(Beethoven: Sonata. Op 10, No. 1, last movement)

articulations to help them.† It is very difficult to know where you are during a period of time as long as the one and a half seconds of that dotted half note. The fact that the first three notes have just neatly articulated a smaller unit of time twice makes it difficult not to use b_1 and b_2.

On the other hand, suppose the whole note were to take only half a second.

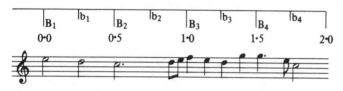

Putting secondary reference points between the B's would mean thinking of the notes in terms of four reference points per second—a rate that most listeners find too exhausting to be useful.

The rate at which reference points occur is called *tempo*. When we measure such rates with a metronome we count the number of beats per minute. Thus, if there is a beat every two seconds, there would be 30 per minute. If we are using a half note to represent the span between two consecutive beats, the metronome marking would be M ♩ = 30. If there are four beats per second there will be 240 per minute or M ♩ = 240. Between these two extremes lies a whole range of more useful tempos. Most musicians would consider a rate around M ♩ = 84 as a moderate tempo. Twice that fast (M ♩ = 168) is very fast but still useful, and twice that slow (M ♩ = 42) is very slow but still useful. A beat per second (M ♩ = 60) seems moderately slow, while two beats per second (M ♩ = 120) seems moderately fast.

number of beats per minute	time between beats	
30	2^1 sec. (2.0″)	too slow to be useful
42	$2^{\frac{1}{2}}$ sec. (1.414″)	very slow

* *Prestissimo* = "very fast".
† See Section 8.0.

number of beats per minute	time between beats	
60	2^0 sec. (1.0″)	moderately slow
84	$2^{-\frac{1}{2}}$ sec. (0.70″)	moderate
120	2^{-1} sec. (0.5″)	moderately fast
168	$2^{-1\frac{1}{2}}$ sec. (0.35″)	very fast
240	2^{-2} sec. (0.25″)	too fast to be useful

If you play our example

at o = 42 your listener will probably understand it in terms of a beat every half note—a moderate tempo is less effort for him than a fast one and there is nothing in these notes that demands a whole-note beat. Similarly, if you play the same example at o = 84 he will probably understand it in terms of a beat every whole note—a moderate tempo is less effort for him than a very fast one, and there is nothing in these notes that demands a half-note beat, either.

On the other hand, if you play the example at o = 60, your listener could either hear it in terms of a moderately slow tempo with a beat every whole note or in terms of a moderately fast tempo with a beat every note.

In a fast tempo, to get your listener to use secondary beats you have to give him notes that are substantially easier to understand with secondary beats than without them; for example, you could anticipate an anticipation or an anticipatory arpeggiation (see above). In a slow tempo, to keep your listener from using secondary beats you have to give him notes that cannot be under-

(Mahler: *Das Lied von der Erde,* "Der Abschied," mm. 433–439.)

* *Sehr mässig*: literally, "very moderate"; understood as meaning "rather slow."

stood in terms of secondary beats—for example, you could segment one span between primary beats into two equal segments and another into three (see above).

Changing the Pattern of Beats • Once your listener has arrived at a regular pattern of primary and secondary beats he will want to keep on using the same pattern over and over again. Getting him to change patterns is often harder than getting him to choose a given pattern in the first place.

It is relatively easy to get him to add secondary beats in the course of a passage. All you have to do is use notes that require more frequent reference points. (See Mozart example immediately below.)

It is considerably harder to get him to suppress secondary beats in the course of a passage. Even though he doesn't need a secondary beat to understand the notes you give him, as long as the secondary beats don't get in the way of understanding the notes, it usually requires less mental effort to continue to use them at the same rate (See Strauss example at the bottom of the page.)

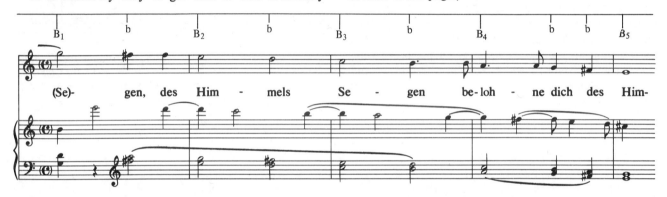

(Mozart: *Die Entführung aus dem Serail,* Act II, "Martern aller Arten," mm. 109–113.)

(R. Strauss: *Four Last Songs,* "Beim Schlafengehen," mm. 56–59.)

To get him to suppress a secondary beat it is usually necessary to make it downright impossible for him to understand your notes in terms of that beat.

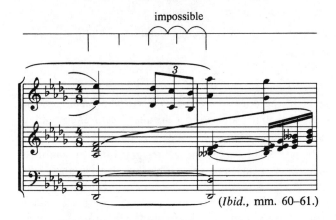

(*Ibid.*, mm. 60–61.)

The trickiest kind of change to project is that in which a point that would have been a primary beat had the pattern continued becomes a secondary beat, while a point that would have been a secondary beat becomes a primary beat. The classic form of such a change is the *hemiola*: suppose that a pattern has been established such that for a given period of time there are six beats of which four are secondary and two are primary.

A hemiola occurs when during an equal period of time there are again six beats, but three of them are primary and three secondary.

To project a hemiola you must make sure that it is either impossible or at least considerably less efficient for your listener to understand your notes in terms of the previously established pattern.

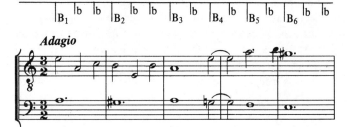

(Handel: *Sonata for Gamba and Harpsichord*, third movement, mm. 1–5.)

Exercises

Use the given note-per-measure structure to generate a pair of lines that will project the given meter at the given tempo.

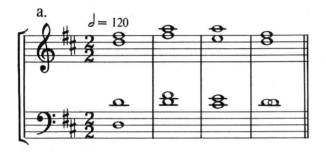

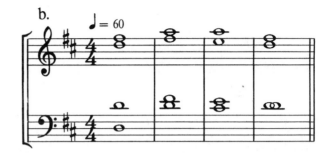

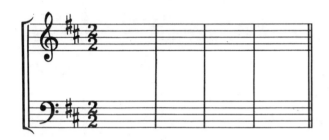

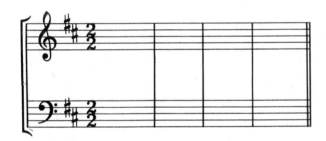

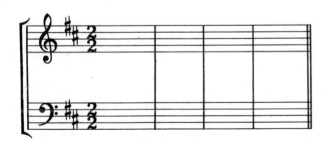

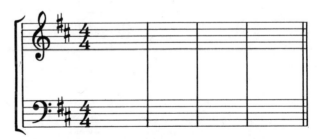

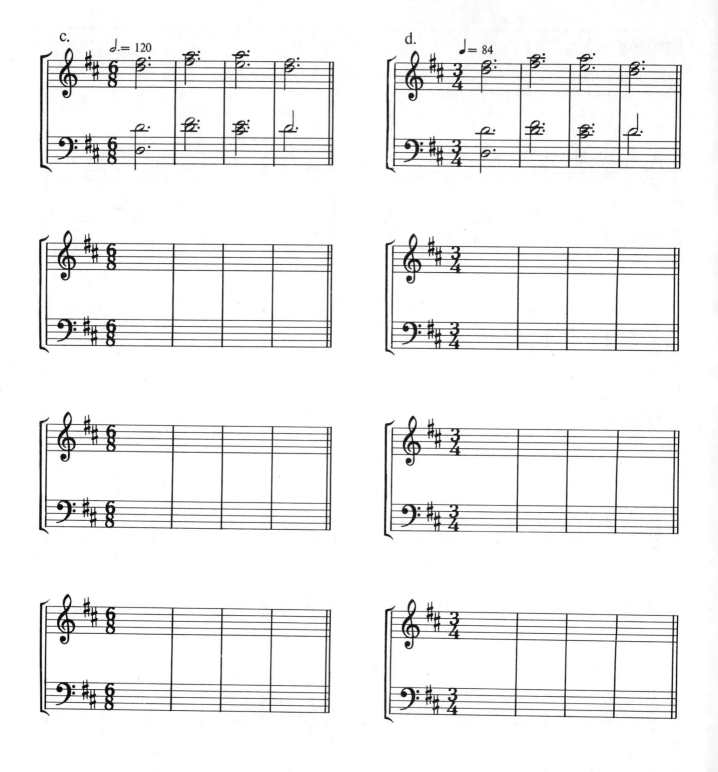

Supplementary Assignment

Examine the examples in the assignment following Section 9.2. Could the pitches and durations of any of them be construed as establishing a different set of reference points from those indicated by the notation? Which and why?

7.6 Non-Diatonic Voice Leading Procedures: Chromatic Neighbors and Chromatic Step Motions

Now that we have established a basic set of temporal constraints under which we can connect pitches to form the fundamental linear operations of tonal music, we can begin to consider some of the other linear operations that are available to us. In particular we can begin to consider how

1. pitch classes outside the diatonic collection may be used, and
2. pitch classes belonging to one line may appear in another.

The first problem will be dealt with in this section, the second in the next.

So far, the pitch material of our examples has been limited for the most part to that used in species counterpoint: the degrees of the diatonic collection plus the raised sixth and seventh degrees in minor. The voice-leading procedures have been essentially those learned in species, although, as we have already seen, the principles of tonal rhythm allow a number of other procedures not possible in species: anticipations, anticipatory arpeggiations, incomplete neighbors, and on-the-beat passing tones and dissonant neighbors. These same principles also allow us to extend our voice-leading procedures to include pitches not in the diatonic collection.

Chromatic Neighbors • A neighbor a major second from the note it embellishes may be altered so that it is only a minor second from that note. For example, in C major [notation] may become [notation] and [notation] may become [notation]. The great advantage of chromatic neighbors is the way they help clarify the function of the notes involved. The relationship of a neighbor to the note it embellishes depends on the proximity of its pitch to the pitch of the other note. By altering the pitch of the neighbor so that it is (1) no longer a member of the diatonic collection and (2) closer to the pitch it embellishes, we increase its dependence on the pitch it embellishes.

Take a passage like

(Haydn: *Quartet* Op. 3, No. 3, fourth movement, mm. 1–4.)

It is easy to understand the C♯ as an incomplete neighbor to the D, with the preceding C♮ as an anticipatory arpeggiation that eventually moves down to B.

becoming

Had both these pitches been the diatonic pitch C♮, their separate functions would have been much less clear.

In general, the more complex the situation, the greater the possibility of unwanted ambiguity and therefore the more useful a chromatic alteration. For incomplete lower neighbors on the beat, chromatic alteration is often absolutely necessary to the sense of the passage. Compare the following:

Allegretto

Allegretto

(Mozart: *Sonata* K.547a, second movement, mm. 1–5.)

Where both upper and lower neighbors are used together and one of them is a minor second from the note embellished and the other is chromatically altered, a diminished third results.

281

becoming

becoming

(Beethoven: *Quartet* Op. 18, No. 4, third movement, mm. 36–40.)

In minor, the double neighbor to the tonic formed by the lowered second degree and the raised seventh is often found in cadences.† The lowered second degree has the advantage of forming a perfect fifth or fourth with the sixth degree.

The bass can then complete the triadic sonority with the fourth degree as a neighbor or step motion to the dominant.

* Note that in this example four upper neighbors, the C, the G, the A♭, and the F, have not been lowered. In general, we can say that for any diatonic collection the degrees further from the start tend to get lowered most often. This tendency is particularly strong in minor.

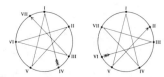

For any diatonic collection, the first two pitch classes to be generated will always be only one semitone above the last two to be generated. In major this means that there is no point in lowering I and IV; they are already as close to VII and III as they can get. The same is true for VI and III in minor; they are already only a minor second above V and II. In minor, VII is already the lower of two available forms; to lower it further would make it enharmonically equivalent to a raised VI. Lowering IV in minor could result in confusion with the raised III borrowed from the major collection (see *Mixture* in Section 8.7). Similarly, lowering I could result in confusion with the raised form of VII.
† See Section 8.2.

Such a collection is commonly called a "Neapolitan sixth."‡

Chromatic Step Motion • Consecutive notes a major second apart may be connected by a note with the intervening pitch to create a chromatic step motion.§ The new note may either segment the span of the original first note,

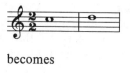

becomes

or the second note may be delayed, with the new note marking the point at which the second note would have occurred.

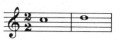

becomes

which becomes

‡ The sixth referred to is the interval between the fourth degree in the bass and the lowered second degree in one of the upper lines. What is so Neapolitan about lowering the second degree is less clear. In any case, the term is in common use.
§ The intervening pitch is usually written as the raised form of the first pitch in the step if the step motion goes up and as the lowered form of the first pitch if the step motion goes down.

Thus

may become

(Haydn: *Quartet* Op. 74, No. 1, first movement, mm. 3–6.)

and

may become

which in turn may become

(Chopin: *Prelude* Op. 28, No. 1, mm. 16–21.)

Chromatic step motion is particularly useful in intensifying the sense of motion in a passage. The principal danger in using it extensively is that the listener may lose the sense of which pitches are the diatonic degree pitches and which the chromatic additions. Given just

how is he to tell that the long notes aren't the original ones?

Of course, the listener isn't given just these notes. Notice the way the bass forms parallel sixths with the short notes

and notice how the pitches forming the sixths can all be understood as members of a single diatonic collection (C major). Notice also that the two places where there is no intervening pitch between members of this collection—between the E and the F and between the B and the C—are handled differently. The E is repeated, the B is skipped from. Finally, the notes in the other lines belong to the C-major diatonic collections and create dissonances with the long notes.

However, if all the lines have chromatic step motion, it may be difficult to discern which diatonic collection is involved. We can understand

in terms of the addition of on-the-beat chromatic step motions to

but no one would claim it is easy to do so. In such a situation the listener must pay sharp attention to such matters as

1. the pitches left hanging in each line (in this case the A that is skipped from at the beginning and the E, G♯, D, and B left sounding at the end) and
2. any form of redundancy between lines (in this case the exchange of G♯ to B and B to G♯ in the upper line in each staff and the F–E's in mm. 1–2 and 3–4).

Otherwise, he's lost.

In each of the preceding examples we showed how you could connect two diatonic pitches a major second apart by the non-diatonic pitch between them. Thus, in each of the preceding examples the non-diatonic pitches were always thought of as subsidiary to the diatonic pitches. But suppose you want to connect two pitches more than a major second apart by a chromatic step motion? You can, of course, do this, but unless you make it distinctly easier for your listener to understand your passage that way, chances are he will understand your notes in terms of whatever diatonic degrees he finds convenient. Of course, if the step motion is very rapid,

(Wolf: *Mörike-Lieder*, "Lied vom Winde," mm. 1–4.)

he isn't given time to think of each non-diatonic pitch in terms of a diatonic one. He will just think of the whole motion as one operation, getting him from one

(Wagner: *Tristan und Isolde*, Prelude, mm. 1–3.)

pitch to another by way of all the intervening pitches. Or if the motion is combined with other motions

(Wolf: *Italienisches Liederbuch,* "Selig ihr Blinden," mm. 19–22.)

that make it relatively difficult to conceive of some of the interior elements in the step motion as conceptually prior

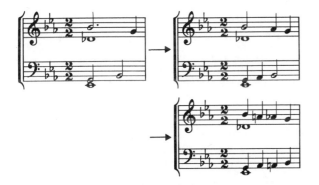

and relatively easy to think of them all as equivalent,

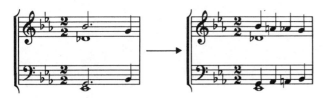

he can dispense with any diatonic basis for the motion and consider it purely chromatic.

One other form of step motion involving pitches outside the diatonic collection should be mentioned here. We saw in species that the sixth and seventh degrees are raised in ascending step motion in the minor. Instead of

we wrote

instead of

we wrote

By altering the pitch of the interior element or elements in the step motion, we made them closer to the destination pitch, thus intensifying the sense of motion toward that pitch. Instead of having the minor second come between the first two notes in the motion, or between two interior notes, it is between the last two notes, thereby intensifying the sense of arrival at the last note. The same principle is used in actual tonal music.

(Beethoven: *Quartet* Op. 95, first movement, mm. 1–2.)

Exercises

Fill in the missing notes in the successive stages according to instructions.

 l = lower neighbor
 u = upper neighbor
 s = step motion (interior element in a step motion)
 ant. = anticipation
 etc. = continue the pattern of arpeggiation shown

Which of the neighbors and interior elements in step motions *must* be chromatic to be understood properly?

How many of the neighbors and step motions *can* be chromatic without damage to the sense of degree identity?

287

7.7 Some New Principles of Linear Generation: Doubling, Borrowing, Exchange, and Transfer

So far, we have been treating each line in a set of simultaneously sounding lines just as we did in species—as a separate structural entity. To be sure, we understand the notes of all the lines in terms of the pitch classes of a common tonic triad and its diatonic collection and a common set of beats. But so far we have taken pains to show how the structure of each line is based on its own specific group of triad pitches which have been connected and embellished by nontriad pitches to form its own specific span structure. To be sure, the specific structure of one line can influence the way we understand the structure of another line. But so far, we have avoided using the pitches of one line to show how another line is constructed. To understand tonal music, however, we must develop a far more flexible concept of line than the one we used for species counterpoint.

We will use the word "line" to refer to any series of notes that we have reason to understand as connected to form a single strand.* There are different kinds of reasons for understanding one note as connected to another and, hence, there are different kinds of lines. Where a series of notes is played by a single instrument or sung by one voice, we speak of an instrumental or vocal line, for example, the clarinet line or the tenor line. When a series of notes maintains the same registral relations to the other notes present, we speak of a registral line, for example, the top line or the middle line.** Finally, when a series of notes forms a span and pitch structure that gives us a way of understanding other notes in terms of that structure, we speak of a structural line.

Doubling and Borrowing • In Section 4.3 we made a distinction between parallel octaves or unisons and doubling. Thus, in a passage like

(Beethoven: *Quartet* Op. 18, No. 1, first movement, mm. 1–4.)

we do not think of the first-violin line as forming parallel unisons with the second-violin line or parallel octaves with the viola and cello lines; we think of the other three instruments as "doubling the cello line."† Doublings are common in tonal music, not only between instrumental lines as in the example above, but between registral or structural lines as well. Thus, in the following example

(Corelli: *Sonata* Op. 5, No. 10, third movement, mm. 1–4.)

the bass line can be understood in terms of a single note-per-measure structural line, doubled by another line with the same structure but in a different register.

The octaves formed by these two lines are then arpeggiated

and the upper note delayed a beat.

Either or both of the lines involved in a doubling may be subjected to further operations:††

---

* By series I mean the notes do not sound simultaneously. By connected I mean they are to be understood as consecutive rather than contiguous. See Section 3.0.
** Unfortunately the words for vocal lines are commonly used for registral lines: the alto line in a piece for piano means "next to highest line." This terminology is confusing for pieces using singers; there is no reason to assume that the altos will always be singing the next to highest line.

† Or of the other three instruments as doubling the first violin line, for that matter. There is no way we can tell from these four measures which line is the original one and which the doubling lines. See the next page.
†† Note how difficult it is to explain the D in m. 2. If we want to think of it as a neighbor to C♯, we must imagine a C♯ on the second beat:

We will discuss some of the implications of this D for the *Menuetto* as a whole in Section 8.6.

becoming

The practice of doubling creates a new type of structural ambiguity: how is the listener to know which line is the original line and which line is merely a doubling of that line? Such ambiguities can usually be resolved by examining what the lines in question are doing just before or after the doubling. It usually proves more convenient to regard whichever line has the greater continuity of structure before or after the doubling as the "original" line. Thus, given two more measures of the Mozart example just cited,

(Mozart: *Sonata* K.331, second movement, mm. 1–4.)

we would presumably understand the upper structural line in mm. 1–2 as the original line and the lower lines as doubling, since the upper line continues the pattern of m. 2 in m. 3, while the two lower lines rest and then take up new functions. Similarly, given four more measures of the Corelli example,

we would understand the lower of the two registrally defined lines as the original structural line, since its A is connected to the dominant in m. 7 by step motion. Finally, given four more measures of the Beethoven example,

we would assume that the cello line is the original and the others doubling, since only in the cello line is the underlying structural line—C–D–E–F—completed.

In each of the foregoing examples we showed how a new line could be created by doubling an already existing line at the unison or octave. It is, however, also possible to get more pitches for the structure of an already existing line by *borrowing* them from another already existing line.

Suppose you wanted to write a phrase with two lines based on the following structure:

You can avoid the parallel fifths by arpeggiating in a downward direction all the thirds except the first and last in the bass.

To make the bass move at a uniform eighth-note rate you can use rearticulation, neighbor embellishments, and step motions.

It is harder to get a line with any sense of motion out of the upper structure. The problem is that there is nothing to arpeggiate, and rearticulations and neighbors don't create much sense of motion.

Suppose, on the other hand, you were to get some other pitches for the upper structure by *borrowing* them from the lower structure.

(Note that since the upper line is in a different register from the lower line, the borrowed pitches are not exactly the same as those in the line from which they were borrowed, but are rather members of the same pitch class.) You can then use these pitches in arpeggiations to create a more interesting line:

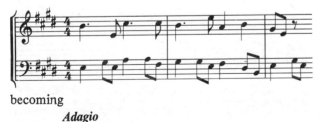

becoming

Adagio

(Corelli: *Sonata* Op. 5, No. 11, first movement, mm. 1–3.)

In this example the note with the borrowed pitch occurs *during* the span defined by the note from which the pitch is borrowed.

In such a case the note with the borrowed pitch forms one segment of a span defined by whatever note was present in that line prior to the borrowing operation.

It and the other segment (or segments) of that span are subject to the law of segmentation. Thus, for example:

might become

or

but not

However, it is also possible to place the note with the borrowed pitch *just before* the span defined by the note from which the pitch is borrowed.

291

In such a case the note with the borrowed pitch both segments the span defined by whatever note was present in its line at that point prior to the borrowing operation and anticipates the span defined by the note in the other line from which it gets its pitch.

Here the duration of the note with the borrowed pitch is subject both to the law of segmentation and to the law of anticipation. Thus

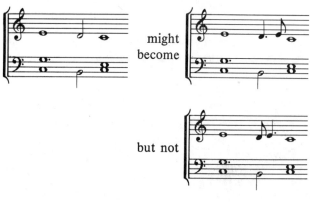

and

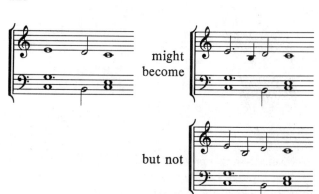

Borrowing is common in tonal music. Note that
1. the pitch need not be the exact same pitch, it need only be a member of the same pitch class.

becoming

(Corelli: *Sonata* Op. 4, No. 6, first movement, mm. 1–3.)

2. If the line from whose structure the borrowed pitch comes moves to another pitch,

becoming

(Corelli: *Sonata* Op. 5, No. 11, first movement, mm. 2–3.)

or has a rest,

becoming

(Corelli: *Sonata* Op. 5, No. 10, third movement, mm. 1–4.)

no octave or unison between simultaneously sounding notes will occur. But if the line from whose structure the borrowed pitch comes does not move,

(Corelli: *Sonata* Op. 4, No. 6, first movement, mm. 1.)

or returns to that pitch just as its borrowed form appears,

(Corelli: *Sonata* Op. 5, No. 11, first movement, mm. 1–2.)

a unison or octave between simultaneously sounding notes will occur. If two or more consecutive notes in a structure are borrowed for another structure, this may result in parallel unisons or octaves.

(Corelli: *Sonata* Op. 4, No. 6, first movement, mm. 1–2.)

(Corelli: *Sonata* Op. 5, No. 9, second movement, mm. 1–2.)

As long as the second of the two parallel intervals falls off the beat, such parallelism is considered perfectly respectable.

3. Where the borrowed pitch is a member of the tonic triad,

(Corelli: *Sonata* Op. 5, No. 11, first movement, mm. 1–3.)

or where the last of a series of consecutive borrowed pitches is a triad pitch,

(Corelli: *Sonata* Op. 4, No. 6, first movement, mm. 1–4.)

borrowing creates no new conceptual problems for the listener. Indeed, we could even think of the borrowed pitches as part of the underlying structure of the borrowing line. For example:

and:

But when the pitch is a non-triad pitch, functioning as a neighbor or interior element in a step motion in the structure from which it was borrowed, it may be left hanging in its new position.*

Consider the following situation in which the first-violin line borrows a G from the viola line, while the viola line borrows a B from the second-violin line.

(Haydn: *Symphony* No. 104, first movement, mm. 17–18.)

The G in the viola and the B in the second violin are perfectly comprehensible within their own lines as interior elements in a step motion. But the G in the first violin and the B in the viola are left hanging. That is, they are given no destination in their respective lines within the time spans they imply.

It might be possible to understand the first violin's G as a neighbor to the F♯ in the next measure,

becoming

becoming

but the viola has rests for the next five measures. Two factors keep the total situation comprehensible:

1. There is no question about the function of the B and the G in their original lines. Both notes get where they are going at the expected time.

becoming

becoming

becoming

2. The B and the G are not left hanging in the borrowing lines forever. The cadence seven measures later brings G down to F♯ and the viola moves from the F♯ (the pitch the line had before the five measures of rests) to an A (a pitch that would have explained the B as a neighbor).

The first of these two factors shows a precondition for any borrowing procedure: whatever the borrowed pitch does in the line for which it is borrowed, the original pitch must form part of a completed structure in the line from which it was borrowed. Without this precondition, borrowing would easily result in a situation in which any pitch could happen at any time and the whole set of constraints by means of which we understand tonal music would come tumbling down. The second of these two factors is an example of one way in which composers have used borrowing to set up pitch connections *outside* the span system.

---

* A situation that was rare in the music of Corelli's time but common in the music of Haydn's time.

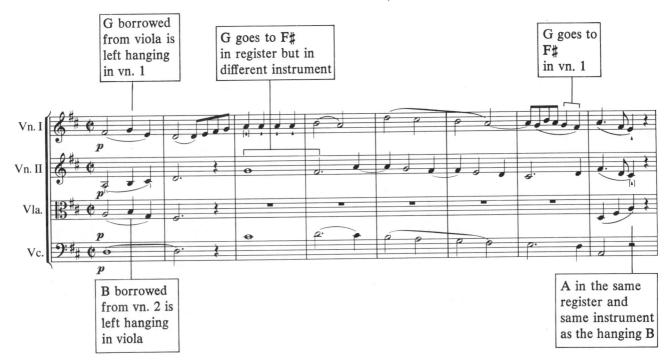

By leaving a pitch hanging in one line you can whet your listener's appetite for certain pitches in certain registers. If you then avoid pitches in that register for a while (or, as in the viola example, use no notes in that line for a while), when you do return with just the pitches your listener has been deprived of, he will attach that much more importance to them (see above).

Exchange • One particularly useful form of borrowing is the exchange.* In an exchange, two lines simply borrow from one another at the same time, that is they exchange pitches, or at least pitch classes.

The exchange may be used to create contrary motion spanning identical intervals

(Corelli: *Sonata* Op. 4, No. 5, third movement, m. 11.)

or similar motion spanning intervals that are octave complements of one another.

becoming

(Beethoven: *Symphony* No. 8, third movement, mm. 45–46.)

---

* Sometimes called by the German term *Stimmtausch*: literally "exchange of voices." We used this technique to create pairs of compound lines in Section 6.2.

Transfers • When the process of borrowing results in what is best described as a permanent loan—that is where the linear structure from which the pitch has been borrowed makes no further use of that pitch, while the linear structure for which it has been borrowed makes it a point of further departure—we say the pitch has been *transferred* from one line to another.

instead of

we have

(Beethoven: *Quartet* Op. 18, No. 1, first movement, mm. 4–6.)

In a transfer, the line that receives the transferred pitch takes over any structural obligations the pitch had in the line it came from. Thus, if the transferred pitch is a neighbor or an interior element in a step motion in the line it came from, it must go to its destination pitch in the new line instead of the old, and it must get there on time.

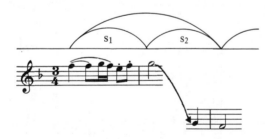

Thus, the line taking over the transferred pitch carries it to its destination, but as a result, the last pitch in the other line may be left hanging.

Such a pitch may, of course, eventually get to where it was going in that line, but it need not do so within the time limits set by the local span structure.

Transfers may occur between instrumental lines, between registral lines, or between structural lines. However, when a transfer occurs between two lines in one of these categories, we can usually understand the notes on both sides of the transfer as forming a single line in some other category. The single line is thus more fundamental to our understanding of the passage than the two lines between which the transfer occurs. For example, in a passage like

(Mozart: *Symphony* No. 40, first movement, mm. 44–47.)

we could say that the E♭ is transferred from the first-violin line to the clarinet line, but the point is that there is a single top line whose structure is clarified by changes in timbre.

(The underlying structure of the passage can be understood as

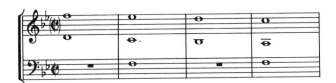

Although the E♭–D is broken by a borrowed B♮ and a borrowed F,

becoming

the connection is still easy to hear because the E♭ is left hanging in the first-violin line until it is picked up some two measures later in the same line.)

Or in the clarinet line of the passage below, we could say that the D is transferred to a registral line an octave lower before moving on to the E♭ and that the same thing happens to the E♭ before it moves to the E♮,

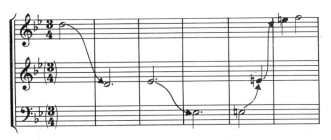

but the point is that there is a simple linear structure—D–E♭–E♮–F—that is being clarified by being passed through various registers.

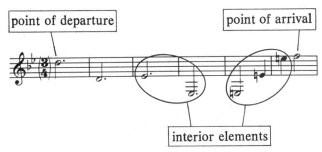

Octave Transfers • The last example shows the most problematic type of transfer, the "octave transfer." In an octave transfer we let a pitch take on the structural role of some other member of the same class. This confusion between pitch identity and pitch-class identity, and between interval identity and interval-class identity can be disturbing. Octave transfers must

(Schubert: *Der Hirt auf dem Felsen*, D.965, mm. 22–30.)

be handled with great care if they are to be understood by the listener as such. Note that in the Schubert example

1. the transfer is made explicit by stating both members of the pitch class

thus

2. the transferred line has an easily grasped relationship to another line that has no transfer

and 3. the notes in the transferred line are doubled in other octaves by other instrumental lines.

Where the first condition is not met,

(R. Strauss: *Four Last Songs,* "Beim Schlafengehn," mm. 1–2.)

it is often easier to understand what might appear to be transferred step motions

becoming

becoming

as arpeggiation with incomplete neighbors.

becoming

becoming

Where the third condition holds, it is usually easier to understand what appear to be transfers within a line as borrowings from other lines (see below). Indeed, this is often the listener's best way of avoiding octave transfers. What appears locally to be an octave transfer can, in the long run, often be reconstrued as an octave borrowing. Thus, I find it easier to think of

becoming

298

becoming

which in turn becomes

the Beethoven example cited earlier in the manner shown above.

In general, octave transfer should be reserved for cases where no other explanation is possible. Take the following:

(J. S. Bach: *Prelude* BWV 924, mm. 1–3.)

We can understand the sixteenths in the right hand as arpeggiating three upper registral lines,

but this combination of lines makes no sense, since neither the suspended C in m. 1 nor the suspended D in m. 2 is resolved correctly. In order to resolve the C to a B and the D to a C you have to use at least one octave transfer per measure. The simplest way to understand the passage is

becoming

Or take the continuation of the Strauss example cited earlier:

(R. Strauss: *Four Last Songs,* "Beim Schlafengehn," mm. 1–4.)

The D♭ in m. 2 and the F in m. 3 are dissonant with the C in the bass—a pitch we have every reason to consider stable—while the notes that follow the D♭ and the F in their respective lines are consonant. Consequently, the only way we can understand the D♭ is as an interior element in a step motion that has been subjected to octave transfer and the easiest way to understand the F is as a neighbor to the E♭'s before and after it, even though the second E♭ is an octave higher.

The A♭ in m. 4, however, has been well established in the previous measures so that even though it forms a dissonant interval with the E♮, we can more easily understand the E♮ as the unstable pitch and hence understand the dissonant G that follows the A♭ as an incomplete neighbor to the F.

This means that we can understand the whole passage in terms of four lines that take us from the pitches of an A♭-major triad with C in the bass to those of an A♭ dominant seventh* with A♭ in the bass. The transfers are all due to borrowings within this structure.

becomes

which becomes

which in turn becomes

* An A♭-major triad plus a G♭. See Sections 8.2 and 8.4.

Borrowing and the Generation of Tonal Lines • While the concept of transfer is highly problematic, the concept of borrowing is extremely useful. Indeed, as we shall see, borrowing provides an excellent means for getting around all kinds of difficulties inherent in the tonal system as we have presented it so far. For example, consider the following problem: a line, by definition, contains only one note at a time. Yet to use one of the four fundamental linear operations—arpeggiation—you need two simultaneously sounding notes. The obvious question is: where do you get the second note? We avoided the question in species by making our linear operations additive rather than divisive.* Each successive operation adds a note of equal duration to the existing notes.

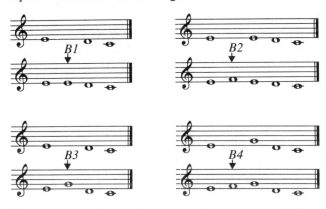

If we try to understand the resulting notes as dividing longer periods of time into equal segments, as we have been doing in this chapter, we would have no trouble understanding the first, second, and fourth cases.†

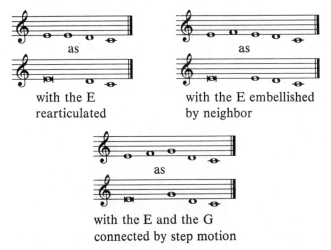

---

* Actually, only the operations for generating simple species lines are additive. The operations for transforming a pair of simple lines into a single compound line are all divisive.

† In none of these cases is the law of segmentation broken. One can, of course, use the *B* rules so as to make it impossible to understand the line in terms of tonal rhythm.

The problem is with the third case. If we want to understand

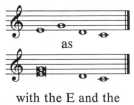

with the E and the G arpeggiated

how are we to understand itself? It is not a line, since it begins with two simultaneously sounding notes. The presence of the D and the C suggest that if only one of the two simultaneously sounding notes can belong to the line, it must be the E. We must consequently assume that the G was borrowed from another line.

In fact, we will find that borrowing fulfills many of the functions that make rule *B3* so useful. Thus, for example, both borrowing and rule *B3* provide a way of relating the pitches at any given point in a line to the span pitches in other lines against which they are to be understood. For rule *B3*, these pitches were always tonic triad pitches, and hence they could be understood as the pitches for the span defined by the entire species composition. Consequently, the use of rule *B3* automatically makes a line "sound tonal" in some rough sense, because it makes you hear whatever happens in the line with reference to inserted triad pitches. In the case of borrowing, the pitches are, of course, not limited to the tonic triad pitches, nor are the spans limited to any particular size.

Both operations provide an easy source of skip-related pitches with which to create secondary step motions. In species, without rule *B3* we would have had no use for rule *B4* and would have found it difficult to construct lines of more than minimal interest. In real music, without borrowing there is no way to create secondary step motions without an enormous increase in the number of underlying lines.

Borrowing also affords us a handy way of getting around the problem of arpeggiating a fourth in the bass. It would be difficult to imagine tonal music without structures like:

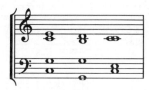

Yet how are we to understand the bass? If we generate the bass by arpeggiation

301

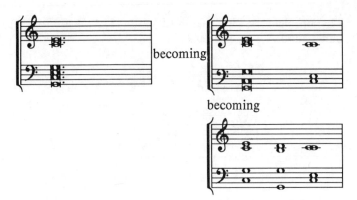

then we are left in the uncomfortable situation of having a dissonance between the lowest sounding span pitch and various other pitches. If, on the other hand, we consider the span pitches to be

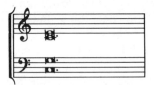

we can then borrow a G for the bass from the next line up, making sure that the listener will not understand a C above it by including notes that are consonant with G but step related to C.

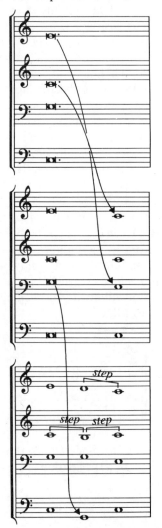

Since borrowing is not limited to triad pitches, we frequently find the bass borrowing a fourth-degree pitch from a neighbor or step motion in an upper line in order to give consonant support to that line.

(Beethoven: *Sonata* Op. 57, second movement, mm. 1–4.)

Note the difference in the way we understand the two low G♭'s here. The first is borrowed from a neighbor in an upper line, the second is itself an incomplete neighbor to the A♭ in m. 3.

One of the great conceptual advantages of borrowing for the listener is the way it reduces the number of pitches necessary to any one span. Such a reduction, however, raises serious questions of ambiguity. When all the pitches in question are consonant with one another, how are we to tell which pitch is the span pitch for a line and which borrowed from the span pitch for another line? Thus, in the example at the end of the preceding page there can be no question of the G being a span pitch in the bass, since it would be dissonant with any C above it. But how are we to tell that the initial E in the top line is the span pitch and not just borrowed from the final E in the next to bottom line instead of vice versa? Here, in fact, the ambiguity can be resolved by internal evidence. We need a G in the next to bottom line for the bass to borrow. Consequently, if we want to keep to one span pitch per line, it is convenient to borrow the final E and hence to consider the initial E as the span pitch. But this need not be the case. Take the following example:

(Haydn: *Symphony* No. 104, first movement, mm. 17–18.)

Here we could generate this passage from two sets of span pitches with equal ease,

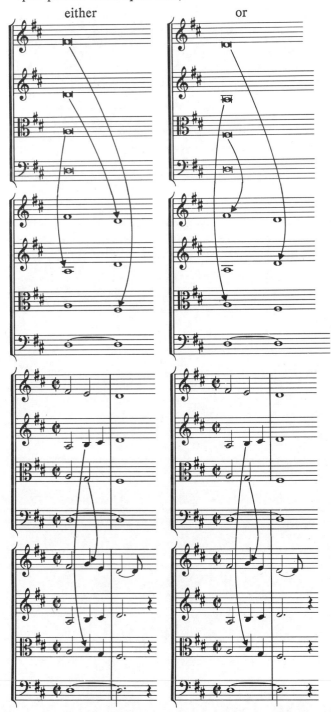

The only way to resolve such an ambiguity is to look further to see which set of span pitches relates more conveniently to the next set of span pitches. Such a search may carry us quite far. For example, in the case at hand even though the pitches of the next span are themselves essentially unambiguous,

they don't really resolve the ambiguity in mm. 1–2.*

Either

or

is conceivable. It is really only at the end of the first eight measures (see the example at the top of page 295) when the F♯ is brought down to an E in the first-violin line that we can see the advantages of the initial span note being an F♯. But to see how, we will need more information about the large spans that will be the subject of the next chapter.

---

* Note, however, that there is never any doubt as to which pitch classes are to be represented as the span pitches. The only doubt is as to their particular distribution among the upper lines; the span pitch for the bass is clear. The larger the span the more characteristic this situation is, and the more we depend on the bass to relate one span to the next.

Exercises

1. a. What is wrong with this way of understanding the passage in the bottom system?

   b. Show how the passage in the bottom system could be understood in terms of the four lines in the top system. (Show the source of any borrowed pitches by an arrow leading from the span pitch in the higher of two adjacent systems to the note with the borrowed pitch in the lower of the two systems.)

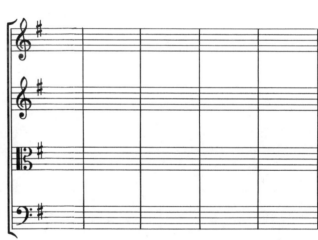

(Haydn: *Quartet* Op. 76, No. 1, third movement, mm. 1–4.)

2. Show how you would use borrowing to generate the four measures in the bottom system from the four measures in the top by writing out a single intermediate stage in which each instrumental line has only one note at a time and all notes begin on the beat and last a beat or more. Show the source of borrowed pitches as in 1b. Your answer should take into account the following considerations:
   a. In m. 1 any of the three pitches that occur during the second beat of the violin line could be generated as a second span pitch from the span pitches in the top system. What influence does the viola's note during that beat have on your choice of a span pitch?
   b. In m. 2 you could generate a C♯ for the second beat of the violin line from either of two span pitches in the viola's upper line—the one in that measure or the one in the next. What factors in the completed passage make you prefer one source over the other?

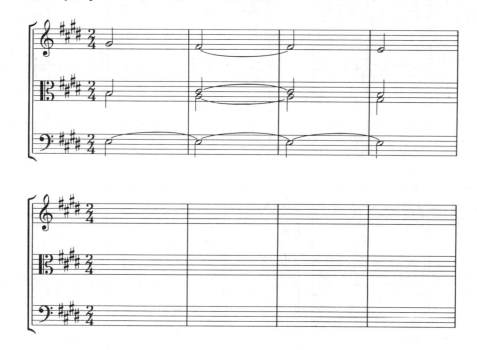

(Haydn: *Quartet* Op. 54, No. 3, fourth movement, mm. 1–4.)

3. The E in m. 2 of the following passage is left hanging.

(Haydn: *Sonata* Hob. XVI: GI, last movement, mm. 1–8.)

Here are two different ways of understanding its relationship to its surroundings. Are there reasons—either in the way the linear connections shown in the bottom system have been generated or in the way these connections are realized in the passage itself—to prefer one explanation to the other?

4.

a. Continue the indicated pattern of transfers so as to maintain contrary motion between the top line and the bass.

b. Use your results in 4a. to generate two lines in $\frac{2}{4}$. The upper line should start one eighth note before the first downbeat.

c. Use your result in 4a. to generate two lines in $\frac{6}{8}$. The upper line should start one eighth note down before the first downbeat.

CHAPTER EIGHT

Phrases, Sections, and Movements

8.0 Spans Longer than a Measure: The Nature of the Problem

In Chapter 7 we established the basis for a theory of tonal rhythm but limited its application to relatively short spans of time—beats and measures. We showed how complex and highly varied structures could be built up from notes occupying these spans by the processes of segmentation, delay, and anticipation. We further showed how these structures could be understood in terms of simple, highly regular sets of reference points and how a given structure could be used to establish a particular set of such reference points in the mind of the listener.

In this chapter we will try to extend our theory to cover longer spans of time—phrases and sections. I say "try" because there is no question but what this extension is the problematic part of the theory. Remember that in order for the listener to understand structures of the kind described in Chapter 7 he must have some way of *comparing* the relative length of the spans of time involved. Consider our capacities as human beings for estimating periods of time: we are most accurate with periods from 0.5 seconds to 1.0 seconds. For periods of 0.7 seconds and less, we can with practice reduce our error to as little as 0.05 seconds. (This minimum error is roughly constant for periods under 0.7 seconds, so the shorter the period of time the greater the percentage of error.) For periods longer than 0.7 seconds, our minimum error increases gradually with the length of the period—negligibly from 0.7 to about 1.0 seconds, noticeably from 1.0 to about 1.4 seconds, and more and more markedly from 1.4 to 2.0 seconds. For periods longer than about two seconds, we aren't very reliable at all.

The fineness of our perception of time is evidently limited by the fact that it takes time to perceive the things we perceive as happening in time. The ear and brain analyze incoming sound waves remarkably quickly, but not instantaneously. It takes around .05 seconds to sort out the characteristic timbre of a note. We are not aware of this period of time as such—indeed, whatever we perceive within this period of time seems to us to be instantaneous. For example, if our ears receive a sound wave lasting only .05 seconds, the sound we hear will appear to have no duration. (If the same sound wave is cut off after only .03 seconds, the sound we hear will not seem shorter, but will have a different timbre.) If our ears receive two sound waves beginning within .05 seconds of one another, we will accept them as beginning at the same point in time.* If our ears receive sound waves, one lasting .05 seconds or less longer than the other, we won't be able to be sure which sound lasted longer. This means that what we think of as a dimensionless "point" in time actually has a certain spread to it, and what we think of as a particular length of time can never be estimated more accurately than that spread will allow.

Our ability to estimate longer periods of time is evidently limited by the way in which the brain processes the information coming to it. Incoming information of the sort collected by the auditory system is evidently held in a kind of short-term storage unit just long enough for the higher brain centers to scan it and send that part that may be needed later on to a long-term storage unit.† The scanning is done very

---

* If the two signals are extremely sharply defined, as, for example, two electronically produced clicks, we may be able to tell that they didn't begin at the same time, but we won't be able to say which came first.

† This is highly conjectural. No physiological bases for the short-term/long-term memory hypothesis have been established.

309

rapidly so that after about 0.7 seconds the information in the short-term unit begins to fade; by two or three seconds it has disappeared to make room for more information.

Presumably this means that information corresponding to events beginning within 0.7 seconds of one another can be dealt with in a single scanning process. So can information from slightly more widely spaced events, but as the period between them is increased, the information from the first event will have had more time to fade and the results will be less accurate.

We can overcome these limitations to some extent by choosing a period of time within the range of greatest accuracy and using it as a unit of measurement. We can then deal with shorter periods of time in terms of how many of them will fit into one unit of measurement, and longer periods of time in terms of how many units they take. However, our capacity for recognizing the number of things contained in something else is also limited. We have no difficulty in distinguishing between two and three of something, or even four and five of something, and we rarely make mistakes; with concentration, we can distinguish between six and seven, but even so we make mistakes; to distinguish between eight and nine of something reliably we must first break down these large numbers into groups of smaller numbers and then compare the smaller numbers. We can, in turn, overcome this limitation by subdividing our unit into some small (but constant) number of equal parts, or building up compound units made up of some small (but constant) number of units. This is, of course, just what we do when we compose, perform, or listen to tonal music. We establish a unit—the beat—usually lasting somewhere between 0.5 seconds (M=120) and one second (M=60) but occasionally as short as .35 seconds (M=168) or as long as 1.4 seconds (M=42). We group and subdivide these units in twos, threes, fours, and occasionally fives, to form measures. We think of very short segments of time in terms of how many it takes to occupy a beat or a subdivision of a beat. Each thirty-second note in the following example takes about a twelfth of a second:

(J. S. Bach: *Brandenburg Concerto* No. 4, first movement, mm. 187–189.)

but we don't have to think of these short periods of time as such. We can think of each note as being one of four notes that fit into any of three equal subdivisions of a basic unit lasting about a second.* Similarly, we think of longer spans in terms of how many measures they take. In the example below the time elapsed from the beginning of the first B♭ in the bass to the beginning of the first F is about 9.6 seconds. Yet we have no difficulty in recognizing it as identical to the time elapsed from the first F to the D. Both last two measures of four beats each.

Thus, the familiar hierarchy of units—measures, beats, and subdivisions of beats—gives us a way of dealing reliably with periods of time anywhere from the shortest period of time between two notes that we can still perceive as consecutive to the longest period of time we can grasp as being made up of a small number of measures.† To deal with even longer

---

* This distinction is of considerable practical importance to the performer, since his error in estimating when to begin each note can be as much as half the duration of the note. Imagine trying to come out with the other players every twelve notes by thinking of the duration of each thirty-second note as such.

† A considerable range: for practical purposes from as little as a sixteenth of a second (notes following one another by less than about a sixteenth of a second blur into one another) to as much as thirty seconds (five measures of four beats each at M=40).

(Beethoven: *Symphony* No. 6, second movement, mm. 1–5.)

periods of time we have to use a unit larger than a measure. In tonal music the next larger unit is the phrase.* A phrase, however, is not just a larger unit than a measure. It is a fundamentally different kind of unit, with a different structure and a different function. A measure is a purely temporal structure, a set of reference points in time in terms of which we can understand whatever notes may occur during that measure. A phrase, on the other hand, has a particular kind of pitch structure that implies a particular type of span structure. A phrase

1. establishes one set of pitches and then
2. moves to a second set of pitches in such a way that
   a. we expect those pitches,
   b. we have some sense of when they are about to occur, and
   c. once they have occurred we know the phrase has gotten where it's going and that no further pitches are needed to complete that phrase.

Such a pitch structure can always be understood in terms of a span structure in which the span corresponding to the phrase as a whole is divided into two large segments, the first occupied by the first set of pitches, the second by the second set.

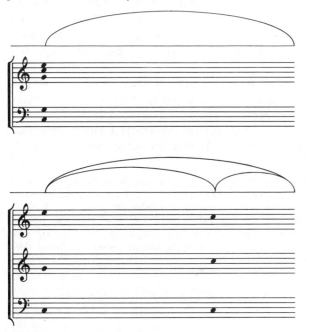

* Unless we include those measure-like structures that are made up of measures the way measures are made up of beats.. Such "macro-measures" are sometimes used in tonal music. For example, the first twenty-six measures of the Beethoven example just cited can be construed in terms of thirteen macro-measures, each consisting of a pair of ordinary measures with the downbeat of the first ordinary measure functioning as the downbeat of the macro-measure and the downbeat of the second ordinary measure functioning as the upbeat. I am ignoring the macro-measure here because, although it is a useful extension of the metric hierarchy, it poses no essentially new problems.

The pitches creating the motion to the second set may be understood as segmenting the first large segment,

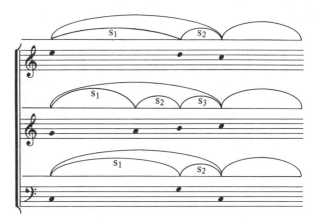

creating an anticipatory segment to the second large segment,

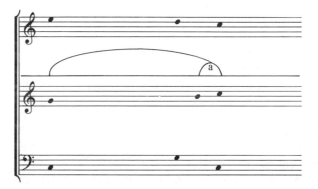

or marking the beginning of the second large segment where the second set of pitches has been delayed.

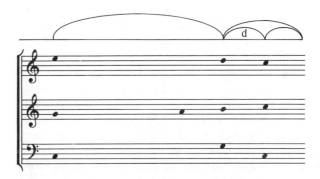

Of course, we understand the span structure of a phrase—like any other span structure—in terms of the framework of whatever reference points are established in the course of the phrase. This means that we will understand both large segments as beginning on downbeats. These two downbeats then take on a special role: they are *the* two points of time in terms of which we understand the phrase as a whole, the primary reference points for that phrase. We can think of any downbeats that fall between such "primary downbeats" as dividing up the time between them into equal periods and hence as secondary reference points, "secondary downbeats." Note, however, that while secondary downbeats may be related to one another and to the primary downbeat, much as ordinary beats are related to one another and to ordinary downbeats, primary downbeats are not related to one another the way ordinary downbeats are. In the first place, there are two primary downbeats in each phrase. They are coupled by the underlying span structure of the phrase in a way that the second primary downbeat of one phrase and the first primary downbeat of the next phrase can't be. In the second place, they are not necessarily equally spaced.* The only constraint on their spacing follows from the law of segmentation: obviously the first large segment of a phrase cannot be shorter than the second large segment of that phrase.

In this second difference lies the root of the two chief difficulties that beset the listener in trying to grasp large-scale span structures:

1. the difficulty in predicting when the next primary reference point is coming, and
2. the difficulty in estimating the lengths of spans longer than a phrase.

As we saw in Chapter 7, the advantage of equally spaced reference points lies in the ease and reliability with which they can be projected. The primary reference points in a series of measures are equally spaced. This means that once you have established two consecutive downbeats your listener knows when to expect the next and the next and the next. He can then use this series of reference points to understand whatever structures you wish to hang on them, including conceptually problematic ones involving anticipations and delays. The primary reference points in a series of phrases, however, are not equally spaced. This means that after you have established the primary downbeats for a whole series of phrases, your listener may still have no way of telling when the next one is coming. Fortunately there is usually no reason why the listener needs to be able to predict the first primary downbeat of a phrase. In most cases the first downbeat in the phrase serves as the first primary downbeat, so he need only understand it as primary in retrospect. That is, he can understand the subsequent downbeats during the first segment as equally spaced from the first downbeat.† There is, however, usually every reason why he needs to be able to predict when the secondary primary downbeat is coming. Our whole notion of phrase structure depends on the idea of arriving at an expected set of final pitches at an expected time.

As we saw earlier in this section, we can extend our ability to estimate periods of time by breaking down longer periods into small numbers of short, equal units. This method still works for the spans defined by most phrases, since any phrase span can always be divided into the same small number of segments (two) and each segment can usually be divided into a small number (seven or less) of measures.‡ But it cannot be expected to work for the spans defined by sections consisting of a number of phrases, since a section might consist of any number of phrases, and each phrase might have a different length. For example, suppose you had composed two spans, one defined by a section consisting of two long phrases and another defined by a section consisting of three short phrases. How would your listener be able to compare their durations? But if he can't tell which is longer, how will he know how to relate them as segments in an even larger span structure? The law of segmentation won't help him if he can't tell which segment is longer.§

Obviously, if we want to make a structure clear to our listener, either at the level of the individual phrase or for a whole movement or piece, we must find ways to help the listener overcome these difficulties. We must

1. find ways to make it clear when the second primary beat is about to occur, and
2. either
   a. find ways of constructing larger units that will make their durations easier to compare

---

* In fact, they usually aren't, or at any rate not for any length of time. When they are, they usually serve to create macromeasures, which can, in turn, be grouped into much longer phrases.

† Any anticipatory spans are usually less than half a measure and hence can be understood within the framework provided by ordinary downbeats. Of course, if the anticipatory span is a measure or more, care must be taken to make it clear that the first downbeat in the phrase is not a primary downbeat. See pages 316 ff.

‡ For phrases whose first segment lasts more than seven measures, we have to find some way of grouping the measures into a smaller number of macro-measures.

§ Without the law of segmentation, the communication of specific span structures is almost impossible. For example, take two consecutive spans in the middle of a piece, the first shorter than the second:

If your listener can tell that the first span is shorter, he knows it must be the final segment of some longer span and hence that the second span begins a new unit.

But if he can't tell which is longer, he cannot be sure that these spans are not segments of some longer span.

or b. find ways for showing the hierarchical relation of one such unit to another that are independent of the relative durations of the sections.

The remaining sections of this chapter will show some of the solutions to these problems developed by eighteenth- and nineteenth-century composers. Section 8.1 deals with the structure of individual phrases and the problem of establishing the two primary downbeats. Section 8.2 deals with a specific technique for letting the listener know when the second primary downbeat is coming—the cadence. Section 8.3 shows how two or more consecutive phrases may be understood as forming parts of a larger structure. Section 8.4 extends the non-diatonic procedures discussed in Section 7.6 to cover whole collections of simultaneously sounding pitches ("chords"). Section 8.5 deals with a non-diatonic procedure that can clarify the subordination of whole passages to one another—tonicization—and tries to show how tonicization can be combined with structural parallelism to create clear large-scale span structures. Section 8.6 presents an overview of the procedures used in Chapters 7 and 8.

8.1 Phrase Structure

Constructing a Phrase • Take a period of time that you can think of in terms of two primary reference points, B_1 and B_2.

Put notes beginning at B_1 and B_2 in two or more lines so as to define a span, S_1, beginning at B_1 and ending at B_2, and a span, S_2, beginning at B_2. Choose durations and pitches in both lines such that S_1 and S_2 can be segments of a superspan, SS.* For example:

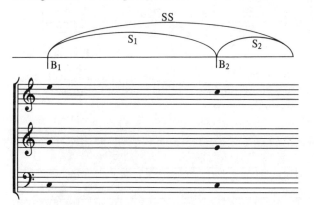

* Note the difference between the two examples. If the segmentation of SS is due to rearticulation and arpeggiation of the tonic triad, as in the first example, the underlying structure will be self-contained. If the segmentation is due to step motion, embellishment by neighbor, or an arpeggiation ending on the dominant, as in the second example, the underlying structure will be incomplete.

or

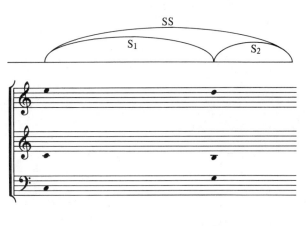

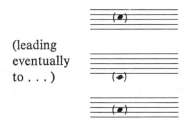

(leading eventually to . . .)

Now measure off the time between B_1 and B_2 with some convenient number of equally spaced secondary reference points, b_1, b_2, b_3, etc.†

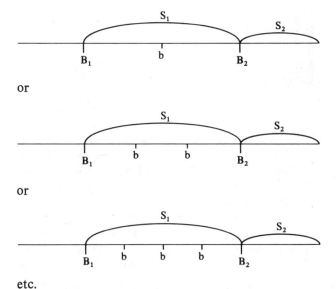

etc.

† Note that these secondary reference points will, like the primary reference points, normally be downbeats. In Chapter 7 we were talking about spans of a measure or less, so that primary reference points (the B's) were always downbeats but secondary reference points (the b's) were other beats. In this chapter we will use B_1 and B_2 for the two primary beats of a phrase (almost always downbeats) and b_1, b_2, b_3, etc., for the secondary beats of a phrase (also almost always downbeats). We will be so little concerned with the tertiary beats of a phrase (almost always the non-downbeats we used to call secondary beats) that we won't set up any symbol for them at all.

313

Extend the succession of equally spaced reference points after B_2 so as to measure off S_2 in the same way.

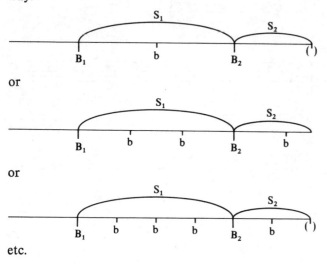

etc.

(If you wish to anticipate S_1 by a span, A, longer than the time between secondary beats, you may extend the succession before B_1 as well.)

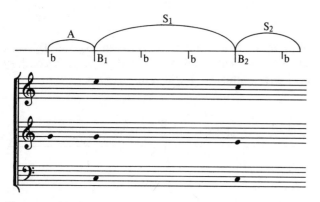

Now apply the processes of rearticulation, embellishment by neighbor, arpeggiation, and connection by step motion in terms of segmentation, delay, and anticipation to arrive at a set of notes your listener can only understand in terms of your set of reference points. What you have is a phrase. (For an example, see the opposite page.)

We think of a phrase as having clearly defined boundaries: a phrase begins at one point and ends at another, and the notes that occur between those two points all belong to that phrase. We think of a whole phrase in terms of two primary beats, one at or toward the beginning and the other at least halfway through. We can think of each note in a phrase in terms of one or the other (or both) of these primary beats—either directly or in terms of secondary beats, which we in turn think of in terms of the primary beats.

Thinking of phrases this way means that the phrase structure of any piece will be subject to three types of ambiguity.

1. Location of the primary beats: which beats are primary and which secondary?

(Haydn: *Symphony* No. 104, first movement, mm. 17–20.)

2. Location of boundaries: where does one phrase end and the next begin?

(*Ibid.*, mm. 17–22.)

3. Position in a hierarchy: is the passage a phrase, a pair of phrases, or just part of a phrase? (See example below.)

(*Ibid.*, mm. 17–24.)

Purcell: *"A Trumpet Tune,"* mm. 1–4, from *A Choice Collection of Lessons for the Harpsichord or Spinnet,* originally a piece for trumpet and strings from *The Indian Queen.*)

We will deal with the second and third type of ambiguity in the next section when we consider problems involving more than one phrase. In this section we will concentrate on one phrase at a time. Therefore we will assume in each of the following cases that the notes under consideration do indeed constitute a phrase and that when they begin and end, the phrase begins and ends.

Establishing the First Primary Beat • The more of a phrase that precedes the first primary beat, the harder it is to establish that beat. If you start your phrase right on the first primary beat, there is normally no problem. Other things being equal, it is easier for your listener to understand subsequent beats in terms of the first beat than vice versa. The same is true if you start the phrase with an anticipatory span shorter than the period between the first primary beat and the first secondary beat.

(Mozart: *Symphony* No. 40, third movement, mm. 1–3.)

As long as you project that period by an unambiguously defined span, your listener should have no trouble locating the primary beat.

On the other hand, if you want to start your phrase with an anticipatory span equal to or longer than the period between the first primary beat and the next secondary beat,

(Mozart: *Die Entführung aus dem Serail*, Act. II, "Wenn der Freude Tränen fliessen," mm. 1–2.)

(Mozart: *Symphony* No. 40, first movement, mm. 1–4.)

you will have to be careful. What you think of as a preliminary secondary beat may appear to your listener as the primary beat itself.

One way of avoiding such a misunderstanding is to wait until the primary beat before bringing in other lines (particularly the bass).

Another way is to show the listener in advance how to place his beats by setting up an accompaniment pattern before the phrase proper begins. Thus, in the following example the fact that the third measure of the accompaniment is identical with the first helps establish the third downbeat as the initial primary downbeat of the phrase.

Establishing the Second Primary Beat • Getting your listener to use a particular point in a phrase as the second primary beat is a different sort of problem. Most, if not all, of any phrase follows the first primary beat; it is easy enough for the listener to refer what he hears back to some previous point in time. At least half of any phrase (and usually more) happens before the second primary beat. It the listener is to refer what he hears ahead to some future point in time, he must have some way of locating that point before it happens. To help him you can do two things:
1. Make sure the equally spaced secondary beats between B_1 and B_2 are clearly established.
2. Make him expect the pitches that are coming at B_2 by creating pitch structures that are incomplete up to B_2 but are completed at B_2.

Neither method is sufficient in itself, but combined they can be highly effective. To see how they work consider the following highly simplified situation: you are trying to construct a phrase that your listener will understand in terms of two primary beats two seconds apart.

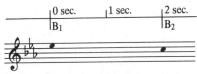

Now suppose you establish a secondary beat, b_1, one second after B_1.

Your listener knows that for b_1 to be a secondary beat, it will have to be one of a series of b's marking off equal segments between B_1 and B_2.

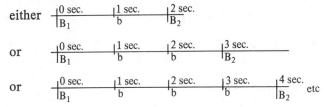

Therefore he can assume that B_2 will have to occur at one of a set of particular points in the future—namely, those points that are some whole number of seconds away from b_1.

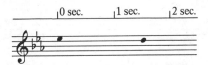

Or suppose instead you put a D 1.5 seconds after the E♭.

Your listener knows that to complete the structure a C or another E♭ will be needed.

Therefore if the C or the E♭ is associated with B_2, he can assume that B_3 would have to come no later than three seconds after B_1.

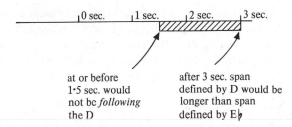

at or before 1·5 sec. would not be *following* the D

after 3 sec. span defined by D would be longer than span defined by E♭

The two methods limit the possible location of B_2 in different ways: the first to any one point in a set of equally spaced points, the second to any point within a short period of time. Neither by itself gives the listener enough information to predict the location of B_2, but together they do.

Consider the following:

Of the points in the set of equally spaced points projected from B_1 and b, only the ones at three and four seconds occur within the period of time determined by the location of the D.

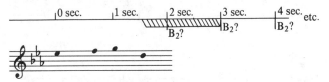

But if B_2 is at three seconds, then the point at two seconds must be a secondary beat, b_2, and there is no way to understand the D at 1.5 seconds in terms of such a beat.

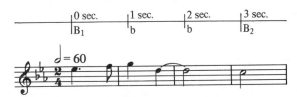

Thus your listener has every reason to expect B_2 at the two-second point.

Now, to say that he expects a primary beat at a particular point in time because of the function the expected pitch would have if it occurred at that point is not the same thing as saying that he predicts that pitch will occur at that point. Other pitches in other patterns could also occur. For example:

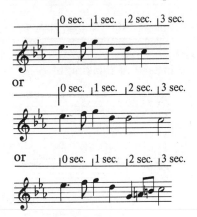

317

But in each of these cases he would still want to use the two-second point as his second primary beat. In the first case he simply understands the expected C as delayed and in the second the D as a rearticulation marking the point at which the C would have begun.

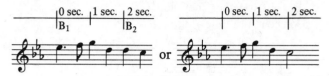

In the second and third cases he would have to reinterpret the D at 1.5 seconds as an anticipation or an anticipatory arpeggiation to the note at the two-second point, that is, as

This, in turn, encourages him to prefer that point as his second primary beat. For example, in the first case

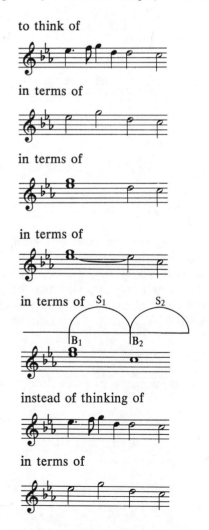

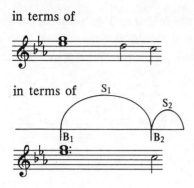

The listener's sense of what is about to happen in a phrase is rarely a matter of knowing exactly what will happen next. It is usually more a matter of having some inkling of the structural features shared by a number of things that might happen next. Of course, that inkling may turn out to be dead wrong. Suppose the line were to continue like this

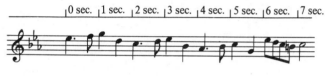

or like this

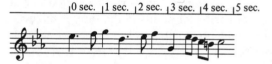

Then the listener would have to reinterpret the notes he has already heard in terms of an entirely different set of beats.

Uncertainties of this kind are less of a problem as soon as you have two or more lines going at once. As we pointed out in Section 7.5, rhythmic differentiation between lines tends to reduce ambiguities of structure. Given two span structures, there is usually only one set of beats that will work for both. It is easier to establish a set of unequivocal secondary beats with two lines than it is with one, and consequently much easier to get your listener to sense the points at which the second primary beat could come. In the same way, the pitches of the other lines can be used to make it clear whether or not the next available point will, in fact, be the second primary beat. If you give your listener,

he knows that the next point could not be that beat, since no structure that the B♭ could take part in could be completed by that point. On the other hand, if you give him,

he knows it could. If you add another line with yet another structure that could be completed at the same point and by a triad pitch, say

he will expect the second primary beat to fall at that point. The greater the number of such structures, the stronger the expectation. Therefore, the surest way of letting your listener sense when B_2 is coming is to combine three or more such structures, each of which could be completed by its final pitch on B_2 and each of which introduces its penultimate pitch either on the last secondary beat before B_2 or somewhere between that secondary beat and B_2. This kind of strategy has crystallized into the technique of the *cadence*, which we will deal with in the next section.

Exercises

1. The two columns show two attempts to generate the measure-span pitches of the first phrase of the third movement of Haydn's Quartet, Op. 76, No. 1 (see Exercise on page 305, question 1) from a simpler structure consisting solely of the pitches associated with the two large segments of the phrase. The pitches are the same in both cases, but the location of the second primary downbeat is not. One of these columns contains an error; find it. Then show why it is impossible to generate the lines in the bottom system of that column from the lines in the top system. Finally, indicate how the lines in the bottom system of the other column have been generated from the lines in the top system of that column.

2. The bottom system shows the measure-span pitches for the opening phrase of the last movement of Haydn's Quartet, Op. 54, No. 3 (see Exercise on page 306, question 2). Use the middle two systems to show how these four lines can be generated from the span pitches for the whole phrase shown in the top system.

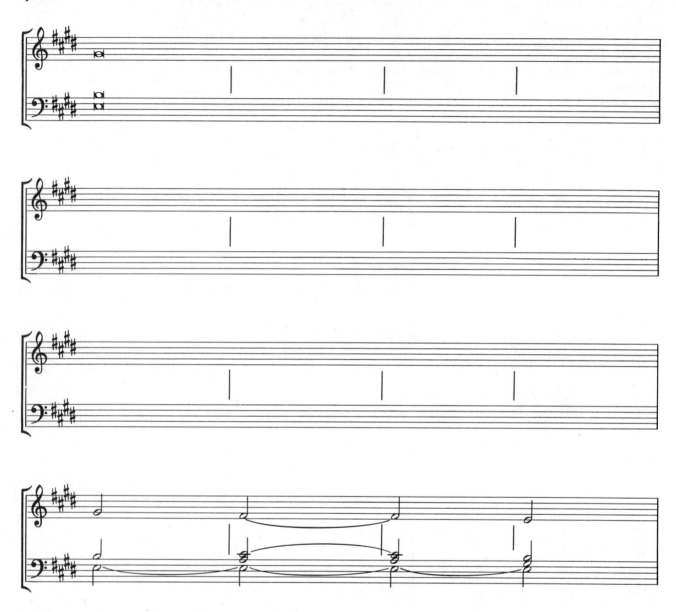

On what measure does your second large segment start? Could it start at any other point? How does the way the various details of the phrase are laid out help project this underlying structure?

3. The following pair of phrases could be generated from four large segments either beginning at mm. 1, 3, 5, and 7, or beginning at mm. 1, 4, 5, and 8. What reasons would you have for preferring one set of segments over the other as a way of understanding the structure of these two phrases? Show how you can generate these phrases from the set of segments you prefer.

(Haydn: *Sonata* Hob. XVI: GI, last movement, mm. 1–8.)

4. Write a phrase in 2/4 based on the measure-span pitches shown in the bottom system in question 1.

5. Write a phrase in 3/4 based on the measure-span pitches given in question 2.

8.2 The Cadence

Imagine that you have already established the first primary beat of the phrase and enough secondary beats so that your listener knows that the second primary beat will have to occur at one of a series of equally spaced points.

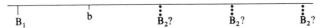

In order to make it absolutely clear to him which of these points is B_2 you are going to combine a number of simple linear structures such that the last note of each falls on B_2 and the next to last falls either on the last secondary beat before B_2 or between that secondary beat and B_2,

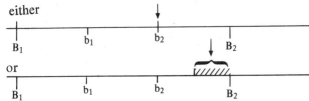

Suppose you were only interested in the kind of complete and self-contained pitch structures that both begin and end on a triad pitch.

Obviously, any combination of such structures would end with a collection of final pitches that would at least partially represent the tonic triad itself. But the collection of next-to-last pitches is also of interest, for it is this collection that tips off your listener that the second primary beat is on its way.

Certain of these combinations—and hence certain of these collections—are more generally useful than others. Consider the bass structure. You could, of course, approach the final tonic by step,

* The parentheses around the key signature means that these examples can be read either in C major or C minor.

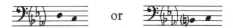

but if you do, you cannot use structures that approach the tonic from that direction in any of the upper lines.

If, on the other hand, you approach the final tonic from the fifth degree

 or

you can approach the tonic from both directions in the upper lines.

Note that in such a case, all three of the next-to-last pitches are consonant with one another. They form the triad based on the fifth degree, the *dominant triad*.

The other scale degrees that are available as next-to-last pitches are the fourth and the sixth degrees. Of the two, the fourth degree is by far the more useful because it can take part in parallel motion with structures using the second degree. It will, of course, be dissonant with both the fifth and the seventh degrees

but these dissonances act to your advantage. Taken by themselves, the members of a dominant triad might be mistaken for stable pitches; by adding the fourth degree —a pitch a minor seventh from the bass—you have a collection of pitches—the so-called *dominant seventh*— that signals to your listener that these pitches are heading for the pitches of the tonic triad.

The dominant seventh has been used as a penultimate collection in cadences since the beginnings of tonality, and composers have long since stopped treating its seventh and diminished fifth with the same care they accord other dissonances. They simply assume their listener will recognize the collection as such. Ultimately the dissonances in any dominant seventh can always be understood in terms of some larger-scale voice-leading situation, although that situation may not be readily apparent from the way the fourth degree is approached. For our purposes we can simply say:

1. in a dominant seventh, the "seventh" (that is, the fourth degree) may be treated as though it were consonant with the other members of the collection.

However,

2. it should lead down to the third degree

unless it is involved in parallel motion with the other upper lines.

(Even in this latter case care must be taken in approaching the fifth formed by the tonic and the fifth degree.)

(questionable) (to be avoided)

The sixth degree can also be added to the collection to form the larger collection known as the dominant ninth.

Because of the voice-leading problems it creates, this collection is less generally useful than the dominant seventh. The line whose note forms the ninth with the dominant must, of course, always move down by step

to get to the triad pitch that completes its structure, but that often creates problems with the structure that has the second degree

unless that structure lies above the one with the ninth

or moves up to the third degree.

Thus, at least in its most fundamental form, a cadence consists of a group of pitches belonging to some dominant collection (dominant triad, dominant seventh, or dominant ninth) followed by a group of pitches belonging to the tonic triad, so arranged in time that the dominant pitches begin either on the last secondary beat before B_2 or between that beat and B_2, and the tonic pitches begin on B_2 itself.

Half Cadences and Feminine Cadences • So far, we have combined linear structures whose final pitches all belong to the tonic triad. Such structures can be thought of as complete in themselves, so we call the cadences that result *complete* or *full cadences*. But we can also create linear structures whose final pitches belong to the dominant triad (or even the dominant seventh). Obviously such structures will not be complete in themselves, but can only be understood in terms of some larger structure. We call cadences ending on such dominant collections *incomplete* or *half cadences*.

So far, we have let the final notes of all the linear structures fall on the second primary beat. The simultaneous occurrence of destination pitches and primary reference points creates a strong sense of arrival. In such a case the cadence (whether full or half) is called a *masculine cadence*. But we can also delay the final notes of all (or most) of the linear structures and even use the penultimate notes to mark the point at which the final notes would have begun (that is, the second primary beat), thereby weakening the sense of arrival. The cadence in such a case is called a *feminine* cadence.

Both half cadences (whether masculine or feminine) and feminine cadences (whether full or half) pose serious problems for the communication of your phrase structure to the listener. For the feminine cadence we can distinguish two central, though related, problems.

1. If you delay the final pitches so they begin after the second primary beat, how is your listener to know that the primary beat isn't where the final pitches begin?

2. If you use the penultimate pitches to mark the point at which the final pitches would have begun (namely, the second primary beat), what do you use to help your listener sense that the second primary beat is coming?

One way to solve the first problem is to make sure the point you delay the final pitches to is not a secondary beat.

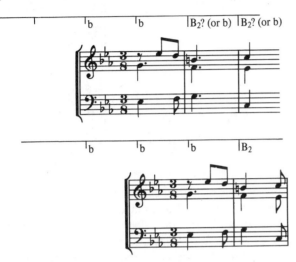

(If the preceding secondary beats have done their job, it will not occur to your listener that the second primary beat could come at such a point.) Another way is to delay the penultimate pitches in the upper lines only, creating one or more dissonances with the bass.

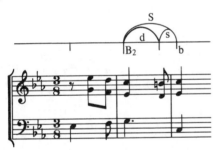

The more your listener has to use that point as a reference point, the more likely he is to make it into a primary reference point. One way to solve the second problem is to introduce, just before the penultimate pitches, other pitches that can only be understood in terms of what is about to happen—that is, to apply the strategy that led us to the technique of the cadence in the first place. All you have to do is apply a secondary operation to one or more of the penultimate pitches, an anticipation

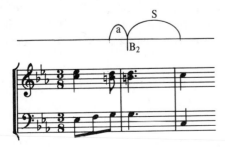

or an incomplete neighbor.

Finally, a way to avoid both problems is to delay the final pitches in the upper lines only, bringing all the penultimate pitches in before the second primary beat and the final pitch in the bass in on the primary beat.

This way the penultimate pitches serve the same function they would in an ordinary masculine cadence, warning the listener that the primary beat is about to occur. The final pitch in the bass marks the moment of the second primary beat, while the dissonances between the penultimate pitches in the upper lines and the final pitch in the bass make it clear that the upper lines have not yet reached their destinations.

For the half cadence we can distinguish a similar pair of problems. If you use the pitches of the dominant triad (or even of the dominant seventh) as the final pitches of your various linear structures,

1. what do you use to warn your listener that the final pitches (and hence the second primary beat) are about to occur? and
2. how can you let your listener know that the phrase has indeed reached its conclusion, that this dominant triad or dominant seventh is not the first collection of pitches in a full cadence?

One way to solve the first problem is to set up a step motion from a tonic triad member to the one note in the dominant triad that is bound to be a tonic triad member, the dominant in the bass.

Whatever the upper lines do before B_2—they might do no more than arpeggiate the tonic triad—such a bass is bound to make your listener expect a dominant at B_2 whether you put the interior pitches of the step motion on the intervening secondary beats

or just before B_2.

Another solution is to introduce a number of pitches that can only be understood in terms of a coming dominant collection, either incomplete neighbors or anticipatory arpeggiations or possibly even anticipations of the pitches in a dominant triad or dominant seventh.

One way of solving the second problem is to chromatically alter those degrees that lead to the dominant, raising the fourth degree or lowering the sixth.*

* In major; in minor the sixth degree is, of course, already only a semitone from the fifth.

By making such pitches closer to the destination pitch, you can make it clear immediately which way they are headed; a raised fourth degree could not be on its way down to the third degree, it could only be on its way up to the fifth degree; a lowered sixth degree could not be going up to the tonic, it could only be going down to the dominant. Raising the fourth degree has the added advantage of creating a collection of penultimate pitches that bears the same relation to the member of the dominant triad that the cadential dominant or dominant seventh bears to the tonic triad.

Such a "dominant of the dominant" is called a secondary dominant. But no amount of chromatic alteration of the pitches leading to the dominant will suffice if your listener has reason to assume there is still time for the dominant to lead on to the tonic. If your listener is used to hearing four-measure phrases and you arrive at the dominant triad on the third measure, he is going to expect you to go on to the tonic on the fourth. What you do to intensify the sense of arrival at the third measure may serve to make that downbeat seem like a primary downbeat, but there is still plenty of time for a feminine cadence to the tonic. If you want to create a half cadence with B_2 as the third of four downbeats, the safest way is to make it a feminine cadence.

Questions for Discussion

What kinds of cadences—if any—do you find in the following passages quoted elsewhere in this book?

Purcell: "A Trumpet Tune"	(pp. 46-47)
Corelli: Sonata, Op. 5, No. 11; Adagio, mm. 1–3	(p. 291)
Beethoven: Symphony No. 6; Second movement, mm. 1–5	(p. 310)
Haydn: Symphony No. 104; First movement, mm. 17–24	(p. 314)
Mozart: Symphony No. 40; First movement, mm. 1–3	(p. 316)
Mozart: Sonata, K. 331; Second movement, mm. 1–10	(p. 335)
Haydn: Sonata No. 9; Last movement, mm. 1–8	(p. 339)

Exercises

Each of the given lines is the top line of a pair of phrases. In the staves above the given line show how you understand its structure by writing notes that define
   a. the two large segments of each phrase
   b. the measure spans
   c. the beat spans

In the two staves below the given line add cadences that would support your interpretation of the given line's structure.

8.3 Consecutive Phrases

General Considerations • In Section 8.1 we saw how we can understand the interior structure of a single phrase in terms of two segments of a single large span. We will see in this section that we can also understand the relationship of one phrase to the next in terms of the way in which their respective spans may (or may not) be considered segments of a single, even larger, span. In general the relationship of any phrase span to the next depends—just as it does for smaller spans—on the relative duration of the two spans and on how we can connect the pitches of the two spans in terms of our set of linear constructs. For example, the phrase spans of the two phrases shown below may be considered segments of a single larger span, since they are of equal length and since their pitches can be construed as forming arpeggiations.

To grasp the relationship of one phrase to the next, however, the information provided by the pitches and durations of the phrases spans is insufficient. We must keep in mind the salient features of the interior structure

(Mozart: *The Marriage of Figaro*, Act. I, "Se vuol ballare," mm. 1–8.)

(Haydn: *Quartet* Op. 3, No. 3, third movement, mm. 1–8.)

of the phrase as well, particularly where that structure is left incomplete at the end of the phrase. Consider the pair of phrases shown above. We think of the second phrase as completing what the first phrase has left incomplete.* By this I do not mean that the A at the end of the first phrase simply serves as a neighbor to the B at the beginning of the second phrase. I mean that the A can be understood as part of a step motion from B to G which is stated in an incomplete form in the first phrase but in a complete form in the second phrase.

The only way we could show this relationship in terms of our system would be to consider the G as the top pitch of the second span, which has been delayed to the second primary downbeat.

This is a rather involved way of explaining such a common phenomenon. It seems to me simpler—and in the long run more fruitful—to say that the fact that we

* Note the importance of borrowing in understanding this passage in terms of a simple structure.

334

expect each phrase to have a particular type of structure allows us to create relationships between consecutive phrases that we could not create between consecutive beats or consecutive measures. Thus, the sense of this particular structure is *not* the same as it would be if the same pitches and relative durations occupied a single measure.

The sense depends on the idea of an incomplete statement of an expected type of structure followed by a complete statement of that structure.

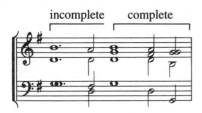

We can use such a sense to *link* two phrases, setting them off from other phrases that have their span pitches drawn from the same triad. For example, when these two phrases are repeated, there is no similar link between the second phrase (first time) and the first phrase (second time) even though the pitches of their respective spans have the same relationship to one another.

Such linking of consecutive phrase spans may be projected at a more detailed level of structure as well. Consider the following familiar example:

(Mozart: *Sonata* K.331, second movement, mm. 1–10.)

Here again, both phrase spans use pitches belonging to the tonic triad:

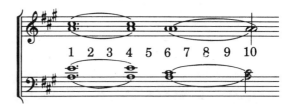

Here the incomplete structures presented by the pitches of the two segments of the first phrase are completed by the span pitches of the second phrase which have been delayed until the second primary downbeats of that phrase.

The E on the second primary downbeat of the first phrase is connected to the G♯ on the first primary downbeat of the second phrase by step motion.

(The transfer helps articulate the G♯ as a phrase-segment pitch instead of an interior element in a step motion from E to B—compare

and

The sense of connection between the two phrases is further intensified by the chromatic step motion between E and F♯ and the on-the-beat passing tones between the F♯ and the G♯.

Embedding • It often happens that what could be considered a pair of consecutive phrases whose spans are segments of a larger span (see the top two systems

(Haydn: *Symphony* No. 104, first movement, mm. 17–24.)

above) could also be considered a single large phrase (see the lowest of the three systems above). Where we wish to consider the spans of the small phrases as the principal segments of the large phrase, we say the two small phrases are *embedded* in the larger one (see below).

Embedding is a useful concept for dealing with long phrases; by understanding a long phrase in terms of a hierarchy of phrase-like structures, you can overcome many of the difficulties posed by long spans and by the lack of regularly spaced reference points for phrases. However, there is no point in using the concept when

1. there is no conceptual need to consider the smaller units as phrases, or
2. its use prevents a more consistent or interesting conception of the larger phrase's structure.

Thus, in the Haydn example just cited, there is no need to consider pairs of measures as phrases. Why go to the trouble of considering all the downbeats in a passage as primary downbeats? As simple downbeats they serve perfectly well as reference points for both structures. Furthermore, by considering mm. 3 and 4 as a phrase, you are in effect placing the second primary downbeat of the larger phrase on m. 4, thereby

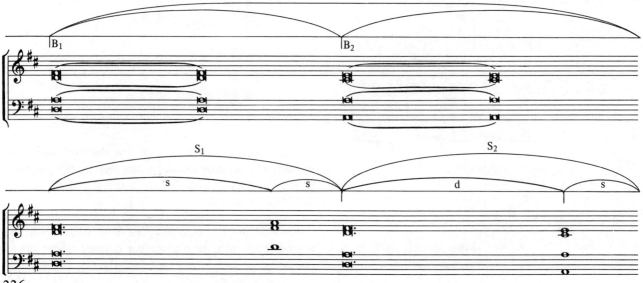

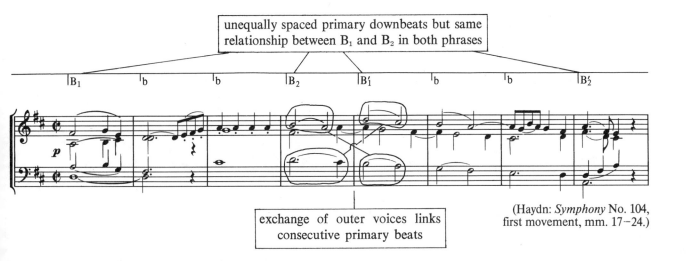

(Haydn: *Symphony* No. 104, first movement, mm. 17–24.)

creating a series of equally spaced primary downbeats

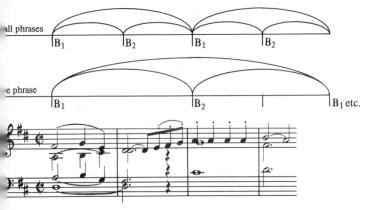

and ignoring the possibility of placing it at measure 20 (see above).

Paired Phrases • Consider the Purcell example we used earlier:

The dots and the double bars mean that this phrase is supposed to be played twice, so as to make two consecutive phrases. Obviously, both phrases will have the same structure (see below), but the second time, that structure will be easier to grasp. Once the listener has realized that the beginning of the second phrase is the same as the beginning of the first, he has good reason to expect that the rest of the phrase will be the

same, and so has a way of knowing where the second primary beat will be. Furthermore, the fact that both phrases have the same structure makes it that much easier to grasp that the superspans defined by both can, in turn, be understood as segments due to one rearticulation of an even larger span.

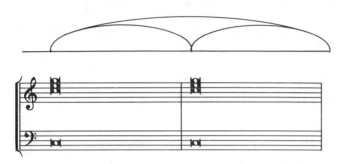

Thus, we have a way of thinking of both phrases as forming a single unit made up of two phrases but, unlike the embedded structures we were just discussing, not itself a phrase. We will call phrases forming this type of unit *paired phrases*. We say two phrases are paired when

1. their spans can be understood as equal segments of a larger span and
2. the rhythmic structures of the two phrases are strongly parallel.

The advantages of paired phrases is that they help the listener grasp relatively long periods of time, much longer than he can manage with the reference-point system alone. The function of the structural parallelism is to make it possible to compare any point during the second span with a point equally far along the first span.

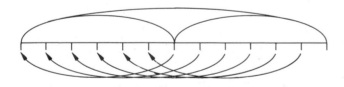

In this way, however long the two spans may be and however irregular their structures, the listener has a way of grasping the relationship of the second span to the first.

Exact repetition is, of course, only one type of phrase pairing. The two phrases do not have to be identical to help the listener understand that their underlying structures are the same.

(Purcell: *Musicks Handmaid*, Part II, "Rigadoon," mm. 1–8.)

Nor do their respective spans have to use identical pitches—a rearticulation is only one way of segmenting a span.

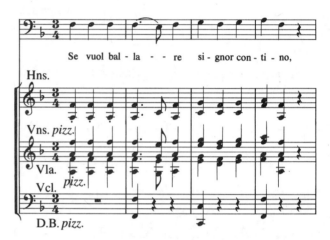

(Mozart: *The Marriage of Figaro*, Act I, "Se vuol ballare," mm. 1–8.)

Phrase pairing is extremely common where the second phrase presents a completed form of the structure left incomplete by the first phrase.

The succession of parallel details makes the listener's task of comparing the underlying structures of the two phrases all the easier. (See the example at the top of the opposite page.)

(Haydn: *Sonata* Hob. XVI: 19, third movement, mm. 1–8.)

Overlap and Extension • Now consider a little more of the excerpt from Haydn's Symphony No. 104 that we used earlier (see above). The structure of the first two phrases is clear. Mm. 1–8 and 9–16 form paired phrases, the second completing the first. But what about the next phrase—where does it begin? Clearly it cannot begin at m. 17 or 18; by then the new structures are well under way. It must begin at the downbeat of m. 16. On the other hand that downbeat is the second primary beat of the second phrase. The solution is of course, that one and the same beat must serve two functions. When one point in time serves both as the second primary beat for one phrase and the first primary beat for the next, we say the phrases *overlap*. Overlapping can have a rather unsettling effect. The new phrase begins too early—that is, earlier than you would have any reason to expect. (In the present example this effect is underlined by the entrance of the full orchestra *ff* at the new phrase.) It can also be confusing, unless there is no doubt as to when the second primary beat is going to occur. (As in this example, overlap is frequently introduced at the second primary beat of the second of two paired phrases.)

Now consider the example on page 340. Again, the pairing of phrases makes the structure easy to grasp. The first phrase has its primary beats at m. 1 and m. 8 and the second phrase at m. 9 and at—well, what does happen at m. 16? We have every reason to expect the structure to be completed at that point, but when we get there we find it's not. Instead it takes another four measures to complete the structure.

What we have here is an example of *phrase extension*. In an extension the listener is made to believe that a particular point will function as the second primary beat of the phrase, only to find that a later point will be used instead. In an extension, the expectation of the earlier of the two points is strong enough so that the earlier point is used as the second primary reference point in understanding the structure of the phrase up to that point. Extensions can easily become confusing. To keep the structure clear for your listener you must

1. give him an absolutely sure sense of when B_2 ought to come, and
2. give him pitches at B_2 that will make it clear that the phrase has not yet reached its destination.

The easiest way to do the first is to use embedded or paired phrases. The easiest way to do the second is to

(Mozart: *Sonata* K.310, third movement, mm. 1–20.)

use a *deceptive cadence*. Note that when Mozart gets to the expected second primary beat of the second phrase, all the lines go where they are expected to except the bass, which moves to the sixth degree instead of to the tonic. He can then repeat the preceding three measures and arrive at the right pitches in all lines four measures later.

Exercises

1. Show how you understand the given passage in terms of
   a. on-the-beat notes
   b. notes falling on downbeats
   c. notes falling on primary downbeats of phrases
   d. notes filling whole phrase spans
   e. even larger spans.

(Mozart: *Sonata* K.311, first movement, mm. 1–16.)

342

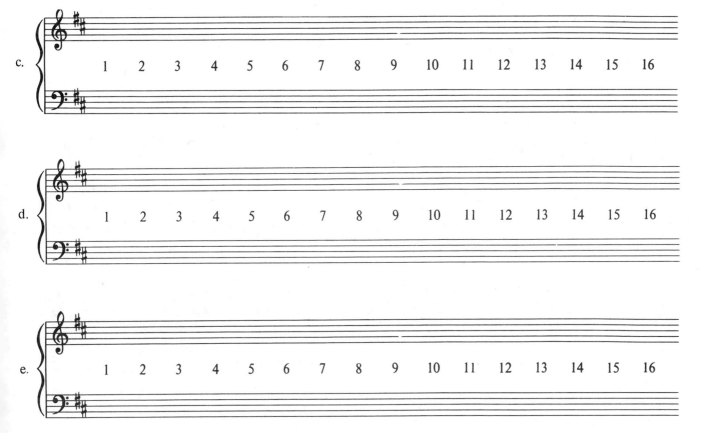

2. Write a 16-measure piece for piano based on the information in 1c, 1d and 1e. The meter should be $\frac{2}{4}$.

Supplementary Assignments

1. Use the concepts of phrase embedding, pairing, and overlap to show the phrase structure of the following passage:

2. Write the beginning of a movement for piano in $\frac{6}{8}$ that uses the same phrase structure as the above.

8.4 Non-Diatonic Voice-Leading Procedures: Secondary Dominants, Diminished Sevenths, and Augmented Sixth Chords; Mixtures

In Section 7.6 we looked at non-diatonic procedures in terms of the structure of the individual line. In this section we will look at a few of the standard ways in which collections of diatonic pitches—either simultaneous or arpeggiated—can be altered chromatically to form *chords* whose intervallic make-up, or "harmonic color", forms a significant factor in the understanding of the passage at hand.

Secondary Dominants • So far, we have used secondary dominants only to allow cadences for phrases that do not end on the tonic. But they can be used in a variety of other roles as well. Any time you have a collection of simultaneous pitches that are consonant with one another you can always put before them another collection made up of neighbors, step motions, arpeggiations, or pitches left over from the preceding notes

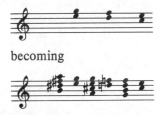

with the same intervallic relationship to the original collection that the elements of a dominant, dominant seventh, or dominant ninth have to a tonic triad.* The added collection is called a *secondary dominant*. It can occur before the span defined by the original collection, in which case its notes occupy anticipatory segments,

---

* Where the consonant collection is limited to thirds and sixths, it is considered to represent a triad without a fifth. Thus

or it can occur at the beginning of that span, in which case the notes of the original collection are delayed and the notes of the secondary dominant are used to mark the point where the original notes would have occurred.†

Like chromatically altered neighbors, the great advantage of secondary dominants is that they help the listener separate out the pitches of secondary structures from those of underlying structures. The difference lies in the fact that a secondary dominant is not just one note but a collection of notes. The intervallic make-up of this collection—its dominant color—helps the listener recognize the subsidiary function not only of the one or two notes that have to be chromatically altered to give it that color, but of the collection as a whole. Secondary dominants are commonly applied to parallel step motions, both to intensify the sense of motion and to hide parallel fifths (see example at the top of the next page).

Diminished Sevenths • You can use chromatic neighbors and passing tones in combination with diatonic pitches to create collections with all kinds of intervallic make-up.

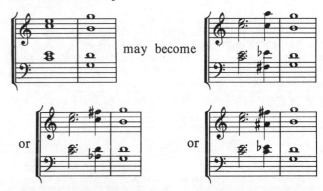

---

† Note the voice-leading: in both cases the parallel octaves are considered "broken" by the pitches of the intervening dominants. The voice-leading of secondary dominant sevenths follows that of dominant sevenths in general (see pages 325 ff.). However, when a secondary dominant seventh is applied to a collection that is itself a dominant seventh, the third of the secondary dominant usually goes down a semitone to the seventh of the more fundamental collection. Thus, instead of

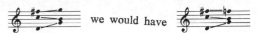

(Schubert: *Ganymed*, D.544, mm. 75–78.)

We distinguish, however, between collections in general use — like the dominant seventh — and collections that are special to a particular piece — like the "Tristan chord" at the beginning of m. 2 in the example on page 284. The advantage of the collections in general use is that the listener familiar with their functions in other pieces can grasp their function in the piece at hand more readily. The advantage of the collections special to a particular piece lies in the way they create for that piece its own special intervallic consistency.* Besides dominant sevenths and ninths, two other types of collections are commonly enough used to merit special discussion. Each type is named after the non-diatonic interval that gives it distinctive color.

Start with two notes forming a perfect fifth. If you approach the upper note with an upper neighbor and the lower note with a lower neighbor, the neighbors will form a seventh. If one or more of the neighbors is chromatically altered so as to be only a minor second from the note it embellishes, the neighbors will form a diminished seventh. If the notes forming the fifth have a third between them, or then a lower neighbor to the third would be a minor third above the neighbor to the bottom note , an upper neighbor would be a minor third below the neighbor to the top note , and the two neighbors to the middle note would be a minor third from each other: Any of these three- or four-note collections

---

* Thus the particular combination of intervals that make up the "Tristan chord" permeates the entire opera, not only as a result of the voice-leading procedures shown on page 284, but as a result of many other procedures as well. For example, in Act II Tristan sings a line whose opening pitches are the enharmonic equivalents of the F, B, D♯, and G♯ that make up the original statement of the chord. Here, however, A♭ and E♭ appear as members of the tonic triad, C♭ as the minor version of the mediant of that triad, and F is an upper neighbor to E♭ (subsequently brought back down to E♭ in the accompaniment).

(Wagner: *Tristan und Isolde*, Act II.)

is called a *diminished seventh chord*. Other ways of approaching a triad will also yield diminished seventh chords.

If the elements of the triad being approached are put in a different vertical order,

the diminished seventh chord may have major sixths instead of minor thirds, augmented fourths instead of diminished fifths, and an augmented second instead of a diminished seventh, but we still think of its intervallic color as essentially the same.

Like secondary dominants, diminished sevenths are often used to embellish parallel step motions and hide parallel fifths.

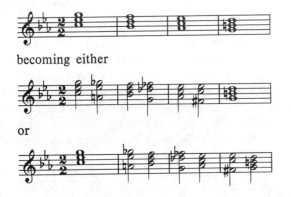

Despite the fact that the diminished seventh is itself a highly unstable collection (there are three augmented or diminished intervals between its four members), its pitches can be delayed to allow dissonant suspension and on-the-beat dissonant neighbors that are understood to resolve into the familiar color of the chord itself.

(Schubert: *Dass sie hier gewesen*, D.775, mm. 1–8.)

Augmented Sixths • Suppose you have two notes an octave apart: If you approach the upper note with a lower neighbor and the lower note with an upper neighbor, the neighbors form a sixth: If you alter either or both so that both neighbors are a minor second from the note they embellish, the neighbors will form an augmented sixth: If there is another note a third above either of the two original notes, or you can approach it by an upper neighbor in parallel thirds with the bottom line: The new collection of pitches is called an augmented sixth chord. If there is also a note a fifth above the lower of the two notes forming the original octave, you can either anticipate it or give it an upper neighbor: *

Both these four-note collections are called augmented sixth chords too. To distinguish among the three we call the first of the four-note chords an augmented six-four-three (after the interval classes starting from the bass and reading from largest to smallest) and the second an augmented six-five-three.

All three of these collections of neighbors could have been arrived at by using other voice-leading pro-

---

* These parallel fifths don't seem to bother composers:

(Beethoven: *Sonata* Op. 57, second movement, mm. 5–8.)

(note spelling, instead of)

Evidently the augmented sixth removes any possibility of the first fifth defining a stable structure in its own right and hence removes the underlying objection to parallel fifths.

cedures as well, as long as the direction of the lines is the same as it was for the pitches in the original collection.* Lines shown here as upper lines could have been lower lines with the same pitch classes,

although most of the time the lower of the two notes forming the augmented sixth is given to the bass. Augmented sixths are frequently used to approach a dominant at the end of a phrase or section. The chromatically altered neighbors forming the augmented sixth intensify the sense of arrival of two of the lines on the fifth degree, while the other line or lines either move directly to the seventh and second degrees,

(Mozart: *Sonata* K.332, first movement, mm. 35–40.)

or are delayed in a double $\begin{smallmatrix}6-5\\4-3\end{smallmatrix}$ suspension.

(Mozart: *Don Giovanni*, Overture, mm. 28–31.)

In a major key, what had been a chromatically lowered neighbor to the second degree may be raised back to the original diatonic sixth at the moment of suspension.

* Where the augmented sixth chord leads to a dominant seventh, the raised pitch may be led down a semitone to the seventh of the next chord:

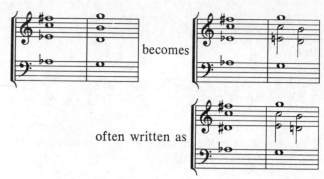

becomes

often written as

Like the diminished seventh, the augmented sixth is so easily recognized that its own unstable elements can be delayed to allow dissonant suspensions or on-the-beat neighbors. In the following example the diminished octave—G♮/G♯—can be thought of as resolving to a diminished seventh—F♮/G♯.

(Mozart: *Sonata* K.331, second movement, mm. 80–82.)

Enharmonic Ambiguity • Diminished seventh chords, augmented sixth chords, and secondary dominants offer ample opportunity for enharmonic ambiguity. Take the diminished seventh chord. We show by the way we write it which interval we think of as the non-diatonic one—the diminished seventh or augmented second—and which interval we think of as the diatonic one—the minor third or major sixth.

But when the performer plays these notes the listener has no way of knowing which intervals are the diatonic ones and which are not until he hears where the pitches are going next.

This means that although the listener can recognize by the color of the diminished seventh collection that the pitches are unstable, although he understands that they must be secondary to another collection of pitches, and although he expects them to lead by step to that collection, he can never be sure which direction the steps will go in, and hence will not be sure what that next collection will be. Indeed, the same diminished seventh chord may be used to approach two different triads in succession.

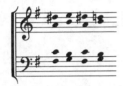

Take the augmented six-four-three. We show by the way we write it which interval we think of as the non-diatonic augmented sixth (or diminished third) and which we think of as the diatonic minor seventh (or major second).

If the bass and some other note form an interval of ten semitones, the listener would normally assume that this will be the non-diatonic interval, since this is usually the case.

But it need not always be the case.

Finally, take the augmented six-five-three. Enharmonically, it has the same intervallic make-up as a dominant seventh. The only way the listener can be sure which it is is to hear where it goes.

Mixture • We use the catch-all term mixture to cover the alteration of one or more diatonic degrees so that a collection of simultaneously sounding notes will form a major triad instead of a minor or diminished one, or a minor triad instead of a major one. Often—as in the example below—the altered pitches can also be explained as forming chromatic

(Schubert: *Die schöne Müllerin*, "Morgengruss," mm. 12–15.)

(Schubert: *Die schöne Müllerin,* "Die liebe Farbe," mm. 6–13.)

neighbors or step motions. But this need not be the case, particularly when it is the tonic triad itself that is subjected to mixture (see above).

Nineteenth-century composers used mixture to create striking effects—effects so striking that the structural role played by mixture can easily go unnoticed. The immediate effect of mixture is to produce surprise at the unexpected color of the altered triad; the listener's attention is drawn to the non-diatonic pitch that created the change. The longer-range effect is—or should be—a better understanding of the structure as a whole. If the listener pays attention to the unaltered pitches in the triad, he should be able to understand its connection to its surroundings despite the change in color. Thus, to take the simplest kind of mixture, when the third degree of a major key is lowered so as to make the tonic triad minor, the immediate effect is that of contrast, created by the altered degree, but the long-range effect is to confirm the identity of the even more fundamental degrees, the dominant and the tonic themselves.

Or, to take a more complicated mixture, when the fifth degree of a major key is raised to make the triad based on the third degree a major one (as in the example below), the immediate effect is that of structural

(Mahler: *Lieder aus "Des Knaben Wunderhorn,"* "Wer hat dies Liedel erdacht?" mm. 41–54.)

disorientation; this new triad seems to have nothing to do with the tonic triad. The ultimate effect is that of structural clarity.* The third degree is the only pitch class these two triads have in common. The underlying structure of this part of the piece exploits the relationship between the bottom two elements in the tonic triad, F and A. The dominant, C, normally a more fundamental element in the triad, is kept in check by being altered to C♯. When the cadence in F major occurs, C♯ returns to C, so in a sense, C♯ functions as the enharmonic equivalent of a lowered sixth degree, D♭, except, of course, that it is consonant with the A, which D♭ couldn't be. Note how Mahler uses the details to reflect the larger structure. By treating the A-major triad as though it were the tonic for a few measures, he can introduce the elements of an F-major triad as a mixture, a major triad based on the lowered sixth degree of A major. This F-major triad is clearly unstable—note the fact that the C is in the bass. The F functions as a neighbor to the E and the C functions as the enharmonic equivalent of a lower neighbor to the C♯. The next twelve measures exploit the reverse of these relationships.

* Here mixture affects not only the pitches of the triad in question (A, C♯, and E replacing A, C, and E) but the pitches forming neighbors to and step motions between members of that triad (A–B–C♯, A–G♯–A). Thus, by using the diatonic collection associated with the A-major triad the composer gets us to understand that triad as though it were—momentarily at least—the tonic triad. See *Tonicization* in the next section of this chapter.

(*Ibid.*, mm. 55–76.)

Drill

For each of the following
- a. identify the intervallic make-up of the given chord ("dominant seventh," "augmented sixth," etc.)
- b. lead the given chord to a triad
- c. write another chord that is enharmonically equivalent to the given chord and lead it to a different triad.

Exercises

Use the following model according to the instructions below.

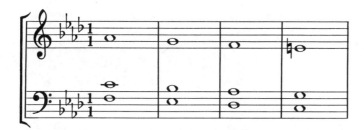

For each of the following write two versions, one with the added chords on the beat and one with them off the beat. (For each version, start from the given model, not from what you got by the previous operation.)

1. Use neighbors, step motions, anticipations, and anticipatory arpeggiations so that each of the given chords is preceded by its dominant, thus breaking the parallel fifths.

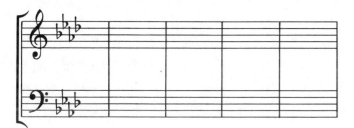
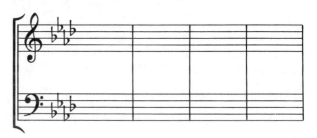

2. Use chromatic neighbors, passing tones, suspensions, and anticipations so that each of the given chords is preceded by a diminished seventh chord.

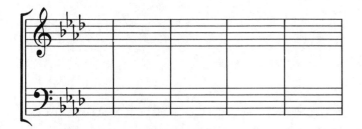
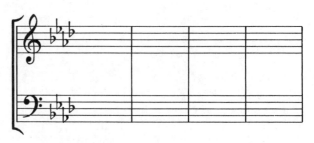

3. Write a phrase using techniques practiced in 1. and 2. but approaching the final chord with an augmented sixth chord.

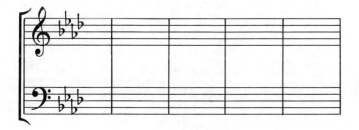
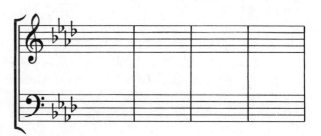

8.5 Tonicization, Structural Parallelism, and Large-Scale Span Structure

We are now ready to return to rhythmic structure itself and consider the problem of the span structure of a whole movement. The listener trying to understand a whole movement must ask himself, "How do I divide the whole into parts? Where does one part end and the next begin? How do I relate the parts to each other and to the whole?" Consequently the composer (and, as we will see in Chapter 9, the performer as well) must ask himself, "How do I make it clear where the large sections of the piece begin and end and how they are related to one another and to the whole?"

This is problematic for both listener and composer because of two factors: the length of the spans and the complexity of their interior structures. As we saw in Section 8.0, the longer the span, the less accurately the listener can estimate its length. The less accurately he can estimate its length, the less he can depend on the laws of segmentation, delay, and anticipation to relate this span to other spans and the more he must depend on its pitches and their relationship to the pitches of other spans. However, the longer the span, the more notes there are apt to be in the span and hence the more opportunities for ambiguity as to what the span pitches are. Consequently, as we pointed out at the end of Section 8.0, the composer must either find ways of making it easier for the listener to compare long stretches of music with one another, or find ways of making it easier for the listener to grasp such passages in terms of a few salient pitches which he can then relate to other such pitches.

In fact, as we shall see in this section, we can do both. We can use the process of *tonicization* to clarify which pitches in a passage are to be thought of as reference points, and the principle of *structural parallelism* to make it easier to relate passages to one another.

Tonicization • Every tonal piece is by definition in a particular key. That is, we understand its structure in terms of a single pitch class, the tonic, a triad built on that pitch class, the tonic triad, and a collection of pitch classes associated with that triad, the diatonic collection. So far we have considered any pitch not in that collection to be a raised or lowered variant of one of the pitches in the collection. We have avoided the possibility of considering these pitches as members of another diatonic collection. That possibility is, however, of fundamental importance to the structure of tonal music, particularly to its large-scale structure.

Tonicization* is simply the process of treating a pitch class other than the tonic as though it were the tonic, at least for the time being. In itself, this is easy enough to do. Just take any collection of simultaneously sounding pitches in your underlying structure. If they are consonant but not all members of the tonic triad, they either form another triad, or, if less than three pitch classes are present, can be made to form another triad by the addition of other pitches.

The pitches of this triad can then be arpeggiated, just as though they formed the tonic, and connected by step motion and embellished by neighbors taken from the diatonic collection associated with the new triad. In short, you can erect the same kinds of secondary structures on pitches forming triads other than the tonic that you can on the pitches that represent the tonic triad itself as in the example on the next page.†

Clearly, the advantage of such a procedure is the way it makes it so easy for your listener to grasp which pitches—or at any rate which pitch classes—are likely to prove fundamental for the passage as a whole. By creating secondary structures with the diatonic collection associated with a given triad you make it easier for him to relate all the pitches in the passage to the pitches belonging to that triad. That triad he can then, in turn, relate to the structure of the piece as a whole. Thus, in the example on the next page we say mm. 11–18 are "in the dominant key", or, simply "in the dominant." That means that we relate all the pitches during mm. 11–18 to the E-major triad as though it were the tonic triad, but we think of the E-major triad within the piece as a whole as the dominant triad, and we relate its pitches in mm. 11–18 to those of the A-major triad in mm. 1–10 accordingly.

By letting your listener know which pitch classes are likely to be the fundamental pitches of the passage you also make it much easier for him to grasp the large-scale span structure. By using the diatonic col-

---

* An ugly word, formed in imitation of the German *Tonikalisierung*, but so well established that we have no alternative but to use it.

† Note the difference here between the concept of tonicization and the ideas implied by the commonly used term "modulation." To say that Mozart modulates from A major to E major says nothing about the way in which a structure in E major can be understood as part of a larger structure in A major.

Mm. 1–10: Two phrases forming a complete structure in A major

Mm. 11–18: Tonicization of the E major triad

(Mozart: *Sonata* K.331, second movement, mm. 1–18.)

lection associated with a given triad you make him suspect that there is or will be a span whose pitches belong to that triad. If you begin your tonicization with a phrase whose first large segment is obviously based on pitches belonging to the tonicized triad, he will understand the span as beginning on the initial primary downbeat of that phrase. Thus, in our Mozart example it is clear that a new span begins on the downbeat of m. 11. On the other hand if you begin your tonicization in the middle of a phrase and end the phrase with a half cadence on the dominant of the triad you are tonicizing, you can make your listener expect a new span to begin with the initial primary downbeat of the next phrase. Consider the example on the next page. Here the tonicization of B♭ begins in the middle of the second phrase (m. 13), which ends with a half cadence in B♭ major (m. 15). This makes us expect the next phrase to begin with a B♭-major triad. Indeed this expectation is so strong that when the pitches of the dominant seventh of B♭ major occur on what appears to be the initial primary downbeat of the next phrase (m. 17), we are willing to assume that the pitches of the tonic triad have been delayed, and that the pitches at m. 17 simply mark the point at which they would have occurred.

Note that in both these cases we do not have to know exactly which members of the tonicized triad are the span pitches and which are just doublings or borrowings in order to know when the new span begins and how it is to be related to the old one. Thus, in the Mozart example, we might at first suppose that the dotted half-note B in m. 11 is the span pitch and the other B's in that measure are doublings or borrowings. At the end of the phrase, however, the B an octave lower proves to be connected by step motion through C♯ and D♯ to the E in m. 18, while the upper B leads only to a C♯ which is left hanging. It is therefore conceptually convenient to regard the lower B as more fundamental for these eight measures as a whole. But changing our mind about which B is *the* B does not invalidate our initial impression that a span with a B had begun at the downbeat of m. 11. Similarly, in order to relate the two spans we do not need to know exactly which members of either of the triads functioning as tonics are the span pitches and which are just doublings or borrowings. Thus, in the Mozart example we can assume that the span pitches for mm. 1–10 will all be members of the A-major triad with A in the bass while those of mm. 11–18 will be members of the E-major triad with E in the bass. Even though we may not know how members of these pitch classes are to be connected to form the upper lines of the underlying structure of this section, we do at least know that the underlying bass line consists of an A followed by an E. Since E is a member of the A-major triad, we have every reason to assume that we can understand both as forming an arpeggiation. If we then attempt to find linear connections for the upper lines that will, like the arpeggiation in the bass, allow us to think of both these large spans as segments of an even larger span, we find there are plenty: we just have to assume that most of the lines form incomplete structures which will be completed later.

Step motion from one element of an A-major triad to another	Embellishing a member of an A-major triad by neighbor	Rearticulation of a member of an A-major triad
C♯–B–(A)	C♯–B –(C♯)	E–E
A –B–(C♯)	A –B –(A)	
	A –G♯–(A)	

We have no way of knowing which of these connections are the relevant ones until the piece is complete, but we don't have to wait until the end of the piece to be fairly certain of the relationship between the first two large spans.

The underlying structure used to tonicize E major in mm. 11–18 of our Mozart example is the same kind he uses as the underlying structure of the whole movement, complete with a basic step motion from mediant down to tonic in one of the upper lines and a basic arpeggiation—tonic–dominant–tonic—in the bass. By using this kind of structure as the basis for a whole series of successive secondary structures you can lend to the pitch class you are tonicizing the strongest possible sense of tonic identity. However, any structure that can be interpreted in terms of one and only one set of diatonic degrees can be used to tonicize a pitch class. The strength of the tonicizing effect will vary with the type of structure you use. It will vary with such factors as

1. the role in the underlying structure of the whole span taken by the pitches of the tonicized triad— Are they the pitches of the first segment of that span? Of the last segment? Is there an arpeggiation of triad pitches in the bass?
2. the depth of structure of the passage as a whole— How many successive sets of operations in the tonicized key are necessary to arrive at the passage? Are the pitches belonging to the diatonic collection just details or do some of them lie deep in the structure of the passage?

Thus, for example, you can to some extent get your listener to identify a triad as a tonic simply by having its dominant precede it.

(Beethoven: *Sonata* Op. 49, No. 1, first movement, mm. 1–33.)

The strength of that identification is, however, so limited that we have invented a special category, namely secondary dominant, so as not to consider such a case a tonicization. But by using the diatonic collection associated with that "tonic" triad to create secondary motions from one element in the dominant to another, we can increase the sense of tonic identity slightly.

Or, to take another tack, by having the dominant follow its triad we can use the pitches of both as the basis of a phrase, ending, of course, with an incomplete cadence.

Such structures are particularly useful in tonicizing pitches whose function it is to lead from one strongly tonicized triad to another. The underlying structures of such "transitional sections" may begin with pitches left over from the preceding section, but their underlying structure usually has the function of preparing the listener to understand what pitch class to expect as the tonic in the next section. For example, consider the next twelve measures of the Mozart example:

(Mozart: *Sonata* K.331, second movement, mm. 19–30.)

We can understand this passage in terms of an underlying structure whose long-range function is to make us identify the E-major triad as a dominant again.*

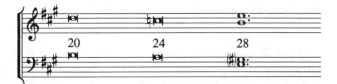

All three groups of simultaneously sounding notes are delayed, the places where they would have begun being marked for the first two by their dominants and for the E-major triad by an augmented sixth.

Step motions from one element of these dominants to another create a weak sense of tonicization of B minor followed by A minor.

The passage is connected to the preceding passage by an E and G♮ that are at once part of the preceding span (they are members of the minor version of the triad just tonicized) and also anticipatory arpeggiations to the dominant that follows (E and G♮ as the seventh and ninth of a dominant ninth in B minor).

* Note that the diatonic collection used is that of A minor; the first eighteen measures give us every reason to suppose that the underlying structure of the whole movement is in A major and hence that, whatever happens in the middle, we will return before the end to the use of A major as a local tonic triad. E major can function as the dominant triad of both A major and A minor. The advantage of using the diatonic collection of A minor to set up E as the dominant is that its tonic triad (here represented by the A and the C♮) cannot be mistaken for *the* tonic triad of the piece, namely the A-major triad.

The E eventually leads to the D in m. 23, but the G♮, instead of leading to an F♯ in that measure, is brought down to an F♮, thereby preventing any sense of arrival at the triad being tonicized and allowing D and F♮ to function as seventh and ninth to the next dominant.

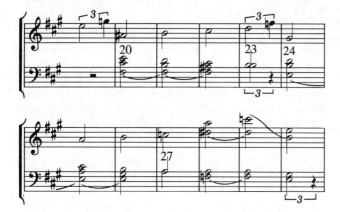

The D reaches its destination (C♮) in m. 27, but the F♮ does not. There is no E in m. 27; instead, F♮ is brought down to E in the bass in the next three measures. Note the way the sense of arrival at the A-minor triad in m. 27 is further weakened by the use of a member of the A-major collection both in a step motion from one element of the dominant to another in an inner line (m. 25) and as an upper neighbor to the second degree in the top line.

Thus, the tonicizations of B minor and A minor serve to help us understand which pitches form the underlying structure of the passage as a whole without distracting us from the function of that structure, namely, to arrive at an E-major triad in such a way as to make us understand it as a dominant and so to expect that a new large-scale span with A-major triad pitches will start on the next downbeat.* Note that neither of the tonicized triads is allowed to begin a span. They are delayed to the ends of spans, and the position of rhythmic emphasis is taken by their dominants. Nor are they allowed to become points of arrival in their own right. While the spans occupying mm. 20–23 and mm. 24–27 may be considered as phrase spans with two primary segments—of three and one measures respectively, in both cases—in neither case is a cadence used to warn us of the

---

* The presentation of the dominant triad of a key in such a way as to prepare the listener to understand the arrival of the tonic triad of the key as the beginning of a large-scale span is called a "dominant preparation." The use of the minor version of the expected major key and the use of the augmented sixth are characteristic means for making sure a triad will be understood as a dominant without actually stating the tonic triad before the beginning of the span in question.

(Mozart: *Sonata* K.332, first movement, mm. 19–45.)

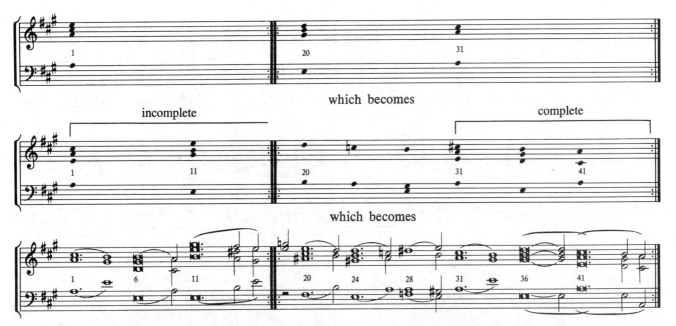

advent of the second primary downbeat and in both cases the second segment contains structures that lead us on into the next span.

Large-Scale Structural Parallelism • In Section 8.3 we saw how the principle of structural parallelism could be applied to consecutive phrases to make it easier for the listener to grasp their relationship. The same principle can be applied to larger units as well. By using the same kinds of structural details in the same order in two subsequent sections you can make it possible for your listener to grasp the relationship of one to the other.

Consider the whole of the Menuetto we have been using. (See the next page.) Mm. 31–48 present essentially the same series of structural details as mm. 1–18. In general, such a parallelism helps us understand the structure of the last eighteen measures in terms of what we already have understood about the first eighteen measures. In particular:

1. We can relate the initial primary downbeat of the first phrase in the last section back to the initial primary downbeat of the first phrase in the movement. We have already understood the downbeat of m. 1 not just as the first primary reference point for the first phrase but as the beginning of the first large span of the piece. The combination of the prepared return to the pitches of the A-major triad functioning as a tonic triad with the series of identical details in mm. 31 ff makes us assume that the downbeat at m. 31 will take on a similar role here.

2. We can relate the underlying pitch structures of the two sections to one another. The fact that the details are largely parallel makes it easier to grasp that the underlying structures are not, that is mm. 41–48 do not tonicize the dominant triad as mm. 11–18 did, but continue to use the A-major triad as the tonic. The effect is essentially the same as that when the second of two paired phrases presents a completed form of the incomplete structure used by the first. (Note also the non-parallel structural characteristics: instead of closing off mm. 31–40 with a full cadence at m. 40, as he did at m. 10, Mozart brings in the D in the bass a measure later [m. 39 instead of m. 38] so he can begin his cadence in m. 40 and arrive at a second primary downbeat in m. 41. That second primary downbeat is, of course, also the initial primary downbeat of the final phrase.)

3. We can identify the span length of mm. 31–48 with that of mm. 1–18 and hence relate the length of mm. 31–48 to the total length of everything up to m. 31. Without necessarily having the slightest sense of how many measures or how many phrases of how many measures each the parallel sections are comprised of, we can assume they must be equal since they are parallel. This means that mm. 1–30 must be longer than mm. 31–48, since the latter section has nothing corresponding to mm. 19–30. Since mm. 19–30 are not longer than mm. 1–18 these durations would obviously suggest the following overall span structure.*

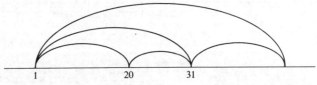

Such a structure fits the rest of our information. In short, we can think of the whole Menuetto in terms of the structures shown above. Note in particular the

---

* Simplified so as to neglect the repeats. With repeats we could represent it as

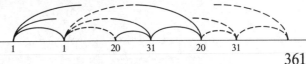

(Mozart: Sonata K.331, second movement, mm. 1–48.)

way the structural parallelism helps us understand the incomplete structure of mm. 1–18 as completed by the statement of a similar—but complete—structure in mm. 31–48. To understand the E-major triad pitches in mm. 11–18 in terms of the A-major triad pitches in mm. 1–10 we assumed (see pages 357 ff) that the structure would be completed in the next span by a set of A-major triad pitches. But the pitches of the next span are *not* those of the A-major triad. The only way we can understand the underlying structure of mm. 1–18 is as an *incomplete* structure, a complete form of which is given in the parallel measures at the end of the Menuetto.*

Structural parallelism between sections has the strongest effect on the large-scale span system when, as in the last example, the first primary downbeat of the second of the two parallel sections coincides with a return of the tonic triad of the underlying structure to its function as a local tonic as well. Such a return, coupled with a parallel series of details is commonly called a "recapitulation" and is one of the strongest methods for clarifying the overall span structure of a whole movement. It is, however, also possible to use structural parallelism to clarify smaller-span relationships as well. Thus in the Trio that together with the foregoing Menuetto constitutes the second movement of Mozart's Sonata, K. 331, the most obvious and extended parallelism is the one between mm. 1–16 and mm. 37–52. (See the next page.) Since the return of the tonic as local tonic occurs on the first primary downbeat of mm. 37–52 (that is, m. 37 itself) this parallelism simply results in an overall structure much like that of the Menuetto. There is, however, also a more limited parallelism that helps us relate the downbeat of m. 17 back to the one at m. 1. The parallelism is limited to a few details and breaks off in a few measures (see below) but mm. 1, 17, and 37 are the only measures in which such patterns are initiated. Obviously there can be no question of a recapitulation at m. 17, since whatever those pitches are they aren't the tonic. However, the first time this downbeat occurs it is equally spaced with the downbeats of m. 1 and the repetition of m. 1 (and easily perceivable as such because of the obvious parallelism between the first sixteen measures and their repetition). Furthermore, these are the only points so far at which phrases have begun on the downbeat. The combined effect of these factors is to make us want to use the downbeat of m. 17 as the primary downbeat of a span, even though the pitches associated with it are not members of the tonic triad or, for that matter, even members of a triad about to be tonicized. Thus, we can think of mm. 17–36 in terms of a single long span beginning on the downbeat of m. 17 and occupied by pitches that are all members of the dominant triad of D major.

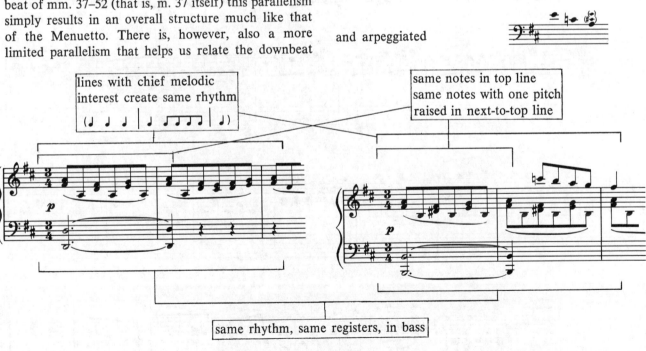

---

* Note that the span starting at m. 11 is too long to be considered as an anticipatory segment to the span beginning at m. 20. Note also that if we were to consider the A-major triad pitches at m. 31 as delayed from m. 20, the second segment of the span of the Menuetto as a whole (mm. 20–48) would be noticeably longer than the first.

(Mozart: *Sonata* K. 331, second movement, trio.)

so as to form three large segments beginning at mm. 17, 25, and 31. The E and the C are weakly tonicized: the E-minor triad is delayed four measures and its place marked by its dominant, but all step motions between elements of either triad are restricted to details in eighth notes; the C-major triad is arpeggiated in the top line, but the bass is limited to a neighbor motion. The A-major triad, on the other hand, is made to sound like the dominant it is: the diatonic collection used is that of D minor with G♯'s functioning as chromatically altered neighbors.

Without the parallelism between mm. 1 and 17 we would assume that the new span begins on the downbeat at m. 21, since that point could be interpreted as the initial primary downbeat of a phrase whose first-segment pitches are members of the triad being tonicized. With the parallelism it is easier to assume that mm. 17–24 are all one phrase whose second-segment pitches are delayed representatives of the span pitches.

The usual effect of such limited structural parallelisms is to refer the listener back to some earlier, obviously more stable, point in the structure. However, they can also be used to refer the listener ahead, if he has ample reason to expect a certain string of structural details to begin at a particular time. Thus, for example, if he thinks a recapitulation is about to occur, you could define an anticipatory segment toward the end of the dominant preparation by using structural details similar to those he would expect to find at the beginning of the recapitulation.

(Haydn: *Symphony* No. 100, fourth movement, mm. 1–4.)

(*Ibid.*, mm. 212–219.)

Exercises

1. Using the rhythm

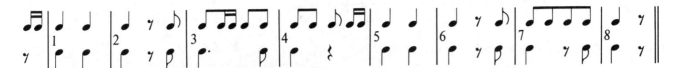

complete each of the given eight-measure sections as follows:
a. Mm. 7 and 8 tonicize F major with a half cadence in F.
b. Mm. 5–8 tonicize F major and end with a full cadence in F.
c. Mm. 3 and 4 tonicize F major by ending with a half cadence in F major.
   Mm. 5 and 6 are structurally parallel to 1 and 2 but in F major.
   Mm. 7 and 8 return to D minor and end in a full cadence.

2. Using the rhythm

and the underlying linear structure

complete the following measures so as to prepare a return to D minor.

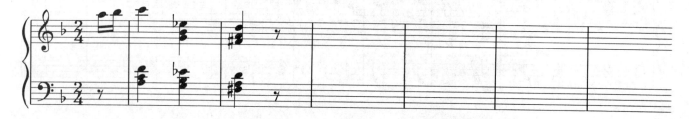

3. Using the rhythm indicated in question 1., write eight measures that could serve as mm. 15–22 of a piece in which your version b. serves as mm. 1–8 and your answer to question 2. serves as mm. 9–14.

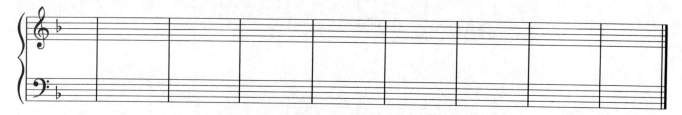

(After you have finished your piece, you might be interested in comparing it with mm. 21–40 of the Finale of Haydn's Piano Sonata No. 7 which have a similar—although not identical—structure.)

4. Show the large-scale pitch and rhythmic structure of each of the following movements in the space provided on p. 373.

(Haydn: *Quartet* Op. 3, No. 3, third movement, minuet.)

(Haydn: *Quartet* Op. 3, No. 3, third movement, trio.)

(Beethoven: *Sonata* Op. 2, No. 2, third movement, scherzo.)

(Beethoven: *Sonata* Op. 2, third movement, trio).

(Haydn: Menuetto)

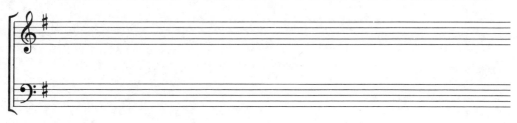

(Haydn: Trio)

(Beethoven: Scherzo)

(Beethoven: Trio)

5. Write a movement in $\frac{2}{4}$ based on any one of the large-scale structures you arrived at in answering question 4.

8.6 An Overview and Some Words of Warning

Levels · In Chapter 3 we presented the view that any piece of tonal music can be understood as a generated structure. That is,
1. we can generate all the notes of any tonal piece from the pitches of its tonic triad by successive application of a small set of operations and moreover
2. the successive stages in the generation process show how we understand the notes of that piece in terms of one another.

In Chapters 4–6 we got some practical experience with this approach by using a related set of operations to generate short compositions within the limited temporal framework of species counterpoint. In Chapters 7 and 8 we have been trying to show how the operations described in Chapter 3 can be applied within the more highly differentiated temporal framework characteristic of actual tonal music. One effect of this differentiated framework is that we expect certain types of structures to be completed at particular stages. We call the particular stages *levels* and name them according to the time spans associated with them.* For the shorter spans dealt with in Chapter 7 we name the level by the shortest span accorded its own pitch. Thus, the structure at the "beat level" consists solely of on-the-beat notes, although some of these may last more than a beat. Similarly, the structure at the measure level consists solely of notes beginning on the downbeat, although some of these may last longer than a measure. For the longer spans dealt with in Chapter 8, we name the level according to the shortest span for which we have complete underlying structures. Thus, the structure at the phrase level will show the principal segments of phrases. The section level will show how span pitches defined by phrases or groups of phrases form structures that underlie a whole section. Finally, the structure at the movement level will provide a simple underlying structure for the whole movement.

Obviously, for longer movements, more than one level will be necessary between the phrase and movement level. We consider all such intermediate levels as section levels in that they do not have phrase-like structures, but we have no regular names for them other than the somewhat awkward "large-section level," "small-section level," "subsection level," etc. Intermediate levels between measure and phrase levels may also prove useful in certain cases. There we may distinguish between a macro-measure level and a subphrase level according to whether the structure at that level resembles those at the measure or at the phrase level. We characterize structures at the beat and measure level as "close to the surface;" that is, they are separated by relatively few operations from the actual notes of the movement. We think of structures at the phrase and section levels as "deeper." We think of the underlying structure for the whole movement as being at the deepest structural level.†

Certain types of structures and certain ways of combining lines are difficult to perceive at deeper levels and are hence more characteristic of levels close to the surface. Anticipations, for example, require some sense of what is about to happen. They are relatively easy to grasp when the anticipated pitch is expected at the next beat or downbeat. At levels where there are no equally spaced reference points, anticipations must be made clear by other means.‡

Delays, on the other hand, require only that we recognize that what has happened at one point could have happened at an earlier point. They can be used at the phrase or section level as well as at the beat or measure level.

Segmentations are found at all levels. However, the longer the segments of a span the less accurately we can compare their relative lengths. Unless strong parallelism at surface levels makes them easy to compare, at the section level only gross differences in segment length are relevant. Furthermore, the more subsequent operations involving doubling, borrowing, and transfer, the less sure we can be of which segment pitches belong in which register and hence in which line of the structure; often the only line for which the segment pitch (or even pitch class) is obvious is the bass. At section and movement levels, therefore, the law of segmentation is often irrelevant and we must rely more heavily on the bass to grasp the structure.

The use of dissonance between simultaneously

---

* The term "level" is a translation of Schenker's term *Schicht*. *Schicht* might better be translated as "layer", but level has gained much greater currency. Note that level in this sense has nothing to do with the word as used in literary criticism, e.g., "allegorical level" or "narrative level".

† Schenker called these groupings of surface, intermediate, and deepest levels foreground, middle ground, and background (*Vordergrund, Mittelgrund,* and *Hintergrund*). While these terms have a wide circulation, I have avoided them because I find the visual analogy confuses people.

‡ For an unusually long anticipation, see mm. 390–397 in the first movement of Beethoven's Symphony No. 3. The E♭ triad pitches in the horn in mm. 394–395 can be considered anticipations of the same pitches in the cello at mm. 398 ff. We have been expecting the return of these pitches in this register for some time (m. 398 is the beginning of the recapitulation). The E♭ and the G in the horn are understood as dissonant against the span pitches of mm. 378–397 which form the dominant seventh in E♭ major. The problem with long anticipations is that it is usually easier to understand them as rearticulations. The same is not true of anticipatory arpeggiations, particularly when they are combined with incomplete neighbors to form dominant sevenths.

sounding pitches helps us to understand which pitches belong to the underlying structure. Where two lines form a dissonance, we seek to understand them in terms of a simpler situation involving only consonance. We would prefer not to have to understand a consonant combination of lines in terms of a dissonant combination of lines. Consequently, while dissonant combinations of lines are common at the beat and measure level, they are unusual at deeper levels. Frequent exceptions, however, are those dissonant combinations like the dominant seventh or even the diminished seventh that are easily recognized as a whole and hence can be used to form the basis of a whole section.

A Structural Map in Levels: Advantages and Dangers • By writing out the structures you understand at each successive level of a movement one on top of the other so that identical points in time are lined up vertically, you are in effect creating a map of the way you understand the entire movement.* Such a map has obvious advantages.

1. It gives us a way of dealing with complex structures in the object language by comparing them with other, simpler structures in the object language.† Since the structure at any level consists of actual notes, we can play those notes and compare what we hear to what we hear when we play the movement itself.

2. It gives us a way of perceiving the structure of a movement independently of our perception of that movement as we hear it unfold in actual time. To a large extent this advantage is simply due to the fact that ordinary musical notation shows sounds in time as symbols along a horizontal axis. If you want to know in which order the sounds occur, you read them left to right, but if you want to study their relationship, you may find that you look in both directions, skipping back and forth from one measure to another. Our map uses the horizontal axis in the same way but also uses various positions on the vertical axis to indicate more completely how time is being structured. The advantage is that one can move back and forth in the time of the piece and back and forth from simple to complex structures in the course of trying to understand the piece.

These advantages can, however, easily lead to misconceptions as to the purpose of such a map. Note that:

1. The only notes that we actually hear when the movement is played are the notes of the movement itself. To say that we understand the notes at one structural level, for example the surface, in terms of the notes at some deeper level is not to say that the notes at the deeper level actually occur as such in the surface level. There is no reason to assume that there are notes at the surface level that have the same pitches and begin at the same points as the notes of the deeper level. Nor is there any reason to assume that notes with the same pitches as the notes of the deeper level will be given any particular emphasis (length, loudness, strong metric position) at the surface level. The worst danger of using such a map is that you fall into the habit of thinking of the structure at each successive level as subsuming all the information at the next level closer to the surface. To say that you understand the notes of the structure at one level in terms of the notes of a simpler structure at the next deeper level is not to say that these structures are equivalent. And note also that

2. The movement itself is designed to be heard in time and its structure perceived as it unfolds in time. Any map of that structure is useful only insofar as it helps us to relate actual musical events as they occur in time.

By picturing the time in which a movement takes place as a single large unit divided into successively smaller units, our map may easily give a false impression of the way we perceive the movement in time. Our map takes little account of the continuity—or discontinuity—with which we perceive the succession of details of the movement itself. Those elements that we perceive as creating a discontinuity may be of far longer-range significance than our map shows. This is particularly true of those details that are discontinuous in that they lack a local explanation. The D in m. 2 of the Mozart Menuetto that we have used so often does not fit our system well. A map would make it disappear at the beat level, possibly by supplying an imaginary C♯. This is simply a way of supposing where a line containing the D would go if it had had a note on that beat. Our supposition receives some confirmation in m. 3, where, just as B went to A in m. 2, D now gets to C♯, and just as D didn't get to C♯ in m. 2, so F♯ now doesn't get to E. However, the lack of a simple local explanation for the D and the F♯ makes us particularly sensitive to what happens to these pitches in subsequent measures and helps prepare us for later events that will appear

---

* Such a map for the Menuetto from K. 331 is shown on the fold out at the back of this book. For a movement like this, it is still possible to put the whole map on a single piece of paper. For longer movements, however, lining up all the levels on a single sheet is impractical. In such cases the best solution is to make maps at more than one scale. For example, one map on a series of pages can line up the actual notes of the movement with the notes at the beat, measure, phrase, and small-section levels; another map on a single page can line up the notes at the small-section level with those at the large-section and movement levels. Note, however, that the two maps must have at least one level in common.

† See the end of Chapter 1 (page 9) for the distinction between object language and metalanguage.

at the deeper levels of our maps, for example the F♯ and the D in the bass of m. 45, or for that matter the D and F♯ of the triad used as the tonic for the whole Trio of this movement.

However, any discontinuity that the system is capable of creating—a change in the operation being used at a particular level, a change in the rate at which structures at a given level flow, a change of doubling, a change in the triad being tonicized, etc.—may be of longer-range significance than our map would show. This is also true of any discontinuity in the succession of sounds produced by the performer as he performs the piece. But that is the subject of the next—and last—chapter.

CHAPTER NINE

Performance

9.0 Some Problems We've Been Avoiding

In the preceding chapters we have been assuming that any two notes that are written the same way—with the same note head, stem, flag, metronome mark, and dynamic—are supposed to sound the same. That is, if you write a series of notes in a line, the performer is supposed to see to it that
1. each note lasts until just before the next note begins,
2. the time elapsed between the beginning of one note and the beginning of the next can be computed from the metronome mark, and
3. all notes are equally loud and have the same timbre.

In fact, nobody who understands tonal music could play a line like that, nor would it be understandable to anyone else if it were played like that.

The intelligible performance of tonal music depends on all kinds of deviations from the norms implied by our notation. Sometimes the composer indicates some of the grosser deviations by specific symbols, but for the most part he depends on the performer's intuitive understanding of the structure implied by the pitches, durations, and beats he notates.

9.1 Articulation: What the Performer Does

Legato means, literally, "bound together" and hence "connected." *Staccato* means, literally, "separated out from" and hence "detached." To connect two or more consecutive notes, the performer must make the transition from the sound at the end of one note to the sound at the beginning of the next note as smooth as possible.* To detach a note from the note before or the note after, he must make the transition to or from the detached note noticeably less smooth—by leaving a silence between notes or by beginning or ending the sound of the detached note more abruptly. How he does either, and the extent to which we can differentiate between legato and staccato, depend largely on the mechanical and acoustical properties of the instrument. These properties differ greatly from instrument to instrument, so before going on to the central problem of the effect that playing some notes legato and others not has on the listener's understanding of those notes, we must first clear up what playing legato actually consists of.

Compare, for example, the violin and piano. Consider how the violin works. Its four strings are all the same length but of different thicknesses and, hence, weights. The violinist tunes them by adjusting their

---

*If you make the transition between two notes with the same pitch as smooth as possible

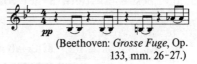

(Beethoven: *Grosse Fuge*, Op. 133, mm. 26-27.)

you may end up with one note.

It is hard to say just what is intended in such a passage. We will avoid this problem by using legato only for consecutive notes with different pitches.

tension so that they will vibrate with fundamental frequencies of

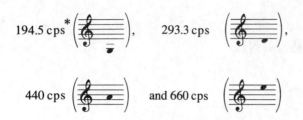

To get a string to vibrate at a higher fundamental frequency than the one it is tuned to, he presses the string against the fingerboard with his fingertip, leaving only a part of its total length free to vibrate.

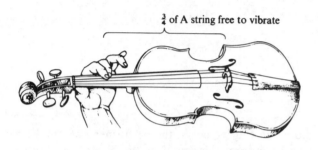

To start the string vibrating, he draws the bow across the string with a single continuous motion. Tiny barbs on the hairs of the bow catch the string and drag it along with them. The more the bow's motion takes the string out of its original position, the more the string pulls against the bow hairs. When the pull becomes too great, the string slips loose and springs back toward its original position, but its momentum carries it past its original position. The further past its original position its momentum carries it, the more the string pulls in the other direction, slowing the string down. As soon as the string has slowed down enough, the barbs catch it again and the whole process is repeated. Each time the process is repeated, the string goes further in each direction. For the first few swings back and forth, the string's motion is irregular, but gradually a periodic pattern emerges as the string begins to vibrate at frequencies one, two, three, four, and five times the fundamental frequency, the multiple being determined by the weight, length, and tension of the string.

But even this periodic pattern is not constant. As the overall amplitude of the motion grows, the relative strength of these frequencies changes. The higher multiples dominate first; it is only after about a tenth of a second that the fundamental frequency becomes stronger than the others.

* cps = cycles per second, i.e. the number of times the wave pattern is repeated per second.

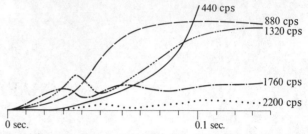

Growth of a violin's A (440) after Fritz Winckel, *Music, Sound, and Sensation*, transl. by Thomas Binkley, Dover, New York, 1967, p. 33.

We hear the first tenth of a second or so as the attack of the note. The violinist can bring the string's vibrations up to full amplitude faster by increasing the pressure of the bow on the string at the beginning of his stroke. This increases the amount of irregular motion and the relative strength of the upper partials and gives the note a "gutsier" attack. He can also cut down the initial irregular motion and make the upper partials grow together with the fundamental by setting the bow in motion before it touches the string and applying pressure only gradually as the string responds. This way, he takes longer to get the string moving at full amplitude, but he can virtually eliminate the initial element of scratch and thus emphasize the sound he gets once the string is moving at full amplitude.

Either way, once the string is moving at full amplitude it settles into a regular periodic pattern, dominated by the fundamental frequency. To keep this motion going, all the violinist has to do is keep his bow moving in the same direction. To stop the motion, he can either lift his bow off the string and let the vibrations die out of their own accord, or stop the bow on the string, damping the vibrations so they stop abruptly. Thus, to make the smoothest possible transition between two notes with different pitches, the violinist plays both notes on the same string (changing the fundamental frequency at which the string vibrates by changing the point at which the string is pressed against the fingerboard) and in one bow (with one continuous motion of the bow). This means that:

1. the sound of the first note will continue at the same level of loudness until the sound of the second note begins; there will be no silence between them and no dip in the level of loudness;
2. while the beginning of the first note is marked by a more or less noticeable attack sound, the second note seems to appear directly out of the end of the first note.

To make the transition less smooth, he can do a number of different things. He can change the direction of the bow for the second note. If he decreases the bow's pressure and increases its speed just before he changes its direction, the amplitude of the string's motion may decrease slightly but it never stops. As the bow changes direction, the upper partials of the new fundamental frequency are favored briefly, but there is little irregular motion. We barely hear the dip in loudness at the end of the first note, and we hear the beginning of the second note as marked by a clear bowed attack without initial noise. If, on the other hand, he maintains full pressure and stops the bow dead on the string, he will stop the string's motion completely in between notes and will have to start it up again with the new bow stroke. We hear an abrupt stopping of the first note followed by a silence followed by what is bound to be a more or less gutsy attack on the second note.

Or he can keep the bow moving in the same direction but vary the way it activates the string. If he releases the bow's pressure against the string between notes, he will get a dip in the level of loudness at the end of the first note and a touch of the attack sound of the upper partials at the beginning of the second. If he lifts the bow off the string between notes, he will get a trailing off into silence at the end of the first note and more attack sound at the beginning of the second. If the notes follow one another rapidly enough, he may actually be able to bounce the bow off the string so that as it returns, its impact helps activate the string faster: this produces a trailing off into silence at the end of the first note and a clear and precise (rather than a noisy) attack on the second.

Now compare how a piano works. Its 243 strings are tuned in groups to vibrate at 88 different frequencies. When the pianist presses a key, two things happen: a damper releases the one, two, or three strings tuned to that frequency so that they are free to vibrate; and a hammer strikes them, setting them in motion. The amplitude of their vibrations is at its highest immediately after impact.* From then on, each vibration will be slightly smaller than the one before. Because a piano's pin board is much more rigid and much less absorbent than the violinist's fingertips, it takes a long time for the vibrations to die away completely. The pianist can stop the vibrations by releasing the key, which in turn allows the damper to press against the strings. That is, however, the only way the pianist can affect the vibrations of the strings once he has pressed the key and the hammer has struck.† Consequently, his ability to control the transition from the end of one note to the beginning of the next is highly limited.

To make the smoothest possible transition, he lifts the first key just as he presses the second key. This means that:

1. the sound of the first note will continue until the moment the sound of the second note begins; there will be no silence between the notes.

However,

2. the level of loudness will have dropped by the end of the first note to well below that at the beginning of the second note, and
3. the beginning of both notes will be marked by identical attack sounds.

The pianist can compensate somewhat for this characteristic of his instrument by putting slightly less pressure on the second key, not so much as to make the listener hear the first note as loud and the second as soft, but just enough to make the beginning of the second note seem a little more as though it grew out of the end of the first note and a little less like an event comparable to the beginning of the first note.

On the other hand, to make the transition between notes less smooth, the pianist presses both keys with equal force but lifts the first key before he presses the second. The longer the period of silence between the notes, the more detached they will seem.

It should be clear that no pianist will be able to make as smooth a transition from one sound to the next as a violinist can. But having heard pianos all our lives, we understand what they can and can't do and consequently, we understand the smoothest transition available to the pianist as a legato equivalent in meaning to the violinist's smoothest transition. Similarly, no pianist has at his disposal the variety of means for breaking up the transition from one sound to the next that the violinist does. But we have come to accept the means available to the pianist as roughly equivalent to some of those available to the violinist.

Really capable performers on any instrument can differentiate many degrees of connectedness, and some composers have taken great pains to specify to the performer just how connected they want any two consecutive notes to be. However, there is no generally accepted *scale of connectedness* that musicians agree upon, nor is there a generally accepted set of symbols common to all instruments. In this book we will limit ourselves to three degrees of connection: *legato* (as connected as possible), *non-legato* (detached enough to be distinguished from legato, but no more), and *staccato* (distinctly, noticeably detached).

---

* It takes the soundboard at least a fiftieth of a second to catch up and still longer to match the string's periodic motion.
† He can, of course, release all the dampers from all the strings by putting his foot on the damper pedal. But that only eliminates what little control he has over the end of the note.

	Legato	Non-legato	Staccato
written	legato slur between note heads also and	lack of either slur or dot* also and	staccato dot also and
as performed by a pianist	No silence between the E and the D. The E slightly louder than the D but not so much as to be noticeable as such.	A minute silence between the D and the C but not so much as to be noticeable as such. The C as loud as the E.	A noticeable silence between the D and the C.
as performed by a violinist	The E and the D in one bow. No fresh attack sound on the D.	New bow on the C. Attack on the C same as on the E but no silence between the D and the C.	A period of silence between the D and the C.

* In this book, absence of a symbol will mean non-legato. In actual scores it may just mean that the composer didn't write a symbol because he thought it would be perfectly clear to the performer what he ought to do.

Questions for Discussion

1. How are sound waves initiated, maintained, and terminated on each of the following instruments?
    a. the clarinet
    b. the organ
    c. the voice
2. How do the clarinetist, the organist, and the singer differentiate between legato, non-legato, and staccato? Are other degrees of detachedness vs. connectedness available on these instruments?

9.2 Articulation: Effect of What the Performer Does on Our Understanding of the Structure

How a violinist or pianist makes some notes sound more connected than others is one problem. *Why* he chooses to connect some notes and not others (or why the composer tells him to do so) is another problem. In general we can say that the function of playing one pair of notes legato and another non-legato or staccato is simply to make it easier for the listener to grasp the structural sense of the notes. In particular, we can distinguish three types of clarification:

1. intensifying the sense of the line as a structural entity by connecting all the consecutive notes in a line as much as possible;
2. clarifying the rhythmic structure of the line by connecting some notes more than others;
3. clarifying the pitch structure where it runs counter to the rhythmic structure of the line by connecting some consecutive notes more than others.

Intensifying the Sense of Line • By definition, any two consecutive notes in a line are to be understood as connected. Consequently, one obvious function of playing two notes legato is to confirm the fact that they are indeed consecutive notes in a line. But note that this function is limited to confirming something we know already by other means. Take two lines that cross:

If a flute plays one line and a violin plays the other, the listener knows which note belongs to which line because of the contrast in timbre and the fact that the sound is coming from two different directions. Even if both lines are played by violins, the contrast in direction enables him to keep track of which line is which. In either case the fact that they are played legato helps intensify the sense of connection between the two notes. But suppose you tried to play these lines on the piano: here playing legato is no help at all, since precisely those factors in a piano legato that would connect the D to the C and the G to the E will also connect the D to the E and the G to the C. The same is true if you play one line legato and the other staccato*:

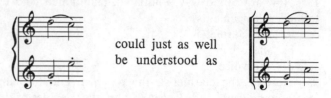

Of course, if the two lines are in oblique motion,

or if their structures or voice leading are such that there is only one possible way of understanding them,

there is no problem.

Clarifying the Rhythmic Structure of the Line • By playing notes that you understand as segments of a span legato, you show your listener in the most immediate way possible how you think of those notes in relation to one another. Take the notes: If you understand the D as creating a step motion between the E and the C in and hence as a segment of the span defined by the dotted whole-note E, then you have only to play the E and the D legato. If, on the other hand, you think of the D as marking the point where C would have been then you will want to play

---

* Playing one line legato and the other staccato has the side effect of creating a timbral contrast between the two lines since the sound of the staccato notes is made up of a much higher proportion of noise factors than is the sound of the legato notes. With just two notes in each line this effect is unimportant, but in more extended passages it can be very useful.

the D and the C legato so as to show the location of the span defined by the original C.*

Or take the notes: Because of the barline, you think of the first quarter note as anticipating a span, S, a half note in length.

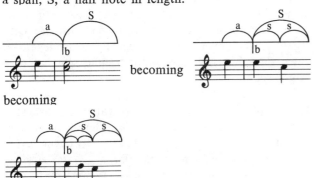

becoming

But your listener can't see the barline, and the first E is longer than the second. He has every reason to understand these notes in some other way.

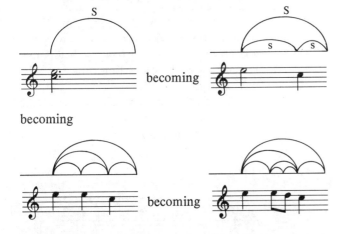

becoming

However, if you play the note you think of as an anticipation staccato and the three notes that you think of as forming the span being anticipated legato,

he should have no difficulty understanding these notes your way.

Clarifying the Pitch Structure When It Runs Counter to the Rhythmic Structure of the Line • Take a line like the top one in

Because of the intervals the up-beat pitches in the top line form with the pitches in the lower line, you understand them as anticipatory arpeggiations to the following downbeats. That is, you think of

in terms of:

rather than thinking of

in terms of

To make this immediately apparent and easy for your listener to grasp, you can connect the anticipatory arpeggiations by playing them legato.†

---

* It will help to begin the D a bit louder too. See pages 391–392.

† Note, of course, that the G is an anticipation rather than an anticipatory arpeggiation; it is consequently played staccato. The span it anticipates must be played legato for its full extent.

Playing notes legato across the boundary of a span will not necessarily endanger the listener's understanding of where the spans begin. The notes in the lower lines define those spans

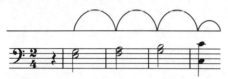

and there is no way they can be understood as delays within spans that coincide with the legato marks.

becoming

Or take the line:

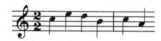

You understand it as the result of arpeggiating two lines

and consequently as having the span structure

But you want your listener to be aware of the linear connections (the arpeggiated thirds will be obvious in any case) in the underlying structure. You want him to understand that the E and the D represent two consecutive notes in the underlying structure, while the B and the C do not, even though they are consecutive notes in the line itself. You could therefore connect the E and the D but detach the B from the C.

Of course, such articulation only works when the span structure is unambiguous.

Now obviously, these three factors are in conflict. You cannot both play all the notes in a line legato to bring out the sense of linear continuity and at the same time play some of them non-legato to show where the spans begin. Nor can you both use non-legato to show where a span begins and use legato to show that that span is also the second segment of a larger span.

What the performer* must do is decide which of these three functions is most critical to his listener's understanding of the notes. While there are no rules for making these decisions that will cover every situation, we can at least describe a general strategy for the order in which such decisions must be made.

1. Begin with all the notes in a line as connected as possible. That is, play all the pairs of consecutive notes with different pitches legato and all the pairs of consecutive notes with the same pitch non-legato.
2. Then, at any point where you think it is important that your listener be able to grasp immediately that a new span is beginning, remove one degree of connection. For example, you may wish to
    a. change the notes on either side of the boundaries of two major spans from legato to non-legato,

change

to

or b. change the notes on either side of the boundaries of any spans within which a delay occurs from legato to non-legato,

change

to

---

* And, of course, the composer, insofar as he indicates the articulations he wants.

and c. change any anticipations from non-legato to staccato.

change

to

3. Finally, where pitch connections are in conflict with the span structure, but the span structure is clear for other reasons, adjust your legatos to clarify the pitch structure.

change

to

Such a strategy gives considerable leeway, particularly at step 2. Your decision there depends on which aspects of the rhythmic structure you think will be hardest for your listener to grasp. Take

* Connecting the D to the G by a legato helps the listener hear the D as an anticipatory arpeggiation.

Here there are no delays and only one anticipation. Hence the hardest spans to grasp will be the larger ones, simply because they include more notes. If they can be clarified by the articulation,

or

the smaller spans will take care of themselves. Indeed, articulating the smaller spans

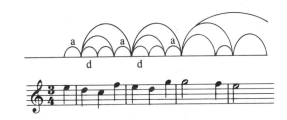

serves no particular function and only sounds fussy.

On the other hand, take

Here the problem lies in the smallest spans because of the delays and anticipations. If they can be made clear,

the larger spans will take care of themselves.

Exercises

For each of the following beginnings of movements
1. show how you understand the structure by generating the top line of the example from a simpler structure;
2. show how you think a listener might misunderstand that structure by generating the top line from another simple structure—possibly one with the beats located differently; and
3. write the minimum number of articulation marks in the top line that will insure that the listener cannot misunderstand the structure.

1.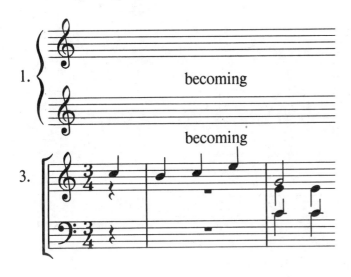

2.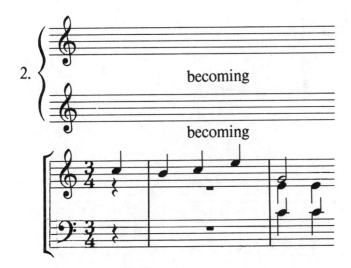

9.3 Contrasts of Loudness and Timbre

One Line Louder Than Another • The chief function of playing the notes of one line louder than the notes of another line is to bring the louder line to the listener's attention. Frequently in tonal music the structural interest and continuity is concentrated in one line—the "melody." If this line is the highest line, there is usually no problem: listeners who have heard tonal music all their lives are used to concentrating their attention on the highest notes. But if this line is not the highest, it may be necessary to make its notes a shade louder to bring them to the listener's attention. Such contrasts are occasionally indicated by the composer

(Chopin: *Preludes* Op. 28, No. 6, mm. 1–2.)

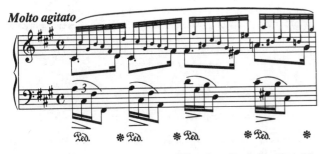

(Chopin: *Preludes* Op. 28, No. 8, m. 1.)

but more often are left to the performer's discretion.*

Some Notes Louder Than Others in the Same Line • The chief function of changing the level of loudness in the course of a line is to clarify the structure of the line. We use abrupt changes in loudness to signal discontinuity and gradual changes to signal continuity.

For example, take

---

* To see just how unusual such indications are, note that Chopin does not use the usual symbols for loudness (*pp, p, mp, mf,* etc.) but relies on such special techniques as verbal instructions and the size of the notes.

(Mozart: *Sonata* K.331, second movement, mm. 1–10.)

When the pianist plays the first two measures *forte* and the next three *piano* with no intervening *diminuendo,* the listener understands that despite the similarity between mm. 2 and 3, mm. 1 and 2 form a unit, and a new unit begins at m. 3. On the other hand, when the pianist changes gradually from the *piano* at m. 6 through the *crescendo* in m. 7 to the *forte* at m. 8, the listener understands these measures as part of a continuous section.† Indeed, if the pianist can make the rate of growth in m. 7 regular enough, he can even get the listener to expect a specific level of loudness in m. 8.

Such large-scale changes in loudness are often marked by the composer.‡ Smaller-scale changes—note-to-note changes within the general level of *piano* or *forte* or even within the gradually changing level indicated by *crescendo* or *diminuendo*—are usually not marked by the composer. Nevertheless they form a vital part of the communication between performer and listener. Take the top line in mm. 3 and 4,

Because of the barline, the pianist understands that the D♯ falls on a downbeat. Because of the pitch and rhythmic structure of the first five measures, he understands that this beat is indeed the second primary beat of the phrase.

---

† *Crescendo* (abbreviated *cresc.*, or ⟨) means, literally, "growing larger" and hence "gradually getting louder." *Diminuendo* (abbreviated *dim.*, or ⟩) means, literally, "growing smaller" and hence "gradually getting softer."
‡ In this case we don't know what Mozart wrote because there is no autograph extant. The first printed editions (Artaria, 1784; Schott, 1784–85) omit the symbols in brackets. They must be inferred from the context and from parallel passages in this movement. See the edition of the Sonatas and Fantasias by Nathan Broder, Presser, 1958.

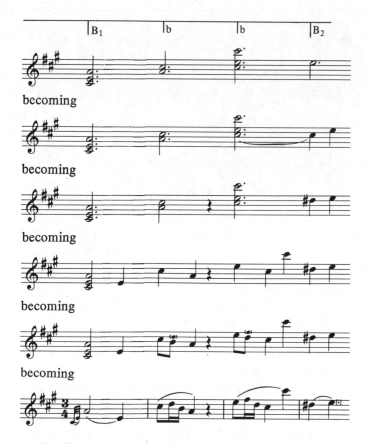

The listener, on the other hand, can't see the barline, but he understands the E as the pitch that the line has been aiming at. The danger is that he might use the moment the E occurs as a reference point, understanding the passage as:

Now, of course, if the listener has understood the first three measures in terms of three equally spaced downbeats, he'll have every reason to expect a fourth such beat at this point:

Furthermore, the position of the legatos should make it difficult for him to misunderstand the span structure in mm. 3 and 4. But a delay is by its very nature always difficult to grasp: to make it easier for the listener, the pianist could play the passage*

The abrupt change from *p* to *mp* helps make sure that the D♯ is not understood as part of the preceding span. The fact that the D♯ begins louder than the surrounding notes helps mark the beginning of the D♯ as a point of reference—the point where the E would have begun had it not been delayed. And the continuous change back to *p* helps make sure that the E is understood as part of the same span as the D♯.

Notes marking the point where a delayed note would have begun are normally played this way but almost never so marked by the composer. He takes it for granted that the performer will intuitively grasp the structure and do whatever is necessary to make it clear to the listener.† On the other hand, if he wants the first note of an arpeggiation played louder,

---

* Note that the *diminuendo* is, strictly speaking, only in the mind of the pianist and listener; of course the D♯ does get gradually softer, but then so does any note on the piano. However, we are so used to hearing instruments that can differentiate between steady and changing levels play a *diminuendo* in a situation like this that we unconsciously impute a diminuendo to the D♯. It helps that the D♯ and the E are legato: we would not understand

It also helps that the D♯ does actually get softer: we would not understand

† That leaves us with the question of just how much louder than the E the D♯ should be, which depends on a number of factors. Making it as loud as the *forte* in mm. 1 and 2 might tend to associate it with those notes and therefore dissociate it from the surrounding *piano* notes. On the other hand, making it only as much louder as the E in m. 3 is louder than the F♯—that is, only as much louder as the legato technique described on page 381 requires—would not be perceived as louder. That is why I wrote *mp*, meaning enough louder than *p* to be distinguished from *p* but not so much louder as to be dissociated from *p*. But there are further variables. If you play the preceding C♯ staccato

you introduce yet another form of discontinuity. The shorter the C♯, the more abrupt its ending and the less need there is to play the D♯ louder.

(Mozart: *Sonata* K.331,
first movement, mm. 9–12
of the theme.)

or an anticipation or anticipatory arpeggiation played louder, he had better say so.*

(*Ibid.*, mm. 9–12 of the
first variation.)

In both cases the ultimate function of making the E's louder than the surrounding notes is the same, but it is considerably easier to see this in the theme than in the corresponding measures of the variation. We can understand mm. 9–12 in terms of two primary beats

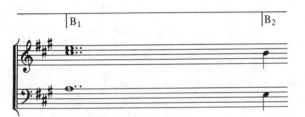

with six equally spaced secondary beats in between them.

The upper lines at the second primary beat are delayed,

---

* *sf* is short for *"sforzando,"* literally, "forced" and hence accented by being attacked more strongly than the surrounding notes.

underlining its role as a reference point. But so are the upper lines at the second secondary beat.

Furthermore, at that point there is room to make the delay a whole beat long. This will create a serious problem for the listener. He can't know during b_1, b_2, and b_3 when B_2 is going to occur. He will want to understand b_1 and b_3 in terms of b_2, setting up a regular pattern in which every other beat is a tertiary beat.

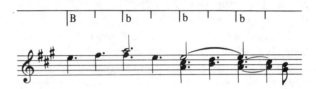

Of course, if he were to continue to use this pattern of beats to understand mm. 11 and 12, he would miss the primary beat in m. 12. He must realize that b_4, b_5, and b_6 are all of equal importance, all secondary beats measuring off the time between primary beats B_1 and B_2. An obvious way of signaling this fact is to arpeggiate all three collections of notes at b_4, b_5, and b_6 in the same way

and to play the on-the-beat notes *sf*.†

---

† Note that the notes at B_2 are not marked *sf*. There are at least two interpretations here. The first is that since the C♯ and the A mark the point where the destination pitches, B and G♯, would have begun, they would be played *sf* anyway. The second is that not playing the C♯ and the A *sf* is a way of breaking the continuity established by the *sf* at b_4, b_5, and b_6 and hence of establishing the boundary between the major spans at B_2. One way of using both ideas is to play the C♯ and the A a shade louder than the delayed notes but distinctly softer than the *sf* E's.

A less obvious way of signaling this fact is to provide the on-the-beat notes at b_4, b_5, and b_6 with anticipations

and anticipate the anticipations *sforzando*.

When an abrupt change in the level of loudness occurs at a point the listener thinks of as a reference point, it usually has the effect of signaling for him that this is indeed the point he will need in order to understand the notes he has just heard or is about to hear. But when an abrupt change in loudness occurs at a point the listener had not thought of or could not think of as a reference point, it usually startles him.* If there is no way he can relate the change to what has happened before (and if it startled him, then presumably there isn't), he tries to relate it to what is about to happen, particularly to what will happen at the next reference point. In the case of these *sf* E's, all that happens is more E's, but some of the additional E's are on the beat. Thus he can understand each *sf* E as an anticipation of an anticipation of an on-the-beat E. The net effect of the *sf* on the off-the-beat E's is to enhance the conceptual rank of the beats on which the on-the-beat E's occur.

Roughly, the listener's reasoning in this case would go: "Those must be pretty important beats to have such loud anticipations depending on them." To put it more generally, if the only way the listener has of conceiving of x is in terms of y, then the more startling x is, the more importance he will attach to y. Clearly, such a principle is not limited to anticipations. For example, take the first eight measures of the theme

Andante grazioso

---

* This distinction is of critical importance in the case of "unstable segmentations." See below.

Consider the two *sf* D's in the bass line. Both those D's can be considered as neighbors to the E's that follow. But note that they are both incomplete neighbors, that is, they are not preceded by an E in that register. We understand them solely in terms of the next note. In both cases the function of the *sf* is to draw the listener's attention to the next note. In both cases the next note falls on what we can understand as the second primary beat in that phrase.†

Unstable Segmentations • In Section 7.1 we arrived at the law of segmentation by making two assumptions: given two consecutive notes, it is easier, other things being equal,

1. to understand the second in terms of the first
and 2. to understand the shorter in terms of the longer.

However, we also saw that if we understand notes in terms of beats, it may be possible to understand the first of two notes in terms of the second. Thus we found we could construct anticipations in which an anticipatory segment, a, precedes the span, S, on which it depends, provided that $a \leq \frac{1}{2} S$ and that either a) S begins on a beat and no beat of prior or equal conceptual status occurs during the anticipatory segment

(Haydn: *Sonata* Hob. XVI : 44, second movement, mm. 1-2.)

---

† A rare example of the secondary primary beat of a phrase *not* falling on a written downbeat.

394

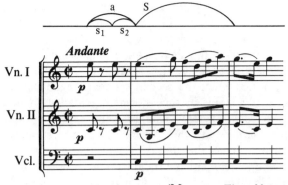

(Mozart: *Eine kleine Nachtmusik* K.525, second movement, mm. 1–2.)

or b) S is one of two or more equal spans segmenting a span defined by two consecutive beats.

(Haydn: *Sonata* Hob. XVI: 44, second movement, m. 4.)

Now it is also possible to understand the longer of two notes in terms of the shorter. Up to now we have avoided doing so, but it is possible to construct an "unstable segmentation" in which a span, S, is segmented into two segments, s_1 and s_2, such that $s_1 < s_2$ provided either that

1. S begins on a beat and no other beat of equal or prior conceptual status occurs during S

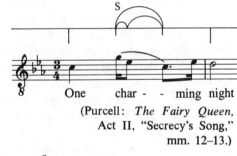

(Purcell: *The Fairy Queen*, Act II, "Secrecy's Song," mm. 12–13.)

(Beethoven: *Piano Concerto* No. 2, third movement, mm. 1–2.)

or 2. S is one of a series of such spans that subdivide a beat into equal parts.

(Haydn: *Quartet* Op. 17, No. 5, first movement, m. 1.)

Such segmentations are unstable in the sense that while they depend on the beat to be understood, they cannot be used to establish or maintain a beat. (Taken by themselves, the first four notes of the right hand in the Beethoven example would be understood as ). They therefore require considerable care from the performer.

There are two types of unstable segmentations. In the first, the initial segment lasts less than half a beat:

One char - ming night

The function of this type is to get the listener to assign greater importance to the beat (or subdivision of the beat) on which the span begins. He has to do just that if he is to understand these segments as forming a single span, since the lengths of the segment would lead him to believe the opposite. The danger, of course, is that he may find it easier to think of the beat as coming a shade later,* which would allow him to think of the first segment as an anticipatory segment to the second:

Therefore the performer must bring the beginning of the first segment to the listener's attention and do what he can to make it clear that these are indeed segments of a single span. The usual method is to play the beginning of the first segment a shade louder and connect the notes of both segments with a legato.

In the second type, the initial segment lasts at least half a beat.

---

* See Section 9.4, Rubato. Tempo deviations of this size are common.

(Beethoven: *Piano Concerto* No. 2, third movement, mm. 1–2.)

(Mozart: *Mentre ti lascio* K.513, mm. 100–103.)

Here there is no danger of the listener assuming that the beat has been delayed, provided a beat has already been established (as in the Mozart example) or is being established simultaneously in another line (as in the Beethoven example). Nevertheless, the effect can still be quite unsettling to his sense of the way things happen in time. Having heard the first note and the beginning of the second, and having registered that the second note began at a point that is conceptually dependent on the beat on which the first note began, he assumes that the second note will be no longer than the first.

When the second note continues, he assumes that it has been lengthened by the delay of some third note.

But the third note begins at a point just after the last possible point that could be explained by a delay—namely, at the beginning of the next span defined by the metric hierarchy. The effect should be to get the listener to connect a point early in one span to the point at which the next span begins. The danger is that the effect will be lost because the listener didn't even notice when the second segment began (since it began at a point in time normally assigned to notes of less consequence). Therefore the performer must make sure that the second segment is clearly separated from the first and that the beginning of the second segment is brought to the listener's attention. The usual method is to play the last note in the first segment staccato and begin the first note of the second segment louder than the surrounding notes.*

To sum up, both the function and modes of performance of an unstable segmentation depend on the length of the first segment. If it is shorter than half a beat, the effect is to direct the listener's attention to the point at which the span begins. The performer plays the first segment louder but joins the two segments with a legato. If, on the other hand, the first segment lasts half a beat or longer, the effect is to direct the listener's attention to the second segment. The performer detaches the two segments and begins the second louder than the first.†

Contrasting Timbres • The chief function of giving the notes in one line a different timbre from the notes in other lines is to make it easier for the listener to grasp that the differentiated notes do indeed form a separate line. When two consecutive notes have the same timbre, while other notes have some other timbre, it is much easier to connect the consecutive notes. This is particularly helpful where two lines

---

* In our examples there have been no operations subsequent to the unstable segmentations, so there is only one note per segment.

† Most composers assume that performers will know how to handle the first type and don't bother to mark more than the legato, if that. Most composers who use the second type, however, take pains to specify the mode of performance, as in the Mozart and Beethoven examples above. A characteristic exception is found in those triple meter dance types (like the sarabande) in which the second segment of a measure frequently occupies both the second and third beat. Here composers rarely tell the performer what to do. However, because so many long segments start on the second beat the listener is prepared for them, so the use of sudden loudness is not only inappropriate but unnecessary.

cross. The timbre of a note is, of course, almost always determined by the composer, and normally the performer's job is simply to maintain the sense of timbral identity from one note to the next.

The chief function of changing the timbre of the notes in the course of a line is to clarify the span structure of the line. Contrasts of timbre can be used, like contrasts in loudness, to set off one phrase from the next

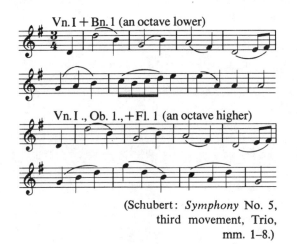

(Schubert: *Symphony* No. 5, third movement, Trio, mm. 1–8.)

or to mark off the smaller phrases embedded in a larger one.

(Haydn: *Symphony* No. 92, third movement, mm. 1–4.)

They can also be used like articulation to show smaller spans*

(Mozart: *Symphony* No. 40, first movement, mm. 44–47.)

or like sudden changes in loudness to create "timbral accents."

(*Ibid.*, mm. 56–59.)

For the most part, the composer makes such changes by changing the instrument assigned to the line. However, sophisticated performers, particularly string players, can achieve similar effects by playing part of a passage on one string and part on another, or by shifting their hand position to use a stronger finger for some particular note.

* Note that in this case the change in color projects something that no articulation could—the overlap between

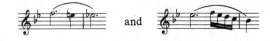

397

Exercises

1. Find examples in the works of Haydn, Mozart, or Beethoven where the composer* has explicitly indicated each of the following:
   a. diminuendo from a note on the downbeat to the next note in that line
   b. an off-the-beat note suddenly louder than the notes preceding it, including the last on-the-beat note. (Or a note falling on a secondary beat suddenly louder than the notes preceding it, including the last note that fell on a downbeat.)

In each case say what structural function the change in loudness serves.

2. Find examples in the works of Haydn, Mozart, or Beethoven where the composer has *not* explicitly indicated the changes in loudness described in question 1, but where you think such changes would be warranted in order to clarify the structure.

---

* Make sure the marks you are talking about are actually the composer's. Use only those editions that have been based directly on original sources (the composer's manuscript, or first editions known to have been corrected by the composer) and that make it clear which marks are in the original and which have been added by the editor.

9.4 Rubato

We think of a note as beginning at a particular point in time and lasting a particular period of time. The proportional symbols of our notation show the relative position of such starting points, and to some extent, the actual length of such periods. Thus a half note followed by two quarter notes means that the time elapsed between the first and the second points should be twice as long as the time elapsed between the second and third points.

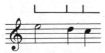

If you play these notes legato, the period of time each note lasts is precisely determined by the symbols, since in a legato passage each note lasts until the next note begins.

If you play these notes staccato, the period of time each note lasts is only roughly determined by the symbols, since each note is cut off before the next note begins, but the next note begins at the same point it would have if the notes were played legato.

Now suppose you were to begin the second note a shade late, so that the time elapsed between the first and second notes is actually a little more than twice the time elapsed between the second and third—not so much as to be understood by your listener as some other simple proportion, like 3:1, but long enough to be understood as an extra-long 2:1.

Or suppose you were to begin the second note a shade early—again, not so early that your listener understands the relationship as some other proportion, say 3:2, but early enough for him to understand the second note as early.

Both cases are examples of *rubato*.*

---

* Literally, "robbed." Presumably in a true rubato, whatever you take from the value of one note you give to some other note. In fact, you often give more than you take.

There are two kinds of rubato. The first affects the location of the beginning of a note with respect to the beat without affecting the beat itself.

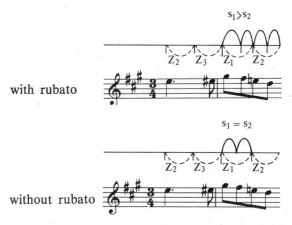

The second affects the location of the beat itself.

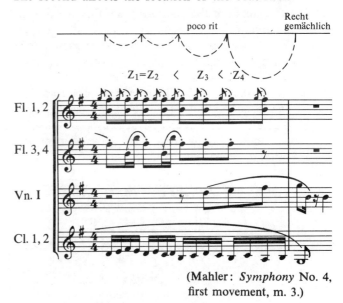

(Mahler: *Symphony* No. 4, first movement, m. 3.)

These two kinds of rubato function in different ways.

Rubato Not Affecting Beats • The principal use of the first kind of rubato is to clarify the span structure by lengthening the first segment in a segmentation at the expense of the subsequent segments

or lengthening a note used to mark the point at which a delayed note would have begun, at the expense of the delayed note.

becomes

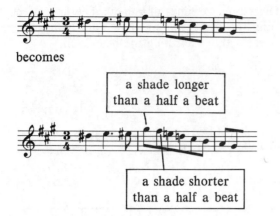

This kind of rubato (sometimes called an *agogic* accent) is particularly useful where
1. the span between two consecutive beats is occupied by notes whose *written* durations are equal;
2. the pitches of the notes are such that the on-the-beat note could be understood as off the beat (as, for example, when a neighbor or passing tone is used to mark the point at which a delayed note would have occurred); and
3. the beat in question is of critical importance to the listener's understanding of the passage as a whole (as, for example, a beat used to establish the meter in the first place, or either of the primary downbeats in a phrase).

(Mozart: *Sonata* K.333, first movement, mm. 1–2.)

(Mozart: *Sonata* K.533, first movement, mm. 1–3.)

Of course, there is no ambiguity for the performer in either of these examples because the notation make the span structure clear to him. But the listener does not see the notation. Even if, as in both our examples, the larger context of the passage would eventually resolve the ambiguity for the listener, the performer will need to use this kind of rubato if he wants his listener to grasp what is going on immediately. How much of this kind of rubato he should apply is another question, and there are as many answers as there are performers. At one extreme is the performer who uses the least rubato that will make the structure clear. At the other extreme is the performer who uses as much rubato as he can get away with without losing the sense of beat.* Indeed, an important side effect of this kind of rubato can be the suppression of a potential beat. Thus, for example, in a passage like

(Schubert: *Die schöne Müllerin*, No. 20.)

the performer can keep his listener from understanding a duple meter at twice the tempo

by lengthening the quarters at the expense of the eighths in the first and third measures

Another common use of rubato is to clarify the relative importance of different lines. By playing the notes of one line consistently a shade ahead of the notes in the other lines, you can bring out a line without actually playing it louder. Such a technique requires great control over the smallest perceptible differences,† but is invaluable where the principal line is not the top line, or where the principal line

---

* Some performers seem to believe that music should be played with absolutely no rubato of this or any other kind. They call it "playing the notes exactly as they are written." But, of course, the notes as they are written carry a great deal more information about the temporal structure than their relative durations alone can convey.
† See Section 8.0.

would easily be covered by other notes or other instruments.

(Brahms: *Intermezzo* Op. 119, No. 3, mm. 1–3.)

(Debussy: *Pour le Piano,* "Sarabande," orchestrated by Ravel, mm. 11–14.)

* The flute's *mf* in this register is no match for the *p* of a large group of violas and cellos.

Rubato Affecting Beats • When you play a passage in an absolutely steady tempo—that is with the beginnings of notes you understand as being on the beat exactly equally spaced—you make it easy for your listener to think of these notes as marking a series of beats. Not only can he understand the notes as you play them in terms of these beats, he can also predict just when each beat will occur. Now suppose he comes to a point in a passage where he begins to suspect that the next equally spaced beat will be not just another beat but in fact the primary beat in terms of which he will find it convenient to think of all those preceding beats. You could, of course, continue your precisely steady tempo, and he might or might not understand the beat in question as primary. But suppose instead you slowed down and made him wait for that beat (as in the example at the bottom of the page). By making him wait for that moment, you intensify his expectation of what the moment will bring—you whet his appetite for that moment and confirm that this is indeed the primary beat he suspected it might be.

On the other hand, suppose you were to speed up just before the potential primary beat and get to it before he expected you to. This would have the opposite effect, destroying any potential for being a primary beat the note might have had. This is what Mahler is warning against when he writes *"nicht eilen"* ("don't rush") in a similar passage later on (see

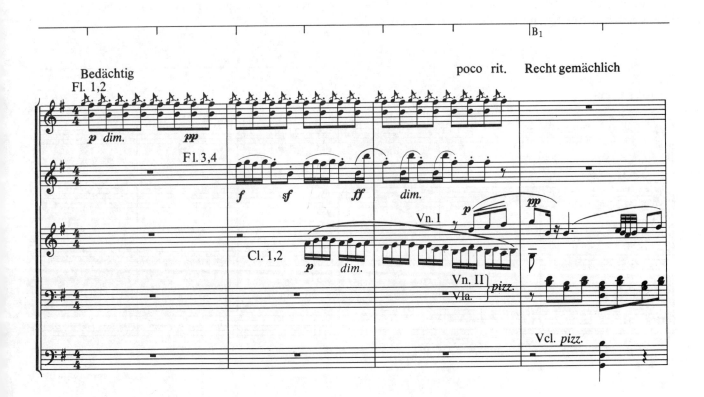

(Mahler: *Symphony* No. 4, first movement, mm. 1–4.)

403

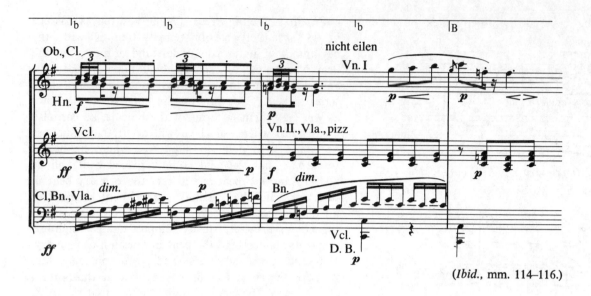

(*Ibid.*, mm. 114–116.)

the example above).

Note, however, that we cannot say that slowing down necessarily makes the listener hear a primary beat, or that speeding up keeps him from doing so. If the process of slowing down occurs directly following what must be a primary beat (see mm. 96–101), the listener simply hears the tempo getting slower and slower. He has no expectations about these beats, which he hears getting further and further apart, and consequently their lateness does not affect the rank he accords them.

Note also that speeding up need not preclude arrival at a primary beat. If the process of speeding up starts long enough before the primary beat so that a number of secondary beats are involved (see mm. 341–346 on following page) and the rate of acceleration is constant, the listener can predict when the potential primary beat is going to come as accurately as if the tempo had been constant.

To sum up, then, making your listener wait for an expected primary beat confirms its primacy, while getting to it too soon destroys its primacy. However, slowing down the secondary beats that follow a primary beat will not make any of them into primary beats, and gradually speeding up a series of secondary beats will not stop a beat at the end of the acceleration process from sounding like a primary beat.

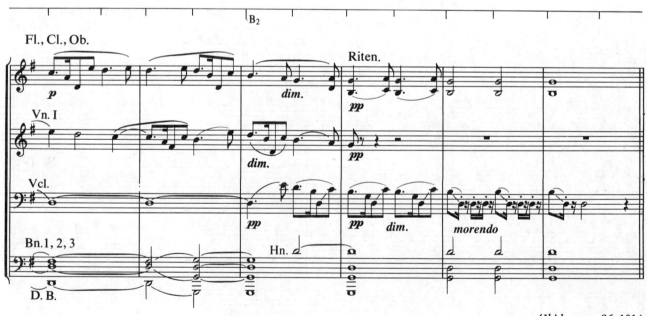

(*Ibid.*, mm. 96–101.)

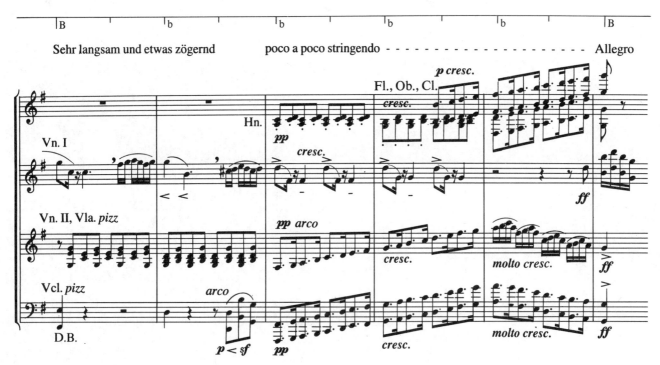

(*Ibid.*, mm. 341–346.)

Exercise

Choose any short piece by Chopin for which a number of different recorded performances are available to you. Choose any passage in the piece that two of the pianists play in a markedly different way. With the aid of a metronome, measure the rubato employed by each. Represent your findings graphically. Is the difference simply a matter of the extent of the rubato, or are the two pianists projecting two different structures?

9.5 Performance Strategies and "Understanding the Structure"

In this chapter we have been dealing with some of the means the performer can use to make the structure of a passage clear to his listener. Some of these means are specified by the composer, but many are not.* It is up to the performer to use not only any means specified by the composer, but also whatever other means he needs to make the sense of the passage clear to his listener. In other words, he must not only understand the sense of the passage, but be able to decide which means are best suited to project that sense. These are both difficult tasks.

The first is difficult since any but the simplest tonal structure is bound to have a degree of ambiguity somewhere: the greater the number of subsequent operations required to build up a structure, the greater the chance that some other series of operations would result in the same structure. The second is difficult since more than one means may produce the same result. Take our Mozart example again:

(Mozart: *Sonata* K.331, second movement, mm. 1–5.)

By playing the notes at the end of m. 3 staccato, the performer can make it easier for the listener to grasp that a span ends there. By playing the notes of the first quarter of m. 4 a little louder, he can make it easier to understand the notes on the second quarter as delayed. By holding back so that the beat at the beginning of m. 4 is a shade late, he can make it easier to grasp that beat as a primary beat. But note that if the listener understands the end of m. 3 as the end of a span, he has to understand the beginning of m. 4 as the beginning of the next span. He will then understand the notes on the second quarter of m. 4 as delayed from the first quarter and hence understand the first quarter as the primary beat. Similarly, if he understands the first quarter as the primary beat, he will have to understand the notes on the second quarter as delayed, and hence understand the boundary between spans as falling at the barline. This means that two approaches are open to the performer. He can apply any of these three means—articulation, dynamics, or rubato—so obviously that the listener will have no choice but to understand the corresponding aspect of the structure properly. (The listener can then, of course, infer the other two aspects.) But the performer can also apply any two, or even all three, of these means more subtly, knowing that the presence of one, however slight, will enhance the effectiveness of the others: if the notes at the end of m. 3 are a little bit shorter than what would be required for non-legato, then the notes at the beginning of m. 4 don't have to be quite so loud to make the delay clear; if the downbeat at m. 4 is just a shade late, the notes at the end of m. 3 don't have to be so staccato, etc. Thus all three factors are in a delicate balance with one another in which one may predominate but no one need do so.

Obviously, the second approach is most commonly used. It allows the performer to communicate the structure of the music unambiguously without interrupting its flow.† But it still allows him to shift the emphasis from one factor to another as circumstances demand. One possible way to describe a general strategy for performance is as follows:

1. Rely as much as possible on distinctions between legato, non-legato, and various degrees of staccato to clarify the local span structure of lines.
2. Where the span structure is difficult to grasp (because it is irregular or because delays are involved), use distinctions of loudness as well.
3. Reserve rubato for large-scale structures or for places where the other two means are insufficient.

---

* In general, the more recent the composer, the more he specifies. Mozart writes legatos and staccatos more frequently than Bach, but the absence of a dot or a slur in Bach's music need not mean that the notes are to be played non-legato. Mahler writes note-to-note dynamic changes more frequently than Mozart, but the absence of diminuendos or crescendos in a Mozart line need not mean that all notes are to be equally loud. And even Mahler, who goes so far as to specify which finger the violinists should use on which string

(Mahler: *Symphony* No. 4, first movement, mm. 3–4.)

(thereby determining completely the quality of the legato), says nothing about rubato between beats.

† Or, more precisely, it allows him to reserve obvious breaks in continuity of any one factor for those places where they are really necessary.

* * *

Throughout the preceding discussion—and indeed throughout this chapter—I have been talking about performance as though it were a totally rational act, as though the performer makes a set of conscious choices within the framework of a consciously planned strategy in order to communicate a consciously arrived at structural interpretation of the notes at hand. Of course, this is a gross oversimplification. In fact, most of the performer's "choices" are intuitively arrived at. Indeed he is often not even aware of the fact that he is making a choice: the "strategies" I have outlined are more accurately described as rationalizations of the habits of performers. Even the fundamental distinction between "understanding what the structural sense of the passage is" and "deciding what to do to make that sense clear to his listener" is misleading if taken literally. More often than not, both are compressed into a single intuitive process. The performer looks at the page and knows what those notes will sound like and proceeds to play them that way. But "what those notes will sound like" already includes all those means that will make the structure clear to his listener.

For the performer, understanding the structure of a passage and knowing what it will sound like are normally one and the same thing: "how it goes." The only time he is aware of a separation is when he runs into trouble: when he realizes, on hearing what he has played, that something "doesn't work" or "doesn't make sense," either because he didn't understand the sense of the passage correctly or because he did not project what he understood strongly enough. The rest of the time he takes the connection between what we have been calling "the structure" and "the way the structure is projected" for granted. That is not surprising—so do we all, as composers, performers, or listeners. The only reason we, as theorists, attempt to separate the two is to see how what we take for granted actually works.

Thus the purpose of this last chapter has been simply to supply the last element necessary to fulfill the purpose of this book: to provide a metalanguage to use when you want to talk about how tonal music works. Please note that possessing such a language does not mean you can write music like Mozart's, or perform Mozart's music as he would have, or understand it in the same terms he would have. It does mean that you are at least in a position to talk more intelligently than the people in the illustration on page 9 about Mozart's music with someone else who knows this language. And I hope it means that you now have a way of thinking about music that will allow you to learn directly from the study of tonal pieces—rather than from books like this.

APPENDIX

Constructing a Pitch System for Tonal Music

A.0 What the Appendix Is For

In Chapter 2, I used the piano keyboard to describe the system of interrelated pitches used in tonal music. In Chapter 3, I arbitrarily assigned attributes such as "consonance" or "step" to certain intervals between these pitches so that I could show what I mean by such constructs as "arpeggiation," "step motion," and "neighbor," or such concepts as "tonic" and "dominant." Without these words we could not have begun to talk about the structure of tonal music.

By proceeding this way, I have left unanswered a host of fundamental questions. For example, with twelve equally spaced pitch classes available, why would you wish to choose just seven to use for a diatonic collection? Why not six or eight or some other number? For that matter, why should there be just twelve pitch classes? It is easy enough to see that it is convenient to divide the octave into equal intervals so that we can use them as units, but why twelve of them? Why not ten or thirteen? And why should the interval we use to define pitch class be the particular size it is? Why should we consider intervals of one size as consonant and those of another as dissonant? Worst of all, why should we consider the same interval (the fourth) dissonant under some conditions but consonant under others?

It is the purpose of this appendix to provide at least partial answers to these difficult questions.

A.1 The Physiology of Pitch Perception

In this section we will describe the human auditory system in a little more detail than was possible in Section 1.1, with a view to understanding a little better how it is we conceive of pitch the way we do.

It is convenient to divide the auditory system into two parts: the ear and the brain. Both receive and transmit information, but they use different types of energy to do so, and in doing so fulfill different functions. The ear uses mechanical energy: fluctuations in air pressure are transformed by successive parts of the ear into various forms of mechanical motion. The brain uses electrochemical energy: impulses generated by mechanical motion in the ear are relayed through a system of electrochemical circuits. The ear's job is to follow the changing patterns of incoming sound waves as closely as possible. The brain's job is to reduce the information gathered by the ear to a usable form.

When a sound wave reaches the ear the fluctuations in air pressure make the ear drum move in and out. The drum is so flexible that the pattern of its motion is essentially the same as the pattern of pressure fluctuation. This pattern is transmitted by a system of tiny levers (the ossicles) to a flexible diaphragm at the base of the cochlea (the oval window). As the oval window moves in and out, it makes waves in the fluid inside the cochlea. These waves have essentially the same pattern as the original sound waves; their energy is distributed at the same frequencies and in the same proportions. The basilar membrane measures this distribution. As the wave travels down the cochlea from the oval window it causes ripples in the membrane. The pattern of these ripples is a map of the way the energy of the wave is distributed. If all the wave's energy is concentrated at a single frequency (as in a sine wave), there will be one ripple concentrated around one point on the membrane.

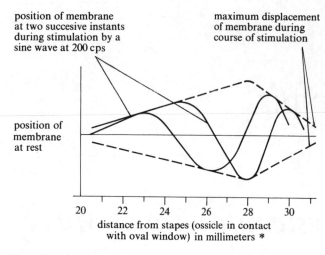

position of membrane at two succesive instants during stimulation by a sine wave at 200 cps

maximum displacement of membrane during course of stimulation

position of membrane at rest

distance from stapes (ossicle in contact with oval window) in millimeters *

The higher the frequency the closer the point is to the oval window.

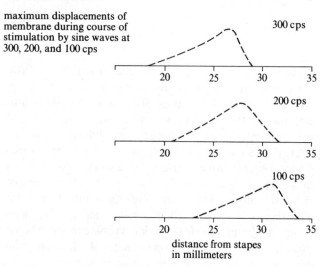

maximum displacements of membrane during course of stimulation by sine waves at 300, 200, and 100 cps

distance from stapes in millimeters

The greater the energy at any given frequency, the bigger the ripple at that point. If a wave has its energy distributed among a number of frequencies (as is the case for any compound wave), then there will be ripples at each of the corresponding points, and the size of each ripple will correspond to the energy at that frequency. If a wave has its energy spread over a wide range of frequencies (as in pitchless sounds like the spoken "s"), the ripples occur throughout the whole stretch of the membrane corresponding to those frequencies.

The hair cells of the organ of Corti convert the basilar membrane's map into a form the neurons of the auditory system can handle. As the membrane ripples, the hair cells in the area of the ripple bend and twist so that they generate electricity. If the charge they generate is great enough, the outermost neurons of the auditory network fire. As the neural impulses are relayed onto the auditory cortex, the information they carry is both sharpened and simplified.

As you can see from the lower figure at left, a wave with all its energy concentrated at 200 cps will activate the basilar membrane and hence the hair cells for about a third of its total length (anywhere from about 20 millimeters to about 31 millimeters from the oval window). But as the impulses activated by the hair cells are relayed through the auditory system, the weaker impulses are filtered out and only those corresponding to the point of greatest activity (in this case the point around 28.4 millimeters from the oval window) get through to the auditory cortex. The particular group of neurons that fire there determine our sense of the pitch of the sound we hear.

A wave with its energy concentrated at a number of frequencies, on the other hand, will activate the basilar membrane and hence the hair cells at a number of points. But we do not hear a number of pitches. We hear only one—the same one we would hear if all the wave's energy were concentrated at the frequency that is the lowest common denominator of the others. This frequency is called the fundamental frequency. The neural impulses from the other points are not simply filtered out. They contribute to our sense of how loud the note is and of what timbre it has.†

How high a sound seems corresponds to the place in the auditory cortex where neural activity is concentrated and in turn to the place or places where the basilar membrane has been activated. This place or places corresponds to the frequencies at which the energy of the wave is distributed. If the energy of the wave is concentrated around one frequency (or around each of a set of frequencies one of which is the lowest common denominator of the others), we get the sensation of pitch—that is, we can say just how high the sound is as though it lay at a particular point on a vertical axis.‡ The higher the fundamental

---

* This figure and the next are adapted from figures in Georg von Bekesy's article "The variation of phase along the basilar membrane with sinusoidal vibrations" (*Journal of the Acoustical Society of America,* 1947). The entire article is reprinted in von Bekesy's collected essays, *Experiments in Hearing* (New York, 1960), and a discussion of its results is available in von Bekesy's summary "The mechanical properties of the ear" in the *Handbook of Experimental Psychology,* ed. S. S. Stevens (New York, 1951).

† They also probably help sharpen our sense of the pitch itself, but how this is done is not clearly understood.

‡ It is not entirely surprising that we should conceive of the sensation of pitch in spatial terms. The brain handles messages from the organ of Corti in much the same fashion it handles messages from the touch-sensitive neurons in the skin. It is also not surprising that the sensation of pitch is limited to one dimension. The organ of Corti is only a few cells wide. It would make no difference if one edge of the basilar membrane were activated more than the other. Why we should conceive of that dimension as vertical and think of sounds whose sound waves have a greater fundamental frequency as higher is another question. The basilar membrane itself is not vertical but coiled in a spiral. In any case we can say that to conceive of pitch along a horizontal axis (with one pitch further to the right than another as on a piano keyboard) would be out of the question since we use that axis to describe the direction the sound comes from.

frequency, the closer the point of maximum stimulation of the basilar membrane is to the oval window and the higher the pitch. As you can see from the lower figure facing, however, the position of the point of maximum stimulation does not vary with the frequency itself but with the log of the frequency * Thus the difference in the height of two pitches—the interval—corresponds to the ratio of, not the difference between, the fundamental frequencies of the two waves. If the pairs of frequencies form the same ratio—

$$\frac{f_2}{f_1} = \frac{f_4}{f_3}$$

—then the intervals formed by the corresponding pitches will be heard as equal—$p_2 - p_1 = p_4 - p_3$. Thus notes whose sound waves have fundamental frequencies of 220 and 330 cps form the same interval as notes whose sound waves have fundamental frequencies of 440 and 660 cps.

The accuracy with which the brain can distinguish among nearby pitches is astounding, although it is more limited at very high and very low frequencies. If the point of maximum stimulation is somewhere between the middle of the basilar membrane and the oval window, a change of as little as .004 millimeters in its position is perceptible. This means that for pitches from around middle C to three octaves above middle C we can distinguish as many as 120 different pitches per octave, ten times as many as we actually use. (As the point of maximum stimulation approaches the oval window itself, this accuracy drops off; although we can hear pitches higher than the highest note on the piano, our lack of ability to locate them accurately makes them less useful for music.) If the point of maximum stimulation is more than halfway along the basilar membrane from the oval window, a change of frequency of as little as 3 cps is perceptible.† This means that as you approach the lowest frequencies we use in music, the sense of pitch becomes increasingly fuzzy. The lowest string on the piano is tuned to vibrate at 27.5 cps, the next lowest at 29.1 cps. If the sound waves produced by these strings were pure sine waves, we would not be able to distinguish between them and would not hear two distinctly different pitches. But, of course, these sound waves are not sine waves; a substantial portion of their energy occurs at higher frequencies—at 55 and 58.2 cps and 82.5 and 87.4 cps. Consequently, we can still hear that one pitch is higher than the other.

The accuracy with which the brain can estimate how much higher one pitch is than another varies with the size of the interval and the ratio of the fundamental frequencies involved. Evidently the brain uses two different processes. For relatively small intervals, it simply gauges the distance between points of maximum stimulation by the fundamental frequencies of the two waves. This process is subject to the same kind of error that human beings are always subject to in estimating distances. Thus, for example, given three successive sound waves with fundamental frequencies of 440, 495, and 550 cps, most listeners would accept both intervals as equal, although of course

$$\frac{495}{440} = \frac{556.9}{495} \text{ and not } \frac{550}{495}.$$

For larger intervals, the brain uses points of stimulation by frequencies other than the fundamental as a kind of ruler. Most of the sound waves we use in music have their energy distributed among a number of frequencies, of which the fundamental is simply the lowest common denominator.‡ Thus, for example, the sound wave for the A below middle C on the piano has the greatest energy at 220 cps, slightly less at 440, even less at 660, still less at 880, etc. Consequently, it is easy to relate such a sound wave to one with its energy distributed at 440, 880, 1320, 1760, etc., cps, since so many of the points stimulated will be exactly the same. Furthermore, we can distinguish between such a relationship and one in which the points stimulated are close but not exactly the same—as, for example, where one wave has its energy concentrated at 220, 440, 660, 880, . . . cps, and the other at 437, 874, 1311, 1748, . . . cps. In general, the accuracy with which the brain can identify a 2:1 ratio between two fundamental frequencies is nearly as high as that for identical frequencies. Where the fundamental frequencies are in a ratio of 3:2, the same principle can be applied. Compare two waves with energy distributed at 220, 440, 660, 880, 1100, 1320, . . ., cps, and 330, 660, 990, 1320, 1650, 1980 . . . cps. Note that they have fewer frequencies in common than two waves with a 2:1 ratio, and furthermore that these common frequencies are not those with the most energy. This means that the brain is a shade less accurate in identifying 3:2 ratios between fundamental frequencies than it is in identifying 2:1 ratios, or to put it more positively, our tolerance for a 3:2 ratio that is slightly off is a shade greater than it is for a 2:1 ratio that is slightly off.

In the next sections of this appendix we will show

---

* Note the way the frequencies are spaced on the right side of the lower figure facing. Note also that while the correlation between the log of the frequency and the point of maximum stimulation is roughly constant for the segment at the far end of the membrane, toward the middle it shifts to a new constant.

† The fact that for lower frequencies the lowest perceptible difference is constant for frequency rather than distance along the basilar membrane suggests that the brain has some way of counting frequencies up to about 500 cps. Whether or not this is the case is a matter of controversy.

‡ Even when this is not the case, as with the sine wave generated by a tuning fork, the outer and middle ear create upper partials in the course of transmitting the wave to the inner ear. See von Bekesy, "The mechanical properties of the ear," in Stevens, *op. cit.*, pp. 1086–1089.

how we can use the three intervals that the brain can gauge most accurately—the unison (frequencies 1:1), the octave (frequencies 2:1), and the fifth (frequencies 3:2) to generate the collection of pitches and pitch relationships used in tonal music.

A.2 The Primary Intervals

Suppose you wanted to write a tonal piece. What intervals would you use? Put this way, the question is foolish. What we understand as tonal music is inseparable from the intervals that are used. But suppose all you knew about intervals in tonal music were the functions these intervals would have to serve. How would you go about determining the sizes of intervals that would best suit those functions? If we could determine appropriate interval sizes for three primary pitch relationships characteristic of tonal music, namely
1. the identity relationship,
2. the relationship between members of the same pitch class, and
3. the relationship between dominant and tonic,

we could use these three primary interval sizes to arrive at other interval sizes as well.

Consider what we mean when we say that two notes have the same pitch. How can we define the size of the interval they form? This question almost answers itself. If we say that two notes have the same pitch ($p_1 = p_2$), we mean that neither note is higher than the other ($p_1 \not> p_2, p_2 \not> p_1$), and hence that there is no difference in the height of the two notes ($p_1 - p_2 = 0$). In short, we need an interval of size zero. We know that when two sound waves have the same fundamental frequency ($f_1 = f_2$) the sounds we hear will have the same pitch ($p_1 = p_2$), so we know that if the fundamental frequencies are in a 1:1 ratio ($\frac{f_2}{f_1} = 1$), the two pitches must form the desired interval ($p_2 - p_1 = 0$). Remember, however, that when we say a sound wave has a particular frequency we really mean that a part of its energy is concentrated around that frequency. Remember also that while the auditory system is capable of making very fine distinctions in locating the frequency around which energy is distributed, its ability is not unlimited. Thus, for example, a sound wave with its energy centered around 1000 cps followed by a second sound wave with its energy centered around 1001 cps will be perceived as $\frac{f_2}{f_1} = 1$, even though $\frac{1001}{1000} \neq 1$. So the safe way to define the size of the identity interval is: two notes form the identity interval when the fundamental frequencies of their respective sound waves are either in a ratio of 1:1 or close enough to a ratio of 1:1 so that we can accept the interval we hear as a reasonable substitute for the interval we hear when they are in fact 1:1.

Now consider what we want to mean by two different pitches being members of the same pitch class. First, we will want to be able to associate them as though they were identical in some sense—we will want to think of them as having something in common even though they are different. Second, we will want to be able to think of any pitch as a member of one and only one pitch class. If p_1 and p_2 are different pitches but members of the same class, and p_2 and p_3 are different pitches but members of the same class, then p_1 and p_3 are either identical pitches or members of the same class. But if p_1 and p_2 are different pitches but members of the same class, and p_2 and p_3 are different pitches and not members of the same class, then p_1 and p_3 are not members of the same class.

What we think of as the pitch of a note corresponds to the fundamental frequency of the sound wave that reaches our eardrums. But that sound wave has energy at other frequencies, frequencies 2, 3, 4, 5, ... times the fundamental frequency. Consequently the basilar membrane is stimulated at points corresponding to these frequencies as well. While we are not consciously aware of pitches corresponding to these other points of stimulation, the brain evidently uses these points to arrive at the sensation of pitch. Thus, whatever the process is, it seems likely that there is some physiological basis for associating pitches of notes whose respective sound waves have fundamental frequencies 2, 3, 4, 5 ... times one another.

Consider, then, a set of possible notes, $n_1, n_2, n_3 \ldots$ with pitches $p_1, p_2, p_3 \ldots$ corresponding to a set of sound waves $w_1, w_2, w_3 \ldots$ with fundamental frequencies $f_1, f_2, f_3 \ldots$ such that $f_2 = 2f_1, f_3 = 3f_1 \ldots$

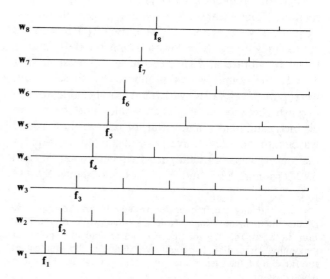

Clearly we could associate any of the upper pitches, $p_2, p_3, p_4 \ldots$ with p_1, since all the frequencies at which any of the upper waves, $w_2, w_3, w_4 \ldots$ have energy are included in w_1. However, we could not associate all of the upper pitches with one another in the same way. For example, the fundamental frequency of w_3 (f_3) is not included among the frequencies of w_2, and the fundamental of w_4 is not included among the frequencies of w_3. However, all the frequencies of w_4 are included in w_2 as well as in w_1. Similarly all frequencies of a w_9 would be included in w_3 as well as in w_1, and all frequencies of a w_{16} would be included in w_4 as well as in w_1. Thus, a frequency ratio of 2:1, 3:1, 4:1, or n:1, where n is an integer greater than one, could be used to define the size of the interval between adjacent pitches in a pitch class. The ratio of 2:1, however, has certain strong advantages. It has the acoustical and physiological advantage that most of the sound waves we use in music have more energy at frequencies twice their fundamental frequencies than at frequencies three or four times the fundamental.* It has the conceptual advantage of corresponding to the smallest interval with the property of association. Thus, if two notes correspond to sound waves with fundamental frequencies in a ratio of 2:1, we can associate their pitches and know that there is no other pitch between them that we would associate so closely with either of them.

For all these reasons we use the interval size corresponding to the frequency ratio of 2:1 to define pitch class.† Two pitches are adjacent members of a pitch class when their corresponding fundamental frequencies are either in a ratio of 2:1 or close enough to a ratio of 2:1 so that we can accept the interval they form as a reasonable substitute for the interval they would have formed had the frequencies been exactly 2:1. This means that a pitch class consists of a set of pitches such that, if the fundamental frequency corresponding to one pitch is f, the fundamental frequences of the others equal $2^n f$, where n is any integer.

Now consider how we think of the relationship of dominant to tonic. We think of the dominant in terms of the tonic rather than vice versa. We think of the dominant as dependent on a conceptually prior tonic. However, note that both the dominant and the tonic are pitch classes rather than pitches. Therefore for each pitch that is a dominant (that is, a member of the dominant pitch class) there will be two adjacent tonics (that is members of the tonic pitch class), one above and one below. Nor is there any reason to suppose that the interval formed by the dominant and the upper tonic will be the same size as the

* A notable exception are the sound waves generated by the clarinet, which have more energy at three and five times the fundamental frequency than at twice the fundamental.
† Such an interval size is of course the one we call an octave, but we can't call it that yet since the name implies the idea that the pitches forming the interval are the first and the eighth members of some set of pitches.

interval formed by the tonic and the dominant below it.

Indeed, if it were, how would you be able to tell which pitch class was the dominant?

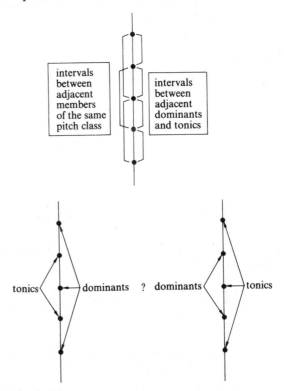

What we need, then, is not just one interval but a pair of unequal intervals that together add up to the interval between adjacent members of the same pitch class. For this to be the case, the intervals in the pair must correspond to a pair of frequency ratios whose product is 2:1.

Many pairs of ratios fulfill this condition, for example,

$1/1 \times 2/1 = 2/1$; $3/2 \times 4/3 = 2/1$; $5/4 \times 8/5 = 2/1$; $7/4 \times 8/7 = 2/1$, etc.,

but the pair best suited to the task will be the pair that ear and brain can gauge most accurately, for the dominant-to-tonic relationships must be easy to grasp if we are to base other relationships on it. As we saw in Section A.1, we can gauge interval size most accurately if we can line up the partials of one wave with the partials of another; indeed the more partials we can line up and the more of the wave's energy is at those partials, the more accurately we can gauge the size of the interval. Since the other partials are simply integral multiples of the fundamental frequency and since most of the energy of the waves we use in music is concentrated in the lower partials, it follows that the intervals we can gauge most accurately are the ones corresponding to frequency ratios that can be expressed in the smallest numbers, 1:1, 2:1, 3:1, 3:2, 4:3, 5:1, 5:2, 5:4, etc. Of the pairs of ratios that fit our two conditions (both ratios must be larger than 1:1 and smaller than 2:1 and the product of the two ratios must equal 2:1), the pair that uses the smallest integers is 3:2 and 4:3.

Consider a set of waves, **W**, such that the fundamental frequency of each wave, w_n, is half that of the wave with the next highest frequency, w_{n+1}.

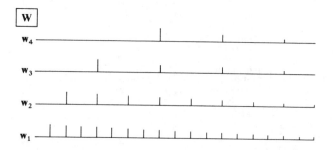

And consider a second set of waves, **W'**, with the same property, so related to the first set that the fundamental frequency of any wave w'_n is 3:2 with the fundamental frequency of some w_n and 3:4 with the fundamental frequency of some w'_{n+1}.

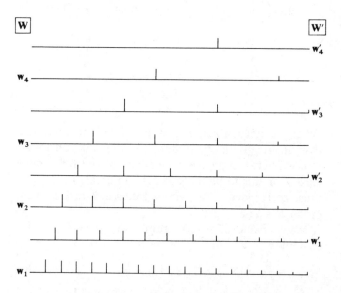

You can see from the way the partials of the waves in **W'** line up with the partials of the waves in **W** why the intervals corresponding to the ratios 3:2 and 4:3 are easy for the ear and brain to gauge and hence why the corresponding intervals are well suited to the dominant-to-tonic relationship. But which set of waves should we choose to consider as corresponding to the dominant pitch class and which to the tonic? Remember that we want to think of the dominant in terms of the tonic. Is there any reason why it would be easier to think of the pitch class corresponding to one set of waves as less fundamental than, or even in some sense subsidiary to, the pitch class corresponding to the other set? Note that for every wave in **W'** those partials that correspond to the fundamental of some other wave in **W'**—that is, those partials on which the sense of the pitch class **P'** depends—are all also included as the third and/or sixth partial of some wave in **W**. But none of the partials in any **W** wave that correspond to fundamentals in other **W** waves are included among the partials of any **W'** wave. Thus, other things being equal, it should be easier to conceive of **P'** as subsidiary to **P** than vice versa. More generally we may say: the set of intervals best suited to the relationship of a dominant pitch class to a tonic pitch class is the one that corresponds to the set of frequency ratios $3:2^n$, where n is any integer. Within this set of intervals we must distinguish between two classes of intervals: those for which $n \leq 1$ and hence the "tonic" pitch is lower than the "dominant," and those for which $n \geq 2$ and hence the "tonic" pitch is higher than the "dominant."

We explained our preference for thinking of one pitch class in terms of the other by showing how we can match up partials corresponding to the fundamentals of one set of waves with other higher partials in the other set of waves. Now when $n \leq 1$ (that is, when the fundamental frequencies form ratios of 3:2, 3:1, 3:½ or 6:1, etc.), the fundamental of the wave we hear as the note with the dominant pitch is higher than the fundamental of the other wave and is hence relatively easy to associate with the upper partials of that other wave. But when $n > 1$ (that is, when the ratio is 3:4, 3:8, 3:16, etc.), the fundamental frequency of the wave we hear as the note with the dominant pitch is actually lower than the fundamental of the other wave and is hence relatively difficult to associate with the higher partials of that wave. This second class of intervals poses certain conceptual problems that will be dealt with in the next section.*

A.3 Consonance and Dissonance, Skip and Step

We conceive of tonal music in terms of such notions as rearticulation, neighbor embellishment, arpeggiation, and step motion. These notions depend on

---

* The interval corresponding to a 3:2 ratio is, of course, a fifth, while the one corresponding to 4:3 is a fourth, but we can't call them that yet because these names would imply the existence of a diatonic collection.

distinctions between two sets of intervallic categories: repetition/step/skip and consonance/dissonance.

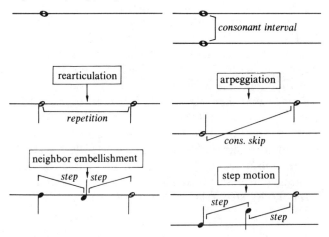

Before we can use such notions to construct music, we must decide which interval sizes we will consider consonant and which dissonant, which steps and which skips.*

Now, although the one distinction applies primarily to simultaneously sounding notes and the other exclusively to consecutive notes, they are nevertheless dependent on one another. In the first place, we have no way of understanding a dissonance except as being related by step to some consonance. When two simultaneously sounding notes form a dissonant interval we have to be able to understand one of the notes as a temporary displacement by step from a pitch that would have formed a consonant interval with the other note, as, for example, in a dissonant neighbor or passing tone.

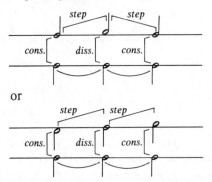

This means that for any interval size that we want to consider dissonant we will have to have an adjacent interval size—one just a step larger or a step smaller—that we can consider as consonant. In the second place, we must be able to tell a neighbor embellishment

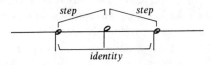

* The only interval size appropriate to the idea of repetition is, of course, the identity interval.

from the arpeggiation of two pitches in which the first is returned to

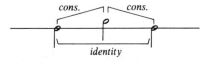

or a three-element step motion

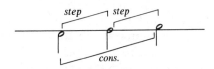

from the arpeggiation of three consonant pitches.

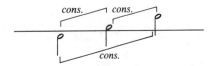

This means that whatever interval sizes we may want to consider as steps will have to be dissonant, for if they were both consonant and steps, we would have no way of distinguishing between essentially different structures.

Thus, if we are going to think of each dissonant interval as dependent via the notion of step on some nearby consonant interval, we will want to consider as consonant those intervals that have functions independent of the notion of step. Furthermore, if we are going to gauge the size of each dissonant interval as being a step larger or a step smaller than some consonant interval, we will want to consider as consonant those interval sizes that are relatively easy for our ears and brains to gauge—in any case, easier than the adjacent dissonant intervals.

Unfortunately, these considerations won't get us very far if we don't know how big a step is. The problem is that the interval size or sizes we will want to consider as steps will be whatever intervals there happen to be between adjacent pitches in the collection of pitches we are going to use. But since we haven't arrived at that collection yet, we can't very well say what size would be appropriate. However, we can set limits on that size. It has to be larger than the interval size corresponding to a 1:1 frequency ratio, so as not to be confused with the identity interval, and it has to be smaller than the interval size corresponding to a 4:3 ratio, so as not to be confused with the smaller of the two intervals we use for the dominant-to-tonic relationship. With this much information we can

1. determine a preliminary set of interval sizes that we can consider consonant, and
2. use these consonant intervals to build a preliminary pitch collection with which we can compose a rudimentary kind of tonal music.

The Primary Intervals as a Preliminary Set of Consonant Intervals • Consider the interval size that corresponds to a 1:1 frequency ratio. Obviously, such an interval must be consonant. We have already assigned it a function independent of the idea of a step—the identity function. It is the interval size our ears and brains gauge most easily and accurately, so there would be no point in looking for another interval a step larger or smaller that would be easier to gauge. Indeed, since this interval is of zero size, there is no smaller interval, and the interval size a step larger would be whatever interval size we eventually assign to the step itself. Such an interval must be dissonant in any case, and we can easily understand it as being the result of a step displacement from the identity interval.

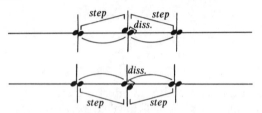

Next consider the interval size corresponding to the frequency ratio of 2:1. Again, such an interval must obviously be consonant. We have already assigned it a function independent of the idea of a step—the function of defining the pitch class. The only interval size easier to gauge is the one corresponding to the 1:1 frequency ratio, and it is much too much smaller, so there is no point in looking for another interval a step larger or a step smaller in terms of which we could gauge this one. Indeed, whatever interval size or sizes we eventually assign to the step, any interval a step larger or smaller than the interval between adjacent members of the same pitch class fits our requirements for dissonance perfectly.*

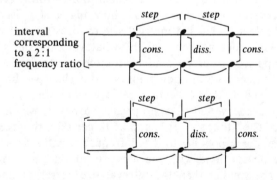

Now consider the interval size corresponding to a 3:2 frequency ratio. We have already assigned it a function: the dominant-to-tonic relationship. The nearest interval size that we can gauge better is the

---

* The same would be true of any interval a step larger or smaller than any interval between members of the same pitch class.

one corresponding to a 2:1 ratio, but the difference between these two interval sizes is too large, since it equals the size we use for the smaller of the two dominant-to-tonic intervals: the one corresponding to a 3:4 ratio.

On the other hand, consider the interval size corresponding to the 3:4 ratio itself. We have assigned it a function: the dominant-to-tonic relationship, but we noted that that relationship is harder to grasp than the larger dominant-to-tonic interval. Furthermore, there is another interval size—that corresponding to 2:3—that is slightly easier to gauge and close enough to be considered a step larger. Under most circumstances, it is easier to think of the smaller interval in terms of its step relationship to the larger,

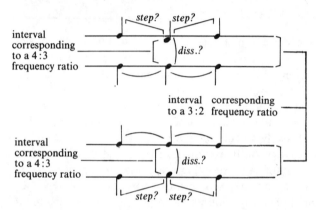

in which case we would want to consider the smaller interval dissonant. However, if the lower of the two pitches forming the 4:3 interval is not the lowest pitch present, and there is a lower pitch that is a member of the same pitch class as the upper of the two pitches,

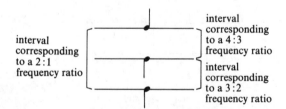

we have a different situation. Here the dominant-to-tonic function of the upper two notes is made unequivocal by the presence of the lower note. In such a case we would want to consider the interval size corresponding to a 4:3 ratio as consonant.

A.4 A Preliminary Pitch Collection

Eventually we will want to construct a collection of pitches with which we can compose tonal music. In order to see the nature of the problem more clearly, let us arrive first at a collection of pitches with which we can create some of the structures we know from tonal music. We can always expand this collection later.

What is the minimum collection of pitch classes we need to create the kind of structures we know from tonal music? Take any pitch class. Consider it the tonic.

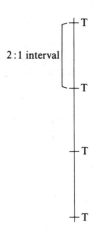

Add another pitch class such that its pitches form the dominant-to-tonic interval with the tonic pitches. Call it the dominant.

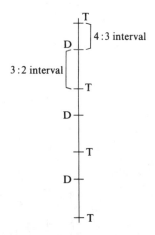

Any combination of pitches from these two classes that has a tonic as its lowest pitch is a consonant combination. This means that you can state its pitches simultaneously

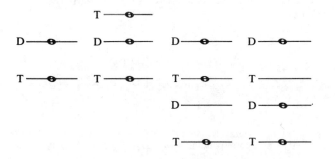

or arpeggiate them. Furthermore, you can distinguish by the order in which the pitches are arpeggiated between "closed" structures, in which the final pitch is a tonic,

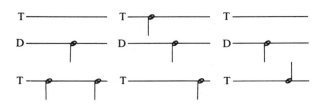

and "open" structures, in which the final pitch is a dominant.

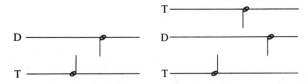

To create neighbors and step motions, we will need pitch classes that are related to some tonic or dominant by step. Suppose we want a pitch class from which we could get upper neighbors to the tonic. Clearly, we need a pitch class whose pitches are a step above the pitches of T—call it T+s.

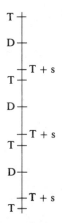

If you're willing to limit your use of T+s to dissonant neighbors,

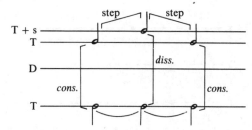

it doesn't make much difference how much higher the pitches of T+s are than those of T, as long as the interval formed is smaller than the smaller of the dominant-to-tonic intervals. But if you want to be able to use T+s to form consonant combinations with other pitches, you must choose it accordingly. There is no way the pitches of T+s can be consonant with the pitches of T, since the intervals they form are those used for the step, and the pitch-class interval is not a step. That leaves the pitches of D. If we make the pitches of T+s and D form an interval the size of the larger of the two dominant-to-tonic intervals,

419

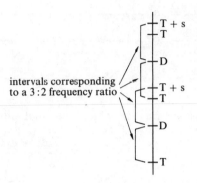

we have a collection of pitches that can be used to create a varied set of structures. T+s can, of course, still be used as a dissonant neighbor to the tonic,

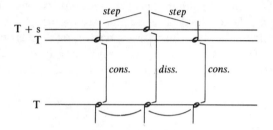

but it can also be used in a consonant combination with a dominant.

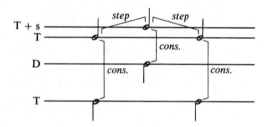

Such a consonant combination can then be used as a basis for other structures: a neighbor embellishment

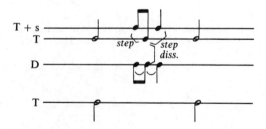

or an arpeggiation.

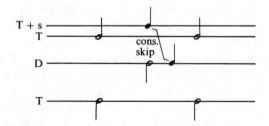

In both cases, note the way in which the structural roles of our two original pitch classes have been shifted. In the neighbor embellishment a tonic pitch is subordinated to a member of T+s, a pitch class that we think of in terms of its relationship to T and D. In the arpeggiation the dominant pitch becomes the recipient of the dominant-to-tonic relationship; it plays the role of tonic to T+s's dominant. Such shifting of roles is essential to our idea of tonal structure.

Following the same reasoning we can add another pitch class D−s (a step below the dominant), such that T and the D−s below it form the larger of the dominant-to-tonic intervals

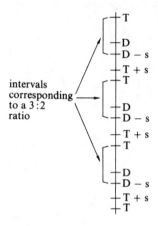

and either a T−s that forms such an interval with the D−s above

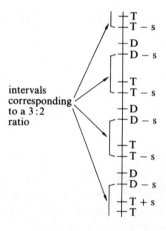

or a D+s that forms such an interval with the T+s below.

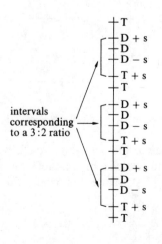

In either case the result is a collection of five pitch classes (a *pentatonic* collection) generated with the interval formed by its two primary members, the dominant and tonic.

starting with the original members T and D,

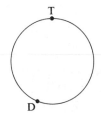

add T+s such that the interval from T+s to D will equal the interval from D to T,

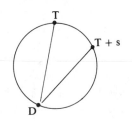

add D−s such that the interval from D−s to T will equal the interval from T to D,

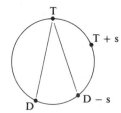

either add D+s such that the interval from D+s to T+s will equal the interval from T to D

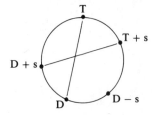

or add T−s such that the interval from T−s to D−s will equal the interval from D to T.

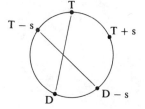

The structural properties of such a collection are directly related to our method of generating it:

1. There are only two interval sizes between adjacent pitch classes and both of these are smaller than the smaller of the two intervals between the primary pitch classes.

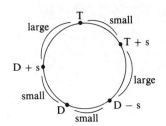
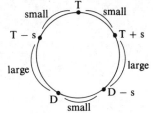

Hence there are two and only two interval sizes to which we can assign the step function.

(If we combine our two pentatonic collections to form a single collection of six pitch classes, we get three different sizes of steps.)

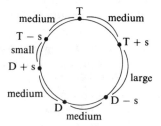

2. There are step-related pitch classes above and below both the two primary pitch classes; every pitch class in the collection is either one of the primary pitch classes or related by step to one of them.

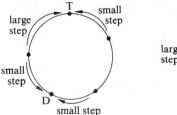
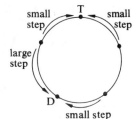

This means that pitches are available for upper and lower neighbors to both primary degrees and to form step motions from one to the other in either direction. Thus, any pitch is either a tonic or a dominant or can be related directly to one or both. (If we stop at four pitch classes

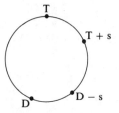

we have no pitch class to put in the smaller of the two intervals between the tonic and the dominant, so we have no way of getting an upper neighbor to the dominant, a lower neighbor to the tonic, or step motion between a dominant and the tonic above it. If we continue to generate pitch classes so that there are more than two pitch classes filling in the larger of the two intervals between the tonic and the dominant,

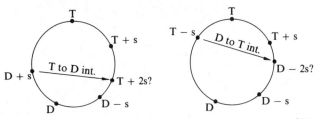

421

we get a pitch class that we have no way of relating directly to either the tonic or the dominant. We could think of it as a step from another pitch class which is in turn a step from the tonic or dominant, or as forming a dominant-to-tonic interval with a pitch class that in turn forms that interval with the tonic or the dominant, but neither of these relationships is direct.)

3. For each primary pitch class there is another pitch class that has the same relationship to it that it has to the other primary pitch class. For example, T+s is related to D as D is to T, and D−s is related to T as T is to D.

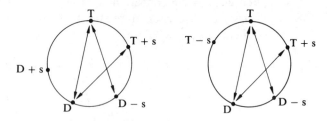

We generated our two pentatonic collections from a given tonic and dominant so as to get this property. But suppose you had a pentatonic collection

and you didn't know which pitch class was the tonic. Of the five candidates only two will yield this property.

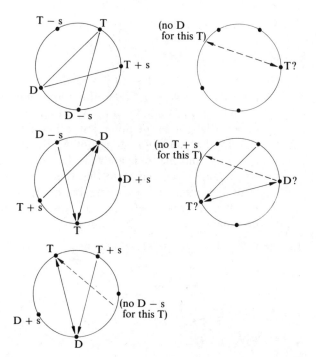

The two structures that have this property are simply rotations of our original two structures.

A.5 Diatonic Collections and Triads

The structural properties of these two pentatonic collections will almost allow us to compose tonal music—almost, but not quite. The main problem lies in the paucity of consonant intervals. Between the zero-sized identity interval and the pitch-class membership interval there are eight interval sizes available: s, s' (the larger of the two step-sized intervals), $2s$, $s+s'$, $2s+s'$, $s+2s'$, $3s+s'$, and $2s+s'$. Of these only $2s+s'$ (the larger dominant-to-tonic interval) is always consonant. This means, for example, that there is no way to combine a step motion from dominant to tonic in an upper line with an arpeggiation of tonic and dominant in the bass so that simultaneously sounding notes are consonant.

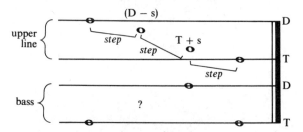

To get more consonant intervals we need more relationships that we can conceive of as independent of the idea of step. To get such relationships we will need a larger collection of pitch classes. Take either of the pentatonic structures just discussed

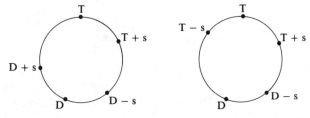

and continue to generate new pitch classes by the same method, starting each case from the last pitch class that was generated.

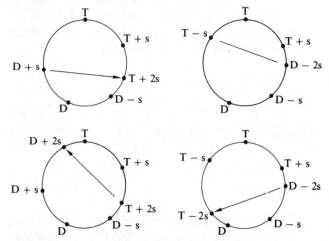

In either case, with seven pitch classes there are again only two sizes of steps

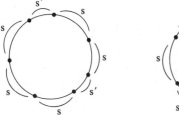

a larger (s) and a smaller (s'). We recognize both as having the same intervallic structure, that of the *diatonic collection*—three large steps, one small, two large steps, one small, three large, one small, etc. However, 1. we have no way of relating one pitch class (T+2s in one, T+s+s' in the other) directly to the tonic or dominant

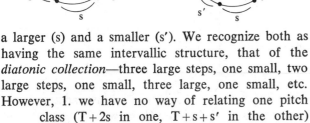

and 2. of the seven pitch classes four could serve as T such that there is a T+s that has the same relationship to D that D has to T, and a D−s that has the same relationship to T that T has to D.

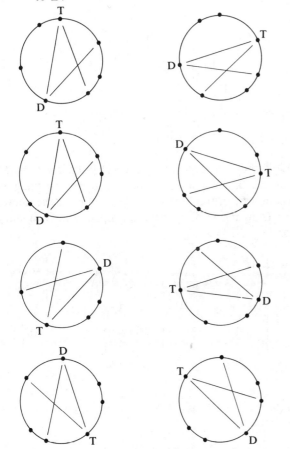

By taking care of the first objection now, we can later arrive at a way of taking care of the second. To take care of the first we must invent some way of thinking of T+2s and T+s+s' directly in terms of T and D. Instead of thinking of either of these pitches as a step from another pitch that is in turn a step from either the tonic or the dominant, suppose we think of each as being midway between the tonic and the dominant, or at least as close to midway as you can get in either of the collections at hand. To fit this conception we will rename T+2s and T+s+s the mediant, M.

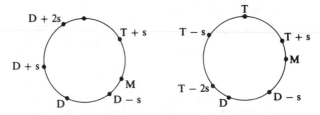

The fact that we can relate M directly to T and D without reference to steps suggests that we might be able to think of the intervals formed between M and T and M and D as consonant. The question remains, are these interval sizes relatively easy for the ear and brain to measure? Consider the sizes of the intervals involved in each case:

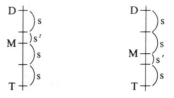

Both the larger M-to-T interval and the larger D-to-M interval are equal in size to two large-step intervals. Hence they should both correspond to a frequency ratio of $(9/8)^2$ or $81/64$. Both the smaller M-to-T interval and the smaller D-to-M interval are two large steps smaller than a dominant-to-tonic interval. Hence they should both correspond to a frequency ratio of $3/2 \times (8/9)^2 = 32/27$. Neither of these ratios looks very promising. However, note that $81/64$ is close to $80/64$ or $5/4$, and $32/27$ equals $96/81$, which is close to $96/80$ or $6/5$. We can gauge the interval size corresponding to a frequency ratio of 5:4 by lining up the fourth partial of one wave with the fifth of the other.

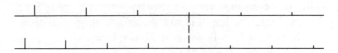

Similarly, we can gauge the interval size corresponding to a frequency ratio of 6:5 by lining up the fifth partial of one wave with the sixth partial of the other.

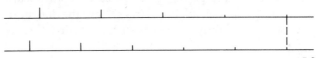

(Of course, since the partials we have to line up are fewer and weaker than those available where the fundamentals are in a 2:1 or 3:2 ratio, the accuracy and reliability with which we gauge these interval sizes is slightly lower.)

Now the question is: how can we use this ability? After all, $81/64$ does not equal $3/2$. Suppose we were to redefine our M's as forming intervals of these sizes with our T's and D's

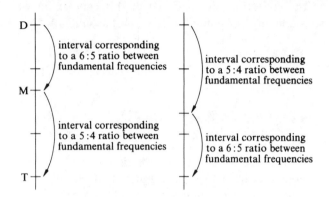

That would make both M's easy to locate with respect to D and T. Unfortunately, it would also mean that one of the dominant-to-tonic sized intervals between members of the collection would have to correspond to a ratio of 40:27 instead of 3:2, or that one of the intervals between members of the same pitch class would have to correspond to a ratio of 81:40.

($6/5 \times 3/2 \times 1/2 \times 3/2 \times 3/2 \times 1/2 \neq 1$; $6/5 \times 3/2 \times 1/2 \times 3/2 \times 40/27 \times 1/2 = 1$ and $6/5 \times 3/2 \times 1/2 \times 3/2 \times 3/2 \times 40/81 = 1$.)

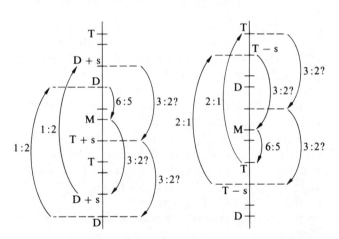

The more easily and accurately we can gauge an interval size the less tolerant we are of approximations to that size. It follows that if we have to fudge on some interval somewhere, we should let it be the one we gauge less accurately, in this case the ones corresponding to ratios of 5:4 and 6:5 rather than those corresponding to 3:2 or 2:1. The alternative then for interval sizes corresponding to 5:4 and 6:5 is to learn to accept intervals slightly larger than the larger of the two and slightly smaller than the smaller. Clearly

if we can do this we can consider both the intervals that M forms with T and D as consonant.

The particular M-to-T and M-to-D intervals we have been talking about are the ones formed when the T pitch is directly below the M pitch and the D pitch directly above.

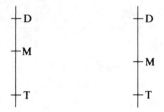

But we can extend the status of consonance to other M-to-T or M-to-D intervals as well. Suppose the M pitch was above the T pitch, but there was room for another T pitch between them

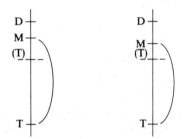

or that the M pitch was below the D pitch but there was room for another D between them.

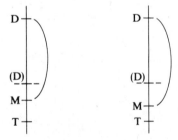

Now if there is room for a T or D pitch near the M pitch, we can imagine it there, and if we can imagine it there we can think of M's relationship to the actual T or D in terms of its relationship to the imaginary T or D.

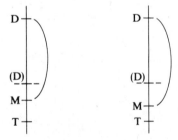

Similarly, if the M pitch is above the D pitch or below the T pitch,

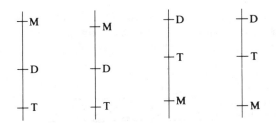

we can imagine another D pitch above the M or another T pitch below the M pitch

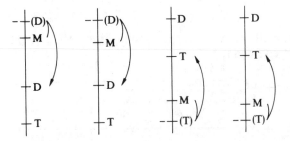

and relate the M to the actual T and D accordingly. The fact that we must supply an imaginary T below the M when the M is lower than the T may affect our understanding of the D–to–T interval. We have been considering the smaller of the D–to–T intervals as dissonant unless there is another T below the D.

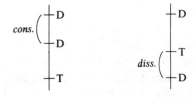

But if we already have to supply an imaginary T to understand the M-to-T relationship, why not use it to understand the D-to-T relationship as well?

In such a case we could understand the D-to-T relationship as consonant.

Where the M is above the D, however, we have to imagine a higher D, not a lower T. In such cases we could not understand the smaller D-to-T relationship as consonant.

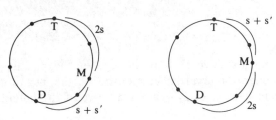

Now, if we consider the interval formed by M and T or M and D as consonant, we can consider intervals between other pitches in the collection as consonant, if they are the same size ($s+s'$, $2s$, $3s+2s'$, and $4s+s'$).

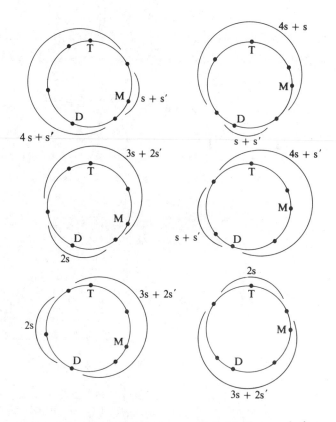

This means that of the eleven available interval sizes between the identity and the pitch-class interval, five (these four plus the larger dominant-to-tonic interval) are always consonant, and a sixth (the smaller of the dominant-to-tonic intervals) is consonant under certain conditions. This in turn means that we can combine members of as many as three different pitch classes such that each pitch is consonant with the members of the other classes. We recognize such collections of three pitch classes as *triads*. Note that while there are six different triads available in any diatonic collection there are only two types—those whose intervallic make-up corresponds to the T–M–D triad with M $2s$ above T, and those corresponding to the T–M–D triad with M $s+s'$ above T. Now, if we consider any triad formed by T, M, and D as a special triad—the *tonic triad*—whose members constitute the primary elements of their respective diatonic collection, we get the following useful property: any tonic triad member is a member of two other triads as well.

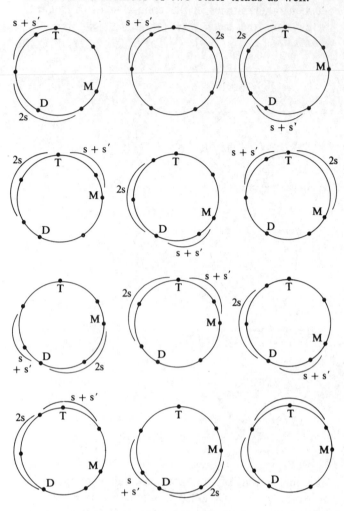

Furthermore, if we assume that a triad, to function as a tonic triad, must yield the above property, then given any diatonic collection

only two of the six available triads can be considered tonic triads.

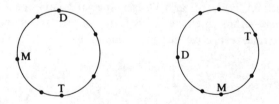

Thus we have both taken care of the paucity of consonant intervals characteristic of the pentatonic system (see page 422) and taken care of the potential ambiguity problem (see page 423). The pitch materials now at our disposal allow us to combine a step motion down from M to T with a complete arpeggiation below it,

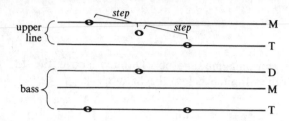

such that each pair of simultaneously sounding pitches is consonant.*

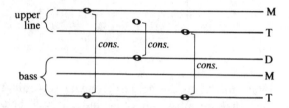

Using this combination of lines as a basic structure, we can compose music with an overall structure like that of tonal music, knowing that each pair of pitches in the basic structure may also be used as the basis for some secondary structure.

More Than Three Primary Pitches • Just because we have arrived at a pitch system with which we could compose music that has a structure like that of tonal music does not necessarily mean that we have arrived at the pitch system best suited to such a structure. For example, the fact that a system with three primary pitch classes embedded in a total collection of seven is better suited to such structures than a system with two primary pitch classes embedded in a collection of five suggests that there might be systems with more than seven pitch classes in the collection and more than three primary pitch classes that are even more suitable. Consider what happens when we add another primary pitch to the collection. Any pitch between T and the M immediately above it is related to both and hence could not be consonant with either. Any pitch in the collection between D and the T immediately above it is either a step above the D or a step below the T. On the other hand, consider what happens when we try to add other pitch classes to the collection. If we continue to use the same procedure to get another pitch class,

---

* Note, however, that we still have no way of combining a step motion down from D to T with an arpeggiation of the tonic triad below, since the pitch between D and M is dissonant with any tonic triad members. It is presumably for this reason that 5–4–3–2–1 lines are so rare in the underlying structures of tonal music.

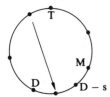
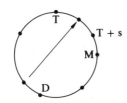

we immediately create a situation in which an interval size that is elsewhere considered a step must here be considered a skip. The s between D and D−s in the left-hand collection and between T and T+s in the right-hand collection is cut roughly in half by the new element. We can get around this problem by continuing to generate new pitch classes, thereby bisecting all the remaining s-sized intervals as well.

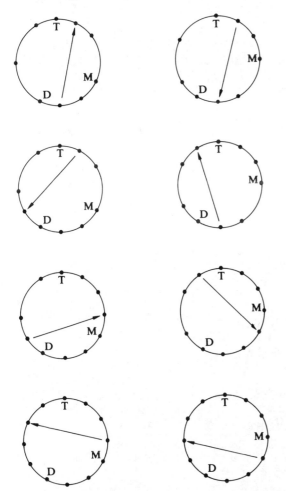

If each new element actually bisected the s interval (that is, if s equalled 2s′), the thirteenth pitch class would be identical with one of the pitch classes we already have.

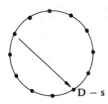
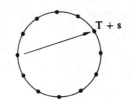

Then we would have a collection of twelve pitch classes with one interval to function as a step, s′. For this to be the case, s′ has to correspond to a frequency ratio of $\sqrt[12]{2}$ so that 12s′ will correspond to a frequency ratio of 2:1. To do this we would have to make all our larger dominant-to-tonic intervals correspond to frequency ratios a shade smaller than 3:2 (actually about 2.995:2) and all our smaller dominant-to-tonic intervals correspond to frequency ratios a shade larger than 4:3 (4:2.995).* Now such a collection of twelve equally spaced pitch classes is extremely useful as a single source for twelve different diatonic collections, as we saw in Chapters 2 and 3. However, as a collection that is to have an analogous function to that of the diatonic collection itself, this "twelve-tone collection" is subject to at least two objections:

1. the pitch class a step above the tonic no longer forms a dominant-to-tonic sized interval with the dominant, nor does the pitch class a step below the dominant form a tonic-to-dominant interval with the tonic;
2. given such a collection you have no way of telling where T is.

The advantages of the diatonic system should be evident.

A.6 A Final Note of Caution

My purpose in the preceding pages has been to show why I think the pitch materials used in tonal music are in fact the ones best suited to the structure of that music. My method has been to sketch out how, given what we know about the physiology of hearing and given some of the ways we like to think about the notes we hear in tonal music, we could, by a series of rational choices, arrive at these particular pitch materials. The results of such a method may appear to be more conclusive than they really are. As I pointed out in Chapter 1, "what we know about the physiology of hearing" is still somewhat limited. And, as you will see if you compare the key concepts used in this book with those used in other textbooks in tonal theory, the number of people included in that "we" in the "ways we like to think of the notes we hear" is still somewhat limited too. Nevertheless, no "Introduction to Tonal Theory" can afford to ignore the questions raised at the beginning of this appendix. I have not answered all of them, but I hope I have at least shown how they are inter-connected.

* Such a deviation is small enough so that we can accept these intervals as reasonable substitutes for those corresponding to 3:2 and 4:3 ratios. Indeed these intervals are the basis of the so-called tempered tuning used for all keyboard instruments since the eighteenth century.

Answers to Drills

Drills on page 60

1. Rule *A1* is incorrectly applied. The diatonic collection indicated by the key signature is that of C major and A minor. E is the tonic of neither.
2. Rule *A3* is incorrectly applied. To form a step motion you must have *all* the intervening diatonic degrees. The B is missing, creating a skip between the C♯ and the A.
3. The choice of F♯ under rule *A1* means that the structure must be in F♯ minor. Thus rule *B3* is incorrectly applied, since E is not a member of the F♯-minor triad.
4. G♯, not G.
5. F♯ and B♭ form a dissonant skip.
6. B♮, not B♭.

Drills on page 70

1. a   3. b   5. c   7. b
2. b   4. a   6. a

Drills on page 81

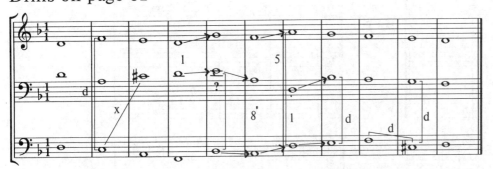

Drills on page 101

1. Given the A in m. 10 of the upper example, there is no pitch available for the bass in m. 9 that would be consonant with the F in the upper line and could be generated by our rules.

In the lower example, the B in m. 8 must be part of a secondary structure (C–B–C or G–A–B–C) applied to a basic step motion. Neither C nor A could occur in mm. 4 or 7 because neither is consonant with the bass at these points. In m. 5 a C would create similar motion to a fifth at m. 6, and an A would both create similar motion and be dissonant with the bass. The last measure in which either a C or an A could occur is m. 3. But if a C or an A occurs in m. 3, there is no place left to put the basic step motion. If the final C in the secondary structure also serves as the final C in the basic step motion, the D in the basic step motion would have to precede the first note of the secondary structure, but D is dissonant with the E in m. 2. The same difficulty prevents the initial C of a C–B–C secondary structure from serving as the final note of the basic step motion.

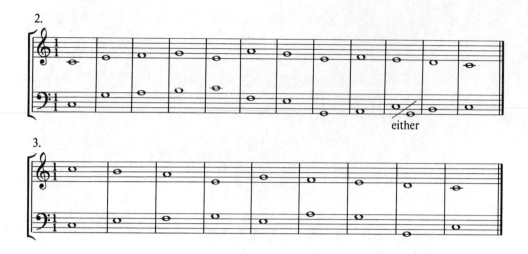

Drills on page 107

Drills on page 117

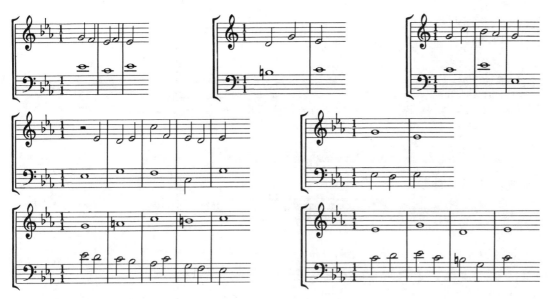

Drills on page 126

Drills on page 133

Drills on page 151

1.
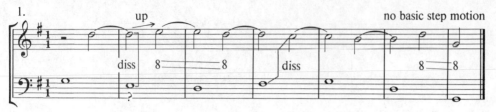

2.
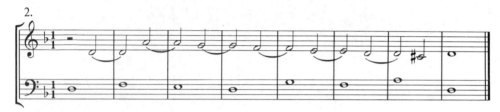

Drills on page 156

1.

(the A an octave lower is also possible)

2.

Drills on page 162

Drills on page 236

1. b, d, g, i.
2.

433

Drills on page 254

1.

2.

Drills on page 263

1. a, c, d.
2.

3.
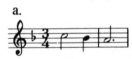
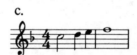

4.

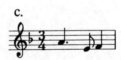

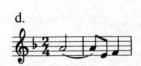

Drills on page 352

a. *augmented sixth* a. *diminished seventh* a. *dominant seventh*

b.  b.  b.

c.  c.  c.

a. *dominant seventh* a. *diminished seventh* a. *augmented sixth*

b.  b.  b.

c.  c.  c.